THE DAWN OF REALIZATION

D1522575

THE DAWN OF

REALIZATION

RONALD BEACH
AND
LEE PITTS

To order additional copies of this book, contact:
Xlibris Corporation
1-888-795-4274
www.Xlibris.com
Orders@Xlibris.com
122134

CONTENTS

TERRORISM IS THE USE OF VIOLENCE, OR THE THREAT OF VIOLENCE TO CREATE A CLIMATE OF FEAR IN A GIVEN POPULATION.

General Norman Schwarzkopf

This book, The Dawn of Realization, was originally published by 1st Books in 2001 with an ISBN of 1-4107-1200-1 (ebooks) and 1-4107-1201-X (Paperback)—it has been re-published with a few minor changes and different cover.

FOREWORD

W E BEGAN THIS novel, which sprang from our experiences in the Army, in the naïve months before the suffering of our nation on September 11, 2001. The book was more than half way toward completion when the tragic events occurred and we felt it was imperative we continue with the book even knowing our country was under attack. It is not our intention to play on the anguish and sorrow caused by the cowardly attacks against our God-fearing nation, but to bring to America an awareness of such actions.

With this in mind we made small changes in our text to acknowledge the cowardly deeds, while attempting to keep to the original theorem, that the majority of Americans share a naiveté about such things happening in their homeland. The original assault on the World Trade Center and the actions of Timothy McVeigh only briefly opened our eyes to such acts perpetrated on American soil. Like in all other developed nations, lawbreakers exist and criminals have always preyed on others and always shall. What we did with this work of fiction was to mix entertaining reading with a possible live scenario. Greed and desire for power drive despots who lack within their hearts a concern for humanity. Our hearts go out to the families and friends of those who lost their lives on September 11th, but those who serve in our military and in the civilian community who hunt for the evildoers deserve our respect, out heartfelt gratitude and praise also. To all of these we dedicate this book. **God Bless America.**

PROLOGUE

__January 4, 1993—Time: 12:30am__—Smoke hung heavy in the dingy motel room in old Las Vegas, the two occupants, men in their mid-thirties, sat at a small table playing poker, the only sound the occasional shuffling of cards. Smoking one cigarette after another, they were apparently waiting for something, only using the card game to while away time. Both men paused at the shrill sound of the telephone. The man nearest the instrument picked it up, simply saying into the mouthpiece, "Hello," he stiffened when he heard the voice on the other end of the line answering with short responses. "Yes, sir." "Tonight, sir." "No mistakes, Sir." With that the line went dead. He looked at his partner, "It's a go, get your stuff." After gathering up their personal belongings, they made a check of the room, making sure there was no evidence of their presence; only the heavy ring of smoke, swirling in the air, left a trace of their existence.

__January 4, 1993—Time: 2:30am__—In the dim light two shadowy figures moved in and out among the small private planes anchored near the hangars located at the end of the airstrip. Dressed in black and moving stealthily, they stopped by a Cessna, anchored by a chain to a ring in the concrete. One of them raised the cowling on the engine compartment, while the other maintained a vigilant watch. Minutes later they silently moved away leaving behind only a silvery object which had been neatly tucked away among the many wires of the aircraft's engine.

__January 4, 1993—Time: 7:15pm__—On Runway 3 West, at McCarran International Airport in Las Vegas, Nevada, its single engine revved to a high whine, sits a Cessna 172. A man and a woman sit inside the tiny cockpit. The man behind the controls awaits instructions from the tower, as the woman sits quietly looking into the darkening night. Receiving the go ahead the pilot revs the engine to maximum torque and prepares for take off, a maneuver he has done many times. Flying is second nature to him, though most of his flying time was in fighter jets while wearing the uniform of a United States Air Force officer. The takeoff is flawless and as the plane ascends it takes a slow turn to the south and climbs to a higher altitude. The glow of the evening sun displays a warm aura in the sky putting to shame the artificial lights of the city below.

WHEN THE PLANE reaches its assigned altitude, the lights of Las Vegas behind, the pilot places the airplane on autopilot and turns to his companion. He reaches over and takes her hand in his. His deep abiding love for her evident in his weathered face, he gazes steadfastly into her face seeing the beauty of the woman who stole his heart long ago. As on him, age has taken its toll on her, but the eyes of love are blinded by what the mind projects.

This woman sitting beside him has been his constant companion for over 30 years, a woman who almost died giving birth to their only child, Reginald. Highly intelligent, she gave up a promising career in the medical field to follow her man to military stations all around the world. Always on equal ground, yet willing to take a back seat when the military beckoned them to pick up and move again, never voicing a complaint, she was always the perfect military wife.

Now, he had to explain one more time that they would have to leave the home that they loved. They must start anew. The beauty, which the Nevada desert offered, reminded them of their final assignment in Israel, a brutal yet beautiful country with a colorful history and friendly people. Not being of Jewish descent and thinking of their son's welfare, making a home there had been out of the question.

Discovering Nevada had so many similarities they had looked forward to living out their days there. As he began to explain his fears and why they must leave, he discovers he is more afraid now than he had been during his forty-five aerial combat missions. He tells her he does not fear for his life, but the lives of the family he loves so dearly. At first the woman looks confused, but as he goes on she begins to understand the anguish and she listens raptly as he tells her what he has hid from her the past few years. As he pauses to gather his thoughts, the woman turns to him in an attempt to assuage his fears, but is silenced forever as a tremendous explosion rips through the fuselage and blows the plane into hundreds of pieces of debris.

Witnesses on the ground said the light was so blindingly bright and the sound so deafening that it seemed only a few hundred yards away. For the couple in the plane all of that did not matter. They didn't even have time to say goodbye. Goodbyes are for the living.

The day had ended, but the *Dawn of Realization* is yet to come.

CHAPTER ONE

The Early Years

"I WILL NOT go!" Those words were spoken by Reginald Nutsbagh, son of Major General Dominic Nutsbagh, when he was told by his father they would be moving again. The General had been nominated for a job in Israel as the Senior Advisor to the Israeli Defense Force, which require him to move there along with his family.

Major General Nutsbagh had spent the last two years at the Pentagon as the Assistant to the Chief of Staff for the United States Air Force, a job he had been recommended for because of his faithful and honorary service to his country for over thirty years.

But, with all Reggie's denials of being unwilling to go, when it came time for them to leave he was the first one on board their charter flight.

Once settled into their home in Ramat Gan, Israel Reggie was still unhappy and stayed that way for the first couple of days that is until he met Joel Garza. This chance meeting on the street in front of his house would turn out to be a happy union and a friendship that would blossom from mere friendship to brotherhood.

General Dominic Nutsbagh was delighted to learn on the first day of work that his neighbor Benjamin Garza, whom he had only met a couple days previously, worked in an office a few doors down the hall. They had met when the general and his family moved in and the Garza family, minus their son and daughter, walked over to greet them and welcome them to the neighborhood.

Three weeks later he was sitting at his desk reading some reports when his aide knocked on his door and told him there was a Benjamin Garza in his outer office and would like to see him. The general had been running around the country meeting the people he would be working with and taking time to get indoctrinated to the country and its people and had finally been able to spend a few days in his office and was delighted when his aide announced Ben was in the outer office.

Smiling, he told his aide, "I know Ben, we're neighbors. The house your government is providing for me and my family is just down the street from his and we share a common problem, teenage boys with raging hormones. You really didn't need to know that, but yes, please send him in."

When Ben walked in, Dom got to his feet and they shook hands in the middle of the room after which Ben turned around and closed the office door.

"Would you like some to drink, Ben?" Dom asked as Ben took the offered chair. "A cold soda or some coffee, I had a fresh pot brewed a little while ago."

"No thanks Dom, I just want to talk to you about something."

"Sure, Ben, anytime."

Then in a hushed voice Ben asked, "Can we talk here in your office? I mean, there is no listening or recording devices in your office, are there?"

"I haven't personally checked," the general replied, "but there had better not be. I can't see as if I have much to hide anyway."

"Chuckling Ben said, "Never forget you are in Israel and everyone is your enemy unless they first come to you in peace. And—"

Breaking in, Dom, looking at Ben with a grin said, "You are starting to worry me. Are you my enemy or my friend?"

"I am your friend but you will have to make your own decision after we have out little talk. I want you to know that I am breaking the rules by talking to you but my superiors will not listen and I need to talk to someone."

"You sound serious when you speak of breaking the rules, Ben, so before you being let me get a cup of coffee and I'll tell my aide not to disturb us."

Getting up Dom walked to his office door and opened it telling his aide he didn't want to be disturbed. Then he closed the door behind him, walked over to the coffee pot, poured himself a cup of coffee then went back behind his desk. Once seated, he took a sip of coffee and then said, "Okay Ben, I'm all ears."

Without preamble Ben began, "Dom, I'm a member of the Israeli Mossad. I was placed in this job about a year ago as it was a perfect cover for me and it gave me a chance to maintain contact with a lot of people who work for our government. I believe I have come across a conspiracy, one I believe that encompasses your embassy and the Israeli Minister of Defense. I don't know exactly who is involved but it has to be either the ambassador or his aide in your embassy or the assistant to the Minister of Defense, or the Minister himself, as no one else could issue the orders that are being issued."

"What in the hell are you talking about, Ben. Conspiracy, embassies and defense involved. What is that all about? And you a Mossad agent, why do you maintain an office here?"

"Let me tell you how this all started. The Mossad moved me into this office to try and keep an eye on all the military personnel working in the building and report any suspicious activity. I visit the embassy and the minister's office all the time and lately have been looking into suspicious shipments going out of Israel bound for your west coast; I think their arrival port is Tacoma."

"What makes them suspicious?"

"It's the cargo they carry and who is manning the ships. Most of the crews on the manifest are foreigners and the cargo is dubious. The crews are always being rotated as they are never the same when that same ship comes back to Israel. I have a feeling the crew who man these ships are taken off at the port in Tacoma and stay in the country, but for what reason I have no idea. Then there are a lot of prohibited items, such as diamonds, gold and even weapons. On one of my many night forays I found some weapons being shipped under the guise of farm machinery, all of these shipments are authorized by either your embassy or the defense minister, or at least under his name. In checking some other paperwork involved in these shipments I found the word DONE. I have no idea what it means but I will find out, but I am thinking that it is either a secret organization in your country or mine."

Here he paused, and Dom said, "That's a whole lot to swallow. I'm a newcomer here in Israel and haven't got into the politics as I have been consumed in doing my job. So, I guess the obvious question for me to ask is why, are you telling me this, and not your leaders?"

"They will not listen to me, they continually want some solid evidence and I have not yet been able to come up with something solid. My instinct is that I can trust you and I needed to talk to someone or

I'll burst. I haven't been in the spy business for long as they recruited me a couple of years ago. They must have felt I had the knowledge and contacts to delve into the shadowy parts of our government. I was previously a university professor in a nice safe job and now I am a spy, how ironic."

"What a jump, from professor to spy." Dom replied. "That sure is some leap."

Before Ben could say anything there was a knock on the door to his office and before he could say anything his aide stuck his head in, "Sir, you have a meeting with the commanders of our air wing in just a little while."

More than a little mad at the interruption the General replied, "I thought I told you I didn't want to be disturbed. I have an hour before that meeting so do as I told you and close the door."

Red faced at the chastising, the aide closed the door muttering to himself, '*I had to interrupt you before that fool Garza spilled more of his guts. Now we might have to get rid of both of you.*'

The interruption broke the mood of the meeting and Ben got up from his chair saying, "I might have said too much already. Maybe we can continue our conversation at a later date and in a safer place where we won't be interrupted."

"I'm sorry about that Ben, and yes we can continue our conversation. To say the least you have stimulated my interest and I still have a lot of questions."

Ben got up and left and the general resumed his work and it wasn't until the next afternoon when the general called Ben, "Hey Ben, I have some time, so why don't you and I take a ride. You promised to show me some more of the city and right now I have some time."

Unknown to the general his phone was tapped but only so his aide could listen into all the conversations taking place in his office and his calls. When he heard the general and Ben were going to take a ride in Ben's car he quickly made a call to his contact and informed the person on the other end of the meeting, giving him a description of the car."

Both men agreed to meet downstairs in the parking lot in a few minutes. After ending the call Dom got up and walked out of his office telling his aide that he was going out for a time and if needed, he could be contacted on his cell phone. Then he headed for the parking lot and his meeting with Ben.

Both men arrived at the parking lot at the same time and were about to get into Ben's car when the General realized he had left his cell phone in his office. "Damn it Ben, I forgot my cell phone. Why don't you move the car around to the front of the building while I run up and get my cell phone and I'll meet you out front?"

"Sure Dom, no problem."

He left to go back up to his office while Ben started his car and pulled around to the front of the building. He was sitting there with the engine idling, when the general, after retrieving his phone, rode the elevator to the ground floor. Watching for the general Ben didn't see the car driving around him roll something under his car then speed off.

The general got out of the elevator and started walking toward the main entrance of the building when there was a tremendous explosion from the front and Ben's car disintegrated right in front of his eyes. The only thing that saved him was that he hadn't made it to the front of the building and was protected by the concrete barricades placed in front of the building.

The fire was still raging around the overturned car when Dom, one of the first ones on the scene, took one look at Ben's demolished car and shook his head muttering, "He never had a chance."

The general's aide, upon hearing the explosion hurried down the stairs with a satisfied look on his face, then walked out of the building and saw the general standing there unhurt, the satisfied looked left his face and was replaced by one of alarm at seeing him alive. Recovering quickly he walked up to the general saying, "Sir, I'm glad to see you are okay. When I heard the explosion I feared the worst. Who was in the car?"

Over the wail of approaching police and emergency vehicles he replied, "Ben Garza, and if whoever had set the bomb would have waited another two or three minutes I would have been in the car and dead."

"I wonder why someone wanted Ben dead?" the aide asked innocently.

Muttering to himself as he walked away General Nutsbagh said, *'I don't know but I do know that what he told me yesterday must have something to do with it and I am damn sure going to find out if what he told me is the truth and who is behind this. I'm also sure I was a target and it was just by luck that I wasn't caught up in the blast.'*

In the next couple of months General Nutsbagh continued to look into the death of Benjamin Garza and trying to verify what Ben had told him during the meeting in his office. When he returned home the evening of the blast, he faced a barrage of questions from his son Reggie about the disappearance of his friend Joel and his entire family.

Being unable to answer his son's questions added to his resolve and he began visiting both the American Embassy and the Israeli Minister of Defense offices, often asking seemingly innocent but leading questions. These visits and questions soon came to the attention of the Ambassador and his assistant and the Minister of Defense and his aide. The Minister, when told about it, merely shrugged his shoulders and said, "It's only the American general looking for information about our country." In the case of the American Embassy, The Ambassador explained, "He needs the information to do his job." But whatever his motives were he was the matter of several conversations between the two assistants.

Remembering what Ben had said about the waterfront, the general, in disguise, took it upon himself to visit several seamen's bars, always buying drinks and asking questions. On one of those nights he found out that a ship, The American Tide, was pulling out later that evening and was still trying to fill their crew. Part of the incentive to get them to sign up for the voyage was that when they arrived in the US they would disembark and there was a job for them. A job, one of his drunken companions said, "Was a mercenary job which paid a lot of money for doing very little. Hell, there are enough weapons hidden in the hold of that ship to start World War III."

With this piece of information the general increased his length of stay around the water front in the ensuing days. During his forays to the port he would always spend time in the bars where the seamen hung out plying those who would talk to him with drinks. He would then ask prying questions and listen to what they had to say.

During the day he also increased his visits to both the American Embassy and the Israeli Defense offices in his capacity as the Liaison Officer for the IDF. He continued, during those visits, asking what he though were innocent questions but geared towards gathering information he needed to fill in the gaps.

One evening while out on another visit to the waterfront, he came across a stevedore who had just finished loading one of the ships in port. He began talking to him all the while plying him with drinks. It wasn't long before he turned the conversation to the ships in port and where they were headed.

During this conversation the stevedore blurted out, "They sure do some strange things at this port. I've worked at a lot of ports and have never seen cargo that was authorized by the assistant to the Minister of Defense. It is normally just some flunky signing the authorization."

Excited by the information the General bought him another drink then ask, "Can you show me some of that stuff? I'll make it worth your while."

"Sure why not. First let me finish my drink."

Ten minutes later with the man leading him they walked down a small alley on the pier and into a dimly lit warehouse. Walking over to a row of crates the man said, "These are the crates authorized for shipment by someone from the American Embassy. Come on let me show you what's really in them."

They walked in between the row of crates and then climbed up on top of a short stack. Pulling a large knife out from his belt the man pried the lid of one of the crates open and pointed inside. The general looked at the label on the crate and saw that it indicated that the crate was packed with farming implements and was stamped with a Star of David. Moving the lid aside he reached inside and felt around then pulled out a brand new sub-machine gun wrapped up with a heavy coating of grease applied to it. Digging further into the crate he saw there were more weapons and even several boxes of hand grenades.

Turning around to his drunken friend Dom said, "I've seen enough you'll get paid when we get out of here."

He had stumbled into something he had been looking for, proof of weapons being shipped out to the US. But in his excitement he missed the cameras which were mounted inside the warehouse so before he got back to his home in Ramat Gan both the assistant to the American Ambassador knew and he immediately placed a call to his comrade in the Israeli Ministry of Defense.

The next morning a call was placed to the Washington, DC with the gist of the conversation being, "General Nutsbagh is getting into things he has no business getting into. He has been doing a lot of talking to the staffs at the Embassy and the Israel Defense Ministry and has made numerous unauthorized visits to the dock talking with a lot of the longshoremen and sailors. All of this interest seems to have stemmed from a short meeting he had with the undercover Mossad agent Garza, who we already put out of business. We meant to get both of them but for some reason the general wasn't where he was supposed to be."

Shortly after the phone call there was a meeting in the US between a high ranking member of the FBI and an Air Force general. The outcome of the meeting was the decision to force General Nutsbagh into retirement rather than kill him. "Killing would be too messy and cause too many questions to be asked."

The Air Force officer immediately called the chief of Air Force Operations and told him he wanted retirement papers printed up for Major General Dominic Nutsbagh immediately, and get them too him for signature.

Within hours he received the orders and then made preparations to go to Israel under the guise of an official visit.

Four days later he met with General Nutsbagh in his office, and as soon as they were seated he said, without preamble, "Dom, you've had a great thirty-one years with the Air Force but we think it's time you retire."

Taken completed by surprise Dom yelled, "What in the hell do you mean retire. Retire! Hell no, I'll not retire."

"Well we think ready or not it's time for you to retire."

"No way! I like this assignment and want to stay to complete it and then I'll think about retiring."

"Then let me be frank with you. Right now, because of your recent activities and your unauthorized investigation into matters that are of no concern to you, you have two choices. Either being brought up on charges relating to your unauthorized investigation, which could turn ugly and cost you your retirement, or you could just quietly retire. The choice is yours."

Not acknowledging or denying the charges concerning the investigation, Dom sat back in his chair his mind trying to comprehend what was happening and then he responded, "I have done nothing wrong or out of the scope of my job, but I'll take what you have said under consideration. Can I have a couple of days before I give you my answer?"

"You have two days and only two days. I'll be around for the next two days and I need your answer. Before I leave I'll do one of two things, either issue you your retirement papers or order a court martial, your choice."

The general got up without another word, walked out of General Nutsbagh's office, nodded to the aide sitting at the desk and then walked out.

Two days later, without fanfare Major General Dominic Nutsbagh retired. The same day dressed in civilian attire the retired general and his family boarded a charter flight bound for Las Vegas, Nevada, where he and his family would settle into a normal life. Or what he thought would be a normal life.

CHAPTER TWO

The Beginning

SITTING IN THE window seat in aisle fourteen of the United Airlines Boeing 727, a man sat looking out as the ground rose rapidly to meet the descending plane. In the distance he could see a small plane on an adjacent runway as it awaited takeoff. An uncontrollable shiver coursed through his body, as he thought of his parents and their untimely demise in a mysterious midair explosion in their small Cessna. Closing his eyes he leaned back and choked back the tears that always presented themselves when he thought of their deaths. With difficulty he cleared his mind and once again glanced outside feeling the slight jolt as the plane touched down. When the flight steward announced the temperature, as a cool 55 degrees, he thought, *'July shouldn't be so cold in Salt Lake City. Especially since I live in the hot arid climate of Las Vegas and just left from there this morning, bringing only lightweight clothes'.*

As the plane of Reginald Von Nutsbagh (Reggie to friends and enemies alike) was taxiing down the runway to the gate area, another plane, in a flight from Seattle, was on its final approach to Runway 6 West. On board this aircraft was a man who would become a lifetime friend. Tobias Wainwright Preston wasn't a particularly good flyer and the turbulence, which had caused him to be buckled in for the final hour of the flight, didn't put him any more at ease. Toby, (he never used Tobias), was anxious to get his feet on solid ground, as were all passengers on the crowded flight. *'Never saw so many unhappy people in one place,'* he muttered under his breath, *'sure hope this conference is worth all of this.'*

Both men were in the city to attend an international conference on terrorism. And both were police officers; Toby, a detective lieutenant in the small town of Bremerton, Washington and Reggie, a pathologist for the Las Vegas, Nevada Police Force.

As Reggie picked up his baggage from the carousel, he had one thing in mind—a hot shower. No, make that two things, the other being a man-sized steak. He was working his way through arriving passengers from other flights, all of them anxious to get their luggage and proceed to their destinations, when he bumped, rather unceremoniously, into a woman towing a reluctant small child. The collision gave the child the impetus she needed to wrench herself from her mother's grasp and immediately race across the room with wild abandon, avoiding the crowd with the skill of the very young. Stopping to help the frustrated mother, Reggie swung around and slammed his briefcase into the midriff of the rather large Toby Preston who held the young child under his arm.

"Oof," he said. "As if this kicking youngster isn't enough of a burden, you incapacitate me with that case, which must be filled with lead." The smile on his face belied his words.

"Well," Reggie countered, "It seems as if helping people in distress doesn't always have pleasant rewards." Extending his free hand, he continued, "Hi, I'm Reggie Von Nutsbagh, I think the Von comes from some Prussian ancestor."

"Toby Preston and with the middle name Wainwright, you can figure my ancestors played games on me too."

Both men had a good chuckle and after making sure the young woman and her child were faring well, walked shoulder to shoulder towards Ground Transportation. Any casual spectator would have assumed they were lifelong friends as they chatted freely.

"So Toby, what brings you to the Great Salt Lake?" Reggie asked.

"Either the powers to be believing a little education about terrorism would benefit our department, or they just wanted to get rid of me for awhile. Any way you look at it, I'm here to attend a three-day seminar. The area, in Washington State, I come from has two major Naval Bases, an Air Force Base, and an Army Base within just a few miles of each other. We're always concerned about terrorism."

"I'm here for the same seminar," responded Reggie, "maybe we can share a seat and some thoughts on the subject. Speaking of sharing, let's save and share a cab. Where are you staying while you're here?"

"The Residence Inn on Broadway," answered Toby. "I wanted to stay where the conference was to be held and was able to book a non-smoking room."

"Well, I guess we're in luck," Reggie stated, "that's where I'm staying also. Let's get out of here, check in and we can talk over dinner."

Toby sized up his acquaintance as 5 foot 10 inches tall, with a weight lifter's body, not an ounce of it fat. '*Sure would hate to tangle with this guy*', he thought. '*If sheer strength doesn't get you, a look from those eyes would.*' His companion's eyes were a piercing hazel color, surrounded by bushy eyebrows, capable of showing tenderness, as well as a 'don't cross me' look.

Climbing into the cab, Reggie said, "Registration begins this evening at five thirty, which means we can go over our schedule as we eat."

After a short time ride, which was spent in idle talk, they arrived at the hotel, grabbed their luggage and walked into the lobby and strode up to the desk.

Hours later over a marvelously prepared steak, with all the trimmings, consumed in the hotel's dining room, the two men spoke of their lives.

During the evening Toby revealed he was recently widowed and raising a twelve-year old daughter, and as his work consumed so much of his time he had hired a Mexican woman as housekeeper, cook and nanny. His wife's family had been pioneers in the Kitsap area of the Puget Sound, with vast property holdings and had left it all to their only child, Esther, after their deaths. For he and Esther it had been love at first sight when first meeting at a church social at the age of twelve. They married at eighteen and Esther worked helping put him through college at the University of Washington, where he had been an All-American linebacker for three years while pursuing a course of studies in criminology. Becoming a police office hadn't been the choice his wife wanted him to make, but after voicing her displeasure she had backed him completely.

Toby sighed, "That's it in a nutshell, how about you?"

"I'm an Air Force brat and spent several years in Israel with my family, prior to my father's retirement. I enjoyed living there only because I was young enough not to be involved in the politics of the area. After that assignment in Israel, we moved to Las Vegas where my father hung up his uniform. I lost both my parents in a plane crash under mysterious circumstances. While I was getting over the shock I attended the University of Nevada at Las Vegas where I got a degree in Pathology.

I've never married, but do have a girl friend, Brandy, a nurse at a local hospital."

"We met when I spent some time in the hospital. She's a wonderful woman, but there's something about the word matrimony that scares me. My parents had a wonderful marriage and when I get married I want mine to be the same."

Reggie's voice broke as it always did when bringing up the subject of his parents. Fighting to control his emotions, he continued, "I have no idea why I was sent to this seminar. I haven't done anything over and above the call of duty. I've helped in several big cases, but I think the chief realized I wasn't satisfied with what I was doing and this is his way of giving me some time away from the office to think it over. How about you, why are you here?"

"I really don't know, unless the chief is trying to get rid of me for awhile until things cool down around the station. The mayor and I have been butting heads for the longest time and no matter what I do I can't seem to stay away from him. I guess the chief is tired of interceding, so he sent me to this seminar to give him a rest. The Chief and I get along real well, but he's caught in the middle of the politics of his office and doesn't know what to do about the situation." Looking at his watch, he said, "I've enjoyed our conversation so much I failed to notice the hour, how does breakfast at seven sound?"

Agreeing upon the time they headed for their rooms and hopefully a good night's sleep. Neither of them suspected that their lives were now interwoven.

The seminar dealt with world terrorism, but a lot of the discussions were centered on the Israel/Palestinian conflict and what was actually happening in that area. The lectures discussed the 'Fatah', jihads, elQuaida and the Palestine Liberation Organization (PLO), their history and why the movement was spreading.

Other discussions were devoted to Israel, its neighbors and a little of the history of the problem. These talks were presented by Samual Leving, Israel's Defense Minister and Abraham Markowitz, a police chief in Jerusalem.

Throughout the three days of the seminar Reggie and Toby were constantly together continuing their discussions of the first night, realizing how much they had in common.

During one of these discussions Toby asked, "You know Reggie, it is none of my business, but I was wondering in all this time since the death of your parents have you tried to do some investigating on your own into what happened?"

"I tried many times," he replied, "but was stonewalled at every turn as none of the investigating agencies would give me any information as to the cause of the crash. I tried as a private citizen and as a member of the police force but couldn't get to first base. It seems like every one is willing to just write it off as engine malfunction or pilot error. Truthfully, there weren't enough pieces of the plane to investigate. I haven't given up hope, though."

When the seminar came to an end it was both a relief and a time of sadness. As far back as he could remember Toby had never met a person he liked as much as Reggie. They were inseparable all of their waking hours. Holding the same enthusiasm for justice, they spent hours talking about cases they had worked on, comparing solutions and techniques.

"Let's talk about dinner," Toby suggested, "It's our last night, how about meeting in the lobby at 7:30 and going out for Chinese, my treat?"

"Better yet," offered Reggie, "Why not Korean fare? Haven't had kimchee since my dad was stationed in Seoul."

"Kimchee?" questioned Toby, "What's that?"

"A very spicy hot type of vegetable, I assure you, you'll like it."

A little hesitantly Toby agreed on Korean food for their farewell dinner and the two separated to finish packing and get cleaned up for the evening meal.

Reggie walked into his room but instead of packing and preparing for the evening he sat down on the sofa and soon became lost in thought. His thoughts drifted back to his parents' death; he knew it wasn't an accident and he wanted to find out why they had died and who was responsible. In his discussions with Toby over the last several days he had come to realize he was no longer satisfied with being a member of the Las Vegas Police Department, now what to do about it?

After a time he came to a decision and because he had taken so long he had hurry to complete his preparations for dinner and arrived in the lobby just a few minutes behind Toby. Walking outside they signaled a taxi; entering the cab Reggie gave the driver instructions to a local Korean restaurant he had learned about from the hotel desk clerk.

"Wow!" Toby exclaimed, as tears streamed down his face, "This is some kind of hot, but good. I'll have to look for a nice Korean restaurant when I get home. Renie likes Jalapenos, so I'm sure she will like this. Pass me some more, will you?"

Dinner continued with a lot of small talk, intuition telling Toby that Reggie had something else on his mind, but not wanting to push he kept the conversation in a light tone. Somehow he instinctively knew if Reggie wanted him to know what was on his mind he would tell him when the time was right. It was during their coffee after dinner that he finally told Toby what was on his mind.

Clearing his throat he began, "Toby, I'm quitting the police force. I know I have a good career going, but my heart isn't in it. I intend on opening my own detective agency."

Toby responded, "Well, I certainly wasn't expecting that, but rest assured I'll help you in anyway I can."

"I really want more than that," countered Reggie. "I was hoping I could interest you in joining me and being my partner. Maybe you could open an agency part time in Bremerton or Seattle and provide me with support. If there ever came a time you wanted to come in full time the door would be open."

Toby responded, "That sounds tempting. I have a love for the law and like you, I often feel we're stymied by the system we swore to uphold and defend. However, I can't answer you right now; there are other things I have to take into consideration. My daughter being the biggest and then I have to ask myself, do I really want to take on the added responsibility."

Reggie was disappointed, but respecting Toby's candor, merely said, "I appreciate that. I didn't expect you to make the decision right now. I don't have many close friends and I've grown to have a tremendous amount of respect for you as a person and would like very much if you would join me in this."

"Thanks," Toby responded, "I'll call you in a few days and give you my answer."

Reggie's revelation of his intention to resign from the police force and asking Toby to join him changed the mood of their evening together, so by mutual agreement the bill was paid and two men stepped out into the night air hailing a taxi to return to the hotel. Arriving at the hotel and as it had been a long night and was very late, both men immediately headed for their rooms and a good night's rest.

The next morning as Reggie's plane left the ground, he mused to himself, '*I think we're going to see a lot of each other in the future, in spite of the miles separating us'*. If he could only have known how prophetic his thoughts would prove to be he would have shuddered.

A short time later as Toby's plane took off he was very happy to be going home to his daughter but there was also the feeling of sadness at the parting from his new friend. But most of all he felt a tremendous amount of trepidation about the decision he must make in the next several days. What was the answer, what should he do?

The next day after his return, Reggie submitted and was granted his release from the Police Department. He immediately began setting up his office and hiring office help. The day after moving into his new office the call, he had been expecting, came. The call from Toby was short and to the point, "Okay, pal, I'll do it. I'm going to remain on the force for the time being, but will provide assistance to you as required." With this call, the private detective firm with the unusual name, '**Broken Dreams We Can't Fix, but We Do Patchwork on Lives'** became a reality.

CHAPTER THREE

Broken Dreams We Can't Fix

IT WAS ONE of those deluges of rain that can come suddenly in the desert. The torrents of rain quickly clogged the drains of Las Vegas, causing the street traffic, mostly tourists, to find the going slow. The honking of horns irritated the locals, who were used to this and seldom slowed for anything, nor did it do much to calm the nerves of the tall man, standing on the corner. Dressed in what once had been a spotless Armani suit, he now looked bedraggled and quite in place with the crowd of people hurrying to locate a dry haven. Spotting a vacant phone booth, the now utterly drenched man quickly entered the booth, looking furtively around. *'I can't go on like this. No sleep, always looking over my shoulder, for whom I don't know,* he lamented, rifling through the phone book.

He knew who he was looking for, but was having no luck in the white pages; when suddenly an ad caught his attention: **'Broken Dreams We Can't Fix, but We Do Patchwork on Lives'.** A catchy phrase, assigned to a private detective agency. This one has offices in Bremerton and Las Vegas. *'It's strange that a branch was located in Bremerton, where the nightmare began,'* he thought. Reading the ad for the detective agency in its entirety his eyes were drawn to the Las Vegas Office. Seeing the name on the ad he knew he had found his man. Looking at his watch he noticed it was beyond normal business hours, but on a hunch that private investigators didn't keep regular hours he deposited his coins and punched in the number, all the while looking suspiciously at the now diminishing crowd. As quickly as it began the rain had stopped and the tourists and locals were going about their business.

The phone was ringing at the other end and after the tenth ring the weary and disappointed man started to hang up when the phone was answered, "Toby, is that you? You know I leave the office at seven. What are you doing, burning the midnight oil? Don't expect an increase in your percentage of the take—."

Interrupting, the irritated man in the phone booth, said, "Hello, this isn't Toby, but I wish to speak to you on a matter of extreme importance. I assume you are Mr. Reginald Nutsbagh?"

Reggie paused for a second trying to place the accent of the caller, maybe European or an Eastern Bloc country. "Yeah, that's me and just who are you? I have an important engagement and don't have much time."

"I'm sorry, I would prefer to not give you my name over the phone, but it is urgent I speak with you tonight. Can we meet some place very public?"

The irritation showed in Reggie's response, "How do I know you aren't some creep trying to score a hit on me because I helped put your mother away for pushing cocaine?"

"I assure you Mr. Nutsbagh, that this is far more important than cocaine. I have not slept for days and am fearful of my life."

"Alright, alright; you'll have me crying in a minute. Where are you now?"

"I can see what looks like a replica of the Eiffel Tower a block south of where I am in a phone booth."

"Okay, just a little further down on the same side of the street is a sandwich shop. Meet me there and make mine a BMT on wheat."

"I beg your pardon?"

"You're messing up my evening, so dinner is on you; coffee, black with two sugars."

Hanging up the phone Reggie lamented; *'I sure hope Brandy will forgive me for being late for dinner'*. With that thought he closed and locked the door to his office. As he walked rapidly to his car he went back over his brief conversation with the stranger on the phone then he chuckled to himself; *'the guys on the force would really make fun of me if they could only see me now.'*

Arriving at his car, he got in and brought the engine of the super-charged BMW to life. *'Think about it, a while ago I was a member in good standing with the Las Vegas Police Department and now I'm running after a total stranger, who says he has something urgent to discuss with me'.*

As Reggie was making his way to the rendezvous with the stranger, fourteen hundred miles north in Bremerton, his partner Toby was at home relaxing with his twelve year old daughter, Renie.

"Hey, Dad, if God loved Mom so much and took her to be with Him, why didn't He take us too?" Never one to just ask, "How was your day?" She had a way of making profound comments which often left him with his mouth open not knowing how to respond.

Taken aback by her question he had to think hard for fear of stumbling over his answer. *'And this child is only twelve years old! What do I do when she turns thirteen and needs to know the boy/girl things?*

"Well, sweetheart, I guess I don't really know, except to say maybe He needed a little time alone with her." Much to his relief the insistent ringing of the telephone interrupted the need for further explanation.

"Mr. Preston, you have a telephone call, the caller would not give me his name."

"Maria, how many times do I have to tell you to call me Toby, like everyone else does?"

Picking up the handset he spoke into it, "Hello, this is Toby Preston, what can I do for you?"

A voice with a distinctly European accent, answered, "Hello, Preston, I am not going to tell you who I am but you need to look into a murder that was committed just a few minutes ago at the Seaside Apartments on Washington Avenue."

"How do you know there was a murder committed on Washington Avenue?" asked Toby. "And why are you calling me at home and not the police if there was a murder?"

"Just go check it out and do not ask questions," was the reply. "Save your questions for later, if and when I call back."

The line went dead. Toby punched his caller ID but there was no number listed for the caller. "What is this, some kind of a practical joke?" he yelled into the dead phone.

"What did you say, dad?" asked Renie.

"Nothing, Hon, but I have to go out for awhile so we'll have to postpone our little talk for a later time. If I'm not back by 10 PM get yourself into bed and we'll talk tomorrow."

Muttering under his breath as he pulled on his green slicker, he pondered, *'I never figured raising a child alone was going to be simple, but sometimes it does take a probable murder to get me off the hook with this kid.'*

Back in Las Vegas, Reggie pulled his car into the Paris Casino and Hotel valet parking area and turned his car over to the parking attendant. He then proceeded to the rendezvous on foot. The humidity was high, causing the air to be muggy, so he removed his coat and flung it over his shoulder as he approached the sandwich shop.

Entering the shop he looked around to see if anyone was watching him. He had no idea who he was supposed to meet and didn't even know why. Then he spotted his party, easily recognizable by his furtive glances and the sandwiches in front of him. When he tapped the nervous watcher on the shoulder the man almost fell off his seat, but then meeting Reginald Von Nutsbagh and looking into those steely eyes for the first time would un-nerve most people.

"Are you the guy who's looking for me?" asked Reggie.

"I am, if your name is Reginald Nutsbagh," the stranger replied.

By his distinct accent Reggie knew for sure this was the same man he had talked to over the phone. Handing the stranger his business card, which contained his name, business address and telephone number, he said, "Careful there, I can see you're awful nervous, but other people might think you're drunk and call the cops. We certainly don't need the police right now, maybe later if I don't like your story."

"Sorry, I am nervous," responded the disheveled stranger, "not knowing who I can trust or who my enemies are is making me jump at shadows."

"Well, before we talk," stated Reggie, "I'm hungry and I see you have my dinner so let me eat first, I don't like to discuss business and eat at the same time."

Removing the wrapping from the foot long sandwich, he began eating while mentally analyzing the man sitting across from him, trying to determine what type of individual he was dealing with. What he saw was a man of medium build, dark brown hair, and well dressed. He looked a little disheveled having just come in from the rain, and appeared very agitated and upset. His deep blue eyes never stopped moving as he seemed to be classifying each individual in sight to determine if they posed a threat.

'One thing I know for sure about this man,' Reggie said under his breath, *'is he's extremely nervous and on edge.'*

After eating half of his sandwich, he looked up at the man saying, "First, let's finish the introductions. You know who I am, now I want to know who you are, after that, you can tell me what's so important and urgent it couldn't wait until morning. And why did we have to meet in a public place?"

Still looking around the busy eating establishment for an unfriendly face, he answered, "My name is John and for now that will have to do," replied the stranger. "As I told you over the phone I have not slept for days and my life is in danger."

"Then why don't you go to the police?" asked Reggie. "It seems to me if someone is trying to kill you then the police would be the place to start and not with a PI."

Ignoring Reggie's comment, John continued, "Was your father's name General Dominic Nutsbagh?"

With this statement Reggie's eyes narrowed as he replied, "Yes, that was his name, but that fact is a matter of public record, so what has it got to do with your wanting to talk to me?"

The man called John took another sip of coffee continuing his constant surveillance of the other customers and didn't reply right away as Reggie's mind went back, for some reason, to the fateful day of the explosion of his parent's airplane and the last time he had talked with his father. He remembered his father telling him he should always watch his back because there were vindictive people with long memories. Why did this come to mind at the mention of his father's name by a complete stranger?

Finally John spoke interrupting his thoughts, "Was your father working in Tel Aviv, Israel as an advisor to the Israeli Air Force?"

"Yes," he replied. "Again I ask, what does that have to do with you and me sitting in a sandwich shop in Las Vegas? Get to the point!"

"Not so fast," John said. "I will get to it in a minute but first I want to make sure I am talking to the right man and that the information will be handled prudently."

"Whoa John, or whatever your name is," he said, "what a prospective client discusses with me doesn't get repeated to anyone unless it involves something illegal and then I'll decide whether or not I need to involve the police, is that understood?"

"That's good to know. Were you with your father during his service in Israel?" John asked, continued with his questioning.

"Certainly I was, as was my Mother, but—"

"Be patient, I will be getting around to the reason for my meeting with you in due time, but for now it is one step at a time."

Reggie had almost come to the end of his patience, but something about the man's manner made him feel the wait would be worth a little listening.

Perhaps it was observing the way that all the time John was talking his eyes never stopped scanning everyone around the shop, paying particular attention to patrons entering. He seemed to be mentally cataloging everyone who entered to try and determine if they posed a threat to him.

"Do you remember anything of significance happening during your stay in Israel?" John further questioned.

A little irritated at why this stranger was asking all of these questions and where it was leading, Reggie replied, "I was young and my father didn't discuss any of his business relationships with me, so the answer is, no."

"How about a big explosion next to your father's office building killing many people? Do you remember that?" John asked. Not waiting for an answer he continued. "Do you remember how often your father was missing from family dinners during that time and how often he was on the road?" John insistently questioned.

Reggie frowned then closed his eyes deep in thought. He seemed to recall there had been a large explosion in downtown Tel Aviv. Afterwards there was a period of time just before they were due to come home that his father was terribly distracted, working late into the night. One time he remembered asking his dad what he was doing and why he was gone so much and was simply told it was Air Force business.

Two days later they were flown as a family to Las Vegas where his father bought the house in Summerlin and they assumed a normal life after his retirement. His father began work in an investment firm and his mother resumed her role as a housewife. They lived a normal life until the airplane explosion, which killed both of his parents.

"Yes," replied Reggie. "During that time he did spend a lot of time away from the house, but that was his job. He was the US Air Force

Senior Advisor to the IDF (Israeli Defense Forces) for the Israeli Air Force."

"But," John insistently asked, "Wasn't he away from the house more than normal during the period just prior to you and your family moving back to the United States?"

Reggie was silent, he didn't want to give this man any more information about his family then he already had, until he found out where this conversation was going.

John again asked more insistently, "Well what about those times? What do you remember about your father and what was going on?"

Reggie wanted to put a stop to this questioning and absorb what John had ask him, so rather than answer his question, he said, "Look I have to go call my girlfriend, we were supposed to have dinner and it doesn't look like I'm going to be able to make it."

Reggie could have used the cell phone in his pocket but wanted to get away, so he stepped outside the shop to the pay phone and placed a call to Brandy. He dialed the number and on the third ring Brandy picked up the phone, "Hello."

"It's me," he began, "I know I'm a little late, but I'm out on business and don't know when I'll be finished."

"Well," replied Brandy, "seeing as how we were supposed to meet two hours ago I figured something was going on, but I'm not going to let you off that easy, so it will cost you more than a dinner."

Returning to the table, Reggie discovered it was empty. The only thing at the table was his coat, two half-filled cups of coffee and the remains of two sandwiches.

He hurried went to the men's room hoping John had to heed the call of nature. But the men's room was empty.

Returning to the table he beckoned to the waitress, "Did you see the man who was sitting here with me?" he asked.

The waitress replied, "Yes he got up and left like he was shot out of a cannon. He was running when he reached the sidewalk."

Nodding at her response, he picked up his coat and walked out of the shop and began walking down the sidewalk looking for John. Not seeing him he picked up his car and drove to his apartment in Henderson, all the while trying to make sense of his recent conversation with the man calling himself John. He made another call to Brandy begging off for the night, then lying down on his bed fully clothed he went over the night's events in his mind. Sleep would be hard to come by this night.

CHAPTER FOUR

A Murder in Bremerton—Toby Resigns

OUTSIDE A SOFT rain had started, and Toby as he had grabbed his slicker. The dark green one Esther had given him on his thirtieth birthday. Why was it, everything brought her back to mind? Shrugging the depressing thought aside, he rushed out of the door heading for Washington Avenue. Placing the portable red light on the roof of his unmarked police car, he sped to the scene of the alleged crime. Going back over the conversation with the mysterious caller he tried to place the voice, the caller hadn't used perfect English and showed a trace of an accent, European possibly German.

"Move over, you idiot," he barked at the driver of the silver Lexus just in front of him, "don't you know what it means when a red light is flashing on top of a car?" As he roared past the car, which had finally pulled over, he caught a glimpse of the mayor, His Honor Elton Norton, the third. *'Wonder what he's doing out this time of night?'* He questioned, as he pulled in alongside the apartment complex.

Located in what was now one of the more seedy neighborhoods in the Navy town of Bremerton, Washington Avenue had once been the residential hub of a now dying town. The waterside windows of the homes and apartments strung out along the avenue offered a spectacular view of Sinclair Inlet with its water dotted with sailboats, and a picturesque view of majestic Mt. Rainier. Now the area was rundown and known for its drug deals and open prostitution. The majestic view was still there, but more often the eye was drawn to the decay of the neighborhood. It had become a place where the police dreaded responding to 911 calls. A domestic quarrel in this neighborhood usually involved a knifing or worse. There always seemed to be something happening.

Climbing out of his car he noticed the mayor had pulled in behind him. *'Now what's that jerk up to?'* There was no love lost between the two men. The current mayor was a former police officer who had campaigned for and won the privilege to serve the people of Bremerton. Toby's opinion (and that of several others on the force) was that he had been a lousy cop and made an even lousier mayor. Out of respect for the office he walked back to the mayor's Lexus and tapped on his window. "What brings you out here, Mayor?"

Stepping out of his car, Mayor Norton, responded, "It seems, Officer Preston, you were in a hurry and with no evidence of a backup, I thought I might offer assistance."

"It's Detective-Lieutenant, your honor, and as a former member of the force, you are aware of the rules regarding civilians at a crime scene."

"What crime scene, Detective? Am I missing something here, and I again question the lack of backup."

With a sigh, Toby yielded to Norton and strolled back to his car. Picking up his handset, he spoke into it, "Dispatch, this is 61 Alpha, come in."

"Go ahead, 61 Alpha."

"I'm at the Seaside Apartments following up on a possible homicide, send backup immediately."

"On its way, 61 Alpha, is an ambulance required?"

"I haven't gone inside yet; I just arrived, but it might be a good idea to put one on standby until we see what we're up against."

Resignedly he turned away from his car and headed back toward the mayor who still sat in his vehicle with the engine idling. As he walked the short distance he sifted through his mind why he detested this ex-cop with such a fierce passion. *'Not jealousy, I was never in the running for mayor. Has to be how he conducted himself while carrying the shield.'*

"Well, your honor, help is on the way. Now we can see what is going on. Don't like people knowing my unlisted number and using it to interrupt what precious few hours I have with my daughter."

"You mean to say you received a call about something going on down here?" the Mayor questioned.

Toby didn't have time to answer as a black and white, with lights flashing and siren blaring came roaring down Sixth Street, followed by the Chief of Police, Commander David Fisher. Screeching to a stop the two uniformed officers bailed out, with their service revolvers at the ready. Corporal Thad Vince and his rookie partner Will Dunphy must have been nearby to have responded so quickly.

Addressing himself to the Chief of Police, Toby, said, "Evening Chief, I didn't know you would still be up this time of the night."

"Must have eaten some bad shrimp and couldn't sleep, so when I heard your call on the scanner I rushed right down. What do we have?"

"Not really sure yet, sir, it came into my home by way of an anonymous call. The caller said a murder had been committed. I need to get inside, so would you stay out here and act as control?"

"Sure, but do you think you might need me inside?"

"No sir, Vince and I will take the inside with Dunphy as cover. If you could keep the mayor contained that would be a big help."

"If that's the way you want it, Toby. Go ahead and do what you have to do. There will be no interference from out here."

Turning to his support team, Toby said, "Okay fellows, you've been through this drill before. As there has been no official report of a homicide we have to go in prepared for anything. An anonymous call is often no more than a prank call, but we'll go in with our weapons drawn, safeties on. I go in first, followed by Vince. Dunphy you stay outside the building for now."

"We have three floors to canvass, so let's do it quickly, but thoroughly. Any open or unlocked door gets special attention. The locked ones mark, so we can come back to them if we haven't found a body or bodies. We'll start with the manager's office."

The door to the manager's office was slightly ajar. The squeak from opening it further was loud enough to wake the dead, which it didn't do for the unfortunate soul lying face down on the floor. Being careful not to disturb anything Preston used his foot to turn over the body. What appeared to be a gunshot wound delivered at close range had sucked the lifeblood out of the very dead person. The upper chest revealed a huge cavity and in the dim light given off by the streetlight it was hard to tell whether the victim with its scraggly, shoulder-length hair was male or female.

"Don't touch anything with your hands. Use your nightclub to turn on the light, then go outside and ask for more officers; send the coroner in if she has arrived. Have someone call downtown and see if the desk sergeant can find out who owns this building and get them here. Bring me some gloves, too."

Cpl. Vince left to do as instructed turning on the overhead light as he left. When the light came on Toby saw he was looking at the body of a middle-aged man, probably the manager of the establishment.

Toby continued to explore the room. All the drawers of the lone file cabinet were dumped on the floor; the desk underneath the window was completely ransacked, other than the injury sustained by the victim there were no signs of a struggle. Whoever the killer was he or she posed no perceived threat. This didn't look like a drug-related murder because there was a jar almost full of coins on the desk, and the victim's wallet lying on the floor still had some bills inside. '*Think, Toby, what happened here and who called and why you?*'

It was going to be a long night and a long day tomorrow. '*Renie isn't going to like this. I promised her we would take the ferry to Seattle and do some clothes shopping. God, I need some answers.*'

To hear Toby Wainwright Preston talk to God wouldn't be unusual to those who knew him. A deeply religious man, he was the kind of person who prayed over his meals even in public. Having attended church all of his life it wasn't difficult to believe his minor in college had been theology. The University of Washington wasn't known for its conservative teachings, so he spent many class sessions arguing with his professors over theological differences. Weighing two hundred and thirty pounds and standing six foot three inches, he had been an All-American linebacker for the University of Washington for three years and didn't let the lecturers push him around in the classroom any more than he let players on the field. Off the field though, he was as gentle a person as you could ever meet.

"Hey, Lieutenant, we have reporters outside, what do you want to do with them?" asked Corporal Vince, as he came back into the room.

Shaking himself from his thoughts, Toby replied, "Who is it? If it's that woman reporter normally assigned to the beat, don't let her in. If it's one of the guys—never mind I'll be right out."

Being as careful as he could, he stepped through the doorway and out into the hallway. Using the gloves Vince had handed him, he shut the door behind him and proceeded down the hall and out the door. It was two AM, yet the front of the apartment building was ablaze with lights. At least five patrol cars, all with lights on, lined the street, along with an ambulance with its crew awaiting instructions. A news van from

Channel Four, a Seattle TV station was also there. *'How in the world did they get here so fast, was it another anonymous phone call? Well, the old saying, 'No rest for the weary', sure works here. Getting out of here without giving an interview would be a trick for Houdini. Maybe I should let the Chief or Mayor take over that part.'*

"Vince, were you able to find the owner of the apartment building?"

"Yeah, Lieutenant he's right over there."

Following the direction in which Corporal Vince was pointing, Toby could see two easily recognizable people. "Are you telling me the Chief owns this place?"

"No, Lieutenant, the Mayor."

With a puzzled expression, Toby turned back to look at the apartment building. "Now why do you suppose he never mentioned that during the time we were together?" Toby mumbled under his breath.

"Vince, I need to get over to His Honor without having to answer a lot of nosy reporter's questions. Step over to your squad car and get everyone to gather around you."

"What am I supposed to say?"

"Tell them what they want to hear, there's an unidentified dead body, lying in a pool of blood in the manager's office and that it's an apparent homicide; committed by an, as yet unidentified assailant. Wing it man, this could be your big day. Imagine your handsome puss on national TV. I need some time alone with the mayor, and as soon as I get out of this doorway I'm going to be swamped. I'll try to come and relieve you if I can get some satisfactory answers from His Honor. Just do it."

Vince was already into his oratory as Toby hurriedly walked over to where the mayor and the chief were huddled under an umbrella.

"Mayor, why did you fail to tell me you owned The Seaside?"

"I didn't think it was necessary and don't see how it's any of your business," was the retort of the disheveled Mayor.

"Well, now that's where you're wrong. This is a homicide and I'll be digging into a lot of your business. I'm not declaring you a suspect yet, but your actions tonight are suspect."

"Lieutenant," a somewhat perturbed Commander Fisher commanded, "this is the Mayor, show a little respect and tact. We are all tired and need some rest. I'll have Captain Jones finish up. You've done enough. Go home, get a couple of hour's shuteye and I'll see you at 9 a.m."

DAWN OF REALIZATION 43

"Sir, we have more than a simple murder here. Diplomacy needs to be thrown out the window. Questions need to be asked and answered. I can't just walk away from this."

"Consider yourself removed from the case, Lt. Preston," the Police Chief said, "I'm officially placing any further investigation in the hands of Captain Jones. Now go home, have a stiff hot chocolate and go to bed. We'll continue this discussion in my office first thing in the morning."

"No, Sir, we won't."

"Are we seeing insubordination here, Lieutenant?"

"Not by any means, sir. What you are seeing is grounds for my resignation. You'll have it in writing on your desk first thing Monday morning. You can explain to His Honor here that he gets his wish of having a thorn removed from his side. I like you Chief, but I don't like the way you do your job, or the company you keep."

With those last words thrown over his shoulder, he stalked off in the direction of his car.

A big sigh emanated from the throat of Chief Fisher, as he realized the impact of losing such a valuable member of the force.

Speaking more to himself than the Mayor, who was still standing at his elbow, he said, "Maybe he'll cool off in the morning and change his mind. He's too good a man to lose."

"I wouldn't worry about him right now, David. Besides I believe you'll be better off without him. He has a tendency to be too easy on the criminals."

"You're wrong there, Mayor. There's no better policeman around than Toby Preston, and there's not an officer on the force who would hesitate to follow him through a hailstorm of bullets. Trying to play this politically correct with you has caused irreparable damage to the department. Goodnight. I'm going to follow my own advice, have a drink, a little stronger than hot chocolate, and try to get a couple of hours of sleep."

Doing an abrupt about face, the now dejected, veteran police chief walked over to where Captain Joe Jones was standing with a small band of uniformed officers.

"Joe, can I speak to you for a moment?"

"Sure, Chief."

"Joe, I am pulling Lt. Preston off this case and I'll need you to take over here."

"Sure, Chief. Is everything all right with Toby?"

The Police Chief just shrugged his shoulders and wearily trudged off to his car and the dreary ride home. His wife, Helen, thought the world of Toby, and his daughter Jennifer and Toby's daughter Renie were the best of friends. "I'm getting too old for this," he mumbled, as he climbed into his car, "I sure need that stiff drink."

For Toby, who was almost home and deep in thought, it wasn't a time for despair, but a time of joy. His dislike for the mayor had begun when the, then sergeant had used unnecessary force while dealing with a couple of teenagers he apprehended for smoking marijuana. The dislike had escalated during Norton's run for mayor. Toby and the majority of his fellow officers refused to endorse him when requested. In spite of the failed endorsement Norton won over a weaker opponent and life had been miserable ever since. Toby had begun to think about termination and now the chief and mayor, with their politics, had just paved the way. Now Toby had a call to make—to Las Vegas!

CHAPTER FIVE

Toby Takes a Blow

TOBY WOKE WITH a start as two bony knees slammed into his stomach forcing the wind out of him.

"Come on, daddy, are you trying to sleep the day away? You promised me a shopping trip to Seattle, and it's already 8 o'clock."

"Give your poor old man a break; I didn't get in until after three."

"Poor old man?" the precocious twelve-year old countered. "Most of my friend's parents are older than you. Besides five hours sleep is all anyone needs. Come on, time is wasting."

Moaning as he threw his legs over the edge of the bed, he rubbed the sleep out of his eyes and padded to the bathroom. A splash of cold water and a quick mouth rinse with Listerine and he pretended he was ready to make an effort to keep up with this bundle of energy. Twelve years old and she still liked her dad, which couldn't be all bad. Turning around he almost knocked her down.

"Hey, can't a guy have a little privacy while he gets dressed?" he grumbled good-naturedly.

"Okay, Mr. Grumps, but don't crawl back into bed."

Selecting a pair of black Docker pants and a blue pullover shirt from his wardrobe he stumbled into the bathroom. "Hope she allows me the time for a shower. What a kid."

Breakfast was coffee and one of Maria's biscuits for him and a bowl of Cheerios and orange juice for Renie. This meal was downed in less than ten minutes to allow them time to reach the ferry terminal for the early ferry run to Seattle.

On the short trip to the ferry for the ride to Seattle, Renie couldn't contain her enthusiasm. It wasn't that she hadn't been to Seattle before, but the time spent with her dad would be the longest time since her mother's death. He rarely left the property any more, except to go to work and church. Maria did all the family grocery shopping and Chief Fisher's wife took her shopping for the normal clothing and school supplies. This was really a treat to have her dad all to herself. She realized life hadn't been easy since mom went away. It was hard for her, too, but it was different for men. Daddy had cried so hard for the first few days after Mom died that she had really became concerned about him. It was the best thing for him when they sent him to Utah for that class, where he met Reggie. He came back a lot happier, and except for still working too hard, he managed to make it through each day.

Toby hadn't yet told his daughter of his resignation. It hadn't quite sunk in for him yet. He had always been one for saying what he thought regardless of the consequences. His predilection of saying the first thing that came to mind had gotten him into hot water in the past and no doubt would in the future, but he didn't regret his decision. He had thought about getting out, but without a sense of false pride he knew he made a difference on the force, but he also knew no one was indispensable. There would be time for confession and any regrets later. *'Let's make this a fun day,'* he thought.

Fun isn't what he would have called walking innumerable city blocks, pouring through dozens of shops, and finally leaving downtown Seattle laden with bags stuffed with shoes, jeans, shirts, and bras. The latter garment had presented him with a brief moment of embarrassment, but a perceptive female clerk sensing his predicament had taken charge freeing him to wander over to men's shoes and purchase a pair of Reeboks for himself. The whole shopping experience created a bond between father and daughter, which made all the seeming miles of walking bearable. "But," he muttered, "I wouldn't want to make a habit of it."

After a late lunch of halibut and chips at Ivar's Seafood Bar, the weary shoppers boarded the ferry for the trip home. Renie fell asleep on one of the benches while Toby went over the events of the previous evening. There were too many things bothering him. The phone call, the Mayor's involvement, the condition of the room where the victim was discovered, but mostly the nagging thought that there was evil loose in his beloved town. While in one of the many stores they had visited, there had been a news flash about one of the dogs in Bremerton's K9 Unit, having been killed so that, in addition to more drive-by shootings being reported every day, and an increased number of meth busts made him question his decision to quit the force. *'Am I quitting at the right time? Did I really make a difference?'* These questions went through his mind as he glanced at his reflection in the window. He was roused from his thoughts by the announcement over the PA system of the boat's arrival in Bremerton. Gently shaking Renie, he said, "Come on, little girl, time to wake up. How does a hot fudge sundae from Baskin and Robbins sound?"

"Can I have a mocha shake instead?" Renie replied.

"Coffee?" Toby replied, "I didn't know you liked coffee."

"Mama used to give it to me all the time, didn't you know?" was her tart response.

"I suppose you and your mother did a lot of things I wasn't aware of," he sighed.

"Yes," she said, "so now I guess you and I will have to do them. There's just you and me from now on, daddy."

Toby looked at this twelve year-old and knew it was going to be hard keeping ahead of her. With her insightful probing she was more like twelve going on thirty was his quick assessment.

It was some time later after he had tucked Renie away for the night that he was able to get his thoughts back on the murder. Death in itself isn't something most police officers have a hard time coping with, though it isn't a thing you seek out. A murder, on the other hand is different, it's an affront to a good cop to think this crime was committed in his town. Therefore solving the crime by apprehending the perpetrator is foremost in a police officer's mind. Such was the case with Toby. He would soon submit his resignation and would no longer be a member of the force, but it happened on his watch. He was still puzzling over the events when the grandfather clock in the foyer began to toll the twelve o'clock hour. It's Sunday, he thought to himself and knowing Renie wouldn't let him miss church, he shut the lights off and headed to bed.

Sleep didn't come instantly, for he remembered hearing the cuckoo clock in the hallway loudly proclaim it was one a.m. before finally dropping off into a restless sleep.

He had hardly begun tossing and turning when he bolted up, sitting upright in bed, he declared, "It wasn't what was missing from the murdered man's room, it was what was there! It was there all the time and I failed to notice it."

Hastily he jumped into his clothes, and quietly, so as not to disturb his sleeping daughter, went down the stairs and out into the night, locking the door behind him he jumped into the family Buick Roadmaster. As he sped the few blocks to the Seaside Apartments, he hoped the Chief hadn't announced his pending resignation and that he would be able to convince the officer on watch to let him in.

Pulling up behind the squad car sitting outside the apartment building, he opened his car door at the same time as the officer in the police car. Toby recognized the officer as being Sarah Shelley, one of the Reserve Officers, who wanted to go on the active duty list.

"Good evening, Lt. Preston," she said, throwing him a snappy salute.

"Evening, Officer Shelley. Tell me they don't have you here by yourself?"

"No Sir, I'm here with Corporal Vince. He thought he saw a shadow at the corner of the building and went to investigate. He's been gone about fifteen minutes and I was beginning to worry. He told me not to leave here, but he has been in there so long I became worried and was just getting ready to call the station when you pulled up."

Speaking rapidly to the young reserved officer, he commanded her, "Sarah, get on the radio and call for backup, I'm going in so hand me your shotgun as I brought no weapon with me. Then I want you to get back in your car and stay there."

Without waiting for response, he took the proffered weapon and stealthily made his way to the front of the former hotel. The concrete steps leading up to the doorway helped in his efforts at silence, but the creaky sound when he opened the door took away any chance of surprise. He sprang through the door, where the murder had been discovered earlier, stepping quickly to the side as he came through the door, he stumbled over an object on the floor. As he tried to maintain his balance he caught a glimpse of a figure out of the corner of his eye and then felt a wicked blow striking him along side the head. As he fell, he thought, *'Now why would the Mayor hit me?'*

If pain could be measured on a scale of 1 to 10, Toby felt what was coursing through his head would be off the scale. Reaching up to touch the area of pain his fingers came away sticky. Groggily attempting to arise he found himself touching what felt like a body and in the dim light filtering through the window he made out the form of Cpl. Vince. Reaching to feel for a pulse he felt a small flicker of life. Stumbling out of the door he headed for the patrol car, where Officer Shelley obediently sat in the passenger seat, her service revolver on the seat beside her. He was just preparing to tap on the car window when two more police vehicles pulled up, with their sirens blaring. Gasping through his pain he managed a yell at one of the approaching officers, "Call dispatch; officer down."

Without waiting for a response he turned to Shelley, who had pulled herself out of the patrol car, and asked, "Did you see anyone come out of the building?"

"No, sir, and I was looking all the time."

Turning quickly away from her, he yelled at the approaching officers, "Surround the building. Whoever the assailant is could still be in the building, there should be no one on the premises other than official personnel. I'll get more officers here and start a search of the rooms."

Turning again to the trembling Reserve Officer, he instructed her to call for all available officers to get to the Seaside Apartments. By his own calculations he had been out for only a couple of minutes, and in this short period of time the person who slugged Vince and himself couldn't have had time to get away.

His thoughts were interrupted by a yell, "Halt," and then gun fire. Waving Shelley to the ground he rushed toward the sound, fearful he would find another downed officer. Instead he found Officers Todd Jessup and Terry Sloan standing over a form dressed in black lying in a fetal position on the narrow path leading to the rear of the building.

Jessup spoke first, "He came around the building running, when I yelled 'halt', he shot at me and I shot back. He missed. I didn't." His voice quavered, "I couldn't just stand there and let him shoot me," he lamented.

Nodding in agreement, Toby gently rolled the inert body over, face up. Sure of whose face he would see so it was no surprise to see the eyes of Mayor Norton staring up at him. The shots by Jessup had been expertly placed, there would be no more campaign signs bearing the name of Elton Norton. Clutched in the dead man's hand was his Day-Planner, the item that had roused Toby out of sleep. Taking off his jacket, he spread it over the face of the former police officer and then picking up the Day-Planner he slid it under his shirt. Standing over the body he was aware that all the energy had been drained out of him and the loss of blood and the shock of tonight's events left him weak. If not for the alertness of Officer Sloan he would have collapsed and fallen to the ground.

"Shelley," Sloan thundered, "Send one of the EMT's back here, now!"

Additional officers were now on the scene and each officer quickly assumed a task, expediting the process of cleaning up the scene of the night's event. Two of their own were injured. One of their fellow officers had been forced to shoot in self-defense and they all felt pride in themselves. Not proud because a person had been killed, but proud that the motto, 'Proudly We Serve', had been upheld.

A person was dead, and that the person was the mayor of the city and the circumstances surrounding his death would surely cause a media frenzy and that coupled with an investigation would definitely shake this small town of 38,000. However, the furor surely to ensue came with the territory and they had sworn to uphold the law to the best of their ability. There was no reason to be ashamed and they could hold their heads up high in the community. They had taken more than their share of flack lately because the citizens had awakened one day to find crime had invaded their little community. Once voted the most livable city in the country, now Bremerton was a city headed for the dubious title of 'ghost town'.

While an EMT from Medic One patched Toby up, Chief Fisher walked up to him, "What happened here, Toby? I know you're banged up, but this can't wait until later. The Mayor of a city isn't killed without questions being raised, what was he doing here? What are you doing here? What—."

"Hold on, Sir," Toby interrupted. "A lot of this needs sifting through before we have all of the answers. Vince will give you some of the details if and when he recovers. I'll fill you in with what I know."

Despite the throbbing in his head, Toby began to relate to the Chief everything that had transpired from the time he was ripped out of a restless sleep, to catching a glimpse of the Mayor slamming him alongside the head. Knowing the question would come out soon enough he revealed what had awakened him. "During the time in the room where I discovered the murder I was disturbed by the lack of motive. It was evident that robbery wasn't a consideration since there were valuables and money readily accessible. It didn't register at the time, but I remember seeing a leather-bound Day-Planner on the window ledge. It didn't come to me until being roused out of sleep, that it was Mayor Norton's. I saw it on his desk, during the Friday morning briefing on the upcoming visit to the Shipyard by the Secretary of the Navy. Every time I came across him at City Hall, he was carrying it; except for the night of the murder, that is." Reaching inside his shirt he pulled out the item in question and extended it to the Chief, "I took it off his body and here it is."

"I sincerely apologize for our misunderstanding the other night, Toby, but we need to dig a little deeper into tonight's shooting and the Mayor's involvement. We can't keep this incident quiet for long and at this time, without more information, we can't imply any impropriety on the Mayor's part."

"I fully understand, sir, and I believe we need to keep this under wraps until we see what we have. If he was willing to risk his life and even take other lives to recover the Day-Planner, then we need to find out why it was so important. After all he owned the building and had every right to talk to the resident manager."

Realizing the frustration Toby was experiencing the Police Chief agreed that any investigation or release of information should be postponed for a couple of hours. Toby was an injured officer, in a lot of pain, yet he was concerned about the department and the city. '*I certainly hope this new development causes him to reconsider resigning,*' thought the harried chief. '*I would hate to lose a person as valuable as he.*'

It took nearly twice as long to negotiate the short two-mile drive back to the house, but he arrived without mishap. Normally he would have pulled into the four-car garage, which housed a 57 Corvette, in pristine condition, a 37 Chevrolet Cabriolet, which he was in the process of restoring, and a new Jeep Wrangler. Beside the garage there was a facility that housed his 32-foot RV. But in his haste to check on Renie he pulled into the circular drive and slowly removed his aching body from the car.

The first thing he noticed as he walked into the house was the unlocked door. Knowing he had locked it upon leaving earlier, he called out, "Renie, I'm home." Getting no response he hastily went back to her bedroom. The bed was unmade and her bureau drawer was open, leading him to believe she had dressed in a hurry. Calling out for her again he headed toward the kitchen. As he went into the kitchen he saw a bloody towel lying in the sink and drops of blood on the floor starting from the back door. He headed in that direction imagining the worst but he could only fault himself for leaving without awakening her.

With trained eyes he observed the blood led from the outside into the house. Not knowing what to think by this time, he strode to the wall phone to begin a check of the local hospitals when he heard a sound coming from the vicinity of the pantry; as he opened the door he saw both Renie and Jeremiah Norton.

Taking her hand, he queried, "What in the world are you doing in there and what happened to you, son, why aren't you home in bed?"

Not giving Jeremiah time to answer, Renie chimed in, "Jeri has a key to his dad's warehouse and was playing around in the warehouse and fell asleep. When he woke up there were some men moving big crates around. He saw a lot of big wooden boxes, one was open and he saw lots of guns and even some rocket launchers. He said there were so many that it looked like something from the Arnold Schwarzenegger movie Combat. He—"

"Whoa, slow down. You're talking so fast your not making sense. Okay, Jeremiah let's hear it from you and slowly."

Stammering at first and with an occasional sob in his voice, the boy went over the night's events. Renie might have been excited when she related the story, but she had it right. The boy saw heavy weapons, even a couple of rubber assault craft and what looked like uniforms. He managed to sneak away unnoticed, but in his haste stumbled on the curb, bloodying his nose. He had been so frightened by all the weaponry he had run all the way to Renie's house afraid of what he had seen.

"How long ago was that Jeremiah?" Toby questioned.

Answering for the quivering boy, Renie piped in, "It was 3 o'clock. I remember the cuckoo clock going off just after he rang the bell."

"Very good, sweetheart, that makes it only twenty minutes ago. Why don't you make some hot chocolate for the two of you while I make a quick phone call?"

"You aren't going to leave me again, are you daddy?" she asked.

"I may have to, but I will be back as soon as I can. Let Jeremiah sleep in the spare bedroom. And you get back into bed also."

As his daughter hurried off to start the water boiling for the hot drinks, Toby grabbed the phone and quickly dialed the Chief's home phone number. He sighed with relief when the Chief himself answered. "Sir, we have a big problem. No time for questions. We need a SWAT team at the warehouse located at Fourth and Warren, call the FBI and send for them also. Something big is going down and we need to hurry. Have all units go in silent and park a block away and wait for me to walk in. I'll fill you in more when I get there. And ask your wife if she would mind dropping by and checking on Renie. I have Jeremiah Norton here also. We need to get on this now." With that last curt statement he hung up the phone, not waiting for acknowledgement.

By the time Toby arrived at the staging area on Fifth Street, a block away from the warehouse there were several city police cars, as well as two Sheriff Cruisers and the SWAT van there. He wasn't the ranking officer there, but they all knew him, and already had been instructed by the Chief to let Toby handle the operation, so he assumed control of the situation.

Telling them he had information from a very reliable source that there was a large cache of weapons along with armed men in the warehouse, he urged extreme caution, "I'll try to gain access through the alley door, which I just happen to have a key for. You know the drill, weapons drawn, and safeties off with the weapons pointed up. Know who is with you, and watch each other's back. Okay, let's do it."

Turning to Sergeant Frank Gibson, the SWAT Team's commander, he said, "Frank how about quietly positioning a man on the roof by the skylight." Turning to the others he said, "Okay, let's do it."

Leading the way, Toby didn't dare tell the men behind him he was taking the word of a thirteen-year old boy. From what had already gone down today, he experienced no doubts or misgivings. Moving quietly up to the warehouse, he saw a semi tractor backed up to a loading ramp. The loading door was down and a man dressed in dark clothes was lounging against the small door leading inside. Toby beckoned to the two officers beside him and motioned for them to take the man down. The man was caught totally off guard and was handcuffed and removed from the area in short order.

Sending two other officers to check the cab of the large Volvo rig, he and the remaining task force moved toward the small side door. As silently as possible he inserted the key, unlocking the door. Now, he thought, is the time to pray for oiled hinges. Leaping through the doorway he immediately went left and into a crouch. The others behind him followed suit and were scattered on the deck or against the wall. The little hallway, which revealed a door at the end, wasn't lit and it took a few minutes for the men to adjust to the dark.

Noise could be heard coming from the larger storeroom. Moving stealthily, Toby and four officers behind him made their way forward.

'*Thank God for concrete floors,*' he thought, as they inched their way along the wall. Standing in front of the door, he gingerly tested the knob. "Great," he breathed, with a sigh, "it isn't locked." Releasing his hold on the doorknob he turned to his compatriots, and whispered, "We are going in not knowing how many people are in there. Be ready for anything, don't shoot unless you have to, but take anyone down who shoots at you. Take no risks; we don't need any dead heroes here."

Orders given, he grasped the door, opened it swiftly and then dove to the left and as he rolled, he yelled loudly, "Drop what you're doing and raise your hands above your shoulders, you are all under arrest."

Completely caught by surprise, all but one of the three men immediately visible complied. That one grabbed for an assault rifle standing nearby, making his first and last mistake of the day. As he reached for the weapon the SWAT member stationed at the skylight above neatly placed a hole in his forehead. The other two men seeing their companion die from a bullet knew they didn't stand a chance and resigned themselves to keeping their hands up. The two prisoners immediately began babbling in an unknown language, but to no avail, as Toby knew they understood some English from their having understood his earlier command.

"Separate them so they're not able to talk with each other. They are evidently not U.S. citizens, but read them their rights, any way."

As the officers read the Miranda rights to the suspects Toby walked over to the crates of weapons hoping to find some clues as to why such a massive arsenal had arrived in Bremerton. Each crate had the name of a firm in Tel Aviv emblazoned on it. A Star of David had been stamped on the lids and the words 'Farm Machinery' were stenciled below the symbol.

While he was studying the crates of weapons the officer assigned to search the two suspects walked back over to him with a slip of paper in his hand, which he handed to Toby saying, "Hey, Lieutenant, have any idea what this means?

Toby looked at the piece of paper and saw the word DONE printed on the paper in bold letters. He scratched his head and said, "I have no idea, but put it with the other items taken from them."

By now the Chief and the rest of the task force had entered the building. Ignoring the Chief for the moment, Toby ordered the rest of the team to start inspecting the boxes stacked throughout the warehouse.

Turning to the Chief, he said, "Well Sir, it looks like somebody was trying to start World War III. From the looks of things there are enough weapons here to make an assault on every military installation within the Puget Sound area. Still something puzzles me about this whole situation, surely these four men weren't going to attack a military base alone, there are more people out there, but where and who? I'll wager my separation check the Day-Planner of Norton's will tell some tales. I'm not sure if we will ever know what turned him, but he was a traitor of the lowest kind."

Not having a response to the evident truth, the Chief turned and gave the order for the police photographer to come in and start with her pictures. "And I left Topeka, Kansas to come to this nice quiet town," he mumbled.

"With your permission, sir I'm going to go home and pick up my daughter and Jeremiah, I'll take him to his grandmother's house in Port Orchard and then take Renie to the park and tell her what I should have told her yesterday; I quit. She'll be glad to hear that, I think."

"You're sure you won't reconsider, Toby? After the way you handled today's operation I'm sure a promotion to captain is in the offing. Maybe you could even have my job.

"No thank you!" Toby shot back. "From now on it's going to be the easy life for me."

CHAPTER SIX

More Confusion

ONFUSION REIGNED IN the young captive's mind. "If this is America why am I being treated in this manner?" he questioned. What had begun as a fun trip with college buddies had ended up with his being tied up and thrown into this dark and cold room. A small beam of sunlight gleamed through the cracks in the wall of the windowless room. His blindfold had been removed, but the rope holding his hands and chafing his wrists remained. He had become separated from his hunting friends and in the process of trying to find his way back to their camp had stumbled into three tough looking men with automatic weapons. His greeting was answered with a clout to his head and the next thing he knew he was thrown into this room. Was it still the same day? He had no concept of time as they had taken all personal belongings away, even his belt was removed. For Thomas Lincoln Graden, the third, it seemed as if his world of pampered living had suddenly turned into a nightmare.

Reggie woke early, not at all well rested; he had spent the night tossing and turning, his mind whirling with his encounter at the sandwich shop. John, the dubious name he went by, and his questions about his family had caused the turmoil as his thoughts turned to his parents and their questionable deaths. After a long hot shower he dressed in his normal attire of jeans and golf shirt and made his way to the coffee shop across the street from his apartment. When he entered the shop several of the regular customers greeted him as he made his way back to where he normally sat in the corner. After greeting him they continued their conversations and from the bits and pieces of the talk he could hear, they seemed to be discussing a murder, which had taken place last night on the Strip.

He paid no further attention to their conversations, as he was still trying to process the information he had heard from John the day before. The waitress brought him his usual order of black coffee and a bagel with cream cheese, along with the newspaper carrying the story of the murder, which was the topic of the other patron's discussion.

Spreading the paper on the table he scanned the headlines. Not finding the story of immediate interest he turned to the Business Section of the paper to check on his latest investments, hoping the Stock Market hadn't plummeted beyond where it ended yesterday.

"Holy cow," he mumbled, "what can a fellow do to make a few bucks in the market? Looks like I lost some more money yesterday."

Laying the paper aside he began eating his now cold bagel. After a few chewy bites he again picked up the paper and started reading the article concerning last night's murder. An unidentified white male, approximately 35 to 40 years old was found dead in an alley behind the Paris Hotel and Casino. The details were sketchy, but did say the police released a statement saying even though he had been severely beaten the cause of death had been a single gunshot to the head.

'*Probably owed the mob big bucks and when they saw they couldn't make him cough it up, took their payment in finality,*' he thought.

He continued to eat his breakfast trying to putting aside his thoughts of yesterday's meeting and attempted to figure out what he needed to do today. Unable to get his thoughts in order he pulled out his cell phone and made a call to his office knowing his secretary, Hilda Crump would be there and hoping against hopes the stranger, John had called this morning.

On the third ring his secretary, Hilda answered, "Good morning, Reggie Nutsbagh's office, can I help you?"

"Morning Hilda, this is Reggie, are there any messages for me?"

"Let me see," she responded, "You had a call from Mrs. Redmond concerning your bill for the work you did for her in locating her runaway daughter. Then there was a call from Brandy; she sounded kind of put out and another call from Phil, your friend from the police department. And here's a message from me; when you finally get here there are some things we need to go over concerning several of your latest cases."

"I will answer those calls and your concerns when I arrive in about 35 minutes."

Finishing his breakfast, his thoughts once again went back to the events of yesterday, not wanting to let go of the strange conversation he had and still trying to figure out what it was all about. He placed another call to Brandy's work and after apologizing profusely, he promised her they would get together in the evening.

When he left the coffee shop he was so caught up in his thoughts he failed to notice the two men sitting in a parked car across the street watching him.

He got into his car, brought the engine to life and drove to his office unaware he was being followed.

"Good morning Hilda, how are you this morning?" he asked, as he entered his office. Without waiting for her response he continued, "Any more calls?"

"Mrs. Redmond called again, still wanting to know about the charges on her bill. Plus we do need to talk about some things concerning your last case."

"Okay, we will talk in a few minutes. Would you please bring me a cup of coffee and the Redmond file?"

He sat down and was going through the files lying on his desk, when the intercom squawked and Hilda's voice came through, saying, "Boss, there are two gentlemen here to see you."

"Give me a few minutes and then send them in, "he replied.

A few minutes elapsed and then there was a knock on the door and Hilda escorted the two men into his office. One of them held out his hand and said, "Mr. Nutsbagh, my name is Samuel Lebowitz and this is Jerod Abbott."

Lebowitz was short of stature, barrel-chested with a thick neck and the expensive suit he wore gave an impression of a successful businessman. His companion was a tall man, who towered above his companion. He had a girth that made his belt work overtime and the flowered sport shirt he wore strained against the buttons and could hardly contain his broad shoulders. Both men appeared to be in their late 50's or early 60's. Other than Abbott's girth there was nothing in particular that separated them from the hundreds of tourists that visit this town annually.

"Good morning, gentlemen," addressed them, "can I offer you some coffee?"

"Yes please," replied Abbott, "we both drink it black, same as you."

"Hilda," he yelled through the open door, "When you bring in my coffee bring in two more cups of black coffee for these two gentlemen."

"Don't think I didn't catch your comment," he continued. "It's apparent you took the time to get to know things about me, so maybe we should get right down to business, instead of playing games."

Abbott replied, "We're here on a very important matter. I want to make sure what we're about to tell you is kept completely confidential."

"Okay gentlemen," he said, his hackles starting to rise, "I'm listening; but I'll be the one who decides what I do with the information you give me, so why don't you stop beating around the bush and tell me what's going on and why you're in my office?"

Through the open door Hilda heard her boss's voice rise, which meant he was starting to get annoyed, so she, wanting to break the tension used that moment to bring in the coffee and asked Reggie, "Is there anything else you need? If not, I have some business at the bank so I will be gone for awhile."

Looking at her, he winked and said, "No, that's okay, Hilda, you go ahead and take care of business. Please close the door on your way out."

He had calmed down, and asked of the two, "Just what is your business with me?"

"We were retained by a very influential person," responded Abbott, "whose identity we're not at liberty to disclose at this time, to look into something that happened in Northern Montana."

"Beautiful country, Montana," he replied, "but what has that got to do with me, and why you're in Las Vegas?"

Abbott began, "It's a rather long story but we'll try to simplify it. Not too long ago a young man disappeared while on a hunting trip into Northern Montana. We were hired to go to Montana and try to find out what happened. We checked with the local authorities and they launched an investigation into his disappearance, although I must say it was half-hearted, but they couldn't find him. And as there was no hint of wrong doing, according to them, they scaled back their search but kept the case open as a missing person."

"So, what has to do with me?" he said, breaking into Abbott's story. "You two don't fit the bill of any investigator I've ever seen."

Abbott continued, "Both of us, like you, are retired police officers and do a little investigative work on the side. Now back to the story; our employer insists the missing young man wouldn't intentionally disappear because he had too much going for him, so we continued with the investigation."

"Again I ask, what has all of this to do with me?" he repeated. "You still haven't told me what brought you to Las Vegas." Laughing he asked, "Did you take a wrong turn on the freeway?"

At this point Lebowitz entered the conversation, "Initially we went to Montana and did some looking around. We stumbled across an old abandoned Air Force Base complete with hangars and other buildings. We didn't get to look around too much, as we were encouraged to leave by a group of people who looked like derelicts from a prison yard. After that things got a little warm and we had to leave."

Abbott again entered the conversation, "After we left Montana and gave our report to the person who hired us, we were instructed to hire another private detective to proceed with the investigation of the missing young man. We did that and the PI went to Montana where we know he encountered some problems, we think with the same people who gave us problems, and he too left in a hurry."

"Are you ever going to get to the part that tells me why you are here in Las Vegas and what all of this has to do with me?" Reggie retorted, getting a little hot under the collar.

"Jerod, let me break this down," insisted Sam, who then continued with the story, "You met with a man last evening in a Sandwich shop, I believe he called himself John."

"That was the name he gave me, but—"

"Let me finish," broke in Sam, "This man, you call John was the PI who worked for us. He called us from Vegas explaining that someone was following him and he was going to contact a PI named Nutsbagh. During the conversation he sounded extremely agitated. We believe he was followed out of Montana to Vegas because of what they think he knows. We need to contact him and get him out of town to a safe place for his own good. We feel responsible for him, after all we hired him."

"Hold it a minute, Sam," Jerod said, jumping back into the conversation, "We must insist, what we are telling you, doesn't get out of this room."

"I have no intention of repeating anything you've told me, because you haven't really told me anything, especially anything which explains why you are in Las Vegas talking to me about a stranger called John, and something happening in Montana."

"If you'll give us a chance we'll get to it," countered Lebowitz.

"Okay," Reggie asked, "But first, where are the local law enforcement agencies in all of this and do they have any idea what's going on?"

Jerod jumped back in explaining, "As I said before, the local law is in the picture only because we have reported the disappearance of the young man. I think we've said enough for now, at least until we check with the person who hired us."

"And this is all you are going to tell me?" Reggie spoke with anger.

"I'm telling you we can't tell you any more until we check with our employer," Jerod said. "We know how you feel, but there is nothing we can do about it. We'll go back to our hotel and make a few calls and find out how far our employer wants us to bring you into this. But I believe, like it or not, you are already in the middle of it, since you were seen talking with John. Think about it, if we saw you then others could have seen you two together, also."

Disgusted Reggie said, "If this doesn't frost the cake, last night I meet with a stranger who gave me a lot of information that meant nothing, then this morning I met a couple more strangers who add more to the information that means nothing and then all three walk out on me. Now on top of that, you warn me I may be knee deep in it—in what I asked you!" yelling the last, as he lost control of his temper.

"I'm sorry," said Lebowitz with a frown. "We'll talk with our employer and if we get the go ahead we'll call and set up an appointment with you."

Having cooled down somewhat, Reggie opened the door escorting them through his office and out into the hall, saying, as they retreated down the narrow corridor, "Well, I hope you do get back to me and don't leave me wondering what the hell this is all about."

"We will for sure," both men said at the same time.

Right after the men left Hilda walked in. "It was a good thing you chose to leave," Reggie told her, "I sure didn't want you to hear me yelling at them. Get Toby on the phone and then bring in the Redmond file so I can look at it before I call her."

As she turned away, he called to her, "Delay that call to Toby, get Phil on the phone, I need to find out what he wants before I talk with Toby."

Going back into his office, now more puzzled than ever, he wondered what was going on. "I can't call Toby until I know what's going on, but it would be nice having him here beside me, or at least working with me full time. Sure be glad when he decides to resign."

CHAPTER SEVEN

Murder at the Paris

"**B**OSS," HILDA YELLED through the open door, "Phil is on line one."

Picking up the phone Reggie said, "Hey, Phil, how is Las Vegas's finest this wonderful morning?"

"I'm glad you can call it a wonderful morning, "Phil responded sarcastically, "I'm up to my neck in dead people, the dog is sick, got a parking ticket this morning and you want to call it a good morning."

Phil Warren and Reggie had been associates on the police force and even after Reggie had resigned they remained friendly. When Phil continued, he said, "You may have read about the dead guy they found behind the Paris this morning. Identifying the body is going to be hard enough, as he was badly beaten, but I'm faced with another dilemma. The Medical Examiner, during his examination, found a substance in the clothing of John Doe, which they have been unable to identify. I know you're no longer with us, but we hoped you could find the time to lend us a hand in identifying it."

"Sure," replied Reggie, "but it's going to cost you lunch. Give me about an hour to clear up some things around here and I'll be right there."

"Great, see you in about an hour," said Phil.

When Reggie hung up the phone, Hilda announced, over the intercom, that Mrs. Redmond was on the other line. Punching the button for line two, he said cheerfully, "How are you this morning, Mrs. Redmond? I trust Michelle is okay." Then not allowing her time to interrupt he explained how it had been an easier job than he had anticipated and felt he couldn't accept the agreed upon amount. After listening to Mrs.

Redmond thanking him for his generosity he hung up the phone and begun working on the files on his desk.

"You know boss, if you keep working for peanuts, that's what we'll be eating shortly," piped up Hilda from the outer office.

"I just couldn't make myself take her money," he answered. "She's a widow with a fixed income and all she wanted was for her daughter to be found. Chalk it up to Community Service and see if the IRS buys it."

Resuming work on the mountain of paperwork, his mind kept returning to the events of the last few hours, trying to find the common denominator which would tie the events together. He had been a police officer long enough to know there's always one piece of information or a clue, which, when brought to light, would help understand the events of the last couple of days and tie them together enough so he might be able to make sense of them.

A short time later, leaving the office, he said to Hilda, "I'll be at police headquarters with Phil and will be unavailable for the rest of the day, but if a person calling himself John calls give him my cell phone number."

It took him forty-five minutes and almost as many bouts of road rage before reaching the police parking lot and then he made his way to Phil's office. The gilt writing on the window of the door indicated this was the office of Senior Detective Phillip G. Warren, Chief of Homicide.

Warren, an old style policeman, promoted up through the ranks from beat cop to his present position; was in actuality more like a bulldog then detective. He and Reggie went back a few years, but Phil's association with Reggie's father went back even further. He had served with the 'General' during his first command, when he was only a lieutenant colonel. During that time Phil had been a Chief Master Sergeant in charge of the flight line mechanics. From that assignment to retirement Phil had traveled with Reggie's father through numerous commands.

When Reggie entered the office he said, "Hey Phil, glad you called me, was starting to think you didn't love me anymore."

"Hello Reggie, have thought about you often, but been way too busy to fit you into my schedule. Phones go both ways, you know. So how have you been?"

"My day was going along pretty well until I was forced to drive downtown and fight all of the tourists flooding the streets," he said laughing. "What you need is a helicopter to get around in, or a more competent police force to control the traffic."

"Since it took you so long to get here," Phil responded, "we'll have to go to lunch before we see the Medical Examiner. Josh locks his door promptly at noon and doesn't open, even for the Mayor, until straight up one o'clock."

Later as they were eating Phil said, "Let me tell you what we need your help with. I'm sure you read in the paper about the dead man we found last night. A delivery truck driver found the body around 3:15 AM in an alley behind the Paris Hotel; he was the one who called the police. The man had been badly beaten, but what killed him was a single shot to the head with a large caliber pistol. The Medical Examiner has the body and is in the process of performing an autopsy. We're attempting to identify the man through the FBI finger print files and other national agencies. We have three problems with this John Doe. One—why was he tortured before he was murdered? Two—what is his name? Three—and this is where you come in, what was the substance found in his coat pocket?"

"Sounds interesting and like you have your hands full working this one. I'll do what I can to help you along with your investigation."

When they finished eating and were getting up to leave, Reggie's cell phone rang, he said, "Hello, this is Reggie."

Hey boss," Hilda began, "hate to disturb you; this isn't about John, but you just received a call from one of the fellows who were in your office this morning. Mr. Abbott called to say he and Mr. Lebowitz would like to meet you tonight at the Paris Hotel Registration desk around 9:00 pm. And as a side note, if you're going to make the meeting you had better call Brandy and let her know. I think groveling is in order."

Laughing, he replied," Okay Hilda, but groveling is better done with flowers sitting on the table. So how about calling the florist and having a dozen red roses sent to Brandy's apartment, then when I call her, maybe telling her I can't make the date again tonight won't be so hard."

After the call was completed he and Phil left the lunchroom and went directly to the ME's office. Entering the outer office the ME, Josh Bartlow, greeted them.

"Hey Josh, how are you?" Reggie asked, shaking the hand of his former workmate. The two of them had been friends since Reggie joined the force.

"I'm fine Reggie; good to see you again. Of course I'm up to my rear end in dead bodies and working my tail off, but other than not having a home life, I'm doing as well as can be expected," replied Josh. Laughing at his own comments, he continued, "Let me get right into it; we have a John Doe, white male, medium build, approximately 5 foot, 11 inches tall, weighing around 172 pounds, blue eyes, dark brown hair. He was dressed in an Armani suit, with no identification and a large amount of cash in his pants pocket. The evidence shows that he was tortured because at least 4 fingers were broken and he had a multitude of contusions and cuts all over his face and chest. He was killed by a single shot from a .38-caliber pistol directly to the head from a short distance. Evidence also shows that he was killed somewhere else then dropped in the alley behind the Paris." Stopping to take a breath he continued, "When we removed his clothing we found a powder like substance inside his jacket pocket and some more in his front pants pocket. Traces of the substance were also found on his hand and under his fingernails. Our lab folks are pretty good but they have been unable to identify it. We aren't even sure you would be able to identify it, but with your knowledge and experience we're hoping you could help us."

Phil spoke up, "We have submitted the fingerprints to the FBI and other federal agencies and are running his photo on the wire in an attempt to put a name to the face, but nothing yet. We didn't find anything else in his pockets or on his person, other than what Josh told you about, not even a wallet."

"Well, "said Reggie, "Just for the fun of it let me see the body then I'll go to the lab and look at the slides."

The three men entered the examination room and approached the body of the man lying covered on the examination table. Josh removed the covering and said, "Reggie, meet John Doe."

When the body was uncovered it took all of Reggie's self control to stifle the gasp that rose up in his throat; he was looking at the corpse of the man he knew as John. *'I guess he didn't get to run too far,'* he thought.

Taking his eyes off the corpse and trying to keep his feelings in check he asked, "How about taking me to the slides of the substance you discovered? I assume the slides are in the lab?"

Phil noticed the look on his friend's face as he viewed the corpse but attributed it to having been away from the sight of dead bodies for some time so he took the lead and they headed for the lab.

As the three men left the ME's office and walked towards the lab, Reggie's mind dropped into high gear and began to race with the possibilities. He remembered Lebowitz remarking in their earlier conversation that he was involved already. Reggie now knew for certain that whatever was going on he had been caught up in it.

The men walked into the laboratory and were greeted by the Pathologist, Bob Sizemore. "Reggie," Phil said, making the introductions. "This is Bob Sizemore, the newest addition to our team."

Offering his hand, Reggie said, "Glad to meet you Bob, it's my pleasure. I hope you don't hold it against me because I came in with these two characters."

Laughing, Bob said, "I won't. The worst part about this job is trying to live up to the reputation of the last man who ran this office. It's my pleasure to meet you Mr. Nutsbagh."

At that both Phil and Josh, offering their apologies, said they had to return to their respective offices.

Taking him over to the microscope, Bob showed him several slides. "Here's the stuff taken from the dead man's clothing. I'll leave you alone, if you need anything holler; I'll be in the office doing some paper work."

Reggie began to analyze the substance found on the dead man. After about fifteen minutes he was certain he knew what he was looking at. The substance was Trinitrotoluene, more commonly called TNT. He gave this information to Bob and then left the lab to find Phil. Walking towards Phil's office, he thought to himself, *'Now I have another piece of the puzzle, but I'm not sure what it's all about. What was my 'John' doing with TNT? What have I stepped into? I sure hope my meeting tonight with Sam and Jerod helps clear all this up.'*

When he entered Phil's office, Phil looked at him, so he said, "The substance found in John Doe's pocket was Trinitrotoluene, better known as TNT."

Phil's reaction was what Reggie expected as he took it in stride without blinking an eye.

A few minutes later, after saying goodbye to Phil, Reggie walked out and on the way to retrieve his car he assessed these latest developments and thought to himself, *'Maybe it's time to call Toby and give all of this to him. Maybe he can come up with some answers.'* Once again he rejected that idea, thinking, *'No let me wait until I have my meeting at the Paris Hotel tonight, then I'll call him. It's about time for him to quit pussyfooting around and join the team on a full time basis.'*

CHAPTER EIGHT

A Burglary, An Investigation

A NURSE AT St. Rose Dominican Hospital in Henderson, Brandy Thomas had been Reggie's companion for the past several years. They met when he was in the hospital recuperating from an injury sustained during a police training exercise. She had been his attending nurse and had made his stay in the hospital as enjoyable as was possible under the circumstances. They enjoyed each other's company so much at the hospital that the relationship continued even after he left. Many times during the last several months he considered asking her to marry him but it seemed like every time that thought entered his mind he couldn't say the words.

Reggie called Brandy on his cell phone and invited her to have an early dinner with him so he could make his meeting with Abbott and Lebowitz. Dining at one of the local restaurants in Henderson their conversation centered on her work and what was happening at the hospital. She was aware of his occupation but always avoided asking questions about it as the thought of him engaged in dangerous work made her uncomfortable.

Marriage had often entered her mind since dating this extremely attractive man, but working where she did and seeing the dangers of the street, she feared the thought of being a young widow. Soon after finishing their meal the conversation became one sided and she sensed his preoccupation and suggested he take her home.

After dropping her off at her apartment, he proceeded to the Paris Hotel for his appointment with Lebowitz and Abbott. During his drive to the meeting he was so preoccupied with the dilemma facing him, he was unaware that several cars behind he was being followed by two men in a blue Buick. Arriving at the Paris Hotel, he entered Valet parking, turned his car over to the parking attendant and walked to the hotel for his meeting.

Nine o'clock, which had been the time for the meeting, came and went and there was no sign of Lebowitz or Abbott. Beginning to expect the worst, he paced back and forth trying to calm his fears then as 9:30 became 9:45, he suspected the two wouldn't be showing up. In hopes he was wrong he went to the front desk and requested the clerk ring the room of Mr. Samuel Lebowitz or Mr. Jerod Abbott.

"I'm sorry, sir," the desk clerk replied, "both men checked out earlier this evening. I remember as they asked me to get them a cab to the airport."

"Are you sure?" Reggie questioned.

"Absolutely, sir," was the reply.

"Did they leave a message for Reggie Nutsbagh, by any chance?" He asked, hopefully.

"No sir," the clerk replied, "I haven't left the desk since coming on at 7 pm and there were no messages left for anyone."

"Thanks," he said the disappointment showing on his face.

After picking up his car, he drove slowly down Las Vegas Boulevard, towards his apartment in Henderson. As before he was so consumed with the latest events he violated a basic principle of every investigator, that is, 'be aware of what is going on around you.' The blue Buick, with its two occupants, was, once again close behind.

Arriving at his apartment complex he parked his car and went up to his apartment and feeling tired out by the events of the day, decided to retire for the evening.

When waking up the next morning he exclaimed aloud to the world in general, "The weekend at last! I'm going to put everything on hold and take the next couple of days off and not even think about anything that has happened this week. It's beginning to feel as if nothing is going right, with all the disappointments of the last several days I've sure been spending a lot of time talking to myself and now I am even starting to answer my own questions."

After showering he called Brandy, "I was planning on going out to the house in Summerlin, would you like to come along? We can pick up some sandwiches from the deli along with some cold drinks and sit around the pool and maybe even do a little swimming." He chose not to live at the house as he didn't want to be faced with the memories of his mother and father so he had hired different companies to provide for the up-keep of the grounds and to make sure the inside of the house was maintained.

"That sounds great!" she exclaimed. "We need to spend some time together and I just happen to have a couple of days off. I need to get away from here before I get called in for overtime. I'll put my suit underneath my clothes and be waiting for you downstairs."

'*You big baby,*' Reggie thought to himself, as he put down the receiver, '*you just want somebody along when you enter that big house, too many skeletons there for you, huh?*'

After picking up Brandy, they made one stop to pick up a couple of sandwiches and some iced drinks then leisurely drove to his folk's house in Summerlin. Once again he was concentrating on the joy of the moment and was unaware of the continuing surveillance.

It was a beautiful hot day and they headed straight for the pool to cool off. After a few laps and some playful water games they climbed out and collapsed on poolside lounge chairs without bothering to dry off. Realizing he was famished, Reggie took out the sandwiches and, after offering Brandy one, bit into his with relish. Sitting around the pool enjoying their lunch brought him back to earth as he recalled the many times he had experienced such moments with his parents. Remembering why he had come here, he spoke, "If you're finished eating let's go check the house out, it's been a long time since I've been inside and I need to face the ghosts for my own peace of mind."

They left the pool area, entered the house and began walking around. During their tour of the house he was filled with sadness as he remembered all of the good times he had shared with his parents in this house. Coming to his father's den, he hesitated trying to draw up enough courage to enter this once sacred domain. Here his father had spent a lot of his spare time writing his memoirs and taking care of daily tasks. A well-read man, he could often be found dozing in the late evening with a book lying open on his lap. He could still hear his father's voice telling him he could go anywhere in the house without permission, except this room.

Understanding his sadness and the need to be alone, she touched his shoulder saying, "You go ahead, and I will walk around the rest of the house. Take your time."

With this, she began her solitary excursion through the large, silent house. For no reason a shudder went through her as she ventured into the kitchen, which not so long ago had been the domain of a woman she had never met.

When Reggie opened the door, to the study, he hesitated, not quite sure if he was ready to be confronted with the memories going into this room would bring. He finally entered and walked across the room then stood in front of the large oak desk. From where he was standing he could look out into the side yard and behold the beautiful garden area where his mother spent so many enjoyable hours. Full of desert blooms and blossoming roses it had been her crowning joy. Walking around the desk, he pulled away the heavy armchair and sat down, then leaned back, sitting there for a time absorbing all of the pleasant memories of his times with his father. Without thinking he began opening the drawers of the desk sorting through the items as he pulled them out. When he came to the last drawer he found it to be locked, unable to locate a key, he looked around the room questioning why one drawer would be locked. Most of the other drawers had contained items of value and one would think they should have been under lock and key. "I wonder what this one holds that makes it so special?" he questioned.

He couldn't take any more of the sadness, so pushing the chair away from the desk he got up, and started to leave the room still puzzling over the locked drawer. Then like a magnet the conundrum wouldn't let him go far so turning on his heels he walked back to the desk, sat down and began searching for the key. Looking under the desk pad, he found only a hand written note with a poem by Longfellow. He extended his investigation to a more thorough search of the unlocked drawers and once again drew a blank. Reaching for the small note pad on the desk he started to make a list of the places already searched. In his frustration he broke the lead of the pencil he was using and reached into the little container full of pens and pencils sitting on the desk but in his haste he knocked it over and out, along with all the writing apparatuses, came a single key.

Chiding himself, he said, "Fine detective you are Nutsbagh, the key was under your nose all of the time."

Using the key, he opened the drawer and discovered several computer disks and a file folder containing official looking documents. Just as he was beginning to check the documents, Brandy entered the den.

Not wanting to answer her questions, he reached for one of his father's leather brief cases and inserted all the contents of the drawer. Snapping the lid shut, he took her elbow and steered her out of the room.

The ride back to Henderson was done in silence as Brandy sensed her companion's need for solitude. The visit had left Reggie in a depressed state and it was evident he needed some time to sort things out. A polite invitation to come up for a while was refused and after seeing she was safely in her apartment he drove away with his thoughts.

Arriving at his apartment he parked in the underground garage and rode the elevator to his fifth floor penthouse, clutching the brief case as if it were a fragile piece of china. As he was entering his apartment the same blue Buick pulled up and parked across the street.

Once in his apartment he checked his answering machine and turned on his computer to check his emails. After reading and answering most of them he removed one of the computer disks he had taken from his father's den and inserted it into the computer. Before the disk completed loading his telephone rang. The call was from a client, the General Manager of the Club Fortune, a small casino located just off Boulder Highway in Henderson.

Several months ago someone had charged the casino with fixing slot machines to reduce payouts and he had been called in by the casino to help with the investigation. Eventually, due to his investigative prowess, the charges had been dropped. He stated the complainant was back in the casino causing problems. He wanted Reggie, who was still on retainer to the casino, to come up and deal with the problem. Reggie wanted very much to view his father's notes, but felt compelled to deal with the current problem at the Club Fortune. With a great deal of reluctance he told the GM he would be there shortly. Turning off his computer, without removing the disk, he set the alarm in the apartment and left for the casino.

He had driven several miles towards the casino when his cell phone rang. Pulling to the side of the road, he answered, "Hello, this is Reggie."

"Mr. Nutsbagh, this is ADT Security calling, the alarm went off in your apartment indicating there's an intruder. Where are you now?"

"I'm on Boulder Highway a of couple miles from my apartment, I'll turn around and get back to the apartment and see what the problem is; I'll give you a call as soon as I find out."

When he arrived back at his apartment he saw the door wide open, the alarm blaring and saw several of his neighbors standing in the hallway looking toward his apartment. He was cautiously looking in through the open door, when one of his neighbors yelled out over the alarm, "They ran out."

"Who ran out?" Reggie asked.

"The two guys who were in your apartment," he exclaimed. "When the alarm went off they came running out of your apartment with what looked like a brief case."

When Reggie heard what his neighbor had to say he hurried into his apartment, turned off the alarm, called ADT Security and told them everything was okay and to call off their response as the intruders were gone.

He began checking the apartment, noticing that the brief case was indeed missing. Turning to look at his computer he observed, with a sigh of relief that the disk he had inserted into the drive was still there.

After calling the maintenance man for the apartment complex about repairing the door, he turned on the computer. As he waited for the disk to load he tried to make sense of it all. The break-in could have been by design or accidental, if it was accidental and the thieves were just looking for something to steal, why his apartment and why just the brief case? It had no intrinsic value while the apartment contained the normal electronic equipment that could be easily pawned or fenced. The most probable scenario was the intruders knew exactly what they were looking for. Taking the brief case since it was their objective. It was at this point he began to realize he must have been followed. "But why?" he asked himself. He had no idea what the items in the briefcase would yield so how could anyone else know? The implications made him fear for Brandy.

Putting all other thoughts aside he quickly dialed her number. He almost panicked when after the fifth ring he received no answer. Just as he was about to hang up it was picked up and a sleepy voice said, "No, I'm not coming in to work today. I'm off-duty—"

"Brandy," Reggie interrupted, "It's not work, just me."

"Sorry," she answered, "I was taking a nap and thought it was the hospital. We have a shortage of nurses and management figures they can work us to death rather than hire more. You just left me a short while ago, is something wrong?"

He apologized for waking her and not wanting her to know the real reason for his call, he chose discretion over truth and told her how sorry he was for being so pre-occupied earlier and was hoping they could have dinner later. She, of course, enthusiastically accepted and nine o'clock was agreed on.

After hanging up he placed another call to the GM of the Club Fortune and explained his situation and told him he wouldn't be able to see him until sometime the next morning; that was agreeable to the GM so he broke the connection.

"I need to look at the remaining computer disk and see what's on it, before I jump to any type of conclusions about the break-in," he said aloud.

When the disk loaded he began scanning the information and could tell by the way it had been written it was his father's work. He also was able to ascertain by the dates on the disk the information came from the time they had been in Israel. Some of information outlined an organization designated only by the word DONE but there was no indication what the acronym meant. Continuing to read he found his father had accidentally stumbled onto what he felt was a 'conspiracy.' According to his father's notes he began investigating on his own and had developed a theory, which included some high-ranking individuals from several governments being involved in the conspiracy. Evidently he only disclosed his findings to one other individual, a close friend. However, someone with a lot of power had an inkling that General Nutsbagh was nosing around too much and pulled strings to get him transferred out of Israel and into retirement.

Most of the remaining information covered the General's decision to go along with the forced retirement and to discontinue further investigation of the conspiracy he felt sure was beginning to grow. He could only surmise this, but he feared if he continued with any type of investigation, his life and the lives of his family would meet the same fate as his friend; who had lost his life in a bombing incident in Tel Aviv and this is something he wouldn't let happen to himself or his family.

There was another file on the disk, opening it he found more of his father's notes, which told of Israel's imports to Washington State. Among these were raw diamonds and electronic parts. What did the information mean and why were they a part of the General's notes? The last few lines concerned the 1996 Legislative action signed by the President giving Federal Agencies more power to investigate acts of terrorism and how the ACLU (American Civil Liberties Union) and the NRA (National Rife Association) were against the legislation. Following this was a notation concerning an abandoned Air Force Base in Northern Montana; followed by the words, 'check on it.' There was no mention of what bearing these facts might have on the investigation or on the probable conspiracy.

When he completed reading all the notes on the disk, he sat in silence stunned with the information he had read. He had been a teenager during the military assignment in Israel and was unaware of any problems. His parents had always been forthright in dealing with their only child, never hiding even the most private of things.

Reflecting on the happy years spent in Israel he could recall no time when they weren't happy as a family. However, the implications of what he had just read began to flood his consciousness.

He put his thoughts into words, "I sure wish I had the briefcase with the rest of the information in it. This lone disk is just the tip of the iceberg. I'm sure the rest of the information contained in that brief case would have answered all of my questions."

He no longer dwelt on the murder of the John Doe from the sandwich shop. Nor did the disappearance of the two men who were supposed to have met him at the Paris Hotel command his thoughts. They were nothing compared to the nagging suspicion that he may be getting closer to the mystery of why his parents had to die.

One thing about Las Vegas is if you love the sunshine and the heat this town would fulfill all your dreams. This is what Reggie woke to the next morning, the warm sun coming through his window, covering him with a warm glow. Lying there and basking in its warmth, he felt at peace with himself. His relationship with Brandy was developing and now for the first time in a long time he knew what direction he wanted to take. After a weekend of relaxation, minus the irritating break-in, he was ready to get to work. Picking up the bedside phone he dialed his office. During the short time it took to connect he detected several distinct clicking sounds, very faint, but audible to his trained ears. He may have been still half-asleep, but not so much so he couldn't recognize a wiretap when he heard it. Hilda picked up the phone at the other end and answered, "Hello, this is Reggie Nutsbagh's Office, can I help you?"

"Good morning, Hilda, I won't be in for a while as I have some urgent business to take care of. Have there been any calls for me?"

After being informed it was quiet so far, he hung up and began dismantling the phone in search of the suspected tap. As he knew he would, he discovered a listening device had been inserted into the base of the phone. After removing the device from the phone, he thought to himself, *'I guess the thieves who were here in my apartment not only took something from the apartment but also left a little something for me. This is a short-range transmitter so I'll have to see who is out and about. I guess this means that my office phone is also bugged, I'll have to take care of that later.'*

He was headed for the bathroom to take a shower when his cell phone rang and he was pleasantly surprised to hear the voice of his friend Toby.

They exchanged pleasantries and then Toby told him to expect him tomorrow. He had booked the only open flight he could find, which would take him by way of San Francisco. When the conversation ended he said to himself, "What a guy, he must have been reading my mind, here I have been saying all along that we needed to get together and bingo, he decides to come to Vegas. Great! Now I can discuss these latest happenings with him and see what he thinks."

After his shower he walked across the street to the coffee shop, entered and headed for his usual seat by the window and as soon as he sat down the waitress brought his usual order of coffee and a bagel with cream cheese.

Looking around he saw two men, not usual customers, sitting at a corner table drinking coffee and talking, but continually looking around as if expecting someone to come in. Finishing his breakfast, he got up, placed money for the food and a tip on the table and then walked out of the coffee shop and back across the street to his car. The two men came out of the coffee shop right after him and got into a blue Buick, which was parked in front of the shop. They didn't, however, drive off immediately, seemingly interested in a street map.

The car itself was nondescript, but Reggie was sure he had seen it in the neighborhood before. Nonchalantly, he crossed back over the street and tapped on the window, asking, "May I help you find an address?"

Caught off guard the men stammered out they were just passing through and were looking for directions to the Strip. From the license plate, Reggie determined they were driving a rental car, leased out of McCarran. Suspecting foul play he chose to go along with them, so instead of confronting them he gave them the directions to the Strip. Walking away he said aloud, "Bet I don't see that particular car again which means, if my suspicions are correct, I'll have to be on the lookout for a different vehicle hanging around."

He wasn't totally correct in not seeing the car again, for as he headed out to make his visit to Club Fortune, he spotted the same car at a distance behind him. He thought, *'Now I won't have to look for a different car.'*

Arriving at the club he parked his car near the main entrance, pausing inside the door long enough to see the Buick pull into one of the handicap spots alongside the building. "At least I know where you are."

Completing his business with the manager of the club, he walked to his car, noticing the car tailing him, was no longer there. Getting into his car he headed down Boulder Highway intending to go to his office. He wasn't on the road long when he spotted the blue Buick once again, as it pulled out from a roadside business. *'Think you're pretty clever, huh?'* He thought. *'Well, as long as you feel you're undetected I'll be able to lead you around by the nose.'*

Pulling over to the shoulder of the road and stopping he picked up his cell phone. It had come to him suddenly he had a decision to make, because of all that had happened he needed to talk with Toby and make him aware of all that had been going on. It was evident Las Vegas wasn't the place, so he felt it would be best to meet him in San Francisco, away from prying eyes and nosy people. By intercepting him, as he changed planes in San Francisco, he might be able to shake the two guys following him. Calling the travel agency he normally used he made reservations for a flight to San Francisco, making his arrival time to coincide with Toby's arrival from Seattle.

Still sitting on the side of the highway he made another call to the hospital and told Brandy he had to go out of town and would be gone for several days and that he would get in touch with her in a couple of days.

It took one more call to his office manager to tell her he was going out of town for a couple of days and he would be in contact with her later.

Then he placed a call to a taxi service in Henderson requesting an early pickup in the morning at the Chevron Station at the corner of Lake Mead Drive and Boulder Highway. By arranging the pickup at that location he would be able to lessen the chances of being followed.

The next morning he got up early, showered, dressed and walked out the back of the apartment complex arriving at the pickup point as the taxi arrived. During the ride to the airport he kept a constant lookout to see if they were being followed, not spotting anyone he began to relax.

Once at the airport, he checked the monitor to find out which gate his flight was departing from and proceeded directly to the gate. "It sure will be great to see Toby I have a lot to tell him when we get together but I really wonder what the big fella wants to talk to me about?"

CHAPTER NINE

Friends Reunite

BREMERTON MAYOR SLAIN IN POLICE SHOOTOUT, the headlines of the Bremerton Sun, the town's only daily newspaper, read in bold print. At first glance the headlines would cause the reader to believe a grave injustice had taken place and the police had committed a criminal act. "Leave it to our liberal press to give the public false impressions," grumbled Toby, as he poured his second cup of coffee. "Maybe somewhere on the inside pages they'll tell what really happened."

Reading further into the story of the deceased mayor's involvement in the gun running operation he found no mention of the weapons having been intended for use in an assault on Bangor Sub-base, as the FBI had taken over the investigation and wasn't releasing a lot of information. The captured men had been linked to an extremist group, believed to be planning a wave of terrorist attacks across the country. In a second article on the inside page, the Police Chief released a statement linking Mayor Norton to the murder, that had taken place at the Seaside Apartments earlier. The Chief asked for patience, as everything would be brought to light when the FBI cleared the way.

"Very diplomatic chief, maybe you could run for mayor," Toby chuckled to himself.

Looking out the kitchen window he could see the late summer morning was already shaping up to be glorious and it wasn't difficult to realize why he chose to live in the Pacific Northwest. Thanks to the generous rainfall the area is green year around and even though the Kitsap Peninsula was steadily growing there was still a sense of living in the country. On a clear day he could see the county seat of

Port Orchard, while watching the Bremerton ferry glide into its berth, discharging its cargo of foot passengers and vehicles. The beauty, which he observed around him, had a way of making the events of the past few days disappear.

Scanning the paper further, the euphoria, which had swept over him, was abruptly washed away as his attention was drawn to an article about an explosion at a petroleum refinery outside of Kansas City, Missouri. In an anonymous phone call received by the FBI an organization calling themselves DONE claimed credit for the explosion. No deaths were reported, but there were at least thirty workers injured.

This was the second time in as many days he had heard the acronym DONE. It gave him cause to think, but the moment passed as he heard Renie yell from her bedroom, "Daddy, aren't you late for work? It's past seven o'clock."

Little did either of them know their lives were going to be full of activity as he hadn't yet told her he had resigned and would be working full time in the detective agency and would have to be gone on occasion. "For that matter," he caught himself saying, "I haven't told Reggie about my resigning either. Think I'll give him a call about taking a trip to Las Vegas, a little down would be nice."

With that thought he jumped up from the breakfast table and made a beeline for Renie's bedroom. Using a phrase he had often heard, he began, "Sweetheart, I have some good news and some bad news, which do you want first?"

Supposing it had something to do with his police work, she took a few seconds to respond; hoping that both good and bad didn't bode ill. Finally unable to contain herself and expecting her answer to spoil her dad's surprise, she said, "Give me the bad first."

Bracing himself for the worst he told her of his intended trip to see his friend Reggie and spend a little time relaxing and unwinding from the events of the past few days. He would ask Maria to live in for a few days so she wouldn't be left alone.

"That's not so bad," she declared, "Now out with the good news."

He had barely voiced the words of his pending resignation, when the hundred pound terror jumped into his arms, almost knocking him off his feet.

"I suppose that means you're happy about my quitting," he managed to gasp out. "As hard as you are squeezing me I may die of suffocation before I get to sign the papers."

"Oh daddy, I'm so happy. This means you will be home nights and nobody will be shooting at you and we can have loads of fun. You can even come to my games."

He couldn't remember seeing her happy since before her mother's death. Her eyes were shining and her smile made her face glow. Right at this moment, he thought she looked so much like her mother it made his heart ache.

"Why don't you get dressed and we'll go out for breakfast then you can go to the station with me while I turn in the papers. First I want to make a call to Reggie, if I can find his cell phone number. Seems he's never in his office, but always has his cell phone with him."

He searched through his wallet and finally found the piece of napkin Reggie had written his cell phone number on and punched the numbers on his phone pad. Almost instantly he heard his partner's cheerful voice, "Hello, this is Reggie."

"Well, I'm glad it's you," he responded, "I would hate to think somebody had lifted your phone and was using all your air time."

With genuine pleasure in his voice, Reggie answered, "Hey, Toby, how are you doing? Haven't heard from you in such a long time I was beginning to think you were just a figment of my imagination."

"You can't get off that easy, friend. We are blood brothers now, in fact I was thinking about coming down for a few days; now that proves I must like you. Why else would I put myself through the misery of being on an airplane?"

"When do you think you'll be coming?" was Reggie's response.

"Actually I was going to try for a flight tomorrow, but the only flight I could get was a Continental with a change in 'Frisco."

"Just give me your itinerary and I'll pick you up at the airport."

"Okay, my friend, as soon as I confirm my reservation I'll call you."

"I'm looking forward to seeing you again. Come prepared to have a good time."

As it was mid-week, he had no trouble booking his flight. At the end of his call a series of clicks on the line told him he had an incoming call. Thinking it was Reggie calling back because he had forgotten to mention something, he jokingly asked, "So what's the plan now?"

A gravelly, cultured voice responded, *"The plan is for you to listen carefully to what I'm going to say. Stay out of my way! Because of your interference I have lost a valuable shipment of arms. I do not take losses lightly. This is the first and last warning you will receive."*

Before he could respond the line went dead, leaving him confounded. He was still puzzling over the strangeness of the call when Renie called from the doorway, "Come on dad, I'm starved. I can already taste that Grand Slam Breakfast."

"Okay, sweetheart, I have one more call to make and then we can get on our way." While Renie waited impatiently, he redialed Reggie's cell phone and gave him his itinerary.

"Hold it, Reggie, don't hang up yet. I need to tell you about this strange call I got just minutes ago." Briefly he related to his friend the one-sided conversation with the gravely voiced man.

Reggie paused before answering and then said, "You're right, that's strange, we can discuss it more when you get here." With that both men signed off.

On the way across town to Denny's Restaurant he informed Renie of his travel plans, reminding her of Maria's being available for the few days of his absence.

Because of recent events things were hectic at the police station, forcing Toby to wait for personnel to complete his paperwork. As he sat chatting with his daughter, Chief Fisher came into the personnel office and upon seeing Toby said, "Toby, how are you doing this morning? I know you're here to tell me you have changed your mind about leaving the department."

Before he had a chance to respond, Renie jumped to her feet, answering for him, "No, sir, he hasn't changed his mind. We are just waiting for the slow-pokes in your office to finish so we can go home."

This outburst by this little girl, who was such good friends with his own daughter, left him momentarily speechless.

Toby, smiling, interjected, "No, Chief, this is going to be final. Just as soon as I sign my name to the release form Cindy is typing, I'm history."

"Well," the Chief replied, "As long as you are still in the department, if only for a few more minutes, come on down to my office, there's someone down there who would like to talk to you."

"Okay, Chief," Toby responded.

Addressing the personnel specialist, he asked, "Cindy, would you mind entertaining Renie for a few minutes while I go to the Chief's office? Be warned that she'll talk your ears off."

Cindy, busily typing away at the computer on her desk, glanced up and nodded. Winking at the young girl, she said, "We just might be talking girl stuff and I may not get finished with your paperwork, but we'll manage."

Walking into the Chief's office, Toby noticed two men standing just inside the door. The Chief introduce them, "Toby, I would like you to meet Agents Jones and Samuelson, of the FBI. They would like to ask you a few questions concerning the events of the last couple of days."

After the introductions, Agent Jones said, "Lt. Preston, you're still Lt. Preston, aren't you?"

"Yes," replied Toby, "But not for long."

"Well, we have several questions concerning the events of the last couple of days. Starting with the murder of the clerk at the hotel and then about the weapons found in the warehouse. By the way, that was an excellent operation you handled at the warehouse, it was real nice."

Toby acknowledged the accolades, but gently reminded them time was of the essence and questions had been mentioned, not history. "Not intending to be rude, but my life is starting to take a new direction and there is a little girl out there who wants her father to get on with it."

"Lt. Preston, where did you get the information about the warehouse and what it contained?"

Toby replied, "The information came from the Mayor's son. He had been playing in the warehouse earlier and saw the men and weapons. He became frightened and confused and knowing I was a police officer, plus being a friend of my daughter, he ran to my house."

Seemingly satisfied with the answer, Jones continued with his questioning, "Why did you go back to the apartment the next morning after the murder of the desk clerk?"

"As I explained previously to the Chief, which I am sure he has already told you, something troubled me about the crime scene which

I couldn't quite put a finger on. I thought about it for a long time and was suddenly rousted out of a restless sleep by the realization that, it wasn't what might have been missing from the room, but what was there. I had seen the Mayor's Day-planner sitting on the window ledge in the manager's office and aware of his penchant for wearing it as an appendage, I went back to try and recover it."

"Speaking of the Mayor's Day-planner we have it in our possession and are trying to decipher his cryptic notes."

Then Samuelson asked, "During the raid on the warehouse, where did you get the key for the door?"

"From the Mayor's son."

"A piece of paper was discovered in the pocket of one of the men your officers searched with the word DONE on it," Jones proclaimed. "Have you any idea what it means?"

"In response to that I believe the dictionary would say it means finished, which is what I am with you. I would love to stay and chat with you, but there's a young girl out there who has plans for her father. Who in turn, has plans of his own. Have a nice day."

With this, he smiled, shook the Chief's hand and walked out of the office.

Returning to the Personnel Office he found all the necessary papers ready to sign. After signing them as Lt. Tobias Preston, he departed the building, with young Renie Preston skipping merrily ahead of him, as Mr. Tobias Preston.

Her excitement at her father's end as a police officer set the pace for the rest of the day and after a full day of shopping, eating and talking they were both ready for a good night's sleep prior to his early departure for Las Vegas.

Breakfast the next day was a little more subdued than yesterday's visit to Denny's as Renie wasn't fully awake, but it was pleasant because they were steadily building rapport. A constant stream of conversation wasn't necessary for them to enjoy each other's company, though it wasn't a totally silent meal.

"Daddy, will you bring me back a souvenir," she begged, "and not just a T-shirt either?" she begged.

"What do you mean? I will be bringing me back. That should be enough for you."

"No, I mean something new. You're old."

Rolling his eyes, he tried to feign a hurt look, but only succeeded in making her laugh. She laughed so hard she spewed milk out of her mouth and onto him.

"Thanks a lot," he muttered, "now I need another shower."

At that moment a car horn sounded.

"Well so much for that. Give your dad a big wet kiss and send me on my way."

The invitation was barely out of his mouth before she leaped into his arms and smothered him with little girl kisses.

"Does that mean you are going to miss me or that you and Maria can't wait to get me out the door so you can live it up?"

"You got it, Dad. Now hurry up so the fun can begin."

Grabbing his bag, he threw a mock stern look at his daughter and went out the door, throwing a parting shot over his shoulder, "I'll be baaack."

The ride to the Seattle-Tacoma Airport was a little longer than usual because of commuter traffic, causing him to have to hurry to catch his flight. The rush did nothing to calm the butterflies in his stomach in anticipation of the flight. '*I need to get over this phobia of flying*, he thought as he checked in at the gate.

After an uneventful flight and on departing the plane and clearing the secure area, Toby looked around to see which way he had to go to make his connections and was surprised to see Reggie standing among the throng of people meeting fellow travelers.

Changing his bag to his left shoulder he stretched out his hand for a handshake, only to be grabbed in a bear hug by his friend. He was taken off guard, but being a demonstrative person himself, returned the embrace.

"This is a pleasant surprise and you even brought your bodyguards."

"Bodyguards!" Reggie exclaimed, "What bodyguards?"

"Don't turn around now, but up against the wall by the Men's Room are two guys who are showing an awful lot of interest in our meeting. Here, hold my bag for a minute while I check my airline ticket, as I do you can casually turn around. One of them is over-dressed and too conspicuous while his probable partner is acting so indifferent to his surroundings that it's laughable."

Doing as Toby advised, Reggie slowly turned and picked out the two men immediately. "This is surely a mess," he commented as he swung full circle. "I thought by meeting you here I could shake them. They must have stayed in the crowds and I didn't pick up on them. I've had these two jokers on my tail for the past couple of days."

Interrupting, Toby said, "What do you think they want?"

"I have no idea, but I found a tap on my office and home phones and saw them again across the street outside the coffee shop I use in the morning for breakfast. I didn't think anything about it until I saw them again in a casino parking lot while I was inside doing some business. Well maybe we can lose them as I've booked a flight to Boise, Idaho for reasons I'll explain later. I know the city and surrounding area pretty well and if they choose to follow us there we will make it hot for them."

"What about you," Toby asked, "You'll need personal items?"

"I brought everything I'll need. Forgive me for not telling you sooner, but I decided to meet you here because I didn't feel Las Vegas was safe enough for a meeting. Speaking of meetings, why are we meeting?"

"Let's get our tickets and I'll explain," was his reply.

"Forget the tickets," Reggie countered, "I've already taken care of that and let's hope these two bozos don't get on, for their own sake."

Checking the monitor to make sure of their gate and departure time, they commenced walking down the terminal aisle, attempting to look as if they didn't have a destination in mind. Followed, of course, by the two men, who were apparently oblivious to the fact they had been identified.

The two friends delayed their arrival at the assigned gate until the last announcement for boarding, hoping not to give their tails enough time to purchase tickets. But it seemed all their diversionary tactics were to no avail as they must have produced boarding passes and got on the plane. They walked down the aisle past Reggie and Toby, who paid them no attention, as they chatted with each other, and took up seats three rows behind them.

"I did it, Reggie," Toby began, "I officially resigned, I'm free to make our partnership a true one and I can carry my share of the load."

Glancing over at Reggie, Toby failed to see the expected enthusiasm. Puzzled, he asked, "We are still partners, aren't we?"

"It isn't that buddy," Reggie explained, "There have been some developments beyond my control which mean we aren't going to be able to devote full time to our Broken Dreams business. Don't get me wrong, though, I need you with me now more than ever. These two goons following are part of the scheme of things, I believe. I don't have the full picture yet, but I'll fill you in when we're in a more private place."

Toby then began filling his companion in on the events leading up to his resignation. When he mentioned a piece of paper with the letters DONE in bold letters, found in a pocket of one of the gun runners, Reggie bolted to an upright position. Those same letters were on the computer disk he had taken from his father's desk, still yet another piece of the puzzle to fit in.

'The strange thing about it is the events that occurred in Bremerton with the arms warehouse,' Reggie thought, *'and what my Dad was doing in Israel are tied together by the word DONE. What does this all mean?'*

CHAPTER TEN

Things heat up in Boise

A S PUZZLING AS things were for Reggie, they were twice as much for Toby. He hadn't a clue what the word DONE meant, or how it tied into what seemed to be troubling his friend and why they were going to Boise.

The two had been partners for only a few months and hadn't had the opportunity to work together so it was going to be a new experience working when the time came to confront the two men tailing them.

The gentle nudging of the flight attendant interrupted his thoughts, "Sir, the captain has turned on the seat belt sign would you please buckle up?"

'Another white-knuckle ride in the air,' he worried. *'Maybe I need to see a shrink about this phobia of mine.'*

Reggie was already buckled up and studying a piece of paper he had pulled from his pocket.

"What do you have there?" Toby queried.

Reggie's response was to thrust the paper into his hand saying, "It's a map of a place in Montana. An old military base, which I hoped we might have time to drive up and see. Part of the mystery surrounding this area in Montana, was the disappearance of a hunter; which I heard about from a fellow in Vegas and there was an entry in my father's notes about the same area so it made me curious. We have a Hertz rental car waiting for us when we land and I thought after we shake our friends we could check it out."

"How do you propose to get rid of our uninvited friends?" Toby asked.

"Somehow they have managed to keep pace with us, so we have to assume they have a car waiting also so if we can't lose them in the streets of Boise, we'll have to confront them somewhere between Boise and Montana. There are enough lonely stretches between Boise and our destination, to waylay them. I don't believe they mean us any harm, yet, I think they're just curious as to what we're up to."

After landing they proceeded to the Hertz desk, maintaining their poise while still being aware of everything going on around them. Even though this was their first time together as a team, their instincts gave them an edge. They seemed to be reading the thoughts of the other and rather than duplicating efforts they automatically assumed control of different aspects of the task of spotting any suspicious activity.

It was natural for Reggie to take the wheel of their rented vehicle, as he was the one familiar with the area and as he drove, Toby studied the map. "This military base you mentioned isn't listed in the index of the map under any name. I did find a small town near it and according to my calculations we should take State Highway 2 into Glasgow, Montana. From there we'll have to find the base as it's somewhere in that area."

He continued to study the map as Reggie drove and watched in the rearview mirror for a trailing vehicle. He hadn't detected any, either the tail had been called off or the two men had become smarter, but not willing to let his guard down Reggie decided to try a few diversionary tactics to draw them out if they were still tailing them.

Turning sharply to the left he turned onto South Interstate 84, an action which caught Toby off guard and he cracked his head against the window. "Hey, buddy, give me a little warning next time," he yelped, as he massaged the side of his head.

"Sorry, pal," Reggie responded, "I didn't see our tail and wanted to draw them out, and I did! Check the side view mirror and notice the tan dodge about 100 yards behind in the outside lane. I believe our boys are inside. When I made the sudden turn, they did too, almost running into the car beside them."

"Got 'em," Toby replied. "They seem to be falling back now, even letting a couple of cars get between us."

"As long as we have them identified," Reggie suggested, "why don't we just let them come along for a while. I'm sure somewhere along the road we can find a place to take care of them."

Nodding, Toby returned to his study of the map, "Why are we interested in the base, anyway?" he queried.

"I'm not really sure, but I discovered some papers and computer disks in my dad's desk. I didn't get to read them all before they were stolen but I did manage to hold on to one of the disks. And when I got into it I saw a notation about this military base in the Glasgow along with the word DONE."

Picking up on what Reggie had mentioned about papers and disks being stolen, Toby exclaimed, "What do you mean stolen?"

"Sorry buddy," was Reggie's rejoinder, "I was going to tell you, but haven't really had the time."

For the next hour Toby listened as Reggie filled him in on the events of the past few days. He left out no details even to the heart rendering account of his going to his parent's home and the ghosts it brought up.

When he had finished, Toby reached over and gave him a reassuring touch. "Do you think these two yoyos' back there are involved in any way?"

"I don't know for sure," was his answer, "But I do believe they are the ones who broke into my apartment and took the briefcase."

Leaning back in his seat while still keeping an eye on their shadows, Toby tried to make sense of what was going on around him. Seeking relaxation from his thoughts he asked Reggie if he minded listening to a baseball game. Getting a nod he searched the radio stations for his favorite team—the Seattle Mariners. Finding an Idaho station, which aired his team, he listened with rapt attention and for a time was able to forget the car tailing them. Seattle was playing the Baltimore Orioles, trailing 3 to 1; the bases were loaded with Edgar Martinez, the DH up to bat.

The broadcaster had just excitedly announced, 'Edgar connects sending a ball to deep right—when an announcer from the network affiliate burst in, "We interrupt this broadcast to bring you this breaking news: A bomb has exploded in downtown Dallas, Texas killing 7 and wounding several more. The bomb was evidently left in a car, which had been abandoned near a shopping mall. There could have been many more injuries and fatalities, had it not been for a warning issued by a caller, identifying himself only as being a member of an organization called DONE. More on this as details come in."

Both men looked in shocked surprise at each other, hearing for the first time a public declaration that the mysterious DONE truly did exist. The game was forgotten as Toby switched off the radio.

Evaluating what he had heard, Toby suggested, "Why not forego the trip to Montana for now and devote our time to cornering our shadows to see what they know. Chances are they are nothing but flunkies, but are undoubtedly members of this group. We need to start somewhere and as we think they're members of this mysterious organization we might as well see if we can take them down and find out what they know."

"My thoughts exactly," Reggie eagerly replied. "Check the map to see if there's a secondary road close we can draw them into."

"One step ahead of you," Toby shot back, "I see we're approaching Mountain Home, get off the freeway at Mountain Home head and east toward Hill City; about 5 miles before Hill City there should be an old fire road. It looks like it dead-ends after about 10 miles. If we're lucky we can pull in among some trees before they spot us and get between them and the highway. Since neither of us is carrying we'll have to make do with what's at hand."

Following Toby's instructions, Reggie turned off the freeway at the Mountain Home exit and proceeded toward Hill City. In a short time he excitedly exclaimed, "I've spotted the road, hold on to your hat!"

Not having a hat on, Toby did the next best thing and grabbed the hand strap just above his window as the vehicle fishtailed when Reggie made the hard right turn traveling at close to 50 miles per hour. Leaning precariously the truck negotiated the turn and sped down the dirt road, bouncing over the ruts caused by large trucks.

"Reggie," Toby said, through chattering teeth as the jolting of the truck threw him around, "You certainly know how to give a guy an exciting time."

Ignoring the intended humorous remark by his friend, Reggie stepped on the accelerator with the intention of giving them a considerable lead over their pursuers, who hadn't yet turned down the road. Just as he had begun to give up hope he caught sight of them in the rearview mirror. "Give me another couple of hundred yards and start looking for a place we can get off this road," he yelled above the din of the straining motor, "hopefully a side road just over a rise so we can turn in undetected."

Thankful for seat restraints, Toby scanned the narrow road as far ahead as he could see. "There's a slight crest in the road coming up. Slow down without braking, so we don't give away our intentions."

As hoped for just over the crest they simultaneously spotted a narrow break in the trees where vehicles had passed.

"Let's hope," Reggie, remarked, "they're going too fast to notice the new tracks." Slowing down he crept into the narrow lane until the trees hid them. When they heard the sound of the pursuing car roar by, Reggie found a suitable place to turn around.

"Let me out here," Toby said, "I'll sneak through the woods and try to get behind them. You told me you were a pretty fair pitcher in your younger days, so why don't you arm yourself with some baseball-size rocks while I look around for a club. Stealth and the element of surprise are all we have on our side."

Knowing it wouldn't be too much longer before the pair in the Dodge knew they had been tricked and would be making their way back to them, both men went about doing what it would take to defend themselves against the possibility of firearms.

They soon heard the roar of the car returning. Toby moved through the brush toward where the car seemed to have stopped and Reggie stepped into the trees crouching behind a clump of bushes.

The two men following them quickly left their vehicle and headed down the road; they were prudent enough to spread out and draw their weapons, holding them at the ready. Both men were wearing suits and their grumbling could be heard as they stepped into mud puddles and stumbled over branches lying in the road.

From his vantage point, Reggie could see Toby, as he circled and came up behind the unsuspecting duo. He must have made some noise, for both men turning around spotting him. Leveling their weapons at him, the taller of the two said, "All right Mister, what-ever-your-name-is, drop the stick and put your hands up."

Knowing that for now compliance was the best thing Toby dropped the stick, and in doing so he was able to advance a couple steps closer to them.

"Would one of you guys happen to have some toilet paper?" he asked, pointing in Reggie's direction, "my friend really had to go and he stepped back into the woods."

Both men committed the unpardonable sin and glanced in the direction Toby had indicated, giving him a chance to stoop quickly, recover his club and lean it against his right leg.

The taller man, who was apparently the leader, looked in the direction Reggie had supposedly headed and yelled, "Okay, Nutsbagh, come out of there with your hands empty and stretched toward the sky."

The words barely left his mouth when Reggie began rapidly firing from his arsenal of stones. His first one missed, but not so with the second or third. Both men felt the sting of the fiercely thrown rocks and in the attempt to cover up, forgot about Toby, who grabbed his club and delivered a hard blow to the man nearest to him. As he crumpled to the ground Reggie scored a bulls-eye, catching the remaining man in his temple.

Being the nearest, Toby quickly gathered up the weapons, sticking one in his waistband while pointing the other in the general direction of the fallen men.

"That was some display, Reggie," Toby exclaimed.

"Maybe so," Reggie replied, "but I should have warmed up a little, I think I threw my arm out."

Ignoring his attempt at humor, Toby suggested, "Let's go over and see what our boys have to reveal."

More cautious than their adversaries, the two friends never took their eyes off the men, who were now stirring. When they were fully awake Toby warned them to sit on their hands. Reggie reached down and started searching one of the men and as Reggie reached into the man's inside coat pocket he pushed Reggie hoping to catch Toby off guard. When Reggie fell against Toby the other man leaped off the ground and lunged at Toby but was dispatched by a single shot to the head from the gun Toby was holding.

Not hesitating, the other man attempted to catch Toby off guard but was grabbed from behind by Reggie who applied a choke hold on the man. He continued struggling until his air supply was cut off and then he passed out. When Reggie felt the man's muscles relax he allowed the body to fall to the ground, he then reached down to check his pulse but found the man was dead. Reggie walked over to the other man, Toby had shot, to check him and found he was also dead. "Damn," Reggie said, "I didn't want that to happen I would have liked to talk to one of them."

Without further discussion they searched the dead men in the hopes of finding some useful information. Except for driver's licenses, no doubt fake and a few bills they discovered nothing that would give them a clue as to whom they worked for.

Perplexed, they walked toward the pursuit car, already expecting to be disappointed. Neither one of the two men had felt the need to travel with gloves; therefore extreme caution was used in the search of the car.

Once again their search revealed nothing, the two had been traveling with no luggage, which meant they had a base of operations somewhere close, or maybe a backup team nearby. They were just about to give up the search as futile, when Reggie opened the ashtray and discovered a torn piece of paper. Pulling out the pieces he tried to arrange them in order to reveal the message.

"Looks like we have another confirmation these guys are part of the same group we've been hearing about," he stated.

The word DONE was written in bold letters with the name Israel directly underneath.

"There's that word again," Toby remarked. "What significance could it have to what's going on?"

"I don't know," Reggie replied, "But a dollar to a donut the answer lies somewhere in Israel. Most of my father's writings seemed to point there. I believe that should be our next stop. Montana will still be here when we return. How's your passport?"

"Sitting idle in my safe, waiting for me to travel," was the reply.

Without further talk they moved the car to the side, pulled the two corpses to the edge of the road, taking the two guns along with them to be disposed of along the way.

The trip back to Boise was a somber one as each man was deep in thought. For Toby, it was the reaction he expected to receive when he informed Renie that he was going away again. For Reggie it was all about his parents and revenge. Neither man could even begin to imagine the things facing them.

Stopping on their way back to Boise they disposed of the weapons, and took time to run the filthy 4x4 through a car wash before returning it to the car rental garage at the airport.

Realizing time was critical, both men concentrated on working out the agenda and itinerary for their upcoming travels.

"I know we need to expedite our plans," Toby began, "but I need a couple of days to work out some things as far as Renie is concerned. This is Wednesday so expect me in on an Alaskan Airlines flight Saturday morning. I'll book it now so you'll have the times and flight number. I leave it up to you to get us on a flight to Israel, okay?"

"Gotcha!" Reggie answered. "Do you remember the guys from Israel we met at the seminar? I'll try to contact them and make arrangements for us to be armed while we are there, and I might even ask them to provide guides. I speak a few words of Hebrew, but it would be nice to have a native along."

Reggie's flight left first and Toby could be seen looking out the window as his friend's plane faded into the distance. "We just left two bodies behind us," he mused to himself, "Wonder how many more there are going to be?" With that he headed to his gate and the flight home to Seattle.

Landing at the Seattle/Tacoma Airport, Toby hurried through the terminal to procure transportation home.

Arriving at the security gate of his home, he disarmed the security alarm, letting himself in and once inside the expansive yard he reset the system and made his way along the driveway to the front door. Rather than just walking in he decided to ring the doorbell. Receiving no response, he used the heavy knocker on the oak door—still no sign of stirring from inside. He wasn't easily panicked, but the events of the past few days had left him a little wary.

'Strange,' he thought, 'they can't be in bed this early. It isn't even 9 o'clock yet.' Finally using his key, he quietly opened the door, not knowing what to expect.

"Surprise," yelled Renie at the top of her lungs! Racing to her dad she threw herself in his arms, planting a big wet kiss on his cheek. "Ugh," she complained, "Your face is scratchy."

"Well, I missed you too," he countered. "How did you know I was coming home early?"

"Uncle Reggie called and left a message for you," she replied.

"Where do you get off with this Uncle Reggie stuff?"

"I have no relatives other than you and I thought it would be nice to have one. Since you two are such good friends, I figured Uncle was okay."

"How did you get to be such a mature person without my noticing?" a bemused Toby asked.

Showing her maturity, she responded, "Because I grew up an only child, silly!"

For the next hour they sat in front of the fireplace enjoying its warmth and being together while Renie filled him in on the latest news. Finally Toby broke it off by saying, "Hey, what do you say we tuck you into bed and start over fresh tomorrow. School starts next week, so we need to make the best of our next few days."

With a big yawn she nodded her head, leaning over to give him a hug, she whispered in his ear, "I love you, daddy."

As he scooped her up into his arms, he whispered back, "I love you too, sweetheart."

All this time Maria had stayed quietly in the kitchen, as she knew how much they needed the time alone coming out only after Toby had tucked Renie into bed for the night, she relayed the message from Reggie. There was no emergency, but he did ask that Toby call him when he got in. Thanking her, Toby asked Maria how her schedule looked for the next few weeks.

"I am free until October, at which time I want to go home to Mexico to visit my family. Do you need me again?"

"I'm afraid so. I haven't told Renie yet, but I'll have to leave again on Saturday and don't know how long I'll be gone. It could be days or even weeks before we finish our business."

"Yes," she said, "I will do it. The girl will be sad, but she is young and will recover from her sorrow."

"Thank you, Maria. You go ahead and take some time off. I will expect you back here on Friday night."

After seeing her to her car and safely out the gate, he returned Reggie's call, using his cell phone number as agreed on. Reggie picked up on the first ring answering with his usual greeting, "Hello, this is Reggie.

"Hey, Reg! What's up?"

"Have you seen the news?" his friend asked without preamble. "It seems our friends have struck again; this time in Chicago, and this time with no warning. A car was used once again and left outside a packed theater. The rescue people are still digging through the debris and so far 70 bodies have been found, many of them children."

"How do we know it was DONE?" Toby managed to gasp out.

"The Chicago Tribune received a phone call from someone claiming to be from DONE."

"Have there been any general warnings issued to the public?"

"The Federal Government issued a caution to people, asking them to report suspicious activities," Reggie answered. "Can you imagine all the phone calls that will generate? Neighbors will be spying on neighbors. Not really sure what the answer is, but it makes our mission more important."

The two men rang off promising they would do everything in their power to get to the bottom of these horrible acts.

Lying in his bed a little later Toby's thoughts turned to his friend and partner, *"How could I be so fortunate as to have met a guy who epitomizes what I believe in? We have never discussed religion or politics but I know he respects my beliefs. He seems to have the same open-minded skepticism as me and we do make a good team as proven by our little escapade in Idaho."*

Those were his last conscious thoughts as sleep took over, putting him into a restless sleep, where he and Reggie were being chased by the recently deceased mayor and two faceless men attired in Arabic dress. Always running away but never widening the distance from the pursuers yet never being caught. In the distance could be seen an oasis, which they didn't seem to be drawing closer to.

Waking with a start, he got out of bed realizing that his dream could only be a precursor of things to come. He wandered into the kitchen, where he started water boiling for a cup of tea and began reading the newspapers, which had been delivered during his absence.

Noticing the FBI had stymied the investigation into the mayor's death, he found himself feeling sorry for the police chief. He was certain the city council was on his case every day. *'Stick with it chief,'* he thought, *'you're better than all of them.'* Finding nothing more worth reading, he placed the newspapers in the recycle bin, turned off the tea pot and headed back to bed hoping he could sleep.

All too soon it was time for his departure for Las Vegas. The few days with Renie had been full and she took his departure as a matter of fact, just glad to have him around more.

The weekday commuters didn't hamper the ride to the airport, and except for stops along the way to pick up other travelers; the Airporter made good time. Later as he sat in his seat of the Alaska Airlines plane, he began the process of putting everything else behind him except for the upcoming trip to Israel. It never dawned on him that he was taking another air flight, and that he wasn't full of fear, as he was preoccupied with what lay ahead. *'What do you suppose is in store for us in that war-torn country?'* With that thought he closed his eyes.

CHAPTER ELEVEN

A Trip to Israel is Planned

T HE SUN STREAMING through the curtains into his bedroom finally brought Reggie out of the first really good sleep he had been able to get in a long time. He lay there a little longer then rolled over in the bed and looked at his clock, to discover it was almost 9:30 am. Toby's flight was due in at 12:15 pm and before he went to the airport there were a few things he had to do. After a quick shower he dressed and made his way across the street to the Coffee House for breakfast, after which he called his office.

Hilda answered in her usual cheerful manner, "Good morning, this is Reggie Nutsbagh's office, can I help you?"

"It's me, Hilda, how's everything this morning?"

"No problems, I just finished making the flight and hotel reservations for you and Toby. Your itinerary is just like you wanted it. There are some other things, but we can talk about them when you come in. Joe is here and would like to talk to you."

Joe Morrison, a black man born and raised in the Watts area of Southern California and had been raised by a single mother who worked two jobs to provide for her six children. He was now a retired policeman and a trusted friend.

During high school he had played basketball and became a highly recruited basketball player, who after graduating from high school accepted a scholarship from the University of Nevada at Las Vegas where he spent four years playing basketball finally graduating with a degree in Electronic Engineering. Immediately after graduation he was offered and accepted a position with the Las Vegas Police Department but was forced into retirement at the age of 55, when he was injured in an altercation taking place during a bank robbery. Even though he was classified as physically disabled he felt fit as a fiddle and had set himself up in the electronic business.

Reggie had used Joe many times during his short career as a PI and in fact it was Joe who had located the hidden microphones and wiretaps in the office when Reggie flew to San Francisco to meet Toby.

Reggie had hired Joe temporarily to look after things at the office while he and Toby were in Israel and, more importantly to provide security for Brandy. Since the break-in at his apartment, and the events in Boise, he was convinced the group he was dealing with was highly organized, capable of anything and he wanted to ensure Brandy didn't experience any problems because of his investigation.

"Okay, Hilda," he responded, "Thanks for making our reservations, I don't think I'll be back in the office today, but both Toby and I will be in tomorrow. Now let me talk to Joe, please."

After a short delay Joe came on the line, "Hey Reg, what's happening?"

After exchanging a few pleasantries, Reggie asked, "Joe, could you do me a favor and be in the office around 10 o'clock tomorrow morning? I want you to meet my partner Toby and at that time we can discuss the security measures you are taking for Brandy."

"Okay Reggie, will do," Joe replied. "Speaking of Brandy's security, I'm going to her apartment and begin setting it up this afternoon."

After returning from Idaho Reggie had decided it best to tell Brandy about what was happening with him and his investigation. He didn't go into all details but only gave her the basic facts. Then he voiced his concern for her safety and what he intended to do about it. He had hoped she would move to his family home in Summerlin, which was easier to secure, but Brandy, being a very independent refused, agreeing, however, to Joe's involvement.

It was still early, but Reggie drove to the airport anyway, excitedly looking forward to Toby coming and their trip to Israel. Just maybe this trip would bring out the truth to his parents demise.

Reggie knew Toby was a white-knuckled flyer and for this reason he was shocked to see a smiling Toby as he cleared the security gate.

'*Something is wrong with this picture,*' he thought '*Toby smiling after a flight?*'

When Toby approached, Reggie asked, "What's with the big smile? I know you hate flying and with the reported wind the landing must have been rough."

"No problem what-so-ever," replied Toby nonchalantly. "It was a really nice flight and I loved it. I think it must be a mental thing with me."

"Welcome to Las Vegas, partner," Reggie answered. "May all your flights and landings be so good, glad you finally got into town."

"Ditto and I'm equally glad to be here."

After retrieving Toby's luggage the two made their way to Reggie's parked car. During the ride to Reggie's apartment they discussed the recent events and the apparent stepping up of activities within the U.S. borders. Knowing they were up against an organization of some size, they discussed the importance of coming to some resolution to put these madmen out of business.

Earlier Reggie had invited Brandy to have dinner with them, so after dropping off Toby's luggage they drove to her apartment and picked her up. When Toby and Brandy were introduced there was an immediate bonding between the two; they embraced and began talking to each other as if they had known each other for years instead of just a few minutes.

Dinner was a nice, with the three of them chatting together all through the meal and up until it was time to call it a night. Dropping Brandy off at her apartment, the two friends returned to Reggie's apartment for the night.

"She's a wonderful woman, Reggie, don't let her get away. You should have put a ring on her finger a long time ago."

"You're right Toby, but the time never seems right and she never mentions marriage. Rest assured I'll not let her get away and after this is all over and my mind is clear, I'll pop the question."

With that, both men said goodnight, retiring for the evening.

Reggie woke the next morning when he heard Toby moving around. Slipping into his robe he went into the living room and saw Toby looking out the living room window at the city. Hearing Reggie enter, he turned and said, "Good morning, pal, beautiful weather you have around here but you certainly need some different scenery, nothing around here green except for the apartment building across the street. I don't think I would like living in the desert."

"It's a beautiful morning, Toby. The desert air and landscape kind of grow on you after you have been here awhile. It's about eight why don't we shower and get some breakfast we're due in the office around ten for a meeting with Joe."

They went to breakfast across the street at Reggie's favorite coffee shop. Yesterday they had talked of other things, but now over coffee and bagels, Reggie took the occasion to say, "I want you to meet Joe. He's a retired cop I've hired for his electronic skills, as well as his detective savvy, he has made some security arrangements for Brandy and we'll discuss those. I told you I'm a little concerned about her safety since the incidents in Vegas and Boise. I'm sure whoever they report to know about Brandy and where she lives." He hesitated then continued, "Also I think we should sit down in the office and discuss our plans for the trip to Israel. I know the office is secure because Joe sweeps the place for bugs about every second day. I would like to go over everything I know and you can add anything you know so we at least have some idea of what we intend on doing once we get there."

Toby responded, "I agree, it would only be smart to have a basic idea of what we want to accomplish in Israel."

Finishing breakfast they took Reggie's car to the office, and as they neared the parking lot Reggie said, "I think we've picked up another tail. I'll move the mirror on your side so you can see behind us. Look for a green Olds a few cars behind us."

After a few seconds Toby said, "Okay, I see the car you're talking about."

Reggie made a few turns as if on a sight seeing tour and then pulled into the parking lot of a drug store. Both men exited the car and walked into the store, pausing just inside the front door in time to see the green Olds drive past the parking lot and stop a little further down the street.

"That settles it," Reggie said, "looks like they are still following us around. Didn't take them long to get another team on our tails. Now I wonder what they want."

Toby broke in, "Could be they are still wondering what we know. But I'll bet you, as extensive as this organization seems to be, they'll know we're going to Israel."

"I've thought about this for some time, and as much as I don't like it I'm going to start carrying my gun with me. We can also process the necessary forms so you can carry a concealed weapon Nevada. It won't take long as I'll ask my friends down at the police department to expedite your paperwork."

"We might as well get to the office, there's nothing we can do about them following us," Toby suggested.

Both men walked outside and got into Reggie's car and as he started to pull out of the parking lot a police cruiser pulled up alongside his car.

"Hey Reggie," one of the officers yelled, "Long time no see."

"Howdy Sal," replied Reggie, "How's business?"

Reggie introduced Toby to both men in the police cruiser. They continued with some small talk when Reggie got an idea, "Hey Sal, want to do me a favor?"

Sal nodded then laughed, "Sure, if it's not against the law."

"The favor I'm asking isn't against the law but against a law breaker. Don't look right now, but down the street about a block is a green Olds parked on the street right next to a fire hydrant, which I think is illegal. They've been following me and I would like to know who they are and what kind of ID they're carrying. Here's my card you can call me at the office later."

"No problem Reggie," Sal replied, "don't like to see any laws broken in this city."

The police cruiser pulled off and Reggie did also and it wasn't long before they arrived at the office and Toby was introduced to Hilda and Joe. After the introductions, Joe went into the security measures taken for Brandy and her apartment. Joe had wired Brandy's apartment, to include the doors and windows and installed motion detectors in all rooms. He had linked this system to ADT and then refined a pager for her that would connect her immediately to him if needed.

Joe had completed his briefing when the intercom sounded and Hilda informed Reggie, that Sal was on line one. Activating the speaker phone, he answered, "Hey Sal, you're on a speaker phone. What did you find out about our friends?"

"The car is a Hertz rental and the name on the driver's license was Robert Smith from Montana, address 718 Hill Street, Glasgow, Montana. They said they were doing some sight seeing, so I wrote them a warning ticket for parking too close to the fire hydrant. Smith, has light brown hair, he's 6 foot, 2 inches tall and weighs 245 pounds and has a strange tattoo on his upper right arm, a dagger thru the word DONE. The passenger in the car goes by the name of James McDuffy, with the same address listed in Montana."

Upon hearing the information about the DONE tattoo, Reggie stuttered out a thank you and disconnected the line. He looked at Toby and saw by the look on his face he had picked up on the remark concerning the tattoo. "DONE again!" Reggie exclaimed. "I'm beginning to believe these are the same people my father tangled with as I remember my father telling me one time, 'Watch your back, there are some vindictive people around with long memories. I'll never forget that, because those were the last words he spoke to me."

After a few more minutes discussing the telephone call, Joe departed to complete the security work while Reggie and Toby sat down to discuss their coming visit to Israel.

"Before we begin our planning I need to tell Hilda something." Punching the intercom he said, "Hilda, I gave you a telephone number earlier, the one to Israel. Would you please call the number and let me know when you've made the connection?"

Turning to Toby, he continued, "I think we need to talk about the questions we need answered when we get to Israel. By doing that we should be able to understand what this is all about and what we're up against."

At this point Hilda interrupted him, on the intercom, informing him Mr. Samual Leving's office was on line two.

Reggie punched line two and spoke into the phone, "Hello this is Reggie Nutsbagh, and I would like to speak to Mr. Leving, please. You might tell him we met at the Seminar on International Terrorism in Salt Lake City."

While Reggie was talking, Toby was furiously writing on a pad, when he finished he pushed it across to Reggie. The note said, 'be extremely careful, remember your father said that there were some high ranking people involved from several governments and didn't know who he could trust; can we trust this guy?"

A voice at the other end of the line said, "Hello Mr. Nutsbagh, I remember you from the seminar. What can I do for you?"

"Sir," Reggie began, "My friend, Toby Preston, who also attended the seminar, and I are planning a trip to Israel in the next couple of days. Just a little sight seeing trip and while we were there I was hoping we could stop in for a short visit with you."

Mr. Leving told Reggie he would be more than happy to see them and had his secretary set up an appointment for the day after their arrival in Israel. Hanging up the phone Reggie said, "Thanks, partner, good thinking. If I had said what was on my mind I would have blown it."

Toby replied, "I guess we need to heed your father's warning and not trust anyone. I think we should forget about contacting anyone else when we get there just let nature take its course and talk with people who are willing to talk and trust our instincts about who we can trust."

"I agree," Reggie replied. "But I still would like to go over some of the things we should keep in our minds as we talk with people."

"Okay," said Toby, "go for it."

"I think first and foremost, because we have seen it so many times, we have to find out what or who is DONE? It's evidently an acronym, but what does it mean?"

"All indications are," Toby interjected, "that the weapons found in Bremerton came from Israel. What do they have to do with DONE? Remember, a note was found in the pocket of one of the men in the weapons warehouse in Bremerton, with the word DONE on it; also what was the Mayor's involvement in the gun running?"

Reggie came back, "We need to try and find out who in Israel is involved in this conspiracy, if it is a conspiracy, and what are their goals?"

Reggie, paused giving Toby time to once again jumped in, "Whoa, we don't want to go into information overload. We have covered most of what we need to find out, I think the rest of it will come to us when we get there."

"You're right, besides, I'm hungry and we need to pack for the trip. Our flight leaves at 10:30am, but with all the airport security we need to be there by nine. Anything you want to do this evening?"

"Not really, let's get some lunch. It would be nice to go to dinner with Brandy and then make it an early evening."

When they returned to Reggie's apartment after dinner, Toby called Renie and talked with her for a long time. After that there was little conversation as each man was lost in his own thoughts wondering what the future held for them. They both felt as if they were traveling to meet their destiny.

CHAPTER TWELVE

Israel

TERRORIST ORGANIZATIONS, THROUGH publicity and fear generated by their violence, seek to magnify their influence and power to effect political change on either a local or international scale.

'*Today is the first day of the rest of our lives.*' For some reason this timeworn saying ran through Toby's mind as the flight he and Reggie were on left the airport in Las Vegas. They were on the first leg of their long journey to Tel Aviv, Israel and as the huge jet lifted its nose into the clear blue sky, Toby, who had never left the Continental United States, felt the anticipation of entering the unknown.

The first leg of their journey was uneventful ending at O'Hare International airport in Chicago and, having some time before the final leg of their flight they decided to walk around the terminal to stretch their legs. Not only would they be able to stretch but also the walk would serve to ease the jitters associated with flying into Israel, not knowing what the visit would hold for them. Reggie took time to make a call to Brandy and Toby bought a copy of the New York Times and a Time magazine placing them in his briefcase.

The newspaper and magazine lay forgotten until they were in the air and the flight attendant announced dinner was going to be served. Reggie had fallen asleep immediately after their departure and Toby, deciding not to wake him until the meal was being served, remembering the newspaper and magazine, removed the newspaper and began reading.

Opening the paper his eyes were immediately drawn to the headlines and article on the front page—GREAT FALLS, MONTANA, TWO MEN

KILLED IN A BOMB BLAST. The article went on to say that witnesses to the explosion told the authorities, as soon as two men got into their car and started the engine the car exploded. A waitress inside the restaurant said the two men came into eat lunch and while they were eating had asked several questions about Montana, wanting to know how far they were from the junction of State Highway 87. The local authorities have turned the investigation over to the FBI. "At the printing of this paper no organization had claimed responsibility, but the residents in the area were wondering if this incident ties in with the warnings issued by the Federal Government concerning an organization known as DONE, the same one claiming responsibility for the bombings in both Dallas and Chicago."

When Toby finished reading the article, Reggie began stirring and rubbing the sleep from his eyes, he said, "In my semi-conscious state, I thought I heard someone mention food. I'm as hungry as a bear, I wonder if I can order two of everything?"

Toby, chuckling replied, "I don't know, but when you get fully awake you might want to read this newspaper article. We've had a lot of leads directing us to Montana and here were two guys, evidently heading into Northern Montana, when their car is blown up. There's nothing about who they were or what they were doing in that area. The only thing the authorities know for certain is the car had Washington State tags and there's speculation the guilty party is DONE."

Taking the paper, Reggie read the article and then remarked, "I believe Great Falls is south of Glasgow. As soon as we get settled into our hotel rooms in Israel I'll call Joe and ask him to check with his contacts in the FBI and see if he can get more information about the bombing. I think it would be interesting to know who those two guys were as there has been too much happening in Montana for it all to be coincidental."

Pausing briefly he continued, "If you look at everything happening over the last several weeks I see a pattern developing. First I meet with a total stranger, who knows a lot about my family during the time we were stationed in Israel. After he talks with me he's tortured and killed. The next day two men I don't know walk into my office telling me they are investigators hired by a person, who they will not identify. They give me the story about investigating a missing hunter in Montana during which time they find an old abandoned Air Base, where, in their words, 'things got too hot so we had to leave'. Then they tell me the first stranger, who was tortured and killed, was working for them. Then on the evening when I'm supposed to meet these two men, they run out, catch a plane and leave me high and dry. To top that off, I've been pegged as being in on this whole thing, because the man who was killed was carrying my business card and I don't even know what it is I'm involved in."

Hesitating, to gather his thoughts, he went on, "If that isn't enough, I find some information in my father's desk which points to a conspiracy beginning in Israel. But before I get a chance to read what my father wrote someone breaks into my apartment and steals the briefcase containing his papers and computer disks. I'm tailed around Las Vegas and the surveillance continues when you and I fly to Boise, where we are forced to kill them before they could be questioned. When you and I get to Las Vegas we're once again followed around the city and only God knows what they want and who sent them."

"And let's not forget," Toby interjected, "to add this unknown organization DONE into the equation. How many times have we heard that name either mentioned in conjunction with a terrorist act or some supposedly subversive activity. You first found the name in your father's writings when he was describing activities in Israel. I found the name on a piece of paper in the pocket of a man, not an American, in a warehouse filled with guns and ammunition. We again found the name on a piece of paper in the car of two men following us in Boise and it was tattooed on the arm of the individual who was following us in Las Vegas. Now the next part of the puzzle is the bombings that seemed to be randomly going on around the country. There have been bombings in Montana, Dallas and Chicago, with DONE claiming responsibility for at least two of them that we know of. What's that all about and how do all of these facts tie in together?"

Thinking about what Toby had said, Reggie responded, "If this is what my father was writing about, it isn't difficult to see why he decided to back off, especially when he felt his life and the lives of his family were in jeopardy. If all of this turns out to be true and is coming out of Israel, we could be in real danger."

Before they could continue their discussion their meals arrived and they shelved the talk as they began eating. The conversation wasn't forgotten but with full stomachs they both decided to take a nap and pick up their discussion once they were in Israel.

Twenty hours and fifteen minutes later their flight ended at Ben Gurion Airport in Tel Aviv, Israel. They claimed their luggage, cleared Israeli customs and were headed for the car rental counter when a loud voice, in passable English called out, "Gentlemen, would you please step this way."

Looking around they saw a young Israeli in uniform, pointing to a partially open door, leading into an office, located on the side of the terminal. Reggie looking at Toby with a bewildered glance, then acknowledging the request they both walked into the office.

Standing behind a desk, inside the room, was another Israeli, in the same type of uniform as the first. He was a large man, with an impish grin on his face, and as they entered he spoke in perfect English, "As I live and breathe I did not believe it when I heard. Reggie Nutsbagh back in Israel! We had better make an announcement around Tel Aviv to lock all doors and chain up all of the young girls."

Reggie didn't recognize the officer even though he apparently knew him. The officer continued in an attempt to jog Reggie's memory, "I can not believe you do not remember your sworn blood brother?"

When the officer mentioned 'blood brother,' Reggie's face lit up with recognition, "I'll be hanged, if it isn't my good friend and blood brother Joel." With a big grin, he embraced the large man. "Joel Garza, after all these years you're the last person I expected to see after you disappeared without even a goodbye."

"There were good reasons," Joel said, "but it sure is good to see you again."

Reggie then introduced Toby, "Joel, I'd like you to meet another good friend of mine, Toby Preston."

"Baruch Habah," replied Joel, as he shook Toby's hand, nearly crushing it in a vise like grip. "Any friend of Reggie's has to be a friend of mine."

"Joel," Reggie said, "we've got a lot to talk about, and as we expect to be here at least a week I'm sure we'll find time, but right now we're some very tired tourists who need to find their car and hotel."

"Okay," Joel replied. "Come, I will show you the car rental counters. You can pick up your car then I will ride with you to the Tel Aviv Sheraton Hotel, which is not too far away. My driver can follow us in my car."

When the four men turned and started walking to the car rental counter, a look passed between Reggie and Toby. The look said more than the spoken words, and meant, *'be careful and remember we don't know who we can trust.'*

During the ride to the hotel, Reggie and Joel continued with their conversation, talking and laughing about things that occurred during Reggie's stay in Israel.

"Hey, Joel," Toby said, breaking into the conversation, "I'm curious, how did you know we were flying into Israel and on that particular flight?"

"Nothing mysterious about that, in my duties as a Captain in the Israeli National Police Force I happened to be in the American Embassy one day last week on some police business and needed to speak with the Ambassador. When I entered his office he was on the phone with someone and I heard him mention your name and your request to meet with Samual Leving. Being a good policeman, I went to Leving's office and inquired of his secretary about Reggie Nutsbagh. She told me when you were scheduled to meet with Mr. Leving; so I called the airlines and found out which flight you were on."

When Joel finished his explanation, Toby remarked, "Sounds reasonable, but what I don't understand is, why was the information about our visit, with Mr. Leving, also given to the American Embassy. Is this common practice in Israel?"

"I must confess we try to keep track of Americans who come to Israel during these trying times. But, enough of these questions and answers, we are close to your hotel and I know you both are tired. Reggie, before I forget, Mother told me to invite you for dinner tomorrow night and she would kill me if I did not extend the invitation, which of course, includes Toby. I will pick you up tomorrow evening at 6:00 pm sharp in the lobby."

"Great, we'd love to go. How is your mother doing?" Reggie asked.

"She's doing well, stubborn as usual. She lives in my house along with my wife and sister. She will be very happy to see you again after all of these years. A little apprehensive, considering all of the trouble we used to get into, but happy never-the-less."

Arriving at the hotel, Joel transferred to his car with a reminder about the dinner engagement. Reggie and Toby gave their bags to the porter, turned the car over to the valet and entered the hotel. Before going to their individual rooms they agreed to meet in the lobby in about thirty minutes to catch a quick snack before retiring.

As agreed, they met in the lobby, walked into the restaurant and chose a table in a corner, next to a window. After ordering, Toby said, "I know he's your friend, but for some reason I don't think he was being completely honest with us. I think he knows more than he was telling."

Thoughtfully, Reggie replied, "Even though he was my friend that was a long time ago and things have a way of changing. I agree with your assessment, Joel was very evasive about why the information of us coming to Israel was passed around. I'm wondering if some of the things he said were spoken in the way of a warning."

They had completed eating and were having coffee when their attention was drawn to the large crowd of people gathering around the television in the lobby. "Must be another suicide bombing in Tel Aviv," Toby commented.

"I'm finished and if you are," Reggie responded, "why don't we wander over and see what has the people so stirred up."

Both men got to their feet, and after paying their bill walked in the direction of the crowd of people. Barely able to see over the crowd they managed to glimpse the repeated image of what appeared to be a large crowd engaged in a celebration when all of a sudden the image became blurred as the party was interrupted by a large explosion.

Both men were stunned as they watched the unfolding saga and as the TV station's commentary was in English they could also understand. According to the commentator there had been a large party, consisting of several families, who has just finished witnessing the marriage of family members and were attending a reception when two men walked into the gathering with bombs strapped to their bodies. Once they were inside the party room they detonated the bombs and the resulting explosion decimated the interior of the building causing many deaths and leaving an untold number of people seriously injured.

The two men stood there, transfixed, unable to speak, their eyes glued to the TV screen not believing what they were seeing.

They finally walked away from the crowd, which seemed to have doubled in size, with the commentator saying the prediction of the death toll made earlier could be much higher.

On the way to the elevators Reggie spoke the words that both of them had been thinking, "What a sad day it is for the Israeli people, I'm sure this is the work of Muslim radicals, but I wonder if DONE is also rearing its ugly head, here in Israel. We know they're spreading their ugliness in our country, is it possible they are here in Israel, also?"

"I know the people of this country are aware of the ugliness of terrorists," Toby somberly replied, "but when will the people of our country will wake up to '*The Dawn of Realization*,' that terror has invaded our shores?"

Heads bowed, shoulders slumped, the two men slowly disembarked from the elevator and headed for their rooms. It would be a sleepless night; the graphic pictures of the devastation, coupled with the heroics shown by some of the people in attendance would be etched in their minds for a long time to come. It would be a long time before the people behind this were singled out but they would be found and revenge would be sought when the guilty were finally found.

Breakfast the next morning was a quiet affair as both men tried to shake off the effects of the long flight and the disturbing news of the latest terrorist activity.

Attempting to put their minds back on the task at hand, Toby asked, "Did you get a chance to call Joe about the bombing in Montana?"

"No, I'll go do that now."

While Toby finished his breakfast, Reggie went to make the call. Returning from the call, he sat down and said, "Joe is checking with his friends at the Bureau and will let me know about the two guys killed in Montana the next time I call. Meanwhile things are happening around Vegas. Phil called and told Joe to pass on to me they have identified the John Doe; his name is Michael Laslow, a highly regarded private investigator from the Seattle area. They don't have any information on who the killers were or why he was killed. But there was an anonymous tip that came in on the police hot line leading them to a storage facility on Boulder Highway. There they found several pounds of TNT in a storage locker. They linked the storage locker to Laslow, when they lifted his fingerprints, along with several others from inside the locker. The authorities haven't put names or faces to the other sets of fingerprints yet."

Toby listening intently replied, "I just had a thought, I'm sure you remember those two guys who were following us around Vegas before we left. Do you think your policeman friend, Sal, filed a report about those guys? Remember one of them had DONE tattooed on his arm. Could they be involved somehow?"

"Good point. While you're finishing your coffee I'll go call Phil and give him that information and have him check with Sal about the two guys he stopped, I'm sure he filed a report."

After making the call to Phil, Reggie returned to the restaurant and told Toby of his conversation with Phil and reminding him it was time to leave for their appointment with Samual Leving at the Minister of Defense's Office.

They got general directions to the Minister of Defense Building from the hotel clerk, retrieved their car and proceeded to the meeting. Discussing their appointment as Reggie negotiated the crowded streets they failed to notice they were being followed.

Their discussion centered on what they would and wouldn't discuss during their meeting, one thing they decided not to discuss, was the real reason they were in Israel. They agreed to keep the discussion on terrorism and see where it would lead.

With the directions provided by the desk clerk they had no problem finding the Minister of Defense building and Samual Leving's office. When they were led into his office and were shaking hands with the Minister another man entered the office.

"Gentlemen," said Leving, "this is my deputy, Joseph Abramson."

After thirty minutes of discussing the effects of terrorism, Reggie thought, *'This conversation is going nowhere. There must be a way to shake things up.'*

"Sir, do you by any chance know anything about an organization called DONE?"

When Reggie asked the question, he did so for the shock effect and he closely observed the reactions of both men. Leving, showed no emotion whatsoever, but his deputy's eyes narrowed and for a second his face showed a disquieting look.

Leving replied, "No, I have never heard of an organization by that name. What does it mean?"

Before Reggie could reply, Abramson spoke, "Sir, you have a very important meeting with the American Ambassador in about 30 minutes, you will have to leave immediately, that is if you want to make the meeting on time."

"You are right, Joseph. Gentlemen, I am sorry, but duty calls," replied Leving. "I hope your time here was not wasted and you can enjoy the rest of your visit to our wonderful country."

The partners shook hands with the minister and his deputy then departed.

Walking out of the building Toby said, "Good move, partner; I realized what you were trying to do and believe we both came up with the same conclusions. When you mentioned DONE, it was quite obvious Leving had no idea what you were talking about, but his deputy, Abramson, is a different story. His reaction was minimal, but there was a definite reaction. He knows about DONE and he wasn't happy you brought up the subject."

Reggie looked at Toby with a grin, "Sorry to surprise you, but I wanted to shake things up a bit and didn't have time to tell you what I was attempting to do, but I see you picked up on it. Abramson's eyes got real hard for a split second, when I asked the question. He's one tough cookie and at least knows something of DONE."

"We're going to have to be extremely careful," said Toby. "Now I think its time for lunch. I didn't eat much breakfast and I'm starving. There must be a good place to eat in this town."

Finding a restaurant close by the two partners were enjoying lunch and were so engrossed in their conversation they were totally unaware of the two men sitting at a table behind them seemingly more interested in them than they were in their food.

Relaxing after their lunch and enjoying their coffee they discussed their remaining itinerary for the day. Reggie reminded Toby of their dinner engagement that evening with Joel and said he would probably take a nap before they had to depart for the dinner.

Acknowledging his comment, Toby replied, "I think tomorrow we need to take a trip to the American Embassy and try to stir something up. Remember Joel said it was the Ambassador's aide who took the phone call informing him we were coming to Israel. I still want to know why he needs to know that and I think I will ask him. Might even take a page out of your book and ask him about DONE."

Once back at the hotel they went to their rooms, promising to meet in the lobby at 5:45 to wait Joel's arrival and the trip to his house for dinner.

At the designated time both men met in the hotel lobby and as they waited Toby's eyes were drawn to an article on the front page of the European edition of the New York Times. Stooping to pick up the newspaper, he showed it to Reggie, saying, "Here Reggie, take a look at this."

Reggie began reading aloud, "In a breaking story the Director of the FBI released information there had been a recent attempt at sabotage of a military installation in the State of Washington. Until now the Bureau suppressed all details of a police raid in the city of Bremerton, which uncovered a large cache of assault weapons."

Returning the newspaper to Toby, Reggie observed, "I think I know now why the Embassy was made aware of our trip to Israel. Your involvement in the raid and contact with the FBI is known by the State Department who alerted the U.S. Embassy. It's a wonder they haven't been watching our every movement."

Making this comment, Reggie looked suspiciously around the lobby catching two men who seemed to be looking in their direction. "Don't look now but I think we have some people who are a little too interested in us. Dressed in suits and ties they look like CIA type."

Nonchalantly, Toby put the paper back on the table where he had picked it up from and glanced toward the decorative palm tree under which the two suspected men were sitting.

Turning to Reggie he said; "If the CIA is tailing us we may have stumbled into something much bigger than we've imagined!"

"I only said they look like CIA type. DONE is a big outfit, as we are finding out, it could be them, instead of CIA."

"One thing is for sure," Toby replied, "We need to be on the alert at all times. Do you suppose we should inform Joel?"

"Not just yet," answered Reggie. "If he's as sharp as I suspect, he'll pick up on the tail on the way to his home. Let's sit back and see how he handles it."

At that moment Joel walked into the lobby and spotted them. As he walked in their direction the two men watching Reggie and Toby turned their faces away as if afraid of being recognized; noting this Reggie thought, '*Now why would they not want to be seen by Joel?*'

"Well, my friends," Joel's voice boomed, "Are you ready for the biggest meal any American has ever eaten?"

"I can't speak for Reggie, "Toby responded, "But I could eat a sow's ear, I'm so hungry."

With this Joel roared, laughing so hard that most of the people in the lobby stared. "This friend of yours will steal my heart from you, if you are not careful," he said, wiping the tears of laughter from his eyes. "Come, we must go or mama will be upset."

Walking briskly he led them out to his waiting car. "Because of my position," he said, "I am assigned a driver, but my superior's must hate me for they give me Saul. Do not mind Saul's driving as he is still in training. Is that not right, Saul?"

"Begging your pardon, Uncle Joel, but I am an excellent driver. Did not you yourself train me?"

"Pardon me, my friends for his rudeness, but this young man is my mother's brother's son. He actually is good, but I must teach him humility so his head does not swell."

Reggie interceded on the young man's behalf at this point, saying, "He certainly has your mother's looks, never having met his father, I would say her intelligence also."

Having taken the front seat for the journey to his home, Joel turned to address his American friends, with a feigned look of pain on his face. As he started to address Reggie his eye caught the car tailing them.

Turning to Saul he said something in a Hebrew, which Reggie was unable to pick up, but from Saul's quick look in the rear view mirror he got the drift.

"Trouble, Joel?" he asked.

"I do not think so, but we have a car following us. I would have seen them if they had been with me earlier. Do you know anything about this?" he questioned.

Reggie admitted they had spotted two men in the lobby of the hotel, "I assume it's those two."

Turning back to Saul, Joel gave his nephew instructions to lose the car. Over his shoulder he advised the two backseat passengers to hang on.

Saul showed his expertise as a driver by darting in and out of traffic on the busy thoroughfare and then turning down a narrow alleyway. His skills would have made a New York taxi driver envious as his skillful diversionary tactics soon lost the tailing car.

Soon after that Saul pulled in front of an attractive, split-level house in Ramat Gan which Reggie immediately recognized from his youthful days. As soon as they got out of the vehicle, the front door of the house opened and a slender woman, appearing to be in her early sixties stepped out.

Spying Reggie, she wiped her hands on her apron and moved rapidly to him, enfolding him in her arms. "I would know you anywhere, my little cookie snatcher," she exclaimed in broken English.

Throughout this exchange, Toby uttered not a word. Not out of emotion for the tender moment, but because framed in the doorway of the house, was one of the most beautiful women he had ever seen, olive skin, dark hair and a body, which could have graced any model magazine. Toby's eyes remained focused on this vision of loveliness and the others, caught up in the reunion of the 'little cookie snatcher,' failed to notice his rapt attention on the woman in the doorway. Everyone, that is, except the young woman, for her eyes had never left the face of this tall, handsome American.

Suddenly realizing he wasn't being the gracious host; Joel grabbed the arm of Toby and pushed him toward his vision, saying, "Toby Preston, this is my sister Ruth. She is a teacher at Bar llan University here in Ramat Gan. You will like her for she teaches English and has agreed to be your guide during your stay here in Israel." Pride was evident in his voice as he continued, "She is very smart. Ask her anything about our history and she knows the answer."

Looking into the dark eyes of this beautiful young woman, Toby could see her face flush under the dark skin. Hoping to make her comfortable, Toby remarked, "It will be hard to keep my eyes on the scenery with a guide as lovely as this." This comment deepened the blush on her face causing her to hastily retreat back into the house.

"Haw, Toby, you have made a conquest of our little Ruth," Joel jovially commented. "Be careful, she is one tough cookie, as you Americans say."

Dinner was a pleasant affair. The huge mounds of food were passed around with Mama going back and forth into the kitchen replenishing the platters of the delicious Jewish fare. Once dinner was over they moved into the living room to enjoy coffee and traditional Jewish pastry, with the exception of Mama and Ruth who retreated to the kitchen to clean up the dishes. Toby's ears would have turned red had he heard the discussion going on in that room. "Well, my daughter," Mama began, "You and that tall American seem to have hit if off very well. Too soon you have forgotten your fiancé Isaac."

"Ex-fiancée, Mama," the normally respectful daughter lashed out. "Isaac was killed more than a year ago, remember? I am going to be an old maid if I don't find someone who will have me. I like him and I think he likes me."

"Forgive me, my daughter, I desire your happiness, but you have only known this American for two hours. He is not of your religion and I hear from your brother that he is only to be here for less than a week. Be careful of your heart, my child."

As soon as the work in the kitchen was finished the two women joined the men in the living room. Once seated Mama said, "Reggie, I am so ashamed of myself, I have been running, as you Americans say, off at the mouth and I was so happy to see you I completely forgot my manners, how is your dear Mother and Father?"

The mood changed from happy to somber as Reggie answered, "They both died a few years ago in an airplane accident. He and my mother flew out of Las Vegas, where we lived, headed for San Diego, California, when shortly after taking off the plane my father was flying blew up, under suspicious circumstances, killing both of them."

As Reggie was telling his story, Toby was listening but also concentrating on Joel because he wanted to see what his reaction would be after hearing about the death of Reggie's parents. When Reggie came to the part about the airplane crash happening under suspicious circumstances, Joel's head jerked around to stare at Reggie and his eyes became slits and his expression was that of incredulity.

When Reggie finished speaking the room was silent, each person lost in their own thoughts. After several minutes of silence, Mama spoke up, "Poor Dorothy and Dominic, it is a shame. They were such a vibrant couple and loved each other so much. Reggie, I am truly sorry, I really loved your mother she was such a wonderful woman."

Pausing briefly Mama continued, "My poor Benjamin was also taken from me. Some poor misguided person detonated a bomb and killed him. I knew he and Dominic were in over their—"

"Mother!" Joel interrupted, "We need to change the subject, this is supposed to be a happy occasion and we should be enjoying the fact there are friends here with us tonight."

Joel was talking fast trying to cover up what his mother had let slip. But both Reggie and Toby had picked up on what she had said and both understood the implications of her comment.

Toby took the opportunity of the silence, to say, "Reggie, we should be calling it a night, my mind is still very active but my body tells me it wants to see a bed."

Reggie hugged Mama and thanked her, as did Toby. Good nights were said and the two started towards the car, suddenly Toby turned around and walked back up the steps. He went over to where Ruth stood and gently took her hand and then looking into her eyes, said, "I'm honored to have met you and can only hope we'll see each other many more times while I'm in Israel."

"We will," Ruth responded, "I have no classes for the next two weeks and as Joel told you I will be acting as your guide and I fully intend on honoring what my brother told you."

"Well," said an elated Toby, "you can start by showing us where the American Embassy is tomorrow, if that is okay with you?"

"That is fine I'll be at your hotel tomorrow at 9:30 am, if that is a good time for you."

With this exchange they looked into each other's eyes and that look said more than either of them could have said.

The trip back to the hotel was completed in silence as they all reflected on the evening's events. Once back at the hotel Reggie and Toby said good night to Joel and walked into the hotel. Once inside lobby they looked around the lobby to see if the two men they had seen earlier were back. Seeing no one they went up the elevator to their rooms, after agreeing to meet for breakfast at 9:00 in the morning.

Sleep wouldn't come easy this night for either of the two, Reggie, because the evening had stirred up buried memories about his parents and their time together in Israel. Then, Joel's mother had unintentionally provided an insight into something he hadn't known. She had indicated, quite by accident, that her husband, Benjamin, and Reggie's father had been working together on something and that her husband was killed by a bomb blast. His mind kept drifting back to the time when he first met Joel and how their friendship developed.

When his father first told him they were being assigned to Israel, Reggie rebelled for the first time in his life and told his father he didn't want to go. After several long talks with his father he finally accepted his decision. They rented a house in the town of Ramat Gan (meaning Garden Heights) and as chance would have it, just down the street lived the Garaza family. On the second day after their arrival Reggie met Joel and from that day forward they had been inseparable. Vaguely Reggie remembered that one day there was a tremendous explosion in down town Tel Aviv and when Reggie came home from school his friend Joel and the entire Garza family was gone and he never saw them again.

Toby's restlessness was a combination of guilt for pushing memories of his beloved Esther into the background for the present thoughts of the lovely Ruth. The redeeming factor was that Esther, knowing she was dying, had encouraged him to find a new love for Renie's sake if nothing else. His last conscious though as he dozed off was of Ruth framed in the doorway.

The two partners spent the night with their thoughts of old memories and dreams of love while across town in a drab, rundown house two men sat around a dilapidated table discussing death and destruction. There was nothing distinctive about the two, except each man had a large tattoo on his upper left arm which depicted a dagger through the word DONE.

CHAPTER THIRTEEN

Truths Revealed

WAKE UP CALLS in rooms 5614 and 5615 of the Tel Aviv Sheraton Hotel sounded simultaneously informing the occupants it was time to face the day. The occupants of those rooms, Reggie Nutsbagh and Toby Preston, had spent a restless night; Toby because he had been captivated by the beauty of Ruth Garza, and now she had invaded his dreams; for Reggie it was the memories of his parents and their deaths, which had been revived during the conversation last evening

After completing their morning toiletries, and as planned the night before, the two men met in the hallway, rode the elevator to the lobby and entered the dining room. They had just been seated in the restaurant when they saw Ruth Garza entering, she paused at the entrance looked around and spotting the two men she walked up to their table a smile playing across her face. Both men got to their feet as she approached, and as she did Toby's face lit up with his own smile. He pulled out a chair for her, saying, "Good morning Ruth, you sure do brighten up an otherwise drab room. Won't you join us for breakfast?"

"Thank you, only coffee for me. I had breakfast before leaving the house."

After being seated she exchanged greetings with Reggie and then turned once more to Toby, inquiring about his evening and asking if he was ready for the day. It didn't take a very smart man to see that Ruth and Toby were smitten with each other. While she was polite to Reggie, she only had eyes for Toby.

Breakfast resumed and, with Toby and Ruth engaged in their own intimate conversation, Reggie took the opportunity to scan the restaurant looking for the two men they had encountered the day before, he didn't see them but that didn't mean they weren't around.

Finishing his second cup of coffee, he said, "I hate to interrupt, but we do have a few things to get done this morning and the sooner we get to them the sooner we'll be able to have some time for ourselves."

"I am sorry Reggie," Ruth, showing her embarrassment, laughed nervously, "You are right. I understand you want to go to the American Embassy?"

They left the hotel in her car and after a short drive arrived at the American Embassy where she dropped them off; saying, "I have a couple of errands to run and I'll be back in about twenty minutes." Toby and Reggie entered the building and within a matter of minutes were passed through security, then ushered into the office of the aide to the Ambassador, Robert Sandoval. After the introductions, Sandoval said, "I'm a very busy man; I know you were at the Israeli Minister's Office yesterday now what can I do for you, gentlemen?"

The tone of his voice was such that Reggie and Toby realized he knew everything that had transpired at the Israeli Defense Minister's office, which meant he was going to be cautious about what he said. Toby opened the dialog, "Mr. Sandoval, we'd like to know several things; first, why was it necessary for you to know we were coming to Israel? And secondly, why is it necessary for you know what transpired at the Israeli Minister's office, during our visit there? Is this something that's usually done, or was it because of who we are or something we did?"

"I will be brief and to the point. I have no intention of discussing the business of this Embassy with you or any other person. If I want to know why American citizens are visiting Israel, then I will find out. Furthermore, while in this country you will conduct yourselves in a manner above reproach, nothing short of that will be accepted. As citizens of the United States you had no right interviewing the Israeli Minister of Defense. Your conduct has been reported through official channels to Washington."

"We don't need to explain anything to you, either," Reggie declared angrily, "our visit to the Minister was completely on the up and up. We have nothing to hide, we met the minister at a conference in Salt Lake City and while we were here in Israel we wanted to renew that friendship."

"From what I understand you were rude, asking questions you have no business asking."

"I'm sure it wasn't the minister who accused us of rudeness," Toby, angrily retorted, "but if we had no business there, according to your policy, then let me be the first to apologize. We intended no harm to our country's relationship with the Israeli government. I do have one more question for you, and then we'll leave you to your important business of spying on American citizens. What do you know about the organization called DONE and what does it stand for?"

"I assure you I have no idea what you're talking about and I'll not entertain any more of foolishness or impertinent questions. This interview is over. I remind you to keep your noses clean while in this country. Have a nice day gentlemen, my secretary will show you out."

The aide turned his back on the two and walked out of the room to be replaced by his secretary, who motioned for them to follow him out the door.

Once outside the building they sat on a bench, close to the entrance, to wait for Ruth's arrival. Once seated Reggie spoke of his impressions of the meeting, "We know he was briefed on our visit with the minister, I'm sure by Abramson. I'm also sure he knows what's going on and was ready for us. I wonder if he and Abramson could be the two who my father was talking about when he mentioned people in high places in governments were involved."

"I agree, Reggie," Toby said, then added, "Also remember what Mama Garza blurted out last night talking about her husband and your father, the comment which had Joel scrambling to cover up. You might not have noticed last night, but when you talked about your parent's death under unusual circumstances, Joel's face took on a look of disbelief. It's as if the information caught him by surprise and the news of your father's death hit him real hard."

Watching people go in and out of the embassy he paused then continued, "Let's put the facts together; your father and Joel's were working together on something dealing with a conspiracy; Joel's father died from a bomb here in Tel Aviv and your father died when his plane blew up, those two incidents must be connected. Israel's aide to the Minister of Defense and the aide to the American Ambassador were both upset when asked about DONE. This coupled with the fact that both of us believe Joel knows more then he's telling, leads me to conclude, as you pointed out, both men, at both offices are up to their necks in the conspiracy your father wrote about and are deeply involved in DONE, one way or another."

He had finished his comments when they saw Ruth approaching so Reggie said, "Let's hold the rest of our discussion for another time."

Ruth parked the car and came to where the two men were sitting, when she arrived, Reggie said, "Why don't you two drop me off at the hotel and then Ruth can take you around Tel Aviv to do a little sight seeing. I have some phone calls to make and a little shopping to do. We can meet back at the hotel this evening about six for dinner."

"Okay," Toby responded, "if you're sure you don't mind?"

"Its fine, Toby, I need some time to myself to try and figure out what is going on."

After Ruth dropped him off at the hotel he went up to his room to make several phone calls. The first call was to Joe, "Joe, did you get any information from your FBI contacts putting names to the bodies found in the bombing in Montana?"

"I sure did," replied Joe. "Their names are Ronald Bowers and Lee Robertson both men residing in Seattle, Washington. They were good friends and just graduated from college several months ago. My sources tell me they had returned from a hunting trip in Northern Montana; spent a few days at home and then for some reason decided to go back into that area and died for their efforts."

"Stay on top of that investigation if you can," Reggie replied, "and keep me informed of any new developments the next time we talk. I don't know if this is a clean line, so I can't explain what's going on right now except to say you really need to tighten down on the security, not only for yourself and the office, but Brandy. I think Toby and I are stirring up a hornet's nest."

"Okay Reg, will do," answered Joe. "Are you going to call Phil? He called the other day with some information for you, but it would be better if you heard it from him. I heard what he said and took notes, but most of it's Greek to me."

"I'll call Phil right away. I appreciate what you are doing and I'm sorry about putting you in this position without telling you what's going on."

"No problem, Reggie, I understand; don't worry about the home front, I'll take care of things around here. Rest easy in the knowledge I'll insure all involved are safe and secure. Brandy has been a real trooper about all of the security measures I've taken and she's getting along real well. I know she misses you as she's been calling me every day asking if I've heard from you; you really should call her."

"Thanks for the information, Joe. Keep in contact with your friends at the FBI and let me know if they come up with any more information concerning the bombings, not only in Montana but the others that occurred in Dallas and Chicago"

Hanging up he placed another call to Phil, "Hey, old buddy, how are you doing?"

"Not so good right now," Phil answered, "I think you've been hiding something from me and it's bothering me."

"Tell me what you're talking about," Reggie said, concerned about his friend's feelings, "so I can at least defend myself. Believe me; I wouldn't knowingly keep important information from you."

"Remember the other day when I told you we put a name to the John Doe we found tortured and murdered behind the Paris Hotel?"

"Yes, but what has that—"

Phil interrupted, "I told you his name was Laslow, a PI from Seattle, well we found out he was staying at Vacation Village at the south end of the strip. When we searched his room we found your name written on a piece of paper."

Before he could continue Reggie broke in, "Phil, just because he had my name written on a piece of paper doesn't mean I knew him nor had anything to do with him. My name and office number are in the phone book and he was a PI just like me. Maybe he wanted to contact me with a business proposition or something like that."

"You're right, Reggie," replied Phil, "I'm a little tense right now, I've been getting a lot of pressure from the mayor's office to find out what is going on with Laslow and the explosives. By the way here's something you might be interested in. We checked with his office in Seattle and found out from his partner he was in Tel Aviv two weeks before he was found dead in Vegas."

When the information was disclosed about Laslow and Israel, Reggie was taken completely by surprise and was unable to respond immediately.

His hesitation was so long that Phil asked, "Reggie, are you still there? Did you get that last piece of information concerning Laslow and his visit to Israel?"

Regaining control Reggie replied, "I heard you Phil, we must have been cut off momentarily. I can see you have your hands full, so I'll get out of your hair. Thanks for the information. I'll do some checking around here to see if I can find out anything about Laslow and what he did while he was here. I'll call you in three or four days and let you know if I find out anything."

"Don't go yet, I have some more information you might like to know. You asked me to check with Sal and his report about the two guys who had been following you before you left for Israel. We got a big break there, we checked with Hertz and even though the car had been cleaned we found two distinctive sets of fingerprints on the center console of the car. Checking with the FBI we put names to the prints, one was Robert Smith and the other was James McDuffy, both from Glasgow, Montana. Those fingerprints are identical to the ones found at the storage locker which means they had something to do with Laslow and his death. They're both known anarchists and are believed to be heavily involved in the militia movement. If you have any contact with them, be careful." With that last bit of information the phone call was terminated.

After Phil hung up Reggie sat on the edge of the bed, trying to regain his composure. He wanted to call Brandy but couldn't with his mind whirling from what he had just heard. The information from Joe and Phil had helped to fill in some gaps and in turn had left a lot of fingers pointing at Joel. There was no other place Laslow could have gotten the information about Reggie's family. This was a very complex puzzle they were working on, yet the part in Israel was beginning to fit. *'It will come together better after a discussion with my Israeli friend,'* he thought.

He finally calmed down enough to make his call to Brandy. After exchanging the normal pleasantries and both expressing the fact that they missed the other, Reggie did something completely out of character for him; he told her how much he really loved her. The line went silent as she was caught off guard at his admission.

She had known for a long time she loved him, but the time had never been right to tell him. She was about ready to respond to his confession of love when the line went dead, and an operator came on the line, after a short pause, apologizing, saying there seemed to be difficulties with the connection in Israel. Still reveling in his admission of love, she sat by the phone hoping the connection could be re-established.

What he had told her was the truth but he never contemplated telling her over the telephone, so the line going dead was a blessing as he feared her answer to his disclosure. Glancing at his watch he saw it was several hours before he was to meet Toby and Ruth so he chose not to try and reestablish the connection with Brandy, lying down on the bed instead, wanting to evaluate his emotional outburst, as well as, digest the latest information he had received from Joe and Phil. He needed to get his thoughts together before talking to Toby and especially before confronting Joel.

Meanwhile Toby and Ruth were enjoying the sights of the city while reacting to love's first bloom. Ruth was proud of her heritage and city, and showed it by her exuberance as they toured different sites within the city of Tel Aviv. They visited the Eretz Israel Museum, took in the old city of Jaffa and the Carmel Market. When hunger came they ate at a typical Israeli restaurant called Tchelet. Sometime during the afternoon, they went from walking side by side to walking hand in hand.

The day was drawing to a close as they walked down the beachfront at Taylet, stopping for coffee at a small café and watching the sun set on the placid Mediterranean. As they sat, Toby impulsively leaned over to his beautiful companion and kissed her on the lips. It must have been the right thing to do for she responded, making the moment one of mutual consent. At the display of passion Toby became flustered and stuttered out, "I'm sorry. I just couldn't resist the urge. You look so beautiful with the sun shining on your face that I—"

Reaching over she tenderly touched his lips, saying, "Please do not spoil the moment, I was hoping you would do it. From the time I saw you standing in the yard looking like a lost puppy something happened to me and I became extremely attracted to you. I know our lives are so different and we may not see each other again, but I believe I am in love with you."

Taking her hands in his and in front of the amused people in the little café he affirmed his love for her, taking the time to tell of his life in Washington and, of course about his daughter Renie. He was in the middle of telling her about his life when they realized it was time to go, Ruth to home to get dressed for the evening and Toby back to the hotel, Reggie would be waiting.

Arriving at the hotel he got out of the car, regretting they must separate, but pleased with the knowledge that she would come back and join them for dinner that evening.

Entering the hotel, his mind still on Ruth so he was startled to hear his name called, looking in the direction of the voice, he saw his partner sitting in the lounge with a cup of coffee in his hand.

Waving him over Reggie asked, "What truck hit you? I yelled your name twice before you heard me." Not waiting for a reply, he went on, "I have some important information to discuss with you and I think it would be best to find a more private place to talk. Why don't we step outside in the garden and sit there?"

Finding a quiet shady place in the hotel garden, the two men sat down. Looking around to insure no one was within listening range, Reggie began, "I talked to Joe and he had some information concerning the two men involved in the bombing in Montana. The two men were identified as Ronald Bowers and Lee Robertson, young men fresh out of college. Evidently they just returned from that area and after several days at home, for some reason, decided to return."

"It's mighty coincidental," Toby said, "that a hunter would disappear in the vicinity and then two more men headed into that general area are killed when they return to the same area."

"You're right," Reggie interjected. "Joe is going to do some more checking and try and see if he can get more information about those two guys who were killed in the bombing."

"This is turning into an international investigation which seems to be growing in scope," Toby responded. "Every time we hear news about people connected to our investigation they end up dead. Did you happen to talk to Phil about the murder and explosives?"

"Sure did. I talked with him and he said they identified the two sets of fingerprints found at the storage locker. They got lucky and based upon our suggestion they got the information from Sal's report and went to Hertz, found the car they had turned in. The rental company had cleaned the car, but they were able to lift two sets of fingerprints from the console between the seats. The finger prints matched the ones found at the storage locker and now they've put names to the prints. One is Robert Smith, the driver of the car following us, and the other is James McDuffy, the passenger, both of them are known anarchists and heavily involved in the militia movement."

"And I suppose," Toby added, "Their last known address was Glasgow, Montana or somewhere in Northern Montana?"

"You got it, partner," Reggie replied. "We know these anarchists are also members of DONE. I guess this lends further credence to what we've suspected all along, we're up against a large organization, one that seems to be well funded. I wouldn't be surprised if we find out part of the funding and training is coming from this part of the world." Pausing for a second, he continued, "I have saved the best for last."

"You mean there's more?"

"Absolutely! Remember me telling you they put a name to the John Doe who was killed in Las Vegas after talking to me? Well his name is Michael Laslow, a PI from Seattle, and after making the identification, Phil checked with his office in Seattle and was told that approximately two weeks before his body was found behind the Paris Hotel, he had visited Tel Aviv."

Toby's eyes widened at the news, "Ouch; I guess this means our friend Joel may know a whole lot more than he's telling."

"I agree," Reggie responded, "And I for one think we need to get Mr. Joel and attempt to level the playing field by asking him some questions. We need to be blunt and pull no punches in a discussion with Joel. Lay it on the line and find out where he's coming from and how much he knows."

"When Ruth joins us for dinner tonight we can find out how to contact her brother. She's picking us up in about an hour and a half, so we had better get a move on if we want to freshen up a little before dinner."

The two men went up to their rooms to prepare and a short time later, returned back to the lobby to find Ruth waiting for them. Seeing Toby her face broke into a smile of greeting as she walked briskly towards them. Saying B'Shalom to Reggie she turned to Toby with a smile still on her face and shyly gave him a kiss on the cheek, saying, "That is to thank you for this afternoon, I had a wonderful time. The best time I have had in a long time."

Blushing beneath his tan, Toby responded teasingly, "Is that the best you can do? I can think of better ways of saying thank you."

Growing uncomfortable under Reggie's steely gaze, she replied, "But in Israel that is not permitted in public."

Breaking into their by-play Reggie said, "I find this conversation most stimulating, but my stomach thinks my throat has been cut and I need to be fed. Thanks to the overseas operators, I didn't have time for lunch, so I'm hoping we can get something to eat, before I pass out for the lack of nourishment."

Toby, replied through his laughter, "Ruth, let me tell you about this guy, he's the only person I know who asked the flight attendants on our flight to Israel for two dinners. So it would be in our best interest to find some place to eat. I don't know what he will do when he gets really hungry and I don't want to find out."

With that comment the trio walked outside and climbed into Ruth's car. When they were all seated in the car she asked, "I know Toby likes Mexican food, because that's what Maria serves him at home, how about you Reggie? I know this great place that serves wonderful Mexican food if you are agreeable we will go there." Reggie agreed and they were soon on their way.

The short ride to the restaurant was filled with small talk and laughter as each partner tried to outdo the other with quips and jibes. The levity of the moment took their minds off the gravity of the situation, causing them to not notice the sedan, which followed them from the hotel.

Dinner was completed and after Reggie had finished his second cup of coffee, he cleared his throat trying to get the lovers' attention, "I don't know about you two but I'm kind of tired and tomorrow is another day. If you like, you can take me back to the hotel, or I can get a cab."

"Don't be silly," Ruth responded. "I will drive you back to the hotel; Toby and I can continue our conversation there in the coffee shop or we can walk across the street and stroll on the beach. The moonlight on the water is beautiful this time of night."

Paying the bill they returned to the car and headed back to the hotel still engaged in idle chatter, so again they didn't notice the car following them. They had driven a short distance from the restaurant when Ruth, who was driving, suddenly stopped. Looking across the street, she exclaimed, "Look over there. I wonder what that is all about."

Looking across the street at the unfolding scene they saw an elderly man being assaulted by two young men. With their attention focused on the altercation they failed to notice the car behind them, running in the dark with no headlights, hadn't stop when they did but rather began picking up speed as it approached their car.

Seeing the man under attacked galvanized Reggie and Toby into action and they jumped from Ruth's car to go to the assistance of the elderly man. On his way out of the car Toby's jacket got caught on the door and he hesitated trying to free his coat, while Reggie continued on toward the altercation, intent on taking a hand in what appeared to be a mugging.

For some reason, he couldn't later explain, when Toby finally got his coat free and he started toward where Reggie was engaged in ending the mugging, he took a quick look back at Ruth's car and saw a car approaching at a fast speed with no lights on. Then he saw something being thrown from the car and roll under Ruth's car. Immediately, Toby sensing danger, yelled at Ruth to get out of the car and run but she was unable to hear him over the sound of the other car's engine as it accelerated past them.

Seeing Toby was gesturing at her, Ruth climbed out of the car and started walking towards Toby. She was half-dozen steps from the car when an ear-shattering explosion filled the air, catapulting Toby backwards, as the bomb, which had been thrown under her car exploded.

Toby felt a sharp burning pain in his left leg and right side, but ignoring his injuries he rolled over and got to his feet, looking for Ruth. He saw her lying motionless in the middle of the street where she had been thrown by the blast. When he saw her lying there he roared with anguish, not because of his injuries, but for the woman he loved, who was lying on the ground, possibly dead. It was more than he could bear. Ignoring his injuries, he limped to Ruth's side and felt for a pulse. With his own heart beating so loud and fast it was a miracle he could feel anything but he finally felt a fluttering of a heartbeat coming from the still form laying on the ground.

Finding it hard to concentrate, as his own loss of blood was causing dizziness, he managed to feel again for a pulse and found, this time, it was stronger. He yelled at Reggie, who had been shielded from the bombs effects, to call for an ambulance. He gently began to check Ruth to try and ascertain the extent of her injuries. It appeared she might have two broken legs and there were minor burns were on both her arms and legs. The explosion from the bomb had ignited the gas tank and only the clothing she wore had kept the burns from being worse. Remembering his first aid he knew he had to try and prevent her from going into shock so he placed his jacket under her feet and covered her up with a jacket from one of the bystanders. When he completed making her as comfortable as he could he heard the sound of sirens approaching.

After calling for help, Reggie came over and placed a hand on Toby's shoulder, "How is she partner?"

"She's alive, for the moment. Her pulse has been getting stronger and that's a good sign."

"Are you okay? You're bleeding."

"It feels like I took a couple of pieces of shrapnel but the bleeding has stopped, but don't worry about me, please get the medics over here to take care of her."

She began making little moaning sounds, so Toby leaned over to reassure her that the doctors were here to take care of her and that she was going to be okay. At the sound of his voice, her eyes opened and she struggled to say something. Leaning down he put his ear close to her lips, trying to hear what she was saying. When he looked up there were tears in his eyes and Reggie could tell by the look on his face that he was praying to God with all his might.

The ambulance, with its team of paramedics and the police arrived at the same time. The medical personnel immediately began to attend to Ruth. One of them, seeing Toby nearby covered in blood tried to take care of him but he refused their assistance asking them to make sure that Ruth was attended to first.

After about half an hour of working on Ruth one of the paramedics told Toby she would make it and he saw no evidence of internal injuries. Her recovery would be long, but she would survive with a few visible scars. With this news Toby allowed them to bind his wounds. He had taken fragments of the exploding car in the side and left leg so using field procedures they removed the shrapnel and ascertained no vital organs had been punctured.

Toby requested to ride in the ambulance with Ruth, leaving Reggie to answer the police officer's questions.

After the ambulance departed Reggie attempted to tell the police officers what had happened but that turned out to be an impossible task as none of the officers spoke English and Reggie wasn't able to converse in Hebrew. Finally a sergeant who spoke English arrived and took over the questioning. He answered all of his questions except the one the sergeant asked as to why someone would want to kill them!

Three hours later the police dropped Reggie off at the hotel where he found Toby in the lobby drinking coffee.

Walking over to him, he said, "Partner, you look like death warmed over."

"She's going to be fine," Toby, responded. "I don't think I could live with myself if she had died. You know this happened because of us, don't you?"

"I know and I've been kicking myself all night. I should have seen it coming. These guys must have been following us all the time and were just looking for the right time to take us out. It was just dumb luck that you and I got out of the car and didn't get caught in the blast."

"I guess we're getting on someone's nerves, or getting too close to whoever or whatever is going on, or at least someone thinks we're getting close."

"Where did you get hit?" Reggie questioned.

"I took some shrapnel in the side and a small piece in the leg. Other than being a little stiff and tired from loss of blood, I'm okay. Were the cops satisfied we knew nothing about what's going on and why this happened to us?"

"Satisfied, no; I'm sure they'll be getting back to us, either way we can't leave the country until they let us. They will be here in the morning to confiscate our passports unless we can get Joel to help us."

Reggie continued, "I'm glad to hear you are okay physically, but how are you mentally? Will you be able to go with me to confront Joel about what's going on?"

"Partner, I'm right as rain. Tired, hurt, but with what I heard earlier from Ruth all of that doesn't matter. Right now the only thing that does matter is she's going to be okay."

"Wonderful Toby, now I think we had best try and get some sleep, if we can. I'm going to try and set up a time and a place for a meeting with Joel."

With this comment the men entered the elevator and went to their rooms. There would be no problems with them getting to sleep tonight. Reggie was mentally exhausted from all the events that had happened in the last 48 hours and Toby was extremely tired from the loss of blood, but the tiredness and weakness were all over shadowed by the knowledge that during the time of crisis, with Ruth lying bleeding and hurting in the street she had told him she loved him.

CHAPTER FOURTEEN

Things heat up

THE SUN WAS up and shining brightly across the Mediterranean Sea and even though its rays shone through the drapes of their rooms Reggie and Toby managed to sleep soundly. Both men were worn out by the events of the previous evening but Toby much more so because of the pain pills he had taken prior to going to sleep. An insistent pounding on the door to his room slowly brought Toby awake, *'Boy the maid service in this hotel is sure demanding,'* he thought. Groggy from his drug-induced sleep, he sat up and attempted to drag himself from the bed when the loud pounding was replaced by an even louder voice, "Preston, open this door before I break it down!"

The pounding and yelling on Toby's room door was so loud it also woke Reggie, who was sleeping in the adjacent room. "Now what the hell is that?" he grumbled, as he rolled over and got out of bed.

"This is the police! Open the door," yelled the now recognizable voice of Joel Garza.

Reggie was just emerging from his room when Toby opened the door admitting a visibly angry Joel. Feeling he needed to be with his friend during this apparent confrontation, Reggie followed Joel through the open door into Toby's room.

Storming into the room without hesitating, Joel grabbed the front of Toby's robe, as he screamed, "What do you mean putting my sister in danger? Your stupidity almost got her killed and you didn't even have the common decency to notify me. What the hell is going on?"

Before Toby could answer, Reggie spoke up, "Joel, instead of asking Toby that maybe you should be asking yourself."

Joel, startled as he hadn't known Reggie was behind him, wheeled around, still gripping Toby's robe, to confront Reggie, "What is that supposed to mean? Are you trying to tell me I am the one who almost got my sister killed? Are you out of your mind?"

"I meant just exactly what I said. If you remember correctly, last evening on the way to your house someone was following us and you were aware of it. The fact alone tells me you know more about the reason someone would want to kill us than anyone else. So I repeat, you should ask yourself the question," Reggie said, yelling the last sentence, on the verge of exploding with his own anger.

"Joel," Toby managed to calmly say, "Why don't you go down to the restaurant and give us some time to dress? Then we'll come down and talk about this in a reasonable manner without yelling and screaming."

Having calmed down, Reggie spoke in agreement, "Joel, please do as Toby asked, we only need a few minutes to get dressed and we'll be right down and join you. All this yelling and screaming isn't going to solve anything. Take a few minutes, sit down, get a cup of coffee and we'll be right there to discuss the situation."

Still angry Joel release Toby and without another word stormed out of the room. Reggie then returned to his own room hastily dressed as did Toby, both of them hoping Joel would give them the time they needed before barging back up to their rooms. Toby could understand Joel's anger, but he had tried several times to contact him from the hospital but no one seemed to know Joel.

He had even tried the National Police but they wouldn't give him any information. It was as if Joel wasn't a member of the Israeli National Police as he had told them.

Toby finished dressing and hurried next door to Reggie's room, when he knocked on the door Reggie yelled for him to come in. Toby walked into the room saying, "Well, Pal, we wanted to lay it all out on the table with Joel and there's no time like the present. I meant to tell you last night but in all the excitement, I forgot; I tried many times to contact Joel, I went so far as to call the headquarters of the National Police and they either didn't know who I was talking about or wouldn't give me the information. Either way I couldn't get a phone number or find any way to contact him or his family."

Completing his dressing, Reggie replied, "I wouldn't worry about it, he isn't going to be happy with anything we tell him. He no doubt has been to the hospital and has probably talked with Ruth and thinks it's our fault she got hurt. I guess we had better hurry and get downstairs before he comes raging back up here and creates another scene. Let's take him for a walk while we talk. I don't want to take any chances or discuss anything where there's even a remote possibility someone could overhear our conversation."

"I agree," replied Toby. "I'll let you take the lead in our discussion with him and I'll add information as necessary, that way we won't be stepping on each other."

Departing the room they got in the elevator and rode it to the lobby. Entering the restaurant they located Joel and walked over to him and as they approached he started to say something but Reggie interrupted him saying, in a very polite tone of voice, "Let us get some coffee first, so we can wake up. Then after coffee we're going to have to find a more private place to talk or we'll not talk at all!"

Sighing Joel said in an equally calm voice, "Okay, we do need to slow down a bit."

After finishing several cups of coffee and a few bagels the three men paid the bill and left the restaurant. Once outside Reggie said, "I think we can find a nice quiet place on the beach across the street."

Agreeing, they walked across the street onto the beach and located a secluded place, which allowed all of them to sit in the shade of a towering palm tree and have an unobstructed view of the clear blue water and the surrounding area. Once seated Joel opened the conversation, "You guys call yourselves policemen? How could you allow this to happen! I don't know what they teach you about being cops, but the newest rookie on our force would never be caught in such a predicament and allow someone to get close enough to throw a bomb."

Angrily, Toby responded, "There's something you seemed to be forgetting, in our country, until recently, there has never been a need to look over your shoulder for people throwing bombs. As policemen we're taught to prevent and investigate crimes, not watch out for bombers."

"What Toby said is absolutely true," Reggie interjected, "we come from a different world then yours. Throwing accusations around isn't going to get us anywhere but angry at each other. I'll be the first to admit both Toby and I blew it, and you're right we should have seen it coming. But if what we both think is going on, you probably could have prevented this from happening by coming clean with us in the first place."

"I don't have the faintest idea what you are talking about," he replied, not looking at either man, but keeping his eyes focused on the near by water.

"Are you really a member of the Israeli National Police?" Toby asked.

"Yes, I am."

"Okay," Reggie stated, "We'll leave it at that for now. I have a more important question to ask, do you know or have you ever met someone named Michael Laslow?"

When Reggie mentioned Laslow's name, Joel couldn't disguise his look of surprise, but he still answered, "No."

"Joel, you're going to have to start telling the truth," Reggie admonished. "We know you're lying. We also know Laslow was in Israel several weeks ago and when he returned to the United States I met him in Las Vegas. When we met, he told me some things about my family and things that happened while my family and I were in Israel that only you could have told him. Laslow is now dead and the two men who hired him are missing. He was probably killed by the same organization that claimed responsibility for setting off bombs in Dallas and Chicago."

"What has that got to do with me?" Joel questioned.

Reggie, showing his anger for the first time, yelled, *"THE TRUTH, JOEL! THE TRUTH!* How the hell would Laslow, a PI from Seattle, get information about events concerning my family and me which occurred during our stay in Israel, except from you?" Reggie stopped in mid-sentence as the realization of what he was trying to say hit him. "Unless the Mossad had information and gave it to Laslow, who really worked for the CIA. Joel, tell me the truth are you working for the Mosaad?"

Joel quickly replied, "As I told you before, I am a Captain in the Israeli National Police."

"And pigs can fly," said Toby in a voice full of venom. "Several times I tried to get a hold of you from the hospital. I called the Israeli National Police headquarters on three different occasions and was told they didn't know of a Captain Garza. The other time I was told you were unavailable. What kind of police force is it that doesn't even know their captains? Those guys who threw the bomb at us last night knew exactly what they were doing and it's only by accident they didn't kill all three of us. I guess captains aren't privy to reports, so let me tell you exactly what happened; we had stopped the car to assist an old man who was being mugged by two young punks. Reggie and I jumped out of the car; I was momentarily held up when my coat caught in the door and saw the car coming with no lights on. I yelled at Ruth to get out of the car," Here he paused to regain control, as he mind flashed back to that terrible incident and he saw in his mind's eye Ruth lying, unmoving in the street then with a catch in his throat he continued, "but she didn't hear me, I tried to get back to her, but I just wasn't fast enough."

Hearing and seeing Toby's distress Reggie took over, "Joel, your mother, bless her soul, let the cat out of the bag last night at dinner. I know you tried to cover it up but she said enough and no matter what you think of our abilities as policemen, we did pick up on what she said about your father and mine working on something and getting in over their heads."

With a hint of amusement, Joel said, "I never thought either one of you were or are stupid, but what she said about my father getting killed has nothing what-so-ever to do with what went on last night."

"We all know that isn't true, she said something about Benjamin and Dominic being in over their heads. Just for the fun of it let's consider this; your father and mine were working together trying to get to the bottom of a conspiracy they had stumbled onto. The conspiracy was developing in Israel and involved some players who were working at high-level jobs in your government and mine. A bomb kills your father and I can assume it was also meant for mine too. The conspirators decide, after they got rid of your father and missed mine, that they didn't want to bring any more attention to themselves and decided not to kill my father, but put him in 'cold storage'. They pulled some strings and had my father transferred and forced into retirement."

Drawing a deep breath to steady himself Reggie continued, "Someone must have found out my father took notes and kept computer records which made him an obstacle to be removed and the records had to be found. It must be a large organization, as the leaders of this organization wanted General Nutsbagh eliminated and it was promptly accomplished. Not only was my father killed but my mother also and she didn't have an enemy in the world." Hesitating in his narrative, as the finality of losing his parents caused his sorrow to surface, but drawing a deep breath to collect himself, he continued, "Since the time I talked with Laslow in the sandwich shop in Vegas I've found listening devices in my home and office and had people following me around and, now with an attempt on our lives, I think it's time to hit back. It seems that someone is concerned about how much I know, and now that Toby is associated with me he is also under scrutiny. Now this trail of information we followed led us to Israel and you."

"Is there more to this fairy tale?" Joel questioned.

Ignoring his comment, and at Toby's suggestion, that they break and get some coffee, they got up from where they were seated and walked over to a snack shop, purchased coffee and returned. Sipping his coffee, Reggie continued, "After the death of my parents I found some information in my father's study, but I was only able to see part of it because someone broke into my apartment and took the briefcase, containing the rest of the information. The only thing I had was a computer disk with enough information to lead Toby and I here. The disk mentioned an organization known by my father by the name DONE. It alluded to the possibility of some high-ranking government officials from several governments involved in a conspiracy."

Once again he had to stop as his emotions over losing his parents began to surface. He looked around the beach, then looked back at Joel and, continued, "Now this is where you come in; you told us you overheard our names going between the Minister of Defense's office and the American Embassy. Being good policemen, retired policemen I might add, we went directly to the horse's mouth, so to speak. We made an appointment with the Minister of Defense Leving, and his deputy just happened to be there. We asked Leving about DONE and we're told, truthfully, I believe, he knew nothing about the organization. Now with Abramson it's a different story, when I mentioned DONE, we thought he was going to have a heart attack but he covered up by immediately telling Leving he had another appointment. From this we surmised not only does Abramson know about DONE, but he also runs that department and the Minister is just a figurehead."

At this point Joel said, "With the theft of the rest of your father's notes, it must have left you up in the air?" Making a point of ignoring Reggie's last comments in references to the two men and DONE.

Knowing Joel was evading his comments about DONE and the two men, Reggie continued with his narrative, "The next day, after having dinner at your house, we went to the American Embassy and did the same thing to Sandoval, aide to the Ambassador, he didn't bite when Toby mentioned DONE. The reason he didn't take the bait was he had been fully briefed by Abramson. Now to answer your question about being left up in the air, we understand what is going on here, but DONE has made several critical mistakes. First they made Toby and I mad as hell and second they are using amateurs to take care of business, evidenced by the fact that Toby and I took two DONE operators out in Boise, Idaho. This was done, not with the guns or knives but with what nature provided for us, rocks and sticks?"

Toby, who had been silent during Reggie's discourse now interrupted, "I also ran into several interesting items where I live, items which can be attributed to DONE. We found a warehouse full of weapons, of all types and sizes shipped in crates marked as coming from Israel. During the raid and the subsequent search of the men in the warehouse we found a piece of paper in the pocket of one of the guys with the word DONE on it. Then the Mayor of Bremerton, owner of the warehouse, was deeply involved but he will never see any more payments from DONE or the results of his efforts, because he was killed."

"All of this sounds real interesting," Joel smirked, "is there more to this amusing fairy tale?"

Reggie, in a voice filled with disdain, rose from his chair and looking at Joel said, "Joel, I thought you were my friend, but times and people change. You have lied to us and are continuing to lie to us. But mark my words we will get to the bottom of this and bring these people down no matter what the cost."

Toby, also got up and looking directly at Joel, said, "I have one more thing to say, I'm in love with Ruth and no matter what you say I will have a relationship with her and she is the only one who can stop me. She is a wonderful woman and has given me more happiness in the past several days then I have had since my wife Esther died."

Reggie looked at Joel, his look of disdain turning to a smirk, "I thought we were blood brothers. If this is what blood brother means to you then you can have it. Come on Toby let's get out of here." At this both men turned and headed back towards the hotel.

"*DAWN of a NEW ERA*," Joel said quietly to their departing backs. "*DAWN of a NEW ERA*, that's what DONE means."

Both men turned, not understanding what Joel had said, and walked several steps back to where Joel still sat.

When they closed the distance Joel said, "You have put me in an impossible position. My existence and that of my families depend on no one finding out that I have said that name or told you anything about what is going on. If either side finds out I have talked to you, I am a dead man and my family along with me. Just mentioning that name, *Dawn of a New Era*, could sign my death warrant."

Reggie was the first to speak, "It's not our intention to put anyone in danger or in any more danger then they're already in. We want to put an end to the evil that is starting to spread around the United States."

Joel sighed, "I need your assurances that what I am about to tell you stays between the three of us. My job, my family's lives and my life may well depend on your maintaining that confidence."

"Speaking for Reggie and myself," Toby replied, "any information you give us will go no further, of that you can be sure."

Nodding his head, accepting Toby's assurance, Joel continued, "We have known for a long time that Abramson and Sandoval were involved in DONE, but it was better, in the long run, if we left them alone so we could try and put the whole network out of business forever. You are correct in your assumption about my father's demise. Your father and mine were working together to uncover the conspiracy and the only reason your father did not get killed by the bomb blast, which killed mine, was at the last minute he was called back to his office. My father started his car to move it and the bomb went off. When it happened the Mossad moved my family out of our house within two hours, which is why I disappeared."

"So," Reggie inserted, "My father was a target also?"

"Most definitely, you see my father was an undercover Mossad agent, working under deep cover trying to discover what this conspiracy was and who was behind it. The only thing he uncovered, according to his notes, is what was going on in Israel and that the financing for the conspiracy comes from somewhere in the Pacific Northwest of your country. We know part of the financing is coming from goods that are being smuggled, into your country through a port on the West Coast. The smuggled items include industrial diamonds, electronic goods, drugs, arms, and people."

"People?" Toby questioned.

"Yes, people, that is probably the most important commodity DONE is exporting from Israel and surrounding countries. After all this part of the world has been engaged in acts of terrorism for years, so what better place to find trainers for terrorism in the United States?"

"And my father and yours stumbled onto this many years ago?" Reggie asked.

"It started by accident, from what I understand in reading my father's notes. Your father uncovered some strange happenings while visiting the Minister of Defense Office and as he was a good friend of my father he told him about it and the investigation went into high gear. We know the exports from this country are shipped out aboard American ships, with the blessing and by direction of the aide to the American Ambassador, with assistance provided by Abramson, and both are getting wealthy doing it."

"Why don't you put a stop to it, if you know so much?" Reggie asked.

"That is why Laslow was here. We asked for some help from the American Government and they sent him. As hard as I tried to cover Laslow's tracks while he was here in Israel, Sandoval found out about him and he left the country under duress. As to why he was killed, I am sure all of us can understand, but the problem I am having, as well as my superiors are having, is what is the CIA doing about it? I am sure someone that Laslow reported to knows about DONE, so we must assume someone in the CIA or your FBI is also on DONE's payroll. It would have to be a person in a high enough position to squelch the investigation and have Laslow killed."

"Did Laslow or anyone else you know of mention the names of Lebowitz or Abbott?" Reggie asked.

"Laslow mentioned their names briefly, during one of our conversations. I believe he told me they had hired him, in his undercover role as a PI, to look into something that happened in Montana."

Toby interrupted, "Is there anything you can tell us about who is leading this organization in the States?"

"Nothing specific," Joel answered, "If you find out who is banking the proceeds from the sale of the exports into the US, I am sure it will lead you to the boss of the organization. Sounds like one of the minor bosses was taken out when the mayor of Bremerton bit the dust."

"I don't know," Toby responded. "He was dishonest enough and very money hungry, but I don't think he had the brains to be in something this big. I believe he was only being paid to store and move the stuff around."

Joel sighed, "Then you are going to have a big problem. We have to shut this operation down real quick, which means we have to shut the suppliers down and when we do that it will send the rest of them in the US into hiding. The Mossad would like to provide assistance to your CIA but now the way things are happening, who can we trust?"

"Joel," Reggie asked, "would it be possible, or could you convince your superiors, who ever they are, to let things run as they have been for a while longer? Give Toby and I some time to put our hands on the chief players of DONE in the US."

"I do not know," Joel, answered, "My superiors are getting impatient and have wanted to close this end down for a while. I keep asking them to give me more time; I guess I could try again, especially with these new developments."

"I have a few more questions I would like to ask," Reggie said.

"Go ahead; I will answer if I can."

"Do you have any idea who gave the order to have my father killed?"

"We found out the order to take my father out came from the United States and we can only assume from the head of DONE. We also found out that those involved here in Israel were told to back off and put your father on ice, not kill him. We both know it would take more than the aide to the Israeli Minister of Defense and the Aide to the American Ambassador to force a four star general into retirement."

"I can buy that, I guess, do you know of anyone in the U.S. Government, outside of Israel, who is involved with DONE?"

"No, and that is going to be your biggest problem. I would suggest you follow the money. It seems to me if you can find out who consigns the exports from Israel and where these are going once they get into the U.S. you can figure out who is directing traffic."

"I have one last question," Toby added, "Do you have any idea who is out to get Reggie and me here in Israel?"

"No, I can only assume it is DONE, but I caution you, play it safe while you are in Israel. We do not know or have not yet identified all the minor players of this organization in Israel."

"There's a problem with playing it safe," Toby replied with a touch of anger. "Someone tried to kill us and someone I care deeply for got hurt, in my way of thinking it deserves a response."

"I can understand your desire for revenge," Joel countered, "but you must remember you are in Israel and here you are only a tourist. The person you are referring to is my sister and I also desire revenge and I will get it, but it will be done my way or not at all. My suggestion to you two, is to get on an airplane and get out of Israel before we ship you home in a box."

"We'll leave, but under our terms," Reggie replied. "I'm sure Toby wants to hang around until Ruth is on her way to recovery and I want some more answers from you. Can you get your people to delay action and do you have any more information about the initial attempt to kill my father? I'm sure there was an investigation."

"When are you scheduled to depart?"

Toby answered, "We fly out in four days."

Joel was silent for a few minutes, and then said, "I will talk with my superior tomorrow morning. I will present your request about holding off busting DONE folks and then dig further into the initial report of the bombing that killed my father. I will contact you tomorrow around 5:00 pm at your hotel. Meanwhile I think you should stick pretty close to your hotel and be watchful; they missed you once but I would not expect them to miss twice."

With this the three men headed back to the hotel. Prior to entering the hotel Reggie glanced around and saw the same two men, they had seen following them the day before, standing outside the hotel, he called to Joel and Toby, who had preceded him into the lobby, "Outside, I just saw the two guys who were following us the other day."

Joel, with Toby close behind, bolted out the door of the hotel, frantically looking up and down the street trying to spot the two men, only to see a car speed out of the hotel parking lot with the two suspects aboard.

Joel walked back into the hotel shaking his head, "I sure wanted to see who those guys were. Reggie, did you get a good look at them?"

"No," Reggie responded, "but I did get enough of a look to know they were the same two guys who were in the lobby the night you came to pick us up for dinner."

Joel was preparing to leave, when Toby said, "Joel, do you really have heartburn with me seeing Ruth? Not that it's going to stop me, but I would rather have you on my side than against me."

"No, what I said was said in anger. I know how Ruth feels about you and she is a big girl and can make her own decisions. I am sure you both know about the religious complications should this affair proceed to the next level."

Then bidding goodbye to Joel the partners decided they would each do their own thing for the rest of the day and meet at six in the hotel restaurant for dinner.

Later, at the agreed upon time, the two partners met in the lobby, and Toby greeted Reggie with a smile, "Hey pal, how was your day?"

"Well, I'm not crazy about shopping," Reggie answered, "but I think I managed to buy everything I needed, at least I hope I didn't forget anyone. "I can guess by looking at your face I don't have to ask how your day went. How's Ruth doing?"

"She's getting along better than expected. The burns are not as bad as previously thought and both her legs were clean breaks and will mend well. I wanted her to have a private room and she gave me a hard time but I insisted and she was finally moved. I guess you can tell, I'm serious about this lady and I intend to see her as much as possible. It will be hard when we leave, she is a wonderful woman and I really think Renie would like her."

Reggie smiled and responded, "I'm really happy for you and I hope that everything works out for you two. Now I'm very tired and as soon as we finish eating I'm going up to my room, take a hot shower and sleep."

"That sounds like a plan," replied Toby, "I hope we don't get rousted out of sleep the same way tomorrow morning."

With this said both men quickly finished their dinner and made their way to their rooms.

CHAPTER FIFTEEN

Their Welcome is running out

ANOTHER BEAUTIFUL BRIGHT morning was dawning, but once again Toby wasn't awake to greet the sun and the beginning of the new day. The confession by Joel and his visit with Ruth at the hospital and the encouraging news of her recovery eased his mind and allowed him to have a restful night's sleep. Yesterday it was the persistent pounding on his room door by Joel that had awakened him, but this morning it was the insistent ringing of the bedside phone that woke him. After several rings he rolled over and by stretching himself full length he managed to pick up the receiver and mumble into it, "This is Toby."

The cheerful voice of his friend Reggie responded, "Hey, pal, throw on a robe or something and come on over for breakfast, it's on me. Room service is bringing it in right now."

Hanging up the phone Toby rolled out of bed and splashed water on his face then climbed into a pair of old jeans and threw on a shirt and walked next door to Reggie's room. He reached for the door and attempted to open it but it was locked; *'why would Reggie invite me over and then lock the door?'* He knocked and almost immediately Reggie opened the door, saying, "Good morning," and then he put his finger to his lips indicating he shouldn't talk. Walking over to the coffee table he squatted down and pointed under the table. Toby looked at where was Reggie pointing and saw a tiny device, which Toby immediately knew was a listening device, firmly planted on the underside of the table.

It was only then that Reggie spoke, "I hope you had a good sleep and are feeling well rested and hungry because there's a lot of food." As he spoke he was furiously writing on a piece of paper.

Reading the hastily scribbled note, which said, "be careful what we say," Toby answered, "Slept like a rock and I'm hungry as a bear. The breakfast sure looks good, not the usual Continental type of breakfast." Lifting the lid on the coffee container he leaned over and breathed in the smell of the fresh brewed coffee. "The coffee sure smells good and I'm ready to eat. I'm glad you came up with this idea."

Again Reggie scribbled on the note pad, "Follow my lead, we know the bad guys are listening to our conversation, maybe we can use their own device to throw them off a little bit."

Eying the platters of food Toby reached for the coffeepot and poured each of them a steaming mug of the very strong coffee, and then each man heaped their plates with the food and began eating.

"I think we can go home now," Reggie said. "I don't believe there's anything more for us to learn here. I had hoped Joel would give us the information we needed, but he gave us nothing. After breakfast I'm going to go take care of some other business and I'll meet you back here, say around 3:30 this afternoon?"

"Sounds good," Toby responded, "I think I'll spend the better part of the day visiting Ruth in the hospital. I completed my shopping the other day, so I would rather spend as much time with her as I possibly can."

The two men finished eating and then Toby, anxious to get on with his activities, got up and waved his goodbye. When he went out into the hallway Reggie followed and quietly suggested Toby check his room for listening devices. Toby nodded in agreement and they made plans to meet down stairs in about forty-five minutes.

At the agreed upon time the two friends met in the hotel lobby, and walked outside before Reggie asked, "What did you find?"

"The same listening device planted in the same spot. These people sure aren't original or imaginative at all. Of course there could be several more of the devices around the room, but that's the only one I found. Knowing it's there puts us on the alert. How did you spot the bug?"

"Nothing scientific about it, I dropped some coins out of my pocket and several of them rolled under the table, when I went to retrieve them I saw the bug. I didn't look for any more; one was enough to tell me someone is interested in what's going on in our rooms."

On their way to the parking lot, the partners carefully observed everything going on around them and when they reached the car they did a thorough check to insure it hadn't been tampered with in any way.

Once they had pulled out into the street and figuring it was safe to discuss business in the car, Reggie, who was driving, said, "While you're at the hospital with Ruth I'm going to make some more phone calls back to Vegas and see if there are any new developments in either one of the cases."

"Sounds good," Toby responded, "I might even make a call back to Chief Fisher and see if there are any new developments on the warehouse case. Also I want to talk with Renie and let her know I'll be home in a couple of days."

"When I get back to Vegas I'm going to try and find out how the explosives got into Vegas and from where. I also want to try and find out more about Laslow's murder. We need to find out if there's a US government connection to what's going on."

"That sounds like a good idea." Toby responded. "I'll do some checking with Laslow's agency when I get back and try to find out what else he might have been working on. I'll also try to find out what I can about other shipments into Washington from Israel. Before we leave we probably should ask Joel if he can give us any information about the shipping and what specific ships are being used to move the stuff. I also might try to find Lebowitz and Abbott and see if they can shed any light on what they were doing, who they were working for and why they left Vegas in such a hurry. Maybe the information could lead us to someone who knows about the conspiracy in the U.S."

"Putting this all together might lead us to the head of DONE," Reggie added.

"Yea, but the only thing this organization wants from us is for us to disappear," Toby replied. "We may put them off for a while, but as long as we're around we're a potential problem for them."

"You're right, partner," agreed Reggie. "I really would like to find out if Smith and McDuffy are still around. I'd like to talk to them in private. When I make my call to Vegas, I'm going to ask Joe to check with Phil to try and get a more detailed description of those two guys, and then maybe he can check around to see if they're still in town.

Later, arriving at the hospital both men went in and up to the 3rd floor to Ruth's private room. She was sitting up in bed and when Toby walked into the room a smile spread across her entire face. Both of her legs were in full-length casts and part of the lower half of her body was covered in a dressing for the burns. Never taking her eyes off Toby, she greeted Reggie asking, "How are you Reggie? I hope all is well with you."

"I'm doing just fine, Ruth. I'm glad to see you're doing better than the last time I saw you. I guess Toby is taking good care of you?"

"I think he has accepted the fact that I am an invalid and he is going to have to take care of me." At this point she had to stop talking as her voice cracked and tears came to her eyes, "At least for as long as he is here in Israel, which I know will not be long."

Toby hurriedly replied, "Ruth, the doctor told you that a part of your recovery is your mental attitude and that you must keep a positive outlook. Even though I may have to leave Israel, what we have will not end." When he finished his comment he took her hand in his and kissed her gently on the lips.

"I have to go," Reggie said, smiling, "I just wanted to see for myself that Toby is taking care of you."

Reggie kissed Ruth on the check then said, "Listen to what Toby is telling you. Don't worry about tomorrow or the days after that, just take it one day at a time."

Reggie then walked over by the window, which provided him a view of the parking lot below. Looking down at the parking lot his attention was drawn to the vicinity where their car was parked. He saw some pedestrian traffic, but his eyes were drawn to two men who were slowly walking between the rows of cars. He continued watching them as they got closer to where their car was parked, then he watched them stop close to their car, furtively look around and then walk in between Reggie's car and the one parked next to it. Reggie, realizing what was happening, yelled at Toby as he bolted out the door, "It looks like they're at it again." Not waiting to see if Toby was following, he ran down the hallway to the exit and the stairs not wanting to wait for the elevators.

Toby, seeing his partner bolt out the door immediately followed him.

Reggie hit the first floor exit on the fly. Nearing the parking lot he slowed down, mentally formulating a plan of action. Looking back towards the hospital he motioned for Toby to circle the parking lot and come up on the rear of the cars parked in the lot.

Reggie could no longer see the two potential adversaries, but assumed they were crouched down between the cars. He began to close the distance, moving in and out between the other parked cars. He didn't look up to see what Toby was doing knowing he would be there when needed.

Approaching their car Reggie heard the voices of the men speaking in a language he couldn't understand. Sneaking a look between the two cars he saw the two individuals trying to attach something to the undercarriage of his car. He let out a roar and charged, catching them completely off guard. Startled they dropped what they were holding and tried to run away from Reggie only to run headlong into Toby. Toby engulfed both of them in a giant size bear hug and held them both securely as Reggie rushed to assist him.

As the struggle went on a young man, not involved in the incident, ran up to them, speaking in what appeared to be Hebrew. Shaking his head, Reggie said, "I don't understand, speak English."

The young man struggling for the right words, man asked in passable English, "What is the problem here?"

Reggie responded, "Would you please call the police? We have a situation here that requires their presence."

Nodding, the young man hurried back into the hospital to make the call.

Within a few minutes sirens could be heard indicating the police would soon be arriving. But before they arrived Toby and Reggie heard a familiar voice, "Well, what is going on here?" Joel walked around the corner of the parked cars and saw Toby and Reggie restraining two men and, without asking why, he directed his driver, Saul to secure the two.

Turning to the partners, after Saul took possession of the two men, Joel ask, "I was on my way to see Ruth, when I picked up a call about some type of disturbance at the hospital, so I hurried here and what do I find, my two friends up to their ears in trouble. What is going on?"

Reggie answered, "If you'll look over there by my car, I'm sure what you'll find will provide you with an explanation."

Joel, turning, walked over to the car and bent down to look at a small bundle lying on the ground next to Reggie's car. Shaking his head, he came back toward the group saying, "You are a couple of lucky guys, if that bomb had gone off, it would have taken you out as well as half the cars in this lot. Are these the two guys who were trying to put the bomb under your car?"

"Yes," Reggie responded, "they sure weren't too smart about it. I was looking out the window of Ruth's room and saw them approaching the car. The way they were walking and looking around told me they were up to no good, so Toby and I ran down and collared them."

"I know both of these guys; they have the brains of an earthworm. They were most likely hired by someone to do the job."

Walking over to one of the two men Saul now had in handcuffs, he slapped one of them not too gently across the face, asking, in Hebrew, "Joseph, who hired you to do this thing?"

Saul standing next to Toby and Reggie provided the translation as Joel talked to the suspects.

Joseph replied, also in Hebrew, "I do not know their names, they paid us 21 thousand shekels apiece to plant the bomb under that car. We were driven here to the hospital, the car was pointed out to us and then they left. Here is the money in my pocket; it will prove I am telling the truth."

By this time two cars of Israeli National Police had arrived. After a short conversation between Joel and the officer in charge the policemen returned to their cars, but didn't leave the area.

Joel resumed his questioning, "Where did you meet them?"

Joseph replied, "We were contacted by a man on the phone. He told us to meet two westerners outside the Dortel Savoy Hotel, on Geula Street. We met them; they are the ones who told us what we had to do and then drove us here."

Joel quickly walked over to his car and made a call on the radio, then returned to where the two partners waited patiently. Approaching them he said, "I guess Saul has told you what Joseph told me? I placed a call to our headquarters to go check the Savoy, but I really do not expect to find anything. Joseph and his partner David are both well known to us, they will do almost anything for money, but this time I think they went too far."

Joel paused, then taking a deep breath continued, "May I make a suggestion? Since your arrival here you have gained a lot of unwelcome attention. Toby, I know you would like to hang around because of Ruth, but it will not do her any good if you are dead. I still owe you some answers which I will give you later this afternoon. If you agree I will get your flight reservations changed so you can leave on an earlier flight."

"Toby, for once I agree with Joel," Reggie said. "We're getting nowhere here, I for one would like to get back on familiar ground and have more on me than just my hands and legs. I understand your feelings for Ruth, but I think if you explain the circumstances to her she would agree it's best for us to leave. But, you are your own man and I can't force you to leave but right now I think we need to stay together."

With a somber look on his face," Toby sighed then replied, "Both of you are right, of course. There are several hours before we are to meet at the hotel, I will stay here with Ruth and then see you back at the hotel later."

"I am going to take Joseph and David back to the station and see if I can get any more information from them. I will let you know if I find out any more this evening when we meet and give your new flight information.

When Joel and Saul left with the two suspects Toby said, "This is going to be hard on Ruth. She knows I love her, but she doesn't understand the situation we're in and wants me out of it. I've got to convince her it's best for both of us to resolve this situation even if it means our being separated for short time."

Several hours later, having completed some more shopping; Reggie was sitting in the hotel lobby when a smiling Toby walked in. Reggie knew, by looking at his face, he and Ruth had reached a mutual understanding and all was well.

Beaming from ear to ear he walked over to Reggie, sat down saying, "Partner, how did your afternoon go?"

"Great, and by the look on your face I would say yours also went well."

"Fantastic! It took a while but I think Ruth understands I'm serious about my relationship with her and regardless of the temporary separation, with her here Israel and me in the United States, we will make it work. We even talked about religion and both of us agree that our beliefs will be the biggest hurdle, but love can break down any barrier. Besides there will be plenty of time to iron out our differences, hopefully a lifetime."

"Wonderful, Toby," Reggie responded, "I'm really glad for you. Now I'll let you in on a little secret of mine." He reached into his coat pocket and brought out a small jewelry box, he opened it and Toby saw a big beautiful diamond ring. It had one large diamond surrounded by several smaller clusters of diamonds and was absolutely stunning.

"Does this mean what I think?" he asked. "Are you finally going to do the right thing?"

Grinning, Reggie answered, "What happened this afternoon and yesterday got me to thinking. Other than you, there's no one else in my life who means much to me, except Brandy. I now find myself in the position of wanting to be much more to her then an occasional date. I want those things you have, a family and a woman who loves me. I've already told her over the phone I loved her and we were cut off before she could answer, so I'm hoping her answer would have been yes and she will accept this ring and marry me."

Toby was overjoyed at Reggie's disclosure so much so, that he reached over and gave him a big hug, saying, "We had better get upstairs and get our packing done and have some dinner before Joel arrives. After we're finished here, I want to spend some more time with Ruth."

When Toby got to his room he immediately went over to the coffee table and removed the listening device and before placing it in his pocket he said loudly, "A souvenir from Israel," and then began his packing.

In less than thirty minutes, Toby walked back into the lobby to find Joel sitting the in lobby with Reggie. When he approached the two they got up and all three of them walked across the street to the beach. Once on the beach, they stopped to admire the beauty of the sun sparkling on the waves as they crashed onto the shore. They then walked down the beach until they were beyond the crowd of people before beginning their conversation.

"Joel," Reggie asked, "did you get any more from those two guys you arrested at the hospital or any information about the people who hired them?"

"No, we even talked with the people at the hotel and they couldn't give us any more then a general description," replied Joel. "Two well dressed American men in their mid thirties, approximately six foot tall weighing around two hundred thirty pounds, both with brown hair and always wore suits. They stayed by themselves and kept strange hours. The staff of the hotel noticed they were in and out at all hours of the day and night. They had been at the hotel for the same length of time you guys have been here and checked out this afternoon just prior to the capture of the two men at the hospital. We checked their rooms and found nothing, except a small piece of paper in one of the rooms with the word Seattle written on it."

"What's the word about holding off on shutting down DONE's activities here in Israel," Reggie asked.

"I had a hard time explaining to my superiors why I talked with you guys and told you as much as I did. The end result was that they agreed to allow the organization to continue to operate, but not for too much longer."

"That's good," Reggie, responded, "Did you find out any more information concerning the organization and its leaders? Also is there any information you can give us on what ships are being used to transport the items out of Israel to the States?"

"The only ships they use are American ships. So when you look into it, you only have to check ships with American registry originating in Israel. In answer to your other question, we do know for a fact that the order to take out my father and yours definitely came from DONE. No one in Israel has the power to contract a hit on someone as powerful as your father or mine. The organizational arm in Israel is only for one reason and that is to move goods to the United States."

Reggie thought for a moment then said, "I have one other question; is there a way that we can, if needed, get in contact with you?"

Joel took a card out of his wallet and printed a number on the back of the card. Handing the card to Reggie, he said, "Please don't let this card out of your possession, the number I wrote on the back is a twenty-four hour contact number for either me or Saul. Outside of my boss you are the only ones to have the number."

"Okay, Joel. One last thing, do you know anything about our rooms at the hotel being bugged?"

Grinning sheepishly, Joel replied, "Yes, I'm afraid I do. Those were put there at my direction prior to you flying into the airport. I had the rooms wired until I figured out why you guys were here. I apologize, but I did not think you would find them and when they were not needed I did not have the time to take them back out of the rooms."

Reggie, laughing at Joel's embarrassment, said, "As you now know we did find them and made the assumption they were placed there by the bad guys trying to find out what we knew."

"Toby, I have not seen Ruth this afternoon, I assume she knows you are leaving. Is everything okay, between you two?" Joel asked. "You know at first I did not approve of you seeing her, but now I have changed my mind and am willing to help you two in any way I can."

"Thank you, Joel," replied Toby, "She's upset I'm leaving, but understands why I must. I assure you as I did her, that I'm going to be around for the long haul. She is a wonderful woman and I love her."

"Good, I am glad for both of you," said Joel. "I will be back in the morning around nine to take you to the airport. Toby, I know you would probably want to go back to the hospital so I have arranged for a car and driver who will stay with you until you are safely tucked away in your hotel room." He then motioned to a young Israeli and introduced him to Toby. Turning to Reggie he said, "I have also assigned a man to provide for your security until you retire for the night." Another Israeli walked over and was introduced to Reggie.

After completing the introductions all of the men started walking back towards the hotel. After walking a short distance, Reggie, spoke up, "Joel," he said urgently, "I think we have visitors, I noticed since we left the hotel, several men paying a lot of attention to us and what we are doing."

Laughing, Joel replied, "I was wondering if you would notice. Don't worry about them, they are with me and will stay with us until you get on the airplane. We will also look over the aircraft and will very carefully check the passenger list. I want to make sure you guys arrive safely."

The next morning Toby and Reggie met in the hotel lobby prepared to leave Israel. After checking out of their rooms and securing their luggage with the valet, they went into the hotel restaurant for breakfast. They were on their second cup of coffee when Joel arrived.

An hour later they arrived at the Ben Gurion International Airport, where they were escorted through a secure entrance relieved of their luggage by the security detail and led directly to the plane. Joel boarded the airplane with them and informed them he would stay until all passengers were on the plane and it was ready to takeoff.

As El Al Israel Flight 203 lifted off the runway, the two partners were seated comfortably in the First Class cabin. Their conversation was light, but each knew the task still facing them could well impact many lives. Maybe even an entire country.

At approximately 6:00 pm Chicago time, the plane taxied to its docking bay and the partners exited, completed the routine customs inspection required of all international travelers and then Reggie accompanied Toby to his departure gate for Seattle. During their walk through the airport there was no conversation as they were both saddened by the upcoming separation. During their time in Israel they had grown closer and now were as brothers.

They embraced and said their goodbyes as Toby's flight was announced and he proceeded down the ramp to board the aircraft. Reggie then headed down the concourse toward his departure gate. Even though both men were on different flights their minds were swirling with the thought of the coming battle and their shared destinies.

CHAPTER SIXTEEN

Another one down

A S TOBY LOOKED out his window seat on his Northwest Airlines flight viewing the majesty of the Pacific Northwest below, he grudgingly admitted that Israel with its dry humid weather and history was wonderful, but, he thought, *'There is no place like home.'*

Weary from his trip to the war torn country, he wasn't looking forward to a battle with Renie but knew he was headed into one. *'You have a fight awaiting you when you tell that daughter of yours you are home only to turn around and leave again.'*

Sitting in First Class its benefits, one of those being you are in the front of the plane, allowing you to be one of the first off the aircraft. So when the door opened he was the first one off the plane and when he got through security he scanned the crowd for the face of his daughter, however she spied him first and in an uncharacteristic manner shoved her way between a couple of bystanders and threw herself at her unprepared father. This caused him to step backward into the path of a deplaning passenger, turning to apologize he looked into the face of one of the men who had followed Reggie and he in Israel; one whom they had seen several times around their hotel in Israel and might have been involved in the bombing that injured Ruth. He reached out to collar the burly man, but the continuous force of the unloading passengers combined with the insistent tugging of Renie, made that difficult. Realizing this was neither the time nor the place for a confrontation he gave up the effort but his gaze followed the man until he was out of sight in the crowd.

"Come on, dad, move, people are trying to get by," Renie's voice finally penetrated his mind.

Mumbling his apologies, Toby stepped off to the side and devoted his full attention to Renie but before he had a chance to speak, she chimed in, "Aren't you proud of me, dad? I made it all the way here by myself without having to ask any directions."

"Indeed I am, but then you always make me proud. In fact I'm so proud I thought we should spend the night in Seattle and go to a stage play at the Paramount."

"Cool, but we got to call Maria, so she can go home if she wants."

Ever mindful of the uninvited third member of their party he gently guided Renie to baggage pickup and then to a telephone where he called Maria to inform her of their plans and then out of the terminal where he hailed a taxi.

After the driver had loaded their bags into the trunk of the car, Toby instructed him to take them to the Four Seasons Hotel, by way of the waterfront, this was a round-about way but he wanted to spend a little time with Renie. He enjoyed the ride with the sound of her voice as she queried him about his trip and the country, even taking time to ask how Uncle Reggie was.

Renie had never stayed at a hotel before so this was a treat for her and she was filled with excitement and awed at the splendor of the hotel. Once the taxi stopped she was off and running, preceding the bellhop into the lobby of the hotel, stopping only to look around in awe at the grandeur of the premier hotel in Seattle. "Wow," she exclaimed, "are the rooms going to be like this, too?"

Toby checked them into the hotel and then they rode the elevator to their room. After securing Toby's luggage they plotted the rest of the day. Both were hungry and agreed on lunch in the hotel dining room to be followed by shopping at Nordstroms for clothing for the evening.

Rest was out of the question for the weary and sore traveler as his energetic daughter kept him busy until 6:30 pm, which was the time they had set aside to be back at the hotel to get dressed for the evening.

The play, The Sound of Music, starring Richard Chamberlain was a success and had Renie so enthralled she had little time for chatter that is until it was over and then she replayed for him the entire story, including the songs. Not wanting her happiness to end, Toby suggested they walk back to their hotel, hoping to tire her out so he could sleep later in the morning.

They had just rounded the corner of Fifth Street, when he spied the man trailing them. Continuing the pace, with Renie skipping along still recounting the night's play they walked on toward the hotel, had he been alone he would have done some stalking of his own and he vowed he would yet after putting Renie to bed.

Once the father and daughter got to their room it was evident he would have no trouble getting the girl to bed as the day had been full of activities and had exhausted her to the point where she headed straight to her bedroom. After giving her dad a kiss and mumbling goodnight she crawled under the covers and was soon fast asleep.

Toby waited for fifteen minutes to be sure then changed into dark clothes and left the room carefully locking the door. In the lobby he contacted the hotel security guard, quietly explaining he was a private eye and found it necessary to leave the hotel for a while. He was concerned with his daughter's safety and requested the hotel provide security for her until his return. His request granted, Toby then casually walked out of the hotel, acting as if he was out looking for some kind of night action. Knowing the local police patrolled the city streets regularly, he chose to lead his quarry towards the wharf area, where activity was normal this time of the night and a couple of men walking wouldn't arouse suspicion.

His shadow hadn't abandoned his prey and followed Toby as he left the hotel. Acting like he had a mission, Toby walked at a pretty fast clip toward the docks; not once turning his head to check his tail, relying on an inner feeling that he was still there. Feeling it was time for action and spying the open gate of a yard leading to a docked container ship, Toby quickly darted inside the gate, ducking behind a nearby container.

His antagonist must have realized he had been spotted, for he continued to stroll past the area where Toby disappeared, acting as if he didn't have a care in the world. Knowing he would circle back either by climbing the fence further along the way or doing an about face and retracing his steps, Toby held his place, straining his ears for the slightest noise. Twenty minutes passed before he caught the faint sound of footsteps stealthily approaching from within the yard. Not knowing if his adversary was armed, Toby remained where he was listening intently as the sound of the stalking man drew nearer. Toby had armed himself with a piece of wood from a broken pallet upon entering the yard, but knew it would be no match for a firearm so he had to strike fast and hard.

Apparently lacking patience the man stuck his head around the corner of the container, giving Toby an open shot, which he took, hitting the man along side his head rendering him unconscious. Then looking around the only thing he found was a short strand of chain links which he used to secure the man. Handicapped by his wounded side Toby still managed to shoulder the unconscious man and stagger to a dockside crane. When he reached the crane, Toby dropped the man and began searching him clothing for identification. The man's wallet had a driver's license issued to Dale Goins, a Visa credit card with the same name, some currency and a business card with the word DONE on it. Not satisfied with what he had found he removed the captive's shoes and hit pay dirt. Neatly folded inside one of the shoes was a piece of paper with 'POT 0130101001' written on it.

Toby was studying the paper when his prisoner began to moan so putting the paper in his shirt pocket Toby climbed the ladder of the crane, hoisting his victim up until he was approximately twenty-five feet off the ground, head downward. Tying the chain off he waited for the bound man to fully regain consciousness. The wait wasn't long and was accompanied with a loud bellow.

"Let me down from here, you moron."

"Now, that's no way to talk to someone who holds your life in his hands. If I were a moron like you say, then I didn't tie that chain very good and any second now you'll plummet to your death. Not a pretty sight when brains are splattered all over. Just about what you had planned for me and my friends in Israel, isn't it?"

"I don't know what you are talking about," he hollered, "I've never been to Israel."

Not satisfied with the man's answer, Toby released some of the pressure on the pulley making the chain drop rapidly for a few inches. The terrified man yelled, "Alright, so I was there, but I didn't try to kill anybody. Now let me down from here."

"Half-truths," Toby responded, "will only prolong your stay up in the air."

"Okay, okay. What do you want to know?"

Looking down at the man he knew as Dale Goins, Toby asked, "What is DONE and who runs it?"

Responding, Goins stated, "I can't tell you the answer to either question. We never see our handlers. Our only contact is by courier. All our instructions, along with cash and credit cards are delivered to a designated spot by a courier in the city where we are assigned. I retired from the CIA and was recruited over the phone. DONE was never mentioned, but some of their cards were in the first envelope I received. Now, can I get down from here?"

Ignoring the request Toby asked another question, "If you know nothing why are you doing what you're doing?"

Goins, feeling the effects of being suspended head down, replied in a barely audible response, "The pay is good and we're told we would be benefiting the country."

"Now you have really made me angry," Toby lashed out, "How can killing any one aid your country? What do you take me for?"

Realizing his captive's position was not helping the quality of the interrogation; Toby slowly lowered Goins to the pavement below. Throwing the chain to the side of where the tied man lay he hurried down the crane's ladder as fast as the he could. He was still about ten feet from ground level, when he glanced below and saw Goins loosening his bonds.

He reached ground just as Goins freed himself from the last loop of the chain and rose shakily to his feet. Looking over his shoulder at Toby he didn't see the truck, which came around the row of containers, and the driver of the truck saw him too late and was unable to stop. The bumper knocked Goins to the pavement and he rolled under the front wheels which rolled over him, crushing the life out of him.

Knowing he couldn't allow the driver to see him, Toby used the shadows of the crane to slip away. The knowledge he had been responsible for the man's death didn't set well with him, even considering the man's occupation.

Looking at his watch he noticed it was almost four and Renie would probably awake soon and be frightened if she found him missing. He jogged back to hotel as fast as possible. Reaching the hotel he looked through the lobby doors, seeing the clerk on duty busy on the phone he quietly walked toward the door leading to the stairway, not wanting to be seen. Opening the stairwell door at the fifth floor he looked down the hallway and saw the uniformed security guard asleep in a chair outside his room. Taking his shoes off he quietly inched his way to his door and managed to let himself in without disturbing the sleeping guard.

Once in the room Toby checked on Renie then stripped off his clothes, fell into his bed and was asleep as soon as his head hit the pillow.

"Mmmpf," Toby croaked out, as the bony knees of Renie pushed into his midsection. "What two-ton mama just woke me from a sound sleep?"

"Come on, dad, get dressed so we can go get something to eat," the ever hungry girl shrilled.

"Okay, young lady, but you need to get dressed too. So you go get showered and dressed while I do the same and then we'll go downstairs, eat breakfast in the hotel restaurant and walk around for a while before heading home," Toby suggested.

"Cool," the excited youngster exclaimed. "Maybe we'll have time to go to the Seattle Center so I can play some video games."

They had finished breakfast when Renie said, "I've changed my mind about going to the Center, let's just go home and hang out. I can show you some of the moves I learned at Basketball Camp, if you think you can stand being beat by a girl."

"You're on sister, but first I need to stop at an office down by the ferry dock and see a man. It shouldn't take too long and it will save me a trip back over here later.

When he was checking out of the hotel Toby glanced at the morning Seattle Times newspaper lying on the counter. The lead article concerned another bombing, this time a bomb had been placed in the cargo carrier of a Greyhound bus bound for Atlantic City, New Jersey from Washington DC. Fortunately the alert driver was able to stop the vehicle, which held the casualties to a minimum. When DONE claimed responsibility the federal officials issued no statements other than saying no demands had been made by the terrorist.

The story angered Toby and he struggled with his emotions as it brought back vivid memories of the incident in Tel Aviv which almost took the life of Ruth. To him the bombing in Israel made some sense as somebody wanted Reggie and he out of the picture.

So what if a couple of American tourists got in the way of an already volatile situation? It was a different story for the many instances of bombing across the U.S., as there was no pattern readily discernable. The group made no demands thus far and except for the foiled attempt against the submarine base at Bangor, there was no sign of anti-government activity or political statement.

Toby was brought back to the present by the insistent voice his daughter. He shook his head responding, "I'm sorry Renie I was reading the headlines of today's paper and got caught up in what I was reading. "Let's get going."

The short walk from the hotel to the ferry terminal was filled with conversation, mostly one-sided on Renie's part. A block away from the terminal Toby saw the building housing the detective agency of the Laslow Brothers. On the second floor, at the end of a long hallway, he saw a door marked with the logo, Laslow Brothers, Private Investigators. Motioning Renie to stay behind him he opened the door and was immediately greeted by a middle-aged, balding man sitting behind a desk.

"Good morning sir, may I help you?" the man's voice held a trace of a European accent.

"That voice," Toby exclaimed, "I've heard that voice before. You are the one who called me and told me of a homicide that had been committed in Bremerton."

The man quickly arose and walked towards Toby saying, "You must be Toby Preston. I have been trying to get in touch with you for some time."

"Some detective you are if you can't find someone just across the pond, but then I have been out of the country. How is it you were able to be close to a murder in Bremerton and call a police officer with an unlisted number to report it? And why were you so secretive?"

"Hold on Preston. To begin with I called you for my brother, Michael, who is dead, as you know, assassinated by agents from a secretive organization we only know as DONE. My brother was working for the CIA and had been told to keep an eye on activities taking place in Bremerton. He was working with the man who was murdered and witnessed the act. Having to keep a low profile, he needed someone from the local law enforcement agency who could be trusted to discover the body. You had been under scrutiny for some time for use as a potential undercover agent that's how we knew how to reach you. My brother was then sent to Israel to investigate Israel's connection with DONE. After that he was sent to Montana to look into the disappearance of a missing hunter and then to Las Vegas to contact your friend Reggie Nutsbagh. Somewhere along the way his cover was blown and, well, you know the rest of the story."

Toby glanced at Renie to see how she was taking all of this and saw she was engrossed in a copy of Sports Illustrated, seemingly oblivious to the grownup conversation. He then turned his attention to Laslow.

"Boy, I must be some kind of a cop myself to not have noticed I was under surveillance. How long had that been going on?"

The man, whose name turned out to be Sergei, responded, "Long enough to know you could be trusted. Michael was the CIA man, not I. He kept his own files. Would you like to look at them? For some reason after his murder was revealed his superiors never asked for any of the papers he had."

Without waiting for Toby to reply Sergei led him to a back room, with two four-drawer cabinets standing against the wall with a small table and a folding chair as the other furniture.

"My brother's filing system was designed to confuse intruders, so what we're looking for will be not in the expected order. He filed those things under Mother." Looking in the first cabinet he extracted a thin folder and handed it to Toby. "I have honored my brother's wishes and have not looked inside. It would please me if you took it. I am not able to avenge my brother's murder, Mr. Preston, but I hope you in some way can bring those who killed him to justice."

Toby thanked the man and assured him he would do his best. Promising to stay in touch he beckoned to Renie and together they walked out of the office, heading for the ferry terminal and the trip home. The street was busy with midday traffic and there was no reason why Toby should have paid attention to the black Honda Accord or the two men who got out of it and made their way up the narrow stairs to the room at the end of the hall.

Once on the ferry Toby completely forgot about the file folder, having stuffed it inside his duffel. Soon the pleasant ride came to an end and for Toby the walk home would have been welcome, but with Renie, luggage and packages, he felt it best to take a taxi. Signaling for a taxi they made the final leg of the journey, for Toby at least, to home, sweet home, at last.

Toby had just gotten everything settled and was relaxing in the living room when the phone rang. Sighing at being disturbed he answered, "Hello, this is Toby." Reggie's voice broke in. "This is Reggie, quick turn on your TV to ABC News." Toby reached over and turned on the TV to Channel Four catching the tail end of the story about a murder in Seattle. A Sergei Laslow had been found brutally murdered in his office. His office had been ransacked, all desk drawers and file cabinets had been yanked out and all files were missing. The only thing in the way of evidence found was a business card with the name DONE lying in the center of a desk.

Toby stood a moment in shocked surprise then he exclaimed into the phone, "I was just there, Reg. He gave me a file that belonged to his brother Michael. I'm certain that's what they were looking for. I haven't read it yet, so I don't know what's in it, but it must be important. He was the one who called me the night of the murder in Bremerton and you know his brother as the stranger you met in the sandwich shop."

In his excitement Toby continued without giving Reggie a chance to talk, "Also I need to let you know I had a confrontation with one of the guys who followed us in Israel. His name was Dale Goins. I say 'was', because in trying to get away from me he ran into a truck and is dead. Anyway the important part is a note I found in his shoe indicating something big is going to happen at the Port of Tacoma six days from now. I am going to need you here to help me out. Think you can make it?"

There was a moment's hesitation as Reggie waited to see if Toby was finished speaking and then he responded, "I'm glad you got the best of Goins, I have the other guy here in Vegas following me around. I don't know what I'm going to do yet, but I need to poke around here for a bit and see what crawls out of the woodwork. One other thing, I did the deed and popped the question."

Toby gave a loud yelp of surprise. "Congratulations! I couldn't be happier for you and Brandy. Next time you see her give her my love. I've got to go, the warden, Renie is calling me."

"Okay, pal, give Renie a hug for me and keep your head down. See you soon."

After the connection was terminated Toby went to Renie's room and had a talk with her explaining about his new love Ruth and how he was thinking about asking her to come visit them. Much to his complete surprise she was extremely excited about meeting the woman who had stolen her father's heart.

After seeing that she was tucked away in her bed, he walked down the hall and into his study; there he sat deep in thought wondering what the future held for him and his partner.

CHAPTER SEVENTEEN

The Investigation moves forward

SHIFTING RESTLESSLY IN his seat, Reggie heaved a sigh of relief when his United Airlines flight touched down in Las Vegas with a slight jolt of the wheels. Glad to finally be on familiar territory and equally glad that some of the pieces of the puzzle were coming together, but also aware there were still some pieces, which didn't quite fit.

He purposely hadn't informed anyone of his arrival, not wanting to go through meeting and greeting at the busy airport. Getting off the plane he picked his way through the busy terminal to baggage claim. Securing his luggage from the carousel he started to make his way out of the terminal, but stopped when he smelled the aroma of coffee coming from a Starbucks stand and decided to have at least a cup of coffee to wind down from the long flight.

Out of habit borne from his interest in people, he let his gaze pass over the hustling crowd, even while looking at the menu. He was startled when he saw a familiar face and it took all of his concentration and training not to turn and stare. He had seen the man, whose face he recognized, twice before in Israel. Pretending to ignore him, Reggie ordered his coffee and a sandwich, as he thought, *'I see you did follow me to Vegas. Good, I know that you are here and hopefully you don't know that I know and we'll attempt to keep it that way until I am ready for a confrontation. But this time the confrontation will be on my terms.'*

Reggie sat down drinking his coffee and eating his sandwich but not looking at the man and when he was finished he picked up his bags and left the terminal. Outside the terminal he hailed a taxi and headed for his apartment in Henderson knowing the man from Israel would be following. Too tired to worry about the man he knew waited outside, he unpacked, showered and lay down, resting a few hours before calling his office to inform Hilda and Joe he was back in Vegas and would be in the office in the morning. Next on his agenda was to call Brandy, a task that scared him more than being faced with a dozen hostile gunmen. Mentally he chided himself, saying, *'You can face armed gunmen, bombing suspects and other sorts of violence but coming face to face with life scares the hell out of you, come on Nutsbagh, get on with it and stop procrastinating.'*

Calling the hospital he asked to speak to Brandy Thomas; after a brief pause she answered, "Hello, this is Ms. Thomas, can I help you?"

Reggie managed to squeak out, "Hello Brandy, it's me, Reggie."

Brandy, normally a very sedate woman came back with an uncharacteristic yell, "Reggie, are you home?"

"Yes, I finally got home. What time do you get off work today?"

"In about 20 minutes," she replied.

"How about an early dinner or late lunch, I'll pick you up at your apartment in about an hour, if that's okay?"

"I'll be ready. I'm glad you're home, I missed you."

"I missed you too. Sorry I didn't give you more warning, but I wanted to see you and couldn't wait."

A date with Brandy was nothing new, but this one would be special and would mean more to both of them then any other date they had been on and he wanted to make it a very memorable occasion. Because of the existing circumstances, with the man following him, part of his preparations, before meeting Brandy, included arming himself, which he did, prior to leaving his apartment.

A look from his window at the street below revealed nothing out of the ordinary, so he went to the parking garage where his BMW sat, exiting the underground garage he executed several turns and made unscheduled stops to determine if he was being tailed. Reggie didn't see his shadow, but that didn't mean he wasn't there.

Approximately an hour later, armed with a dozen red roses and a small felt covered box he arrived at Brandy's apartment. When he rang the bell it was an overly excited Brandy who greeted him. She flung the door open and fell into his arms, the flowers fell to the floor and they exchanged a very long, passionate kiss.

Several moments passed before they parted with both of them breathless from the passionate encounter. Catching her breath, Brandy finally spoke, "Let me get these flowers in some water before we walk all over them. As you can probably tell, I missed you."

Reggie stood in the doorway, out of breath and unable to speak after such an overwhelming greeting. Finally able to speak he said, "I—I would like to stop by the house in Summerlin before we eat, hope you don't mind."

"No I don't, as long as we're together."

Silence prevailed during the short ride to Reggie's house in Summerlin, as both of them were still savoring the emotion of the moment and the passion generated by their first encounter since Reggie's return.

Arriving at the house Reggie stopped the car in the driveway and escorted Brandy to his mother's oriental garden. Stopping by a bench in a secluded glen within the garden he asked Brandy to sit down for a minute. A puzzled Brandy did as she was asked and sat down on the bench. When she was seated, an obviously nervous Reggie took a deep breath to steady his nerves then he knelt at Brandy's feet and took her hand. "Brandy, over the telephone from Israel, I said I loved you. When I said it, I knew I meant it with all my heart, but was glad the phone call was disconnected because I was unsure of your answer. As the days went by I found myself thinking more of you and I couldn't imagine a day without you in my life and I knew for certain that I loved you very much and I'm now asking you to be my wife and companion."

A totally stunned Brandy could do nothing except nod her head, as tears fell down her face. Reggie was slipping the ring on her finger when she finally collected herself enough to say, "Yes, yes, yes, I would be happy to be your wife. I have loved you for a long time."

They embraced for a long time, then not wanting the moment to end, they again expressed their love. Reggie's heart sang at her acceptance of his proposal and upon hearing her profess her love for him. They sat in total silence for a long time just holding each other and enjoying the moment, then as if one person they got up and walked hand in hand back to the car still not speaking, allowing the moment to speak for it's self.

With the events leading up to dinner setting the tone for the evening the meal proved to be a very romantic affair, with more attention given to each other more than the food. After dinner and during their glass of after dinner wine, Reggie told Brandy about his and Toby's trip to Israel and the reason for it. He explained there might be trouble ahead and she could possibly be on the fringe of it. He further explained his reason for pursuing these people and his driving need for revenge on those who had his parents killed.

During the telling of his story, Brandy gripped his hand tightly and when he finished she said, "Reggie, my love for you knows no boundaries, I'll be with you either in body or soul from this day forward, no matter what."

With a sigh of relief and as no words were necessary he leaned over and kissed her gently on the lips and said softly, "I love you."

An hour later he dropped Brandy off at her apartment, making sure she was safe inside with her alarm set, and then headed for his apartment. It was during the drive back to his apartment when he once again saw he had picked up his tail. *'Stay with me friend, pretty soon it will be my turn.'*

Twenty minutes later Reggie entered his apartment and out of habit turned on his television and was headed for the bathroom when his attention was caught by the mention of the name Laslow in conjunction with a murder in Seattle. Also mentioned was the finding of a card with the name DONE. Continuing to listen he picked up his phone and dialed Toby's phone number.

After several rings the phone was answered, "Hello this is Toby.

"This is Reggie, quick, turn on your TV to ABC News."

The phone went still for a moment while Toby went to turn on his TV. A few minutes later Reggie heard a gasp from Toby and he came back on the phone. With shock evident in his voice Toby relayed to him how he had just been in that office and had been given a file belonging to the brother, Michael, who was the stranger who had met Reggie in the sandwich shop.

Toby continued without drawing a breath, telling him about the man who had followed him and something about a note, which indicated something big, was going to happen in Tacoma. Toby concluded by asking Reggie to come to Washington.

Reggie hesitated and then told Toby he was being followed by the other man from Israel and had to take care of him, and also that there was several other things he wanted to do, but would get there as soon as possible. Before he hung up, Reggie informed Toby he had popped the question to Brandy. Toby's reaction left Reggie with a big smiled on his face.

Ending the conversation, Reggie, completed preparations for the evening and fell into bed exhausted, both mentally and physically but happier than he had been in a long time.

Reggie awoke the next morning and after his usual preparations and normal breakfast, he headed for his office aware he was being followed but took no steps to discourage the trailing man. He wasn't concerned about being followed, as he was sure the opposition already knew the location of his office, but knew that something was going to have to be done very soon about his shadow.

Parking his car and walking into his office he greeted Hilda and Joe then proceeded to his office asking Joe to join him. Over the intercom he asked Hilda to bring him some coffee, he then told her to insure they weren't disturbed for any reason.

Sitting down at the desk with a sigh, he looked at Joe and said," Joe, I owe you an explanation about what's going on. When you know all the details you will have to make a decision."

Two hours and four cups of coffee later Reggie completed his story, not omitting any details. "Now you can see why I wanted you to be careful about security. Right now I have someone following me around Vegas."

"You want me to take care of him?" Joe asked, hopefully.

"No, let him be for now. We'll take care of him later."

"I know you told me before about staying around, but now you know the details, I'm going to ask you one more time, do you still want to be involved with this investigation?"

Joe looked at Reggie with a grin before replying, "I have never ran from anything in my life and won't now. Whatever you need and whatever help I can give you, just call on me."

"Thanks, Joe, why don't you move your operation here? You can use the office next to mine and I'll put you on the payroll."

Later, as Reggie was completing some paperwork the intercom sounded with Hilda telling him Phil was on line two.

Reggie punched up line two and warmly greeted Phil. After exchanging greetings and answering all of Phil's questions concerning his trip to Israel, Reggie asked, "Phil, do you have any more information about the PI, Laslow's murder, who killed him and why?"

"We haven't charged anyone for his murder, but our prime suspects are Smith and McDuffy, the two guys Sal rousted for following you around Vegas. We were lucky when a couple of witnesses came forward and made statements saying they saw Smith and McDuffy along with Laslow sitting in the hotel lounge around 1:30 am the night of the murder. Their statements indicate Laslow seemed to be under duress at the time."

"Have you put out a bulletin on them, requesting pickup?"

"Absolutely, but they seemed to have vanished, at least from Vegas. We put their names and photos on the wire and contacted the Montana authorities, so now it's a waiting game."

Reggie continued his questions, "What about the explosives in the storage locker is there any more information on where it came from and how it got there?"

"No, we have no idea how the stuff got there and who put it in the storage locker other than the identification of the three sets of fingerprints I told you about," Phil replied.

"How much explosives were in the locker?"

"Enough to put a huge hole in that part of Las Vegas, the locker also contained a large assortment of weapons. We're at our wits end trying to find out who it was that put them there and why here in Las Vegas. The FBI advised us about the other bombings and that the organization DONE has claimed responsibility. I sure hope those explosives were not meant for use in Vegas."

Reggie hesitated for several seconds trying to put what Phil said into perspective then said, "So you have no leads into why or who, other than the three men, whose fingerprints you found at the facility?"

"You got it, Reggie. Listen, Reg, drop by and see me if you get a chance, I would like to hear about your trip to Israel and at the same time I can show you the reports."

Assuring Phil he would stop by he broke the connection then ask Joe to come into his office, "Joe, remember the second time I called you and you told me that Phil called and you took some notes of what he said?"

Joe's face flushed, "I'm ashamed to admit it, I not only remember, but did some checking on those two guys on my own. I contacted Phil and looked at Smith and McDuffy's file photos; I wanted to be able to recognize them."

Reggie elated and hopeful said, "That's great, there's nothing to be ashamed of, actually I'm glad, and hope you can shed some light on where they disappeared to or have some other information we can use to locate them."

"Well, I do and I don't; quite by accident I saw them while I was working on another case of mine. I was at the South end of the strip at Vacation Village, doing some electrical work on their security cameras at their hotel when I saw both Smith and McDuffy, along with another man come out of the hotel. I watched as they walked to a car and left. Later, I checked the car license and found it was a Hertz rental registered to a George Rueben. I didn't know this Rueben character until I saw his picture in the Las Vegas Journal in an article about explosives found at the storage facility. The guy being interviewed was George Reuben, who just happens to be the manager of the storage facility and several others around town."

"Outstanding," Reggie exclaimed, "this may be the lead we need to start tracing where the explosives came from and where they were going."

Joe, grinning said, "We could put a little heat on George. With a little pressure he would squeal like a pig."

Reggie laughing, replied, "He probably would, but we don't want to tip our hand right now. I'll have to come up a reason why I need to conduct business with him and not one of his other managers. Maybe I could say we need to rent 10 or 15 large storage lockers and I will only talk with the boss because of the sensitive nature of the things I want to store, we might—"

"Might what?" Joe asked.

Instead of answering Joe's question Reggie said, "Joe, do you know where Rueben's office is located?"

"No, but I'm sure I could find out. Why?"

"Well, if we can find his office I'm sure I could find someone intelligent enough to put a few well positioned listening devices around his office and perhaps bug his telephones," Reggie said, laughing.

"Leave it to me," Joe exclaimed.

"You can get to that later right now I'm going to invite my friend, who has been following me all over town, to a little party which I intend to hold in his honor, and to do that I'm going to need your help."

"I'm with you, what are we going to do?"

"I'm going to leave the office and I want you to position yourself so you can see the parking lot, when you see a car pull out of the lot and follow me, you call me and tell me the make and model of the car. Then meet me at the corner of Russell Road and Boulder Highway. I will be on Russell just short of the Boulder Highway intersection. When you get there I want you to drive about a half mile south on Boulder Highway. When you're in position, I'll leave, going south on Boulder Highway, he'll follow me and then I want you to fall in behind him and stay with us. From then on just follow my lead."

Over the intercom, Reggie asked Hilda to get Phil on the phone. Five minutes later Hilda informed him Phil was on line two.

"Hello Phil, can you spare me a few minutes of your time?"

"Sure. Reggie, what can I do for you," Phil responded.

"I need a big favor, without a lot of questions."

"Tell me what you need and I will be the judge if there are any questions or not."

"I think we have a handle on Smith and McDuffy and will be happy to give them to you, but it has to be my way."

"You were a cop long enough to know what it means for civilians to be playing cops and robbers and withholding information vital to an investigation, you can be put away a long time."

"I know that, Phil, I'm not asking you to do anything illegal, it's just that I may need you to arrest and detain an individual for at least 24 hours. He's following me and is probably armed, I need to get him out of the way for a while; if you can do that for me, I'm almost positive that I can give you Smith and McDuffy."

"Where and when?" Phil asked.

"Can you meet me in the Henderson K Mart parking lot? Joe and I will be there in about an hour. There will be some type of confrontation and it will be up to you to step in and take it from there. How does that sound?" Reggie asked.

"Just what the heck are you going to do?"

"I was afraid you would ask. I don't really know, but whatever I do, I will do it to the guy who is tailing me, so you can take it from there."

"Okay, I don't know what you are up to but we've been friends for a long time and I'm going to trust your judgment on this, just don't put me in a compromising position. Henderson is out of our jurisdiction, as you know, so I'll call in a couple of favors from a lieutenant friend of mine in the Henderson Police Department, we will both be there in an unmarked car."

"Thanks, Phil, I owe you.

Ending the conversation, Reggie spoke to Joe, "Okay, Joe, here is what we are going to try and do. First get the camera out of the file cabinet and take it with you. After we get the tail between us we'll pull into the K-Mart parking lot in Henderson. When we do I want you to ram his car, just hard enough to put it out of commission. Then get a few photos of our friend and wait to see what unfolds."

A few minutes later Reggie departed his office, walked nonchalantly to his car and pulled out of the parking lot.

In a few minutes his cell phone rang, Joe came on to give him the description of the car tailing him; it was a light brown Dodge, with a Hertz rental sticker on the rear bumper. Reggie glanced in his rearview mirror and spotted the car about 100 yards behind him.

They proceeded as planned then once in the K-Mart parking lot Reggie did a quick u-turn just in time to see Joe's truck run into the side of the other car and push it up against the curb. As soon as this happened, Reggie heard a siren and saw an unmarked police car pull up to the site of the accident.

Not wanting to appear involved in the accident Reggie stopped a short distance away where he could observe what was taking place. Phil and the Henderson Police lieutenant were interrogating both Joe and the other man. A second later Phil reached for his gun and held it at arms length pointed at the stranger, telling him to raise his hands; when he did as instructed Phil removed a pistol from a holster on the man's belt. The man was then handcuffed and placed in the police car. Meanwhile Joe was walking around the accident site taking pictures of the accident, which of course, included pictures of the other man.

Reggie's inquisitive nature overcame his desire to stay on the fringes of the developing situation and he walked up to Phil, who said, "Well, you said you didn't know what you were going to do, but it will be enough for me to see that bird jailed for about 48 hours, on a weapons charge. For your information he has a Montana driver's license with the name Ron Johnson."

"Thanks, Phil. If my plans work we should be able to get Smith and McDuffy into your hands in the next couple of days." Reggie walked over to where Joe was standing next to the police car and started to say something, but was interrupted by the man sitting in the police car, "Okay Nutsbagh, the first round goes to you, but you can bet on it the next one will not be so easy. Your mistake was being a softy; remember what happened in Israel, it will only get worse."

Walking away, Joe said, "Reg, he sounded mad, maybe we should have taken him out completely; now we'll have to deal with him later."

Later over lunch Reggie said, "Next step; we need the address for George Rueben's office."

"I have it," said Joe. "When you left the office Hilda looked it up in the yellow pages; his office is at 1725 Paradise Avenue."

"Do you think you can get into his office and plant some listening devices some time today?"

"No problem, I'll get right on it and meet you back at the office when I'm finished."

Twenty minutes later Reggie arrived at Phil's office to find him working on a mound of papers, Phil looked up and growled, "See what you caused! Arresting someone in another jurisdiction and moving him to the city jail creates more paperwork than you can imagine. I hope you didn't come here to gloat?"

"No, I just wanted to thank you, again. How long do you think you can hold him?"

"At least 48 hours on the gun charge; he showed us his license to carry concealed, but it's from Montana and is no good in this state unless you submit the proper paperwork."

"Phil, you're going to have to trust me a little bit longer. Toby, my partner in the agency, working out of Bremerton, Washington and I are working on something which seems to have taken on a life of it own and is growing every time we turn around. It has to do with the explosives you found in the storage facility, Michael Laslow's murder and other things happening around the country."

"Okay, Reggie, I'll let it rest for now. I'll try and warn you when we have to let Johnson out of jail. Meanwhile, here are the files on the Laslow murder and the explosives found at the storage facility; you'll have to read them here."

Scanning the files, Reggie determined they contained no information, which could be useful in his investigation; he thanked Phil and headed for his own office. When he arrived he found Joe buzzing around setting up equipment in his office.

"Hey, Joe, what's going on?" Reggie inquired.

"Well, you wanted something set up in Ruebens' office and I'm putting the finishing touches on the equipment."

"You mean to tell me in this short period of time you were able to establish listening devices on his phones and in his office?" Reggie asked.

Joe replied with a chuckle, "People are gullible, especially when a telephone repairman comes to repair phones that aren't working correctly." Saying that Joe held up a pair of coveralls with a well-known telephone company logo on the back, "I repaired their phone lines, which were messed up for some unknown reason, and as I made the repairs I also installed listening devices around the office. Now as soon as I finish connecting the rest of this equipment we should be able to hear Rueben sipping his coffee from 20 feet away."

Joe finished setting up the equipment then turned it on to make sure all systems were working correctly. Everything seemed to be fine, and when Joe turned on the recorder there was the sound of a telephone ringing and a voice answering the call, "Hello, this is George Rueben's office, can I help you?"

A few minutes later, Hilda came over the intercom telling Reggie Phil was on line two and that she was leaving for the day.

Acknowledging Hilda and telling her to have a good evening, Reggie picked up the phone saying, "Hey, Phil, what can I do for you?"

"Just thought you might be interested in what we took out of Mr. Johnson's hotel room. We found his passport showing he just came back from Israel and an open plane ticket on Alaska Airlines for Seattle, Washington. With all that's going on I'll sure be glad when you can fill me in."

"It won't be long Phil, and thanks for the information. Have a nice evening."

Leaving Joe to finish installing his equipment, Reggie wished him goodnight and departed for his apartment.

Later in the evening, after a refreshing shower, Reggie lay down on the bed contemplating everything that had occurred since his return to Vegas. He was sure they were headed in the right direction in their investigation and hoped Toby was progressing as well.

CHAPTER EIGHTEEN

An Arrest is made

THE SOUND OF a telephone ringing came over the speaker sitting on a table in Reggie's office. After several rings the receiver was lifted and a voice said, "Hello, this is George."

There was a short pause then a gravelly and very angry voice came over the speaker, *"George, what the hell is going on down there? How did the police find out about our equipment in that storage locker? There had better not be any more problems or someone will pay the ultimate price."*

George's voice quavered, "The rest of the items are safe, for now. When are you sending someone to pick up the stuff before the police get ideas and inspect the rest of my storage facilities?"

"Probably early tomorrow morning," the still angry voice responded. *"I will call you later and let you know. Where are R and J right now?"*

"At the safe house," was George's reply.

"Get in contact with them and tell them to be ready to catch a ride when the shipment is picked up."

George replied in the affirmative and the connection was broken.

This was what greeted Reggie the next morning as he settled into his chair in his office. The listening devices Joe installed had already provided invaluable information with more to come.

"Joe," Reggie said, "from now on we're going to have to live in the office. I want to know exactly when they are going to pick up the rest of whatever they have stored."

"Are you going to give the information to Phil?"

"No," responded Reggie, "I'm going to follow them to their destination, I have to know where this stuff is going."

"That could be dangerous, but it's probably the only way to find where it's going," Joe responded.

Later the same afternoon Hilda was preparing to leave for the day when Brandy walked into the office carrying an oversized basket.

"Hello, Brandy how are you doing this afternoon? Reggie and Joe are—" she stopped in mid-sentence when she saw the large diamond ring on Brandy's left hand; grabbing Brandy's hand she squealed, "Wow, what a beautiful ring; does that mean what I think it means?"

Brandy's answer was a nod and the two women embraced.

"I can't believe Reggie proposed to you and didn't even mention it to us; isn't that just like a man." Hilda said. "Joe and Reggie are in his office, do you want me to announce you?"

"No, thanks, I'll surprise them."

Her entrance was a surprise and as with Hilda the first thing Joe noticed was the ring on her finger. He smiled, embraced her whispering in her ear, "Congratulations, take care of him, he needs someone to look after him."

They were eating the dinner Brandy had brought and engaging in small talk about their engagement when the sound of a ringing telephone came over the speaker. After the second ring, a voice answered the telephone," Hello, this is George."

A loud gravelly voice replied, *"I hope we didn't make a mistake putting you in charge of that facility. Losing a container full of goods isn't something I'm going to take lying down."*

George replied, his voice full of fear, "But sir, I did my best, how did I know that guy was CIA. He was with Robert and James—"

"Shut-up, you moron, don't use names. How many times do I have to tell you that? Okay, here's what will happen tonight; get in touch with R & J, make arrangements to pick them up and meet our truck at your storage facility on Boulder Highway at 1:30 am. I want you there so we can go to the other storage facilities and pick up the rest of the stuff."

A stammering George said," Okay, but what about—."

The voice at the other end yelled, *"Don't interrupt me again. Tell R & J to call me, using their cell phone, they have the contact number I want to talk to them about the destination and route for the truck. Do you understand?"*

"Yes sir," George replied.

The connection was broken.

Far away in a mountain retreat one of the many telephones sitting on a large oak desk rang. After two rings a well-manicured hand reached over and lifted the receiver from the cradle. The person on the other end spoke first.

"Smith here, sir."

"Hello Smith. Are you and McDuffy ready to travel?" The gravelly voice asked.

"Yes sir."

"George will pick you and James up around 12:30 AM, be ready. Use the same route as before to get to the camp. When all the containers are empty and loaded on the truck there is one other small detail I need you to do before leaving Las Vegas. I think George has outlived his usefulness, take care of that!"

"I understand, sir. What about Nutsbagh?"

"Nutsbagh and his friend Preston now become a bigger and separate problem and will be dealt with later. Right now do as you were told!"

Brandy was amazed at what she heard but didn't question Reggie as she figured he was on some kind of a case relating to his business, so she gathered up the eating utensils, kissed him and then departed. After escorting Brandy to her car and watching her drive away, Reggie went back up to his office and to the task at hand. He knew they would have to come up with a plan and quickly.

"How are we going to handle this latest bit of information?" Joe asked.

"That's going to be a problem," Reggie said with a frown on his face. "I want to know where the stuff is going but I don't want it to get there. We'll have to make plans on the fly. Right now we have to be at the pickup point around midnight. We'll take two cars and have communication between us using our cell phones and be ready to travel. After the pickup is made I'll follow the delivery truck and get a general idea of where they are headed; once I'm satisfied I know their destination I'll have to come up with some way to stop them."

"Okay, but, what do you want me to do while you are playing tag with the truck?"

"After I pick up the truck and began tailing it I want you to keep an eye on George and try to find out if there more shipments coming in for storage. Keep checking with Phil to find out when he's going to release our friend Johnson from jail as he could become a problem. We can stay in contact by cell phone to make any necessary changes to our plans."

Their conversation was interrupted by the sound of a ringing telephone.

After the second ring, it was answered, "Hello, this is George."

The same gravelly voice said, *"It's all set. Go pick up R & J, they will be waiting for you at 12:30 AM, bring them to the storage facility on Boulder Highway and wait the arrival of the truck, he will be there around 1:30 am. He will be using the usual identification method. Once he arrives, load everything you have there and at all of the other sites, I want all of those containers empty. R & J will go with the truck and I'll get back to you later about other shipments, understood?"*

"Yes, sir" George replied, "What about my payment."

"Don't worry you'll be paid, tonight."

When the call was terminated Joe looked at Reggie, shook his head saying, "That sure sounded like George has lost his job, I don't think he's going to like the way he'll be paid."

"You're right, but we can't get involved, George will deserve anything he gets. I wonder if anyone else in this town is involved in these shipments."

Looking at his watch Joe continued, "We should be going, it's almost eleven and there are some things I need to do before we meet."

"Right, be careful and make sure you check to insure you're not being followed."

At exactly midnight Reggie drove past Joe's pickup parked along Boulder Highway at the rendezvous point. To avoid attracting attention he drove further up the highway to another vantage point where he could observe the storage facility and the truck when it arrived.

An hour later a semi pulled up to the storage facility gate and, after a brief delay was admitted. Another hour passed and the semi came back out of the gate with three men in the cab, followed by a car. When they cleared the gate of the facility George, who had been in the trailing vehicle, got out and secured the gate then got back in the car.

When the semi and following car made their way down the highway, Reggie called Joe, "I don't know where they're headed; but I'll follow for a while, you hang back, then we'll switch so they don't get the idea they're being followed."

Joe acknowledged Reggie's instructions and the convoy proceeded down the highway. The game of cat and mouse went on as the truck and trailing vehicle made several more stops at other storage facilities.

After about 3 hours the routine changed, the truck came out without the car following, a different man got out of the cab of the truck and locked the gate and the truck departed.

Immediately Reggie called Joe, "I'll follow the truck, I think something has happened to our friend George. See if you can get inside and find out. Be careful you don't leave any evidence pointing to you. Call me and let me know what you find."

Joe acknowledged the instructions and then Reggie fell in behind the truck as it headed west, thirty minutes later the truck turned onto the Interstate heading towards Boulder City. Soon after making the turn onto the Interstate Reggie's phone rang, knowing it was Joe, Reggie said, "Yeah Joe."

Joe responded, "Looks like they didn't need George any more, he took a bullet to the head."

"Why don't you make an anonymous call to the police and report the killing then hang around out of sight until they come? I'm about two miles from Boulder City. I can't allow this stuff to get to its destination, so once I get the general direction I'll find a way to pull the plug. One other thing, wait until the killing is printed in the paper then call Phil and try to find out if he has any information about the killers."

"Okay, will do Reggie, you stay in touch. Are you sure you don't need me along?"

"No," Reggie responded, "You need to be there to stay on top of what's going on there in Las Vegas. Be sure you try and monitor what's happening with Johnson."

"Will do, you be careful, it's evident, if they just put the gun to George's head and shot him and they wouldn't hesitate to do it again, to you."

An hour later Reggie called Joe, who answered after several rings obviously wakened from sleep, "Hello, boss, why is it you call me when I'm supposed to be sleeping."

Reggie laughing, said, "Wake up, besides if I can't get any sleep why should you be getting sleep unless you are getting enough for both of us? We have just entered Arizona headed east and if my guess is correct we'll travel toward Albuquerque, New Mexico then head north. I've looked at the map and everything indicates these characters are headed for Montana. I guess sometimes after they hit I-25 and head north, I'll have to do something to get them stopped. What's happening around there?"

"I called 911 and reported the murder, then hung out to see what would happen. Slowly but surely the right people got to the storage facility; Phil must have been called in because of the implications with George and the storage facility. Boy, did he look unhappy. How are you holding up?"

"Tired, but hanging in there. It's important I know the general area where this stuff is headed. I think I know but want to let things play out for a while. Maybe we can help Phil out by killing two birds with one stone. We can give him the killers of Laslow and Rueben all tied up in one package. Looks like they are pulling into a truck stop for fuel, I have to be careful, Smith and McDuffy know me by sight, I'll call you later."

After advising Reggie to be careful, Joe hung up.

Hours later an extremely tired Reggie watched as the semi turned onto I-25 and headed north. At mile marker 75 they pulled into a roadside rest area and parked. An exhausted Reggie pulled in and parked on the other side with a clear view of the truck and watched as all three men got out of the cab, stretched and then got back in, the truck didn't restart so Reggie was sure they would be resting here for a time. *'Now what do I do?'*

He got out of his car and began walking around to try and clear his head. Seeing a phone booth in close proximity to his car an idea formed in his head.

Looking into the phone booth he found listed on the wall the phone number for the local sheriff and information to identify the rest stop. He dialed the number, after the third ring a voice answered the call, "Sheriff's office, Deputy Richardson, can I help you?"

"I'm not going to tell you who I am but listen very carefully," Reggie began. "I'm sitting here at a rest stop identified as Pueblo at around mile marker 75 on Interstate 25, just north of Pueblo. Parked in the same rest stop is a semi truck and trailer, no markings on the trailer, but the cab is marked with Sam Jones Trucking, Billings, Montana. In the semi are at least three men, two of them are armed and dangerous and wanted in Las Vegas on suspicion of murder. The truck is loaded with either explosives and guns, or both."

The deputy responded," Sir, who are you and how do you know this?"

Reggie responded, "I'm not going to tell you that. But what I have told you is the truth. Remember at least two of the men in the truck are armed and very dangerous; approach with caution." He broke the connection and then moved his car to another location at the far end of the rest stop, but still within visual range of the truck.

In less than thirty minutes, three sheriff's cars, three State Patrol cruisers along with two unmarked vehicles silently approached the rest stop and blocked off the entrance and exit.

Two uniformed officers remained at the rear of the truck as two men in civilian attire approached the cab on either side. Simultaneously both doors of the cab were opened and the occupants, who had evidently been asleep in the front seat, were physically dragged from the cab. A search revealed both were armed with several handguns. They were handcuffed and placed in police cruisers. In the glow of the overhead lights of the vehicles Reggie could see the two men were Robert Smith and James McDuffy. A third man, obviously the driver, was also removed from the truck, searched and handcuffed. Seeing the officers successfully complete the operation with no injuries, Reggie silently cheered and breathed a sigh of relief.

Several men in plain clothes, probably FBI Agents went to the rear of the truck, broke the seal and opened both doors. Reggie had positioned himself so it was possible to see into the rear of the truck when the doors were opened, but he wasn't prepared for what he saw stacked inside the trailer; huge crates stacked all the way to the back. The officers pulled one of the crates out and found it loaded with brand new automatic rifles; opening another crate they found blocks of C4, a military type explosive. There was no doubt the rest of the load was made up of similar weapons and explosives.

Fifteen minutes later a very elated Reggie pulled out of the rest stop and headed into Pueblo, Colorado. Arriving in Pueblo he pulled off the freeway and checked into a Holiday Inn. There he phoned Joe, "Well Joe, that's one load DONE won't get their hands on." Then he filled Joe in on the details and asked him to check with Phil later, to see if he knew about the capture of Smith and McDuffy.

Hours later Reggie awoke, rolling over he looked at the bedside clock radio and saw it was 4:00 pm; he had slept the day away. He reached for his cell phone to call Joe, but it didn't work. He remembered he had turned in off before going to bed, so he turned in on and called Joe.

"This is Joe, can I help you?"

"Hey, Joe, Reggie here."

"Holy cow, I was about ready to send out the National Guard to find you, we've been trying to call you for about 3 hours, where are you?"

"Sorry about that, in my sleep deprived state early this morning I turned my phone off, what's going on. I hope there's no emergency?"

"Well," replied Joe, "There is and there isn't, but a lot of things have happened, where shall I start? Phil had to let Johnson out of jail this morning. Phil told me the records check came back stating he was former a member of the CIA; his full name is Ronald Dean Johnson with no known address or other information listed. Phil was notified about the arrest of Robert Smith and James McDuffy and is processing the extradition paperwork as we speak. He called to talk to you, but did told me the Colorado State Police in conjunction with the FBI had them in custody and were holding them on Federal charges of exporting explosives and firearms across state lines without a permit. Phil thinks he has a good chance of getting them back to Las Vegas to face murder charges. With the investigation of Rueben's murder at the storage facility, they got lucky and removed one set of Smith's fingerprints from the gate, which could possibly tie him in with Rueben's murder."

"Looks like things are coming together for Phil," said Reggie. "Is there anything else you can tell me?"

"Yeah, now the bad news, there was a hand written note in with your office mail. I'll read it to you: 'I told you I would give the first one to you but the rest of them are mine, you are becoming a pain in our side and I will deal with you personally even if it means taking out all of those around you.' We don't know how it got in your mail. Do you have any ideas who the author of the note is?"

"Crap," was Reggie's reply, "I know exactly where the note came from. Remember the other day in the K-mart parking lot when Johnson was sitting in the police car, during that time he told me I had won that round, but there would be more rounds. So it has to be from him. You have to get Brandy and make her go to my house in Summerlin and then hire a security firm to provide 24-hour security around the house and at the gate. Don't alarm her but tell her why, just ask her please to go there for my sake and I will explain the whole thing to her when I get back to Las Vegas. Tell Hilda to take off on vacation, with pay. Don't tell her why; make up some kind of a story. Then you're going to have to be extremely careful, he means business."

"Is there anything I can do about this guy?"

"After you get Brandy and Hilda taken care of, see if Phil can give you any more information about Johnson and where he went after being released. Then call in all the favors owed you and me around town and try to locate this guy. He has probably crawled into a hole somewhere; we need to dig him out."

"If I find him then what?"

"When I get back into Vegas you and I are going to pay him a visit and try to persuade him to leave well enough alone."

"And if he doesn't buy that?"

"Before I let him harm someone that's close to me, I'll go against everything I believe in and put him out of business, permanently."

"Okay, Reg, I'll take care of that. Where are you now?"

"I'm still in Colorado, but should be on the road in about an hour."

It was a long trip back to Las Vegas and it was a very tired Reggie who drove up to the front gate of his house only to find out he couldn't gain access because of the tight security Joe had set up. The security guard called Joe and he soon arrived to clear up the matter and vouch for Reggie. After adding Reggie to the access list Joe, turning to him said, "I'm sorry about this but there was no other way for me to insure no one else was allowed entry onto the grounds."

"No apology necessary, Joe, I'm glad you have such tight security. Now on to more important matters; have there been any other developments since the time we last talked and have you been able to find Johnson?"

"No, Reg., Johnson must have crawled into a hole and pulled it in after him, but we'll find him. You look like hell, why don't you go home and get some sleep and we can talk business in the morning."

Five minutes later both men departed. When they left a late model sedan pulled up and parked on a side road about fifty yards from the driveway to Reggie's house with a very sadistic smiling Ronald Johnson inside, thinking to himself, *'I told you my time would come Nutsbagh.'*

Twenty minutes later Reggie arrived back at his apartment, showered and went to bed. He had only been asleep a short time when the insistent ringing of his cell phone finally got through to his brain and pulled him from his deep sleep. Groggily he picked up the phone, and said, "Hello."

"Hello, is this Reggie Nutsbagh?"

Unable to get his sleep-induced mind in gear, Reggie's reply was a short, "Yes."

"This is the security detail captain, you need to get over to your house quickly there's a problem."

This last comment jarred Reggie completely awake, he asked, "What's going on is everything okay at the house?"

"No," was the short reply. "There's a dead man on the grounds, killed by our roving patrol. The Las Vegas Police are on their way."

"How about the lady in the house, is she okay?" asked Reggie, the fear for Brandy's safety evident in his voice.

"The intruder never got close to the house," was the reply.

"I'll be right there."

Reggie dressed and was out the door and into his car in 5 minutes. On the way to his house he called Joe and asked him to meet him there, explaining briefly what he had been told.

Pulling into the driveway, he was stopped by the same security guard as before, but this time he was immediately passed through the gate.

Arriving at the front of the house the first person he saw was Phil and when Reggie got stopped and got out of his car Phil came over, "This is a hell of a way for you and I to get together. I'm sure you're anxious to know what happened, so let me tell you as much as I know. The dead man is Ronald Johnson, yea, the same guy I jailed at your request. He tried to bluff his way onto the grounds through the front gate claiming to be Brandy's father."

"That didn't work, so he went to the back and tried to gain entry by climbing the fence. When he got over the fence he was spotted by the roving security guard, Johnson saw the guard and fired hitting him in the upper arm, the security guard returned fire, hitting Johnson twice, one in the chest and the other in the head. Johnson died instantly."

"Did he get into the house?"

"No, he never made it. My question to you is, why the security?"

Reggie hesitated, trying to think of a way to answer Phil's question without lying to his friend, "Well, if you must know, Johnson threatened me when you picked him up the other day at K-Mart. Then a threatening note was received at my office, which I presumed was from him, so I had Joe move Brandy into my house and set up the security at the gate and around the house until I could get back and deal with Mr. Johnson."

Reggie's explanation was interrupted by a loud scream as an overwrought Brandy charged into the group and straight into Reggie's open arms.

Babbling, obviously confused by all of the police presence, she broke into tears and held tightly to Reggie.

Holding onto Brandy, he moved her to a small bench located in the yard. Sitting down and before he could say anything, Brandy spoke through her tears, "Reggie, I woke up with all the lights shining around the house and didn't know what was happening, I was so scared."

Reggie replied, "I know, I tried to keep you away from all of this, by moving you here, but it looks like I failed. I'm truly sorry you had to go through this experience. I'll explain what happened in a little while, at least you're safe and that's the most important thing."

A few minutes passed with the two sitting on bench holding each other then Reggie was startled when Phil, who had walked up unnoticed, said, "Okay, Reggie, now's the time for you to let me know what is going on around here. Not tonight, but some time in the next few days I expect you to come and see me and let me know in detail exactly what you're involved in, you owe me that much."

CHAPTER NINETEEN

Things heat up at Toby's Homestead

TOBY SAT AT the kitchen table with the folder given to him by Sergei Laslow in front of him. *'What information could possibly be in this file that was so important it would lead to the taking of two lives?'* So much had happened these last few days. He was reasonably sure the U.S. Government itself wasn't involved; yet some of its employees surely were. How far into the workings of the State Department had evil crept?

Opening the folder he spotted his name in the first entry. Reading further he became increasingly uncomfortable to see his every move had been observed by Laslow. From what he could gather Laslow's bosses (the CIA?) had ordered him to maintain surveillance to see if Lt. Preston would make a good undercover agent. One page contained personal information such as his address, his unlisted telephone number, and other information about him, including information about his daughter, and Maria his maid. There was even a short blurb about his church affiliation with a notation that 'this could be detrimental if a moral decision were required.' The rest of the first page was devoted to names of friends and acquaintances, hobbies and the places he frequented.

Just as he was about to turn to the second page, he heard a squeak of footsteps behind him, glancing at the window he caught a reflection in the glass and dove out of his chair just as a hand wielding a semi-automatic weapon struck at where his head would have been. Rolling over he used his legs in a scissor motion, knocking the intruder to the floor. He then drove a crippling chop to the man's throat cutting off his air supply and then ripped the gun from the victim's hand and slammed him alongside the head; rendering him unconscious. Using a rope, he kept in the pantry he tied the man's hands and feet.

Realizing there must be at least one more of the man's associates nearby, he left the house through the side door and crept along the house until he was able to view the front yard and gate area. He spotted the man's partner lounging against a black Honda Accord just outside the gate.

Making a quick decision, Toby went back around the house and entered the woods behind the house. Moving quietly he worked his way through the trees, climbing the fence surrounding the property, out of sight of the unsuspecting man. Quietly, but quickly he advanced on the man, whose attention was focused in the direction of the house. When Toby was within five feet of the man something must have alerted him, for he turned in Toby's direction and at the same time reaching in his waistband withdrawing a revolver. Toby, acting on instinct, launched himself at the man, hitting him high in the chest dislodging the weapon from the assailant's hand, and then struck a sharp judo chop to the side of his neck.

Taking a deep breath Toby removed his opponents' belt, tying his hands and legs with the belt. Searching the man he removed a wallet with identification—most likely false—giving his name as Jerry Tilton. He shoved the bound man under the car, lodging him in so tightly that any movement was nearly impossible, and hurried back to the house to check on his other captive.

The other man was starting to regain consciousness and was struggling furiously against the rope.

Looking down at the man Toby said, "You made a big mistake coming into my house, fella. Now you and the sickos you work for have made me angry and I'm going to do everything in my power to find all of you and eliminate you one by one." With that he took the man's own weapon and pulled back the hammer then pointing it between the terrified man's eyes he pulled the trigger. The loud click of the bolt slamming shut sounded like a thunderclap. The bound man collapsed in a near faint.

"Oh, my, I forgot to put the bullets back in. That's okay, on second thought I don't want your brains splattered all over my kitchen so I guess I'd better take you outside. At least I can use the garden hose to rinse things off. A shame you don't have a silencer on your gun, hate to disturb the neighbors." Grasping the quivering man by his bound legs he dragged him across the kitchen floor, over the threshold and down the three steps leading to the yard. Finally Toby stopped and propped the man up against a tree. For added security Toby bound the man to the tree using a garden hose. A quick search of the man's person revealed nothing unexpected; a Visa credit card issued to Stephen L. Soberg, which he pocketed; hoping it would provide a lead to the people financing the organization, and a business card with the word DONE on it. He patted the man on the head saying, "Now stay here for a few minutes while I go check on your partner. Be a good boy and maybe I won't miss with my first shot."

Instead of checking on the tree-bound man's partner, Toby put in a call to the local police, asking for Chief Fisher. When the chief came on the line he asked, "So what do I owe the honor of this call, Toby? If you are asking to come back to work, you will have to beg. And even then I would start you off on the beat."

"Like to stand here and trade shots with you, chief," Toby replied, "but I have a couple of guys who trespassed on my property and I would like you to send someone over to pick them up. I suggest you contact the FBI agents who are working on the mayor's case, as these are real bad guys and may somehow be related to that case. Don't have time to answer questions now, but hurry."

Not waiting for any response he hung up and went outside. Remembering his encounter with the ex-CIA man he caught in Seattle he took off the shoes of his tree-bound assailant. Finding nothing there he headed out to the other captive. He barely finished his search (coming up with a folded piece of paper this time), when three patrol cars pulled up with sirens blaring and light flashing.

The first officer to climb out of the police vehicles was an old friend, Thad Vince, now sporting the shiny new stripes of Sergeant. Bounding up to Toby he did an uncharacteristic thing by giving him an emotional hug. "Boy, it's good to see you. You seem to have picked up a tan and lost a few pounds. Civilian life must really agree with you."

"Looks like things have been going good for you too. Congratulations on the promotion."

"You know how it is, Lieu—I mean, Toby, you give a little blood in the line of duty and they think they owe you, so what do they give you, a little more money and a lot more responsibilities. What do you have here?"

By then the other officers had approached and listened as Toby recounted the capture of the two men. In the telling he left out the scrap of paper he had found and the credit card he had pocketed.

He had hardly finished when a car with government license plates pulled up. Toby immediately recognized the two FBI agents who had questioned him weeks earlier, Seth Samuelson and Terry Jones.

Filling the two agents in on the details he concluded by saying, "If you check the arms of both men you will find the word DONE tattooed there. If you remember the same organization was involved in the warehouse episode."

At this point Agent Jones interrupted, "You seem to know a lot about this DONE group, Preston. Maybe you could enlighten us further."

"Better yet," Toby returned, "Why don't you take your leather truncheons to the two hoodlums I caught trespassing and by beating up on them instead of harassing me you might get some answers."

Toby walked over to Thad who was preparing to leave with the suspects and pulling him aside he cautioned him on the handling of his cargo. "I can't prove it, but I believe these two are the ones who killed the private investigator in Seattle yesterday."

"Okay," Thad responded and started to leave, but before he could pull away the two FBI agents stopped him and insisted the two men were federal prisoners and demanded they be turned over them. Believing they were right, Toby convinced Sgt. Vince to release them after getting release forms signed. Toby watched the government car's fading taillights and as they disappeared he had an uneasy feeling in the pit his stomach.

"Well, Toby," Vince commented, interrupting Toby's feeling of uneasiness, "you sure do add excitement to an otherwise dreary day. I might even make Lieutenant if you hang around long enough," not waiting for a reply Thad motioned to the other officers and they all climbed back into their cars and departed the scene.

Toby watched as the police cars disappeared from sight and then headed back to the house and after checking to see if Renie was still asleep and all was well he returned to the folder picking up where he had left off.

The second page of the interrupted reading was devoted entirely to Bremerton's ex-mayor, Elton Norton. The notes showed him as an inveterate gambler who had been in debt to the tune of fifty grand, when his fortune seemed to change. He suddenly had enough money to purchase the warehouse on Burwell, clear his debts and buy a new Lexus. Reading on Toby caught the name of the apartment manager, Doyle Dixon, who had been an undercover agent for the CIA. The notes mentioned how Norton found out about Dixon as Dixon, in his eagerness to reveal the information about the contents of the warehouse, had placed a call to Laslow's office, unaware that his phone was tapped. Apparently Laslow wasn't in, and Norton heard the message discovering he was under surveillance. He met his manager later that evening and killed him, not suspecting that Laslow was in the building and witnessed the act, hence his call to Toby.

Then the two ex-cops, Lebowitz and Abbott showed up at the Laslow office to hire someone to track down a missing man last seen in Montana. His brother was unavailable so Michael took the case. There were no notes for the next two days and then Laslow started in again with the words, 'I'M ON TO SOMETHING BIG'. That was the final entry.

'The answers to most of our questions are probably in Montana,' Toby deliberated. 'If Laslow found something in Montana that was important enough to send him to Reggie it could be a very important clue for us.'

Getting up from the table Toby went into his office. Going to a file cabinet in the corner he moved it away from the wall; lifting the carpet he revealed a floor safe, which he opened and placed the file inside.

After locking the safe and putting things back the way they were, he walked to his desk and picked up the phone. Dialing information he asked for the listing of a Samuel Lebowitz in Renton, Washington. After a few seconds a computerized voice informed him there was no listing under that name. He then asked for a Jerod Abbott. This time the voice informed him that the number was unlisted. To himself he thought, 'Headway at last; tomorrow I'll get in touch with Joan at the telephone company and see if she can get the number and address for me.'

This done he headed for bed, knowing tomorrow would be a full day. His last thoughts before dropping off were of Ruth, the sloe-eyed Hebrew beauty.

Toby was awakened the next morning by the smells of fresh coffee and bacon. Maria had quietly let herself in and was getting breakfast ready.

The smells were too tantalizing, so Toby threw his legs over the side of the bed and struggled into his robe as he padded down the hall to the kitchen, the patter of small feet behind him alerted him Renie was fast catching up.

After a morning hug she returned to her bedroom to prepare for school, as Toby continued on to the kitchen thinking, *'that girl really needs a mother to do the girl things with, maybe I should see if Ruth wants to come over for a while as she recuperates. These two have to meet sooner or later.'*

Entering the kitchen he exchanged greetings with Maria, accepting the steaming cup of coffee she offered and then sat down with the morning paper. The front-page story blared out, 'FBI LOSES THEIR MEN.'

According to the article Agent Jones was alone in the car used to transport the two suspects, when they somehow managed to get free of the handcuffs. Knocking Jones out they dumped him out of the car in the parking lot where he had been waiting for his partner. Agent Samuelson found Jones lying unconscious on the pavement and the car missing; the car was found hours later crashed into a tree with no sign of the two escapees. The FBI was releasing no further information at this time.

'How do two securely bound men work their way out of their handcuffs without a little help?' Toby asked himself. *'Can I expect them back here? Is there some collusion in the FBI too?'*

Toby called the Bremerton police station about the possibility of having his house put on the list of places needing to be patrolled. The desk sergeant informed him the chief made those decisions and he would contact him immediately. Toby then turned to Maria, "Maria, I am expecting trouble and would appreciate it if you would stay away for a few days. I'm going to send Renie to Chief Fisher's house for a few days and you won't be needed. In fact it would be a good idea for you to go home to Mexico for a while. I'll keep up your salary and call it a paid vacation."

"Does this have anything to do with the two men who talked to me about my visa, Senor Toby?"

Alarmed Toby responded with alacrity, "Which two men, Maria? And when was this?"

Taken aback by the tone and urgency of his voice, a bewildered Maria answered, "It was the Friday before you came home. I had just come home from early Mass when the two men drove up in a black

Honda; they showed me badges from Immigration and said they needed to know what flight you were on. I was very frightened thinking I had done something wrong and they wanted to talk to you before sending me home to Mexico. They left when I told them your flight number, but they said they would be back. What am I to do, Senor?"

Toby assured the tearful Maria she wouldn't be sent back to Mexico and cautioned her to contact him or the police as soon as possible if they came back. He asked her again if she would like to go see her family in Mexico, but she declined, saying, "I must be here for the little one."

Before they could continue their conversation Renie entered the kitchen for breakfast. As soon as breakfast was finished Toby dropped Renie off at school and headed for the telephone exchange building, hoping he could get an address to go with Abbott's unlisted number. Joan had helped him many times and this time was no exception; after greeting him with a smile and a hug it took less than a minute to bring up the name and address on her computer screen. "Do you need a record of incoming or outgoing calls?" she queried.

"I'm supposed to be the detective here," he teased.

This brought a pleased blush to her face as she began retrieving the information. "How far back do you want to go?" she asked.

"Can you go back as far as July?"

"Sure can," she responded. "It may take me a few minutes longer, though." Looking at him slyly, she said, "Maybe I should retire and become your girl Friday?"

More than half seriously, Toby replied, "I think that would be an excellent idea. But you're hardly thirty-nine yet and I'm not sure I can wait until you turn fifty-five."

Laughing Joan said, "I turned sixty yesterday and have over thirty years in."

Toby hadn't had time to think about his need for office staff, but he knew eventually he would need somebody as efficient as Reggie's Hilda. "Tell you what, Joan, don't quit right now unless you had already planned on it and I will get back to you. I'm on a case right now that's going to take my full concentration. If I survive you're hired."

Getting the final computer read-out from Joan, Toby headed for his car, arriving at the car he reached into his pocket for his car keys, and found the credit card and note he had confiscated last night. The note read, "Gather at the compound Thanksgiving." '*Why was the note so important it had been hidden in the shoe? Why hadn't it been committed to memory and destroyed. What and where is the compound?'* Toby shoved the note back into his pocket and headed for home and the telephone. There would be time enough to figure what and where the 'compound' was. The note seemed important, but first he wanted to follow up on the leads provided by Joan. Focusing on the task ahead he failed to notice the car following a discreet distance behind.

Arriving home Toby tried calling the number Joan had given him but only got an answering machine. Pulling out the list of calls she had given him he scanned it for a number or an area code that would strike a cord, but nothing stood out. His next call was to Israel. After what seemed an eternity, the voice of Ruth Garaza came on the line, speaking in Hebrew. Toby didn't know the language, but he understood two things about the answering party; he recognized her name as she spoke it and he recognized the voice of the woman he loved.

Toby's heart leapt in his throat at the sound of her voice. He answered, "Hi lovely lady, hope I didn't catch you while you were resting?"

Switching to English, Ruth replied, "Oh, Toby, my darling, it is so good for you to call me. I have been missing you terribly. When are you coming back to me?"

"Actually, sweet, that is the reason I'm calling. I think it would be nice if you came to the United States to recuperate. You could get a leave of absence from the University. I would like very much to see you and Renie is looking forward to meeting you."

"I would love to come," she responded, "But I must contact my superior first."

"Superior?" he asked with a puzzled tone in his voice.

"I'm sorry, I meant Supervisor of my department."

"When can you find out?" He quickly asked, forgetting the slip of tongue.

"I will call them right away. It may take some time for they are not always in the office."

"Them, they?" he once again questioned.

"Sorry, my love, I am so excited with your call I keep forgetting my English words. Forgive me. Please do not hang up right away. Tell me what has been going on in your life?"

Never before had he heard her speak in anything, but perfect English. In fact she had made it her mission to correct his enunciation sometimes to an annoying degree. Now she seemed to be using schoolgirl English.

"Toby, are you still there?"

"Sorry, Ruth, I was listening to your voice and my mind started wandering. Most of what I have been doing can't be discussed over an unsecured line. I've missed you very much, though. Letters don't seem to take the place of your nearness and your lovely smile."

"You know, flattery will get you everywhere," she coyly answered. "Keep talking, I feel better already. Not so good that I will not want to come to the States to finish recuperating, though."

"Well, you get hold of your department head and let me know as soon as you do. I'll arrange for tickets to be waiting. Within twenty-four hours we could be together."

After telling her he loved her, Toby hung up with the nagging thought there was something about her attitude that was different, she should have been eager to come. But he dismissed his doubts because of the events that had occurred in the last couple of days he knew he was looking for bad guys behind every bush.

Five minutes hadn't passed when the phone on his desk rang and Ruth's excited voice informed him she had been approved to come.

Pushing aside all doubt he gave her the information she needed to retrieve her ticket, as he had made her reservations before her return call knowing she would be coming. Making sure she could travel on her own, he promised to be waiting at the gate when she arrived two days from now. With parting words of endearment they severed the connection.

Toby's apprehension would have proven founded if he had been able to be a fly on the wall at the Garaza house. After Ruth hung up the phone, Joel observed the look of pain and disgust on her face as she turned to him saying, "I feel so guilty. I'm letting the man I love and wish to marry be used, so you can find out how he and Reggie are progressing. I wish I had never agreed to this. I feel like I'm betraying Toby."

Placing his arm around the slender shoulder of his sister and fellow Mossad operative, Joel said soothingly, "It is the only way, my little dove. He will never suspect and you will have done your brother and country a great service."

Then Joel walked into the other room and Ruth sank down into the couch and sobbed, praying she had done the right thing.

Toby held on to the receiver for a few seconds then when he leaned over to put the phone back on the cradle the windowpane shattered and the sound of a bullet thudded into the wall in line with where his head had been. He dove for the floor just as another bullet hit the wall. Bleeding on the cheek from flying glass, he crawled to the desk, removed the pistol he had stashed in the bottom drawer and was making for the backside of the house when he heard the sound of a firefight at the side of the house; and then silence. A few seconds later he heard the voice of Sgt. Vince, yelling, "Everything is okay Toby. We have the shooters."

Even though he knew the voice of Sgt. Vince, Toby rose slowly and stayed low against the wall until he could look out the window and see Vince and another officer standing over two forms sprawled on the lawn.

"Am I ever glad you guys happened to be in the neighborhood that was too close for comfort."

"We didn't just happen by," Vince responded. "The Chief authorized constant surveillance after these two characters broke away from the Feds. He was certain they would come back and wanted you and Renie protected."

"Are they dead?"

"Afraid so; we hoped to take them alive, but they gave us no choice."

"I'm not sure what kind of statement you are going to need from me, but I need to go back inside and make arrangements for replacing the window and patching some holes. I don't want Renie to see this mess."

Walking back into his office, Toby realized he had acted as if he was a seasoned soldier during the fracas. Even now he could hold his hand out and it was as steady as a rock. *'I sure hope I don't get to like this kind of action,'* he said to himself, *'but it appears the people we are up against are a bloody lot and there may be more to come.'*

CHAPTER TWENTY

A wild ride in Las Vegas

'*WHAT A NIGHT!*' was Reggie's first thought as he opened his eyes to the bright sunlight streaming through his apartment's partially closed drapes. Sleep had eluded him until the early hours of the morning while he relived the rollercoaster of emotions he had experienced over the last twenty-four hours, from the high of seeing several of his adversaries taken into custody to the low of fearing for Brandy's life.

Rolling over in bed he grabbed his cell phone and hit the automatic redial button for his office, after the second ring, Joe answered the phone, "Hello, this is Reggie Nutsbagh's office, can I help you?"

"Joe, don't you ever sleep?" Before Joe could answer he continued, "Actually when I called I forgot we sent Hilda home, sure didn't expect you to be there this early after what went on last night. We probably need to contact Hilda and see if she is free to come back to work with Johnson out of the picture."

"I'll call Hilda as soon as we get off the phone and see when she can come back to work. You know the listening devices we put in Rueben's office are still in place and lucky for us. When I came in this morning the tape was almost full and it picked up some interesting tidbits of information. I'm sure you'll be extremely interested in what the tape caught concerning Boulder Storage."

"That's great, I'll grab a shower and breakfast then be right there."

"No problem," Joe said, "nothing you need to be in a hurry to hear, the tape isn't going anywhere, just think you'll be interested in it."

An hour later Reggie arrived at his office to find Joe sitting at Hilda's desk, involved in what must have been a very serious phone call as his brow was furrowed in deep concentration and as he talked he was furiously writing on a pad of paper. Joe glanced up, saw Reggie, waved his hand hello then continued with his conversation.

A short time later Joe, carrying a cup of coffee, walked into Reggie's office beaming. "Good morning, boss, and how are you this morning?"

"Tired, didn't sleep well last night; I was too busy fighting ghosts until about three this morning, it's been a busy couple of days. What are you smiling about?"

"Let's take these things in order; first I'll play the tape for you and then I'll tell you what I learned about the message on the tape," then Joe turned the tape player on.

When the tape began the first thing heard was the sound of a telephone ringing, after several rings, a woman's voice is heard, "Boulder Storage, can I help you?"

"I want to speak with Mr. Peter Hatcher," a loud gravelly voice demanded.

"Sir, may I ask who is calling?"

"No you can't, just get Peter on the phone, you don't need to know who this is, get him on the phone and right now!" This was the now familiar voice of a man who was used to being obeyed.

"Yes, sir, one minute please."

Several seconds later the woman's voice could be heard through the intercom, telling Peter the phone call was for him and the person on the other end of the line wouldn't identify himself.

The phone was picked up and a voice said, "Hello, this is Peter Hatcher, can I help you?"

"What in the hell is going on down there?" a very angry voice said. *"Rueben must have screwed everything up. How in the hell did the Colorado State Police and the FBI get wind of our truck and stop them in Colorado, arrest all three men, confiscate the truck and it's load?"*

"I have no idea sir. As you are aware, I just came on board about a month ago, I really don't know what Rueben was doing before that time, plus he didn't let me in on a lot of his activities."

"When I find out who is responsible for this screw up, heads will roll and I mean that. Not only did we lose a truck full of goods but R and J have been arrested and are now residing in the Pueblo City jail awaiting extradition to Las Vegas. They are wanted in Las Vegas for the murder of Laslow and who knows what else they are wanted for, those guys have

always been loose cannons. We can't afford for them to be in jail in case one of them turns out to be talkative."

"I agree sir what do you want me to do," asked Peter.

There was a brief hesitation then the gravelly voice came back, *"I only wish I could kill Rueben again, only this time I would do it myself. If there are any more screw-ups down there, more bodies will be found laying beside the roads in Las Vegas. I want you to find the best lawyer in town, give him a large retainer, get the money the usual way and get him on the case of R and J. I don't care how it's done but I want those guys out of jail when they get to Vegas. Once they're out of jail tell them to skip town and get to the compound. If they have any questions they can contact me at the usual number."*

"Yes sir, I'll get on that—"

"Just listen, I don't have time to say this but once, I want you to check through Rueben's files to insure he didn't fill out any type of paperwork on our utilization of those storage units. I told him not to make a record of anything concerning our shipments and storage, but no telling what he did. Now that you're in charge of those storage facilities make sure we have plenty of room when we need it. I will get back to you later to find out about the lawyer and let you know when you can expect another shipment." There was silence as the line went dead.

There was a period of silence on the tape and then a telephone could be heard ringing, Joe walked over to the tape machine and turned off the recorder, saying, "Reggie, this next conversation was recorded several hours later just so you know." Joe turned the tape machine back on.

The woman's voice was heard again, "Boulder Storage, can I help you?"

"Get Peter on the phone," commanded the caller.

Peter was again called through the intercom and came on the telephone, "This is Peter."

Without preamble, the voice at the other end said, *"What is the name of the lawyer you hired for R and J?"*

"His name is John Peterson, sir; he comes highly recommended, and I paid him twice the normal retainer and told him to start on the case right away."

"He had better be good; I'm growing weary of the screw ups in Las Vegas. Now listen up, in about a week we have another shipment coming in, it will probably take three of your largest storage units. Be ready! You

need to nose around and try to find out where the leak is and plug it up anyway you have to. There better not be anymore problems down there or we will come in and take all of you out, permanently."

Fear was detected in Peter's voice as he responded, "Yes sir, I understand."

Then there was silence as the connection was broken.

Reggie sat silent for a time digesting what he had heard then said, "I guess getting that truck and its contents confiscated by the FBI caused some problems with DONE. I have to get on the phone and warn Toby about this latest piece of information it looks like things might be getting tough."

Joe nodded in agreement, "I agree. They're playing for keeps and we're going to have to reply in kind and not let them get the upper hand. When I first listened to the recording I did some digging trying to find out about Hatcher, that's why I was on the phone when you came in the office. Here's what I found out; Peter Hatcher is recently from Tacoma, Washington, where he was previously employed as the Transportation Movement Supervisor, at the Port of Tacoma. I'm sure with him having that job if we look hard enough we'll find some connection with Hatcher and DONE before he moved to Las Vegas. Being a supervisor at the Port of Tacoma gave him access to all of the incoming shipments and he could circumvent any inspection by custom officials. I also did some checking on the ownership of Boulder Storage. Boulder Storage is owned and operated by Rainier Investment Company, headquartered out of Seattle."

"You have been busy," Reggie said. "Do you have any more revelations?"

"I tried calling the Rainier Investment Company to get some more information on Hatcher, but they wouldn't talk with me. I do know he got into Vegas several weeks ago and resides in an apartment in your neck of the woods. It's a complex called South Valley Ranch Apartments, Apartment 615."

"I know where the place is. Now we need to come up with a plan based on this latest information and do something about it before I have to go to Seattle and help Toby. He called me earlier and asked if I was available to help him with something concerning the Port of Tacoma. This information about Hatcher could very useful for us should we end up at the Port." Thoughtfully Reggie paused before continuing, "Joe, we need to continue monitoring all of the calls to the storage company so leave the listening devices in place for the time being."

"Okay, Reggie. I better try and get hold of Hilda about coming back to work, so let me get on that."

Fifteen minutes later Joe came back into the office, shaking his head and chuckling to himself and when Reggie looked up he said, "That Hilda is something else. I called her; and she told me she was ready to come back to work yesterday. I told her in the morning would be soon enough, guess she's not use to being home all day. Now Reggie if you have nothing else for me to do there are a couple of things I need to do so I'll be gone for a couple of hours; I have to tie up some loose ends."

"Go ahead, Joe, I need some time to think about our next step, and then I'm leaving to have lunch with Brandy. Let's meet back here about two and try to lay out what we need to do next."

Joe left the office and Reggie sat down to complete the rest of the paperwork on his desk. He had worked about fifteen minutes when the phone rang. Picking up the receiver Reggie answered, "Nutsbagh, can I help you?"

"Can't afford a secretary anymore?" Phil asked, with a chuckle. "Well, what you said came true, don't know how you did it, but Smith and McDuffy are on their way to Las Vegas to face murder charges. They were picked up in Colorado, but I suppose you knew that already? Also don't think I've forgotten about the other night and our little discussion, you owe me an explanation about what's been going on around town."

"Phil, I promise I'll come clean about everything, but you need to give me just a little more time. I have a few more loose ends to tie up then I'll let you in on our investigation."

"I'm going to hold you to that promise, Reggie. We have been friends for a long time and I know you'll not let me down. I'll talk with you later, bye."

Hanging up Reggie sat for several minutes lost in thought, not only about Phil's call; but now what to do about Hatcher and his connection to DONE. He knew they needed to press the attack and stay after DONE.

Suddenly a bold plan came into his head which would be a shot straight to the heart of the problem and might set DONE back on their heels. He knew he must have a physical confrontation with Hatcher and it had to be tonight. Satisfied, he looked at his watch and saw it was time to meet Brandy for lunch.

Reggie walked into his office at 1:30 pm, just a few minutes ahead of Joe. Evidently Joe hadn't had time for lunch as he walked in right behind Reggie with a sandwich in his hand. Grabbing a cup of coffee to go with the sandwich, he followed Reggie into his office. He took a bite and tried to talk at the same time.

"Well, boss, what's the plan?"

Reggie laughing at Joe's attempt to eat and talk at the same time, replied, "Go ahead and finish your sandwich, when you're finished we can talk."

Twenty minutes later Joe had finished eating and Reggie began to outline his plan.

"Joe, this evening you and I are going to pay a visit to Apartment 615, at the South Valley Ranch Apartments. I think we'll do it around 11:00 pm. We are going to pay Mr. Hatcher a visit and find out what he knows and if the need arises we aren't going to be polite."

Joe, laughing at Reggie's comment about not being polite, asked, "Is there any thing I need to bring to this party."

"I would like you to make a cassette recording of the latest conversations we have of Hatcher and the other guy. Then bring the cassette recorder and yourself to the entrance of Hatcher's apartment complex at 11:00 pm, oh and bring along an old hypodermic needle, if you can find one."

"It looks like we are going to have a party and only three of us are invited. Are we going to try and hide our faces or disguise ourselves in any way?" Joe asked.

"No," said Reggie, "I really don't think at this stage that will be necessary, unless you want to. They already know all there is to know about me, but you might be another story so on second thought it will be wise to hide your face; it could prove to be beneficial to us in the long run."

After finalized their plans for the evening, Joe made the cassette recording and departed.

At 10:45 PM, the same evening, Reggie pulled into the South Valley Ranch apartment complex to find Joe already parked and waiting. Getting out of their cars they approached the apartment, which, luckily for them was on the ground floor. Before Reggie rang the door bell Joe pulled a mask over his face

The door bell pealed and then a voice came from the other side of the door, "Who is it?"

Reggie who was standing so he could be seen through the spy hole, answered, "My name is John Downey, are you Mr. Peter Hatcher? I'm sorry to bother you at home at this late hour. I was given this address for a Mr. Hatcher the manager of the Boulder Storage Facilities. I need a lot of storage space this evening and would like to talk about renting the space. I'm willing to pay a good price."

Not sure who was at the door, but willing to take the chance because of the mention of money, Hatcher responded, "Just a minute please."

Hatcher unlocked the door and started to open it when Reggie forced the door the rest of the way open causing Hatcher to recoil several steps backwards. Joe, following Reggie through the door, grabbed Hatcher before he recovered his balance.

Joe, his voice muffled by the facemask, said, "Okay, Hatcher, just keep your mouth shut and do as you're told and you won't be harmed."

Reggie, meanwhile, seeing Joe had Hatcher under control, closed and locked the door and then cut the telephone cord. Joe dragging Hatcher over to a chair by the dining table slammed him into the chair and then secured him to the chair with handcuffs.

"What in the hell is this all about?" cried a frightened Hatcher. "Who are you guys and what are you doing in my apartment?"

"Shut up," Joe said, lightly slapping Hatcher across the face.

Hatcher realizing he was in no position to bargain with the intruders shut up and sat passively while Reggie removed the cassette tape player from a small bag Joe was carrying. He inserted the tape and let it play all the way through.

During the time the tape was playing Reggie observed Hatcher's facial expressions and saw the look on his face go from wondering how someone had taped his conversations, to fear, knowing someone had taped his conversations with DONE.

When the tape finished playing, Reggie surreptitiously switched the tape player from the play position to the record position then spoke in a voice filled with anger, "You don't need to know who we are the only thing you really need to do is listen and listen real good; I'm going to ask you some questions and I want you to tell me the truth. If you don't, I'm going to have my friend here inject you with something that will cause you to tell the truth, probably for the first time in your life."

Hatcher, having regained a little composure, answered with a renewed confidence, "Sure, I have nothing to hide. The tape you played says nothing about me being involved in anything unlawful."

When Hatcher finished his comment Joe stepped up and delivered a vicious slap to Hatcher's face, saying, "We'll not tolerate lies. You had better start and finish with the truth."

Reggie immediately launched into his questioning, "What do you know about Michael Laslow and his murder at the hands of Robert Smith and James McDuffy?"

Reggie and Joe, as part of their plan had decided to play the 'good guy, bad guy' routine. Reggie to be the good guy and Joe the bad one, ready to provide what force was necessary to get Hatcher to talk.

Keeping the pressure on Hatcher, Joe again stepped in close, pulling a needle from his pocket saying, "Right now you have two choices either tell the man what he wants to know without the injection or take the injection and tell him anyway. The choice is yours!"

"I know Smith and McDuffy killed Laslow," Hatcher said reluctantly, "I was told he, Laslow, was caught snooping around the company's compound in Montana and skipped out just a few steps in front of Smith and McDuffy. They followed him to Las Vegas and picked him up late one evening on the strip coming out of a sandwich shop. Initially they took him up to the storage facility and threatened him by putting explosives on his person telling him they were going to blow him up. The beating, which followed, was very sadistic and meant to insure he was telling the truth. Somewhere along the line they searched him and came up with a business card of Reggie Nutsbagh. Then Smith put the gun to his head several times playing Russian roulette. Finally the pistol reached a chamber with a bullet in it and he died. I helped them load the body in a car and they took it back to Las Vegas and the Paris Hotel."

"The Boss, referred to in the tape, who is he?"

"I don't have the faintest idea, I have never met him. Every time I was contacted by him it was by—"

Once again Joe stepped in, this time delivering a sharp blow to Hatcher's mid-section causing him to gasp in pain and almost fall on the floor. After the blow, Joe said, "We have all night and the later it gets into the night the harder it's going to be on you. I'm not a very patient man."

"I'm telling the truth, I don't know who he is. As far as I know there are only about three people in the organization who know and they are sworn to secrecy."

"I'm sorry about you getting hit, it's hard for me to control him when he gets like this," said Reggie, turning away from Hatcher to wink at Joe. "Okay, I believe you. When you were working at the Port of Tacoma as maintenance supervisor, what were you supposed to do?" Reggie asked this question, knowing full well that wasn't his job title, but wanting to see if Hatcher would tell him the truth.

"I wasn't a maintenance supervisor; I was the Supervisor for Transportation and Movement. I would receive a call about certain shipments and would divert these shipments away from prying eyes of customs until they could be picked up."

"What does the Rainier Investment Company have to do with the Port of Tacoma?"

"I don't—"

Before Hatcher could complete his sentence Joe stepped in and grabbed the handcuffs on his wrist and violently twisted them, causing Hatcher to yell as the pain. "I thought we were going to be truthful, I think you were just about to tell another lie."

Trying hard to ignore the pain, Hatcher, said, "The Rainier Investment Company paid me a lot of money to overlook those shipments."

"We know the Rainier Investment Company owns Boulder Storage, why did they move you here? Did you screw up something at the port?"

"No, evidently they were dissatisfied with Rueben and knew they were going to terminate him, so they sent me down to take his place and put another man in my place."

Joe piped up, "You mean to tell me Rainier Investment Company has enough power to tell the Port of Tacoma who to hire and fire?"

Hatcher, still fighting the pain, spoke through clenched teeth, "Evidently so, they put me in the job and provided a replacement when I left. I remember when I was put on the job there was one man, the assistant to the old supervisor who was supposed to move up, but was passed over so I could take the job. He complained about it and then one day he didn't show up for work and no one knew what happened to him. The guy who was hired to take his place, my assistant, now runs the section."

Reggie thought for a moment, and then asked, "When is the next shipment due at the port?"

"I don't know, you heard the tape they said they would call me and tell me when I was to be prepared to accept the next shipment. Can you loosen these handcuffs; I think you broke my wrist."

Reggie signaled Joe to remove the handcuffs seeing Hatcher was in a lot of pain. Joe walked over to Hatcher, unlocked and removed the handcuffs. As soon as the handcuffs were removed Hatcher pushed Joe aside then bolted out of the chair, ran into the bedroom, slamming and locking the door.

Reggie, pulling the gun from his shoulder holster, motioned Joe to step over to the side, then walking up to the door, he said through it, "Okay, Hatcher, come out of there, we aren't going to harm you unless you persist in remaining in the bedroom."

There was no reply from the other side of the door. Reggie placed his ear against the door and heard Hatcher dialing a phone. Reggie chided himself; he should have known there was an extension in the bedroom. Still listening through the door Reggie heard talking but couldn't make out what was being said until he heard his name mentioned. Signaling Joe they both hit the door at the same time caving it in. Because of the violent impact the lock broke, and the door swung open. They both landed on the floor and Reggie heard two shots. Knowing Joe didn't have a gun, Reggie returned fire, getting off two shots of his own and then there was silence, with the exception of Hatcher's body hitting the floor.

Anxiously Reggie asked Joe if he was okay. Joe responded by saying, "He hit me in the upper arm, just a flesh wound, I'll be okay."

Reggie got up from the floor and went to where Hatcher was lying on the floor beside the bed. Reggie picked up the phone and hit the automatic re-dial; after several rings a woman's recorded voice answered the phone, "This is the Rainer Investment Company our business hours are—" Reggie hung up the phone before the recording was finished.

"What now, boss?' Joe asked.

"Let me bind your wound so you won't bleed all over the apartment then we'll do a quick search to see if we can find anything. First let me look outside to see if any of the neighbors have been alerted by the shots."

Opening the apartment door Reggie took a quick look around, and saw no one. After binding up Joe's wound, they proceeded to search the apartment. Finding nothing of significance, they gathered their equipment and left the apartment locking the door behind them, returning to their cars.

This latest development placed Reggie in a difficult position; what was he going to do about Phil? Surely he would be brought into this investigation because of Hatcher's involvement with Boulder Storage.

"How's the arm?" Reggie asked, "Do you know a doctor who can patch you up without asking a lot of questions?"

"It's only a scratch, nothing a little antiseptic and a bandage won't cure. I can take care of that myself."

"Okay, let's get out of here; I need some coffee and some time to unwind. How about stopping off at the Sunset Casino Café and give ourselves a chance to wind down and talk about what we're going to do about this latest development?"

Having ended another man's life didn't sit well with Reggie as it went against everything he believed in, no matter how evil and sinister the individual was. But when it came right down to it, he did what he had to do to protect himself and Joe. With the killing of Hatcher he realized another DONE agent was out of the way.

Fifteen minutes later both men were sitting in the café drinking coffee and waiting the arrival of their hamburgers. Joe was the first to speak, "Well, boss, where do we go from here?"

"I would like you to go out to the pay phone and place an anonymous call to the Henderson Police and tell them to check apartment 615 at the South Valley Ranch apartments, then hang up quickly."

Joe left to do as requested while Reggie sat at the table drinking his coffee and trying to formulate what he was going to tell Phil. After what just happened he was sure Phil was sharp enough to know Reggie and his investigation was tied into this latest murder. After a few more minutes of silent deliberation Reggie decided to see Phil later in the morning and put everything out on the table.

Joe returned and Reggie informed him of his decision, but that he would leave him out of the equation, if at all possible.

Finishing their food and departing the casino both men headed for their respective homes, a shower and some much needed rest.

CHAPTER TWENTY-ONE

Headway in Seattle

BEING FROM A small-town, Toby had always found going to Seattle an overwhelming experience, one which he avoided when possible. The occasional shopping trip to the city made with Esther and Renie had always been limited to walking distance from the ferry, so it wasn't surprising to find him pouring over a city map as he tried to navigate this city with its many hills in search of a residence on Queen Anne Hill.

It had taken numerous phone calls and the continued assistance of his friend Joan before he had been able to come up with an address and formulate a plan which he hoped, would help him find some answers to his questions. Finally sighting the address he was looking for he pulled to the curb but before climbing out of the car he checked in his rear view mirror to see if the green Ford Taurus, which had started following him when he drove off the ferry, was still there.

Assuring himself the car was still there he emerged from his car without looking in the direction of the tailing car. Knocking on the door of the house, he spoke to the lady who answered and after a few words was admitted. The two men in the car, which had been following him, were satisfied he had arrived at his destination; so they relaxed in their parked car. However, they would have been mad had they known he had gone straight through to the back door. From there he walked two doors down where a door leading to an adjoining garage was waiting open for him. He climbed into the car inside, opened the garage door and pulled out of the drive, heading up the street away from the Taurus and its occupants.

The address, his actual destination, was fairly close by and as he drew up in front of the house he glanced up and saw the curtains drawn aside and what appeared to be a woman peering out. Taking this as a good sign he walked up to the door and lifted the ornate knocker on the oak door. A very regal looking elderly woman answered his knock. "It's about time you showed up, young man. It certainly has taken you long enough to get here." When she spoke, it was in a quavering voice, giving the impression she was on the verge of tears.

Sure she had mistaken him for someone else; he began to explain when she cut him off with an animated wave of her hand, silencing him. She then continued, "I sent those former police officers out several months ago to find my grandson and when they never got back to me I figured they had turned it over to the FBI. Then when that FBI agent came by, saying their investigation was stalled, I knew the CIA would take over. But they never came and I had almost given up hope until that nice Mr. Laslow said he was going to get a man on it. That's you, isn't it?"

"Well, not exactly," Toby explained, "But I'm here to try to find some answers. First, when did the man from the FBI show up and do you remember his name?"

"Of course I remember his name. I thought it strange he would ask so many questions and then tell me there was nothing else they could do. He wanted to know what kind of car my grandson was driving, if I had any correspondence from him and when did he last contact me. He even asked if I had a picture of my grandson. You would think he would have obtained that information from Mr. Lebowitz or Mr. Abbott. He didn't fool me one bit. They were just trying to make an old lady go away."

Not skipping a beat, she said, "His name was Jones. Nice young man, but he asked a lot of questions and continually looked out into the street, as if someone was out there."

Toby wasn't sure if he was ever going to get a word in edgewise, when just as quickly as she had begun, she ceased talking. Her shoulders drooped and gentle sobs wracked her thin shoulders. Not knowing exactly what to do he placed his muscular arm around her shoulders and guided her to a large sofa in the corner of the room. He waited for her to compose herself before he spoke.

He started to speak when she jumped up from the sofa and left the room; returning in a few seconds to place a much-handled photograph and a wrinkled postcard into his hand and then she sat back down.

The photograph was tear stained and showed a handsome youngster, possibly in his teens. The resemblance to the woman was remarkably more like a son than a grandson. On the back was scrawled, "To Grams, you're the best." The words were faded from much handling and so tear stained he could hardly make out the writing, but the picture on the front revealed typical Montana scenery and a small caption which identified the area as 'The Beautiful Porcupine River, near Glasgow, Montana.

Handing the treasured items back to the woman, Toby said, "I may not be the person you were expecting, but I'm his partner. I'm Toby Preston and I think my partner, Reggie Nutsbagh, who is working on a different angle of this case in Nevada, is the one you were expecting. Between the two of us we hope to be able to bring your grandson home to you."

"I'm Lucille Graden. My grandson is Thomas Lincoln Graden, the third. My husband and both his parents were killed while on a mountain climbing trip on Mt. Rainier when he was only two years old. An avalanche took them away. We are the only family each other have, so please find him and bring him back to me."

Toby tenderly touched the grieving woman's shoulder and reassured her they would do their best to reunite her with her grandson

Through glistening eyes she smiled bravely saying, "God bless you, Toby Preston. Thank you for giving an old woman renewed hope."

Driving away he could see her still standing in the doorway. '*I sure hope I didn't give her false hope, but I guess any glimmer is better than none at all.*' With a sigh he retraced his route. He had been gone well over an hour and was certain the men watching the house he had initially entered were getting antsy.

Later walking out to his own car a casual glance down the street revealed the car with its occupants sitting in the same spot. '*Now for a little follow the leader because I really need to shake you before I go to the airport to pick up Ruth.*' Even as he spoke he knew it wouldn't be long before they showed up at his home. This was getting tedious and he found himself wondering if his life would ever return to normal.

Picking up his cell phone he punched in the number for Reggie's office. Hilda answered on the second ring with her usual cherry greeting, "Good Afternoon, this is Reggie Nutsbagh's office. Can I help you?"

"Hi, this is Toby. How are you?"

"Toby," she replied with genuine pleasure in her voice, "It's great to hear your voice. Hold on I'll get the boss for you."

Almost immediately the welcome voice of his friend came on the line. "Hey turkey, what have you been up to? How are things developing there? Feel free to talk openly as Joe has installed a scrambler on all my phones and we're relatively certain they're clear."

"Great, I need to tell you a little about my visit to the relative of the person Lebowitz and Abbott were searching for in Montana. It looks like the FBI is interested in the case also; they questioned the grandmother, but she is one smart old lady. She told them nothing, yet shared all with me. From a postcard she showed me it looks to me like we're going to have to get back to Montana, after all."

"Good going, partner, I'm in the middle of some things here, but I'll be able to be up there on schedule and Brandy will be with me." Reggie then told him about the capture of Smith and McDuffy.

"I can't stay on much longer," Toby, responded, "a couple of our friends are with me and I need to shake them before I go to the airport. Ruth is coming in this afternoon and I don't want them around when I pick her up. I'm glad Brandy is coming with you. It will be good for all three women to meet each other."

"Okay, buddy, do your thing. Keep in touch and if you should need to reach me in the next couple of days use my cell number. I expect to be moving pretty fast and may not touch base at the office very often. Don't take any unnecessary risks."

"Gotcha, pal, I'll see you around."

Starting his car Toby slowly pulled away from the curb heading in the direction of the downtown area. The time was three PM and about now Seattle traffic would be teeming with shoppers and people in their cars trying to get out of town before the heavy traffic started. Hoping to establish a pattern with the men in the car behind him he decided to race through a few yellow lights on the way to downtown. '*Sure hope the local police are off doing something else,*' he said under this breath. '*I don't need them to stop me now.*'

Thinking Toby was unaware of their presence, the couple in the Taurus hung back a few car lengths and this was what proved to be their undoing. Just as he approached the Ballard draw bridge the lights began flashing indicating the bridge was being raised for ship traffic. Stepping on the gas he managed to get underneath the bar being lowered and despite the yelling of the attendant made it safely over before the bridge began rising. Breathing a sigh of relief he proceeded to the airport and his reunion with Ruth.

At the Airport Toby had to wait at the security gate for the plane's arrival. Knowing her airplane had landed he watched as passengers streamed by, all anxious to greet those who were waiting until finally he saw her as she approached the security gate. Dressed in a beige pantsuit with her hair lying loose on her shoulders she took his breath away. Outwardly she showed no physical scars from the bomb, but a slight limp was visible in her walk. Hurrying forward, mindless of others waiting for loved ones; he embraced her with the ardor of one who has been separated for a long period of time. Planting a long kiss on her lips he was aware of the people around observing the exchange and Ruth's complexion couldn't hide her blush, as she wasn't used to such a public display of affection.

"I was beginning to get butterflies in my stomach as the plane began its descent," she managed to breathe out. "I was looking so forward to this moment, I could not eat. And I did not sleep well at all, even on the long flight."

With his arm around her waist and her carry-on bag over his shoulder, Toby guided her out of the stream of traffic, saying, "And I have been feeling like a schoolboy in anticipation and I kept wondering how you could fall in love with me so soon and then love me enough to come to a foreign country where you will be faced with meeting a twelve-year old child who is terribly possessive of her father, but you are here and you will love Renie, as I know she will love you."

The drive to Bremerton was slow because of the afternoon commuter traffic, and for the most part there was silence as both basked in the nearness of the other. As they were crossing over the Tacoma Narrows Bridge, she sat up, oohing and ahing over the spectacular view.

"Look out the back," Toby advised, "It's a clear day and the view of Mt. Rainier is awesome."

Turing in the seat Ruth glimpsed the magnificent, towering mountain with its snow covered peak, that is fabulous," she said. "Breathless! Can we go up there sometime?"

"We might be able to squeeze in a day trip up there," he responded. "The snow level is usually high enough so we should be able to get all the way to Paradise."

"Paradise, is that like in the fantasy books?"

"No," he answered with a laugh. "It's just the name of the area where we park and enjoy the view. And if you are up to a walk, we can walk on then Nature trails."

"Oh, I would love that," she enthusiastically shot back. "We have some mountainous areas in Israel, but nothing like this."

The rest of the way home Ruth bubbled over with conversation. She commented on everything from the trees and vegetation to the green waters of the Puget Sound. It wasn't until they pulled up to the gate across the driveway leading to the house that she became silent. Toby suspected she was feeling a little apprehensive about meeting his daughter.

The car had barely come to a full stop in front of the house before the door flew open and the dynamo better known as Renie came out of the door. "Hi Dad," she said, then turned to Ruth and exclaimed, "Wow, you are gorgeous. You weren't kidding, were you, daddy? You even smell like my mom. Bet you are wearing Chanel No. 5, aren't you?"

By the time he had taken Ruth's bags to the guestroom off Renie's bedroom the two females were deep in conversation in the family room, heads bowed over an old photo album.

Renie, seeing her dad standing in the doorway said, "Hey, dad, while we are visiting why don't you order some pizza? What kind do you like Ruth?"

"I don't eat much pizza, Renie, so you pick for all of us, okay?"

"I will decide on something Kosher for you and pepperoni is what Renie and I like best," answered Toby. "Show her the house, sweetheart."

The afternoon had been such a relaxing time that Toby failed to notice his shadows had once again taken up a position near the house. But as he returned with their evening meal, he spotted them and reminded himself he would have to do something about them soon. He relished his privacy and freedom and was being robbed of it by these goons.

Concentrating on the return of the surveillance car, he wasn't aware that one of the men from the car lay hidden approximately fifteen feet from the gate. This man had a high power set of binoculars and was able to see the numbers as Toby punched in his security code for entrance through the gate.

When Toby entered the house he could hear the voices of Ruth and Renie in the guestroom. Setting the pizzas on the kitchen table he ventured in the direction of the voices, seeing him, Ruth piped up, "I do not know much about pizza, but I think it is supposed to be eaten hot. What do you say we dig in, as you Americans say."

Renie raced ahead of them to the kitchen so Toby took that opportunity to reach for Ruth and gave her a long kiss, "I love you, Ruth," he whispered.

"Okay, so when are we getting married?" Ruth asked, smiling brazenly.

"Is that how they do it in Israel?" Toby answered, completely taken aback by her directness. "Over here the man asks. Give me a few days to get a ring and I will ask you formally."

From down the hall, Renie yelled, interrupting any further discussion, "Hey, you guys, come on. I'm already on my second piece."

"Alright, we're coming. Don't eat it all or we'll have to rent a crane to get you up from the table," Toby yelled.

"This matter is not finished, Mr. Toby Preston," a determined Ruth told the red-faced Toby. "We will resolve this before I go back home. My mother would lock me up if she knew I was being so bold, but I do not want to grow old never having been loved. Now let us go before Renie comes looking."

For the entire mealtime the two girls giggled and carried on while Toby quietly chewed his food, wondering how he was going to survive having two scheming women under the same roof.

The call bell from the gate interrupted the meal. Going to the intercom mounted on the kitchen wall, he spoke into the box. "May I help you?"

"Mr. Preston," the voice on the other end answered. "This is Agent Jones with the FBI. May I come in and talk to you? It's of great importance and I only have a few minutes before I will be missed."

"I'll open the gate for you. Drive on in."

In the kitchen, Ruth, hearing that an FBI agent was on his way in, began to formulate a plan in her mind that would allow her to hear what was going on. She felt like she was betraying a trust, yet her sense of devotion to duty compelled her to assimilate anything, which could be used by the people she worked for in Tel Aviv.

While he awaited the arrival of the FBI agent, Toby went into his office, took his gun from its hiding place and stuck it in his belt behind his back.

When he opened the door for the agent, he asked, "What's so urgent we couldn't conduct this meeting in your office instead of my home? And where's your pal? Thought you guys came in pairs."

"Look, Preston, I know you don't like me and maybe I did come on a little strong the few times we met, but this investigation has had me stonewalled for so long. Evidence is either misplaced or stolen and it seems like every time something new comes up you are in the thick of things. You can't blame me for being suspicious."

Not to be put off with words, Toby retorted, "Your actions almost put you on the other side, what with losing your prisoners, who in turn almost killed me. Your visit to see the lady in Seattle about her missing grandson couldn't have been an official action either, as his disappearance was never reported as a kidnapping. You are either a bumbling fool or on a mission of your own."

Jones' face turned red as he struggled to control himself. "You stubborn idiot, can't you see I'm trying to mend fences here? I want to work with you and have put myself at risk to even come here. Get it through your thick skull I'm not one of the bad guys."

With this outburst, Toby relented a little in his attitude. "Sorry, Jones, but I have been shot at, survived a bombing attempt, have seen the mayor of my city killed because of his complicity in something I'm still in the dark about. Yours may be an official investigation, but mine is that of a private citizen and right now I'm swimming upstream against a strong current. Now what brought you here?"

Ruth had sent Renie on a mission from the room and had removed a miniature tape recorder from her handbag with which she was recording the heated exchange between the two men. She was caught off-guard when the young girl returned sooner than expected catching the Hebrew woman with her ear up against the door leading to the foyer and asked, "What are you doing Ruth?"

Flustered at having been caught in the act, she responded, "Your father and that man were yelling and I didn't know if I should go in and break it up. Your dad went out there with a gun and I was worried."

Apparently Renie hadn't seen the small recorder and seemed to be satisfied with Ruth's answer, for she shrugged her shoulders and replied,

"There's been a lot of strange things going on lately and I think my dad is just being cautious. Come on let's go outside. I want to show you our yard."

"Okay, Renie just let me listen for a few minutes longer, at least until they are through yelling. Could you fix me a nice cup of hot tea and by that time I am sure it will be safe to leave the two alone."

As the girl bounced off to accomplish the task, Ruth placed the recorder on a shelf near the door, behind some large figurines. She turned just in enough time to escape being caught by Renie the second time as she returned from making the tea.

The voices of the two men had quieted somewhat, and Toby was heard to say, "Come on down to my office and we can continue there."

This action caught Ruth off guard, but thinking quickly she turned back to the shelf as if to admire one of the figurines and quickly palmed the recorder. Turning to Renie, she commented, "This is a beautiful piece of art. I have never seen anything quiet so exquisite."

"It was one of my mother's collection she had lots of other collectibles, too. Would you like to see the rest of them?"

Jumping at the chance to stay near the two men she replied, "That would be nice. Will we be disturbing your father and his guest?"

"No, Daddy took the man into his office; we'll be in the den and the family room. Some of them are in dad's bedroom, but I'm not allowed in there unless he's there. He hides my Christmas and birthday presents there."

As they walked by Toby's office door, Ruth saw the door was slightly ajar. Using the guise of admiring one of the antique pieces of china placed on shelves along the hallway, she set the mini-recorder behind a china dish, hoping it was close enough to pick up what was being said in the office, as she followed Renie down the hall she could hear Toby's voice.

"My whole life has changed ever since Norton's demise. It hasn't been only you and your sidekick's interference in my life, but a number of things, so you will have to understand my skepticism. Now for the final time, what is it that brought you to my door?"

Without mincing words the FBI agent stated, "My partner is a member of the DONE organization!"

"How do you know this?" Toby asked in surprise.

"There have been a number of things leading me to suspect there was someone within the local office of the Bureau dealing underhandedly. First the Mayor's Day Planner ended up missing from a secure room; then the two guys we took from here got out of their handcuffs and ended up at your house with weapons we had confiscated from Norton's warehouse. To top it off I discover my line has been tapped. No other phones in the office, just mine. One evening while at home I received a message from an unknown person telling me to back off or my life would be in danger. If Samuelson received the same kind of call he made no reference to it the following day."

At this point Toby interrupted asking, "The voice of the person calling you, what did he sound like?"

"I recall it clearly. Whoever it was is used to giving orders. His voice was gravelly, cold and hard, as if my death was a matter of fact thing, or as if he ordered deaths on a regular basis. There was no background noise at all."

"Hmmm," Toby contemplated, "I've heard a voice just like that several times, giving me pretty much the same warning. You still haven't given me anything that points directly to Samuelson as being one of them."

"I would agree with you, except I received confirmation of my suspicions yesterday. Up until then I had never seen Seth without a coat or long-sleeved shirt. We had just come back from rummaging through some files at the warehouse and he took his coat off to wash the grime from his hands. In the process he rolled up his sleeves and revealed the same tattoo, which the guys your cop friends killed here had. I tried not to stare, but I think he saw me looking and that's why I think I'm in danger from my own partner."

"I guess you had better know you were most likely spotted coming in by a couple of guys in black hats. They have been parking across the street for some time now. Why they haven't struck yet is a mystery for I'm sure I'm on a hit list. If you weren't on a list before you are now."

Toby paused a moment and then continued, "You are a badge-carrying law officer, why don't we lead them away from here and then waylay them somewhere. Who knows we might get some answers."

"I'm game," Jones replied.

Leaving his office Toby went in search of Renie and Ruth. He found them in the family room giggling over some picture in the family photo album. '*Probably telling some new story on her father,*' he grumbled under his breath.

Entering the room he said in his most severe voice, "Agent Jones and I are going out for a while try not to destroy my carefully built image too much, Renie. This lady could be your mother one day so keep a tone of respect when talking about your father."

Giving them both a kiss goodbye, he headed for the door, loudly stating over his shoulder, "I'll lock the door and gate as I leave don't allow anyone in."

Then he and the FBI agent left to implement their plan. They had no sooner gone from sight with their tail close behind, when a police cruiser pulled up to the gate and a uniformed driver leaned out the window, punched in a code and watched as the gate opened. In the house Ruth and Renie heard the buzzer alerting them to someone entering and hurriedly went to the front window, assuming Toby had forgotten something. Ruth lagged a little behind in hopes of retrieving the tape recorder.

Seeing the two men in uniform get out of a police car, Renie opened the front door and asked, "How did you get in the gate?"

The older of the two men in uniform answered, "Your father was worried about you and gave us the code so we could watch over you until he returned."

"My dad would never give anyone the code," argued the young girl, as she quickly attempted to close the door. She didn't get the door shut as the younger of the two men had moved up closer during the brief exchange of words and stuck his foot in the door keeping it from closing. He then forced his weight against the door throwing the young girl against the wall.

Both men entered the house, glancing around, "Are you alone, little girl?" the younger man asked.

Upon hearing the voices, Ruth, on her way to join Renie after getting the tape recorder, hung back in hopes of surprising the intruders. The plan was spoiled by the frightened girl's response. "My father's girl friend is here and she will scratch your eyes out. And when my father gets back he will shoot you both."

Both men laughed loudly with the older of the two commented, "You have spunk, kid. Now tell your friend to come out where we can see her. Hands empty, of course."

When Ruth rounded the corner, the younger of the two whistled and said, "Wow, this is going to be more fun that I thought. You take the kid and I'll take the woman. The boss said to make Preston sorry he ever got involved and after we finish with these two he'll want to shoot himself."

"Take her off into one of the back bedrooms. I expect Sid and Adam will keep Preston and the Fed busy for a while. Before I take care of this little one I want to check out Preston's office."

Yanking both Renie and Ruth down the hallway, the two men searched the hall for the rooms mentioned. Ruth struggled against the stronger man's grip. Unable to wrest herself from his grip she resorted to words.

"Leave the girl alone. I am woman enough for both of you."

"Lady, when I finish with you there won't be enough for Mario to have. Besides he likes little girls. I, on the other hand like the ones like you."

Dragging her into the first bedroom he came to—the guestroom—he began pawing her, running his hands over her full breasts. Beginning to pant from his lust he yanked at her blouse, ripping it off her shoulders revealing the lacy brassiere and the round curve of her breasts. Ruth changed tactics; instead of resisting she became compliant. Pressing herself against the man's body, she said, "I like it when a man gets rough. Let me help you."

Stepping back from her captor she seductively ran her hands down her hips; when her fingers reached the hem of her skirt she slowly began raising it. If the man had been a little more perceptive he would have noticed that the right hand, which was sliding under the skirt, wasn't reaching for the panties underneath. Too late he found himself staring down the barrel of a .32 caliber pistol, which had been strapped against her inner thigh. Without hesitation she advanced on the startled man, jammed the pistol into his chest and pulled the trigger twice in rapid succession.

Pushing the man's body away from her she quickly moved to the door hoping the other man hadn't heard the muffled shots. She knew she only had a short time before he would begin molesting Renie.

Shaking from the experience of killing her first person, she managed to calm herself enough to check the load of the gun. Then praying the floor didn't creak; she slowly advanced toward Toby's office door. Renie was in the corner of the room where her assailant had callously thrown her. Ruth heard her say vehemently, "You will never get away with this my dad will find you and tear you apart."

Scowling menacingly the man turned toward the young girl, raising his hand as if to strike her. It was then that he saw Ruth. "What the—", he bellowed as he reached for his gun. He was never to complete the move, as a small hole appeared in his forehead where Ruth's bullet stuck him. Ignoring his tumbling body Ruth rushed to the young girl and wrapped her in her arms.

"Are you okay, sweetheart?" Ruth asked. "He did not touch you, did he?"

The sobbing girl clung to her benefactor, her body wracked with tremors from what she had just witnessed. "Nnno," she stuttered. "He was too busy looking in daddy's desk and file cabinet. I'm glad you killed him."

"Yes, sweetheart," Ruth answered in a quavering voice. "I have never killed anyone before, but I have to admit this was a pleasure. They were both wicked men. Now we have to call your father, do you know his cell phone number?"

Picking up the phone, the now relatively calm girl said, "I'll dial it and you can speak to him."

After the third ring the phone was answered on the other end. Without giving Toby a chance to speak Ruth said, "Toby, something terrible has happened here at the house. Come quickly, we are both fine but please hurry." Not waiting for a response she hung up.

"I am sure he will call back, but we will not answer and save all the questions and answers for when he arrives."

True to her deductions the phone began ringing as soon as she put the receiver back on its cradle. Averting her eyes from the body of the man on the floor, she went into the guest bedroom where she picked up her torn blouse from the floor and put it on. Closing the doors of the two rooms to shield their eyes from the bodies of the dead men, they walked toward the kitchen, the haven where they would wait for Toby.

When she slouched into a kitchen chair the enormity of what had just taken place hit Ruth like a sledgehammer. Her body began to shake as her head slumped to the table. Huge sobs racked her body as she realized she had taken two human lives. Renie, with a show of maturity, put her arms around the older women in an attempt at consoling her.

Ruth slowly turned to the young girl and tearfully said, "I did the right thing, but I will live with it forever."

At that moment the squealing of tires could be heard coming up the driveway, followed by the slamming of car doors. Toby ran through the open front door yelling as he ran, "Renie, Ruth, where are you? What happened?"

Both women answered in unison and Toby rushed into the kitchen, picking up Renie in one arm and pulling Ruth to his chest with the other.

Excitedly Renie began to recount what had happened; Toby listened to her without interruption, but his eyes were looking at Ruth. He was seeing her in a new light. Not sure where she came up with this cold-blooded ability to kill two men, yet grateful she had.

Leaving Renie with Agent Jones, he and Ruth walked back to the scenes of death. In the hall he saw a mini-recorder on the floor near the wall, stooping he picked it up and slipped it into his pocket, unnoticed by Ruth, who had dropped it when the intruders burst in and in the commotion, which followed, she had forgotten about it.

Ruth told Toby about the intrusion and the shooting of the two men, leaving out the seductive scene in the bedroom. Puzzled, Toby asked, "Why were you carrying a weapon?" Before she could answer, Toby continued, "I had better call the police. They aren't going to like it that one of their cars was stolen and they have two more deaths on their hands."

Before using the phone he pulled her into his arms, kissing her tenderly on the lips. "Thank you for being here. Sorry you have to be mixed up in this, but thank you."

He continued holding her as he used his free hand to punch in the telephone number of the Bremerton Police. She relaxed in his strong arms feeling his hand caress her shoulder. '*This is what a man's touch is supposed to feel like,*' she thought, as she snuggled even closer.

The phone call completed Toby and Ruth headed back to the kitchen where Renie and Terry Jones sat sipping on cups of steaming hot chocolate.

"Why don't you go back and look at the two stiffs before the police arrive," Toby suggested. "You might recognize one or both of them."

After Jones left the room, Toby took the recorder out of his pocket and asked, "What is this?" Without waiting for a response he said, "Looks like a hi-tech tape recorder. Do you think it might have fallen out of one of the guys' pockets? If so it could have some good stuff on it."

Once again he failed to wait for a reply. Switching it on he was startled to hear his voice and that of the FBI agent, shutting it off he turned angrily to Ruth. "This is yours, isn't it? You were spying on me, weren't you? Who are you really? Who do your work for?"

With each question, Toby's voice had risen, until the yelling brought Jones running back into the room.

"What's going on?"

Angrily Toby answered, "This is between the lady and me, and right now I would appreciate it if you would leave; I'll be in touch. There is nothing you can offer the police and its best you are not seen here."

The agent tried to object, but was indelicately led to the kitchen door leading to the back yard by the angry Toby. As the door closed in his face, he yelled at Toby, "Call me right away. We still need to talk."

Inside Toby had turned to Ruth and was about to speak when the sound of sirens interrupted his actions. "We'll clear up this matter once the police have finished."

Renie was completely bewildered by her father's behavior. All she knew was that Ruth had put herself in danger to save them both and now her father was showing anger instead of gratitude.

Looking at the older woman she asked, "What is wrong with daddy, Ruth? He was nice and then all of a sudden he jumped all over you. That isn't like him at all."

Saddened by the turn of things and the loss of trust from the man she so deeply loved, she replied, "I am afraid I have done your father wrong, my darling Renie. I failed to tell him everything about me and he feels betrayed."

"What did you do? Are you really married? Don't you want to be in our family?" The young girl sobbed, sure that her well-ordered world was slowly crumbling around her.

"No, sweetheart, I am not married. And yes, I want very much to be a part of your family. I love your father more than life itself. I would leave with a broken heart rather than hurt him further. Please understand; his anger is justified."

With that she sat down at the kitchen table and put her head on the table and began sobbing.

At the front door Toby greeted the first of the officers. "Well, Sgt. Vince, we meet again under about the same circumstances, come on in, you will find two bodies down the hall. Come into the kitchen when you are ready the person who shot them will be waiting."

"You mean it wasn't you?"

"No," Toby returned. "If I had been here you would have only body parts to cart off. They tried to attack my daughter."

As Sgt Vince made his way down the hall, Toby went back into the kitchen. Silently he looked at the two women; noticing the stubborn set of his daughter's jaw he refrained from speaking. By the way she clung to the older woman, he knew now wasn't the time to continue his interrogation.

When Vince strode into the kitchen the air was filled with tenseness and he assumed it was due to what had taken place in the house resulting in the two intruders being slain.

"The chief is really going to be upset that one of his patrol cards was used to carry off this little charade. The uniforms most likely came from a uniform store, but the car is ours and was parked in a secured lot."

Turning to Ruth he asked, "I guess you're responsible for the two corpses, care to tell me about it?"

Recounting the story Ruth kept a somber face, looking straight into Toby's face as she told her story.

"That was pretty cool on your part, ma'am. From the sound of things you're no stranger to this kind of thing. From your accent I gather you aren't from here and from your description of the hiding place for the weapon I figure you to be in law enforcement."

Neither needing nor expecting a reply Thad turned to Toby, "I'll have the Coroner's people take the stiffs away. I would appreciate it if you would bring the young lady by the station Monday and fill out the paperwork with Homicide."

Once the contingent of police and the Coroner's staff had left, Toby motioned the two women to follow him into the family room. Still using sign language he pointed to chairs, directing them to sit down.

Fearing a continuation of the tongue-lashing she had received earlier, Ruth opened her mouth to speak.

Placing a finger over his lips Toby hushed her, speaking in a subdued voice he began. "I'm not a man known to make rash judgments, but I did. I'm not known as a man who loses his temper easily, but I did. I'm known for logically working things out and I believe I have. Stop me if I'm wrong, Ruth. You are Mossad, aren't you? You work for your brother and he used you to find out where Reggie and I were in our pursuit of the organization DONE, right? I detected something in your voice during the conversation inviting you here. The only thing, which had me puzzled for a time, was how you got through customs with a gun. Then I remembered that it took awhile for you to get to the gate, so then I knew. You had declared yourself on the trip and were allowed to carry the firearm as long as you gave it to the pilot of the plane."

As Toby went on he gave an almost eerie assessment of how Ruth had been roped into helping her brother after their father had been killed. He even had it right as to her reluctance to engage in the surreptitious activities against her love.

When he finished his dissertation he walked over to where Ruth sat. Kneeling in front of her he said in a voice full of contrition, "Ruth Garaza, I love you. Can you ever forgive my outburst? And will you do me the honor of becoming Mrs. Toby Preston?"

The weeping began again, but this time tears of joy as both women jumped at the kneeling Toby, bowling him over.

"Oh, yes, yes, I will. Today! Right now it is I who must beg your forgiveness, my darling. I want you to trust me completely. I will call my brother and resign. He never really used me before Reggie and you came into the country."

Not wanting to be left out Renie piped up with, "Let's celebrate. Why don't we get dressed up and go out to dinner?"

At once the two women began making plans for the evening and together he expected they would try to plan the rest of his life. *'Well, I could be worse off,'* he thought. *'Guess I had better call Reggie and let him know.'*

Lying on the carpet where Ruth and Renie had left him, he watched the two women chattering away as if they had known each other forever. *'Yes, life is looking up.'*

CHAPTER TWENTY-TWO

Brandy takes a hand

THE DEMONS RACED around in Reggie's head and one of them had captured Brandy and was about to pull the trigger of a pistol held to her head. Reggie tried in vain to foil the demon, but every time he did a large man, with the word DONE carved into his forehead, knocked him to the ground.

The chiming of the clock in the hall brought him back to the world of reality and as he lay on his sweat soaked sheets he breathed deeply trying to rid his mind of the lingering effects of his nightmare. Rolling over he looked at the bedside clock and saw that it was 9:20 am. '*I should have been at work already. There are a lot of things I want to accomplish today.*' Jumping up he headed for the shower.

He hurriedly completed his morning toiletries and was heading out the door when it suddenly dawned on him it was Saturday and he didn't need to go to work. Shaking his head at his stupidity he turned back into his apartment, '*that dream was so real I guess it unsettled me. This would be a good day to spend with Brandy and put those demons behind me.*' With this thought he picked up the phone and dialed her number, when she answered he asked, "How are you doing this morning, Brandy? Would you like some company today?"

Twenty minutes later Reggie pulled up to the entrance of his home in Summerlin, and after a short delay he was admitted through the security gate. Before he could ring the bell to announce his presence Brandy opened the door.

Two hours later, after eating breakfast at a local restaurant, the two lovebirds returned to the house, and as they walked up to the front door Reggie's cell phone rang. Brandy had gone ahead and was unlocking the door when she heard the phone ring, she turned back to hear him say, "Hello, this is Reggie."

"Hey Reggie, this is Phil, how are you doing this morning?" Looking up Reggie signaled Brandy to go ahead, so she went into the house leaving the door ajar.

"Pretty good actually, I'm spending the day with Brandy so I'm at the house. We've just finished breakfast and now we're going to spend some time relaxing by the pool. To what do I owe the honor of the call?"

"I have some bad news and some real bad news," Phil responded. "We had Smith and McDuffy, for about six hours. We extradited them from Colorado and filed murder charges. We had them locked up in a holding cell; last night Smith complained of being sick and needing a doctor; the cop on duty got too close to the cell door and Smith grabbed him through the bars, took his weapon and made him unlock his cell. Then using the cop as a hostage, had him unlock the door to McDuffy's cell, then, still using the cop as a hostage, the two got outside the jail, grabbed a car and disappeared. Two hours later we found the car in Henderson with a cop dead inside. We have an all-points bulletin out but they were able to elude us before so I have my doubts about our ability to get them."

"Damn," was all Reggie managed to say at Phil's bad news.

"The real bad news is you are in their sights and are going to have to watch your step," Phil said. "I spent several hours questioning both of them before they escaped, they didn't say much about the murder, but somehow they knew you set them up and had some real disparaging remarks about you, your ancestors and anyone else associated with you, they really don't like you much."

"Well that does sound interesting, but there's not much I can do about what they like and dislike. The security around the house is good, so I'm not worried about it and I can pretty much take care of myself."

"On a different front, what do you know about the new manager for the Boulder Storage Facility, a guy named Peter Hatcher, getting himself killed last night at the South Valley Ranch apartments?"

Acting surprised at the news, he responded, "Don't know anything about someone named Hatcher, in fact I didn't know they moved in a replacement after Rueben's death. Do you think that Smith and McDuffy had anything to do with it, or do you have any other suspects?"

"No," was Phil's response, "the Henderson Police called me in because they knew I was working on Rueben's killing and felt the two were related. The apartment was pretty clean, looked like a professional hit job. Hatcher was hit twice from short range with a 38caliber pistol and must have died instantly. It also looked like there had been a gun battle of sorts, his gun had been fired twice and we found some blood on the rug, so it looks like he might have hit one of his attackers."

Reggie hesitated for a few minutes before replying, "I spent a quiet time in my apartment last night in fact I didn't even turn on the TV. By the way Phil, even though it looks like you're going to have your hands full on Monday, I promised, so I will be in to see you so we can have that little talk. I know I owe you an explanation and will try to clear things up."

"I'll look forward to it; you've kept me in the dark long enough about what you're working on and how you knew about Smith and McDuffy. Seriously, be very careful about those two guys, they would think nothing of killing you and Brandy."

The call completed, Reggie walked back to the security guard station and told him about the events that had unfolded at the city jail, cautioning him to make sure the guards were extremely vigilant. Walking back to the house, he called for Brandy who came out of the bedroom wearing her bathing suit. "I hope the phone call didn't spell work for you this weekend, I was looking forward to spending time with you, today," she said.

"I'm not going anywhere, why don't you go on out to the pool, I'll change and be with you in a few minutes," he replied. Going into the house, Reggie changed into swimming trunks and was about to go out to the pool when he stopped as he thought back to his conversation with Phil, '*I wonder if I should tell Brandy about my conversation with Phil. I think she needs to know what is going on,*' he thought.

Coming to a decision, Reggie finished changing and started to join Brandy at the pool but stopped, turning around he picked up his gun, from the bed and put it along with a spare magazine into a small bag and then walked out to the pool.

Arriving at the pool he sat down in a chair beside Brandy, looking at her he said, "The call was from Phil. It was about a murder and he had some disturbing news for me. I'm pretty sure I told you about the two men who were following Toby and I around Vegas before our trip to

Israel. They are also suspects in the killing of a private investigator from Seattle, killed here in the city. To make a long story short, I found out where these two killers were hiding and then they decided to skip town so I followed them out of town and when I was certain of their destination, turned them into the police. They were arrested in Colorado, extradited back to Las Vegas and placed in the city jail. Several hours later they escaped by taking a cop hostage, later killing him. Somehow they found out I had turned them in and Phil thinks they may be out to get me."

Brandy looked at Reggie, concern showing on her face, "I guess the reason you're telling me this is that I might get caught up in this mess?"

"Yes," Reggie replied. "Evidently when Phil was questioning them, they didn't have anything good to say about me or anyone associated with me. As much as I've tried to avoid getting you involved it is, guilt by association."

Brandy sat quietly for a few minutes evidently mulling over what Reggie had said, then answered, "Let me try and ease your concern by telling you a little of the things you don't know about me. I was the only girl out of six kids. I was born and raised on a farm outside of the town of Minot, North Dakota. Growing up my brothers constantly tormented me, but if someone else tried to give me a hard time my brothers took exception and it never happened more than once. When I was thirteen years old, my parents were killed in a farming accident. All of us kids stayed on the farm and were raised by an Aunt and Uncle." She paused, as if trying to recall those early years, and then continued, "That's one reason I can't believe I got hysterical when that man was killed on the grounds of the house. My brothers taught me all there was to know about using firearms, how to load and shoot them and take care of them. I use to beat them when we had shooting matches around the farm. I killed my first deer at fourteen."

Amazed at the revelation, Reggie looked at Brandy, saying, "I never knew that. Guess there's a lot about you I'll be finding out, as we grow old together. My father kept several guns in the house, they are still there sitting in a gun cabinet in his study, located in the closet behind the desk, so if you ever need to arm yourself you know where they are; ammunition is in the drawer of the cabinet."

Brandy smiled, saying, "I have you to protect me, why would I need to have a gun?"

Reggie laughed, "As if you couldn't take are of yourself, after all this time I find out that you use to be a gun toting mama. I never would have thought that a nice young lady like you grew up knowing about shooting guns. How did a girl from Minot, North Dakota get to Las Vegas, Nevada?"

"I attended the University of North Dakota then took up nursing at a medical school in Bismarck. During our graduation there were representatives from different medical facilities around the country trying to recruit nurses. I chose to come to Las Vegas and have been here ever since. Now you know the story of Brandy Thomas's early life. Would you like to hear the rest of the story?"

This last comment was puzzling to him so he asked, "What's the rest of the story?"

"Now Brandy Thomas lives in Las Vegas and is very much in love with Mr. Reggie Nutsbagh and will not be scared off by some fool who doesn't like him or me. How's that for a wonderful ending to a dull story?"

Reggie smiled tenderly at Brandy's comment, and then replied, "I'm so glad you are and to complete the story I can tell you Reggie Nutsbagh is deeply and sincerely in love with Brandy Thomas."

This tender scene broke up when Reggie picked up Brandy and deposited her in the pool. After about twenty minutes of racing around the pool chasing each other and generally having a good time, it was a winded Reggie who climbed out of the pool and sat at one of the poolside deck chairs. Brandy, who swam like a fish, completed several more laps of the pool then she too emerged from the pool asking, "How about some lunch? I'll go in and take a quick shower then make us some lunch."

"Sounds great, I'll use the shower here in the pool house and as soon as I'm finished I'll come in," Reggie replied.

Brandy left and went into the house and Reggie started walking towards the pool house but stopped halfway, turned around and looked around the area. Suddenly it occurred to him he hadn't seen or heard the roving security guard one time since they had been outside the house. This was strange so Reggie, instead of going to the pool house, turned and began walking toward the front gate. Getting closer to the gate he knew something was wrong because he couldn't see the guard standing at his usual position at the front gate. Reggie hesitated, looking around trying to see if anything else was out of the ordinary. He was looking around, when out of the corner of his eye he caught movement, someone was hiding behind a bush close to the front entrance of the gatehouse. Nonchalantly he turned around and, resisting the temptation to run, leisurely made his way back to the side of the pool, stooping down he picked up his bag with his gun inside. He then turned and started walking back toward the house.

He had only taken a couple of steps when a man, later identified as Robert Smith, stood up from behind a tree a short distance away and yelled, "Nutsbagh, this time it's going to be me who will have the last laugh." With this said he brought his gun up and fired three times, but Reggie wasn't where he was supposed to be. When Smith had opened his mouth to taunt Reggie, his police training took over and he dove behind the corner of the pool house. All three shots missed their mark. Reggie was safe from his pistol fire but what he didn't realize, was behind him was the other part of the duo, James McDuffy.

Believing Reggie was unarmed, Smith moved from his hidden position and when he did Reggie brought his pistol up and fired two quick shots, both taking Smith in the chest dropping him instantly. When Smith went down Reggie heard a growl behind him and as he turned his head he heard a gun go off and felt a sharp pain on the side of his head.

Reggie slowly came back to the land of the living and tried to reach up to his head, which was pounding. Only then did he become aware of the restraining straps that were holding him down. He slowly opened his eyes and turned his head and the first person he saw was Brandy. He still didn't know exactly where he was or what had happened after he passed out.

Trying to move around against his restraints only caused him more pain, so he stopped moving, then his mind cleared and he realized he was laying on a gurney inside an ambulance. From his position on the gurney he could see outside the open door where two medics and several policemen stood, one of them his friend Phil.

Seeing he was awake, Brandy took his hand, saying, "Take it easy, Darling, a bullet creased your head. A centimeter further to the right and you wouldn't be here right now. The two men are dead, you killed one and the other shot you and then was shot and killed in the kitchen."

Reggie, confused, asked, "What do you mean, killed in the kitchen. Who—What?"

Before Brandy could answer his questions, Phil stuck his head inside the ambulance, seeing Reggie was awake, he said, "How are you doing, Reg?"

"Other then having a tremendous headache and a whole bunch of confusion, I'm doing okay; at least I'm not dead, I don't think."

"Brandy, will you excuse me please, I need to talk to Reggie for a minute. I promise I won't keep him long."

Brandy leaned over, kissed Reggie on the cheek and was helped out of the ambulance by Phil.

After she stepped to the ground she walked over to a nearby bench and sat down. She had always been a mentally tough woman, but as the realization of what she had done hit her she began to shake uncontrollably. Tears began to flow, not for the man she had killed but as a way to relieve the tension building in her body.

Phil climbed into the ambulance saying, "You are one lucky individual."

"What's that supposed to mean?" Reggie replied. "I sure don't feel lucky."

"Oh, believe me, you were extremely lucky, one that McDuffy wasn't a better shot and the second one and more important, is that you have such a wonderful and talented woman by your side, you had better never let her go."

"Could you please stop beating around the bush and let me know what happened, my head is killing me and hurts too much for me to solve any riddles," said Reggie, groaning with pain. "The last thing I remember was Smith moving around in the bushes, he got two shots off and missed, I got two shots off and didn't miss, then I heard a growl behind me, which sounded like a dog, and then I turned around and the lights went out. The next thing I know I wake up lying on this gurney tied up like a sick dog."

"Well," began Phil, "To gain entrance to the grounds, Smith and McDuffy killed both security guards. You got Smith then McDuffy got you and started for the house, evidently to even the score and kill Brandy also. There he ran into a problem; when the first shots were fired, Brandy looked out the window saw you shoot Smith then saw McDuffy shoot you. She ran into your father's den and got one of his pistols, loaded it and waited behind the kitchen door. When McDuffy broke into the side door and started into the kitchen Brandy could see him, but he couldn't see her. When he got into the kitchen she yelled at him to drop his pistol, he laughed at her and refused. He then said some unkind things about what he was going to do to her when he got hold of her, and as he approached her with his gun drawn she shot and killed him."

By the time Phil had completed telling Reggie what had happened in the house, Brandy, now composed, was climbing back into the ambulance so Phil tactfully stepped down to let them have time alone.

Reggie closed his eyes as he fought back the pain in his head; after a few seconds he opened his eyes, looking up at Brandy tenderly, he managed to say through the pain, "I love you, Phil told me what you did, you're an amazing woman."

"Be quiet, don't talk right now. I know your head hurts. They're going to take you to the hospital and I'm sure they'll keep you overnight for observation. I'll follow the ambulance to the hospital and volunteer for night duty so I can be on the ward with you during the night."

Reggie smiled and slowly closed his eyes, thankful he could rest with no demons chasing him.

Arriving at the hospital Reggie was examined and the doctor concluded no further tests were necessary, but wanted him to remain in the hospital overnight under observation. True to her word Brandy volunteered for duty and spent the night on duty, checking in on Reggie throughout the long night.

The next morning Reggie was released and went back to the house accompanied by Brandy, who had requested the next three days off. Two new security guards were on duty at the house, so it took several minutes for Reggie and Brandy to get admitted through the gate, as the new guards were extremely cautious in properly identifying both of them after what had occurred the night before.

Several hours later when both of them had rested Brandy went into the kitchen to prepare lunch while Reggie wandered into his father's study and turned on the computer. Browsing through the programs on the computer he came across a file he couldn't get into because it was password protected. This intrigued Reggie and he was determined to find the password and look at the file. For about an hour he tried using every word he could think of to gain access and was so engrossed in the attempt to gain access he wasn't aware that Brandy had come into the room and was standing behind him observing his attempts. Becoming frustrated he started to turn the computer off, when Brandy spoke up, startling him, "What was your Mother's maiden name?"

"Dorothy Jones," Reggie replied; then shook his head in disbelief, "a hell of a detective I am. I've been working on finding this password for several hours, and it was right in front of me all the time." Looking up at Brandy, he said, "thank you," then he entered the name 'Dorothy Jones', and was given access to the file. Before going into the file Reggie turned back to Brandy, "Not to change the subject but in a couple of days I'm going to Seattle for a while and do some work with Toby. Do you think you can swing a leave of absence from the hospital and go with me?"

After a short hesitation, Brandy replied, "That sounds wonderful I've never been to the Pacific Northwest. My supervisor at the hospital will not be overjoyed, as we're short handed, but faced with the alternative of me resigning I think she'll see it my way."

"Wonderful," Reggie responded, "We'll stay at Toby's house along with his daughter Renie and Ruth."

"Sounds good to me, now before you get into that file, let's go have lunch," Brandy said.

After lunch Brandy began cleaning up the table and washing the dishes as Reggie excused himself as he was anxious to get back to the computer and find out what his father had stored on the hidden file. When he accessed the file he saw a bunch of individual entries, appearing to be a journal of some sort. A lot of the initial writings had to do with his father's reasons for leaving Israel and retiring from the Air Force. The file outlining his reasons for retiring was that he was faced with the decision to retire or face disciplinary action for conducting an unauthorized investigation. Although he had done nothing wrong there were people in high positions in the government who didn't like his snooping. Coupled with the pressure brought to bear by the government, and people in the FBI, he made a conscious decision, for the good of his family, to retire. The only thing missing from these entries were names, but at least it confirmed what Toby and Reggie had suspected, the cancer had taken hold not only in the government but also the FBI.

After his father left the Air Force he couldn't let the investigation go. He felt there was a force loose in the United States which threatened the very core of democracy so he made the decision to continue his investigation.

He found someone in Las Vegas was involved in the conspiracy and that weapons, ammunition, and explosives were being routed to and stored in Las Vegas before being moved to Montana and some of the people involved in this movement belonged to a militia organization. He had traced the origin of the arms and found they were coming through the Port of Tacoma and the Rainier Investment Company was deeply involved, because they owned most of the storage facilities in Las Vegas.

Another entry discussed the time he flew his plane to Tacoma, Washington, supposedly on a business trip, but he wrote he really wanted to take a look into what was going on at the Port of Tacoma. He began asking questions at the port trying to find out what the procedures for custom inspections were on in-coming shipments, especially those from Israel. He had been directed to a Mr. Peter Hatcher who had told him the custom procedures used at the port were none of his business. This in itself was suspicious, but more so was the letterhead of a letter lying on Hatcher's desk; indicating it was from the Rainer Investment Company.

Another entry indicated his father then went to the Rainer Investment Company and tried asking questions but was rebuffed at every turn. Evidently while there he attracted some unwanted attention with his questions and he left Tacoma in a hurry.

After returning from his trip he realized there was more to the investment company than meets the eye so he concentrated on finding out all he could about the company, RIC.

Through research he discovered RIC was a comparatively new company with many diverse investments. The company was founded by disgruntled executives of the Boeing Corporation, who left their jobs with their company stock options in hand. They pooled their resources then invested that money in creating RIC. Headed up by a group of individuals who sat as the Board of Directors overseen by a CEO, the directors of RIC for all appearances ran the company but in all actuality the company was ran by the CEO, whose name he was unable to uncover. But under the CEO's guidance RIC flourished and became a very viable company in a short period of time.

The company prospered by making many wise investments, in land, new buildings, shopping malls and a rather large construction company. They also invested heavily in storage facilities around the country to include many sites in Las Vegas. It is said in corporate circles that the board members and the CEO of RIC were some of the highest paid executives in the country.

Other entries in the file indicated that his father decided to tempt fate one more time, so once again he took his plane back to Tacoma on a 'Business Trip'.

The next journal entries were an assortment of incomplete paragraphs. *'Found someone who would talk to me and have found out who the CEO is! I can't believe it! I personally have admired the man for his contributions in the political arena and his sizeable donations to all types of charities.'* Reggie read on hoping that a name would be listed, but his father never put a name to the CEO. After that there was a lone entry containing the name of a company called 'Worldcompt Limited' and a personal reminder to look up the ownership of the company. The rambling stopped there. Then after some insignificant entries he read, *'Just saw an article in the Seattle paper which read, HAROLD JOHNSON, a member of the Board of Directors for the Rainer Investment Company, was found dead in his car, he had apparently been tortured and killed. Cause of death was a single shot to the head, with a large caliber pistol.* "This was the man who gave me the information on the CEO of RIC."

Several days after he returned from his second trip to Tacoma his father began receiving telephone threats against him and his family with reminders of what happened in Israel to his friend Benjamin Garza. The last straw was when he found a dummy bomb planted at the back of the house under the kitchen window, with a note saying, "Back off, or else the next one will be real."

Facing this threat, his father then made a conscious decision to once again uproot his family and move out of Las Vegas. But first he had to finally, after all of these years, tell his beloved wife what was going on. His last entry read, *'I'm flying to San Diego tomorrow and will take my beloved Dorothy with me so I can explain what has transpired and why we have to move out of the house she has grown to love.'*

With this last entry in the file Reggie began to weep silently knowing his father had carried a heavy load during the later years of his life and gave his life because of his beliefs. Sitting back in the chair, Reggie said in a voice racked with emotion, "Dad, if it's the last thing I do, I will track your killers down and put an end to what you started."

Several hours later, after transferring all the information from his father's computer to a disk Reggie claimed a headache, but he really wanted to be alone to go back over the information contained in the file, so he said goodnight to Brandy and left for his apartment.

It was in the early hours of the morning when he finally laid his head on the pillow. From the time he had arrived at his apartment he had looked over the information from the file many times trying to get the bigger picture in his mind. He never came up with anything new, but every time he looked his resolve to find those responsible was strengthened.

After only an hour of sleep Reggie woke up, completed his preparations for the day, had his breakfast and then drove to his office. He walked into his office and was greeted by both Joe and Hilda.

Greeting Hilda first, he said, "Good morning, Hilda, glad to have you back. Were there any calls for me this morning?"

"No, boss. Would you like me to get you a cup of coffee you look like death warmed over this morning?"

"Sure! Joe, grab your coffee and come on back, we have to talk."

A few minutes later both men settled into chairs at a conference table in Reggie's office and Reggie related the details of the events surrounding the deaths of Smith and McDuffy.

After Reggie finished his narrative, Joe, looked at him and said, "I agree with Hilda, you look like hell, now I understand why. What I find hard to believe is that Brandy took McDuffy out, I suspected she was a strong woman, but this takes the cake."

"You're right about Brandy, she certainly knows how to handle herself, I guess that shows me what I'm in for when we get married," Reggie said with a smile. "And you're right about me, I didn't get much sleep the last two nights, it's awful hard to sleep in a hospital and with a great big headache. That's one reason I'm leaving shortly; you and Hilda can take care of things around here. Right after I see Phil I'm taking off; if you need me for anything you can call me on my cell."

Reggie yelled through the open door, "Hilda, see if you can get Phil on the phone for me."

Several minutes elapsed then Hilda came back across the intercom, "Boss, Phil is on line two."

"Hey Phil, I sure hope you're in a good mood this morning. I'll be down to see you in about an hour; will you be available so we can talk?"

"Sure, I'll make time."

Fifteen minutes later, after taking care of some business in the office and instructing Joe on several of his pending cases, Reggie started to leave the office, but was stopped by Hilda,

"Boss, you have a phone call. The caller wouldn't give his name, but says it's extremely important he talk with you."

Reggie walked back and picked up Hilda's phone, "This is Reggie."

The gravelly voice at the other end of the line immediately began speaking without introduction, *"Nutsbagh, your father was snooping into things which had nothing to do with him and look what he got. The men you faced in Israel and other encounters you have had were with the second team and up to now you have countered every move. I have a few surprises left and neither you nor your partner will survive the next round with the first team."* With this the connection was broken.

Reggie couldn't believe what he had heard. He was standing staring at the phone when Joe's voice finally penetrated, "Boss, hey boss, what's the matter?"

Hanging up the phone, Reggie motioned to Joe and they both walked back into Reggie's office. Closing the door he told Joe about the threat he had just received. Joe immediately said, "Maybe from now on I need to travel around with you until this thing is cleared up, an extra set of eyes won't hurt."

"No Joe," Reggie replied, "I don't think that's necessary, but thanks for the offer."

Reggie then walked out and headed for his meeting with Phil at police headquarters.

After the normal exasperating drive he arrived at police headquarters and walked into Phil's office. When he came in Phil called his secretary and told her he didn't want to be disturbed for any reason, unless the Chief or the Mayor called. Then looking at Reggie, he said, "Okay Reggie the floor is all yours."

Reggie began, "Let me start from the beginning. It all started the day my parents were killed flying to San Diego in my father's plane."

For two uninterrupted hours Reggie related the story of his investigation to Phil not leaving out anything. From the day at the morgue when he didn't tell Phil he had met with the John Doe (Michael Laslow) to trailing Smith and McDuffy out of town with the load of guns, ammunition and explosives. He told him, although he didn't see the killing of Reuben, he had followed the truck around town as it picked up their cargo from other storage sites and how on the last pickup George Rueben failed to come out and he figured they had killed him. He told him of finding evidence, on his trip to Israel, that there was an organization which was a threat to democracy and has been utilizing people within militia organizations. Smith and McDuffy had been a part of the organization and killed Laslow because of what they thought he knew about the location of a so-called compound in Montana.

"You're telling me that Las Vegas is a way station for illegal arms, ammunition and explosives being shipped to a final destination in Montana?" Phil asked, not believing what he had heard. "And this organization had Rueben killed because they felt he was incompetent for having some of the illegal goods confiscated?"

"Phil, I'm sure you trusted my father, as you worked for him for many years. Let me show you a file I found on his computer just yesterday. Then I want you to hear taped conversations between Rueben, Hatcher and a mysterious man giving orders to both of them. Before you ask the obvious question, yes, I had the manager's office wired for sound and have known for a long time what has been going on at the Boulder Storage facilities. That's how I knew where Smith and McDuffy were and when the truck left Vegas and I was the one who called the deputy sheriff in Pueblo, Colorado and caused them to be picked up; as a matter of fact I was sitting in the rest stop at the time they were arrested."

Reggie put the disk in Phil's computer and scrolled down the file so he could read the information. As Phil read through the file the only thing he could do was to shake his head in disbelief. Once the file was finished Reggie immediately turned on the portable tape player, he had brought with him and played the entire tape of all the conversations, with George Rueben, Peter Hatcher and the mysterious caller giving orders.

After the tape was finished an astounded Phil sat silently shaking his head in disbelief for several minutes before he could say anything. Finally he spoke, "Reggie, you should have let me in on this a long time ago, I could have helped. I always admired and respected your father and would have done anything in the world for him. Why didn't he come to me for help? During all those years I served with him he helped me out more times then I can count. Now I feel like I let the General down."

Reggie carefully thought about what he was about to say and then finally spoke, "The reason I didn't talk to you Phil is, I know you're a good cop and believe in the letter of the law. There are some things I have done to get this far in this investigation which were a little bit outside the law and it would have been hard for you to turn away from it."

"Reggie is that all or is there more? You might as well lay it all out on the table. It can't get any worse, can it?"

"I'm the one who killed Hatcher! I really didn't have a choice. Before you say anything let me tell you what happened. You heard the tape so I thought it best to confront Hatcher so I went to his apartment late that evening. He opened the door when I told him I was a salesman looking for a lot of storage space and would pay a good price and when he opened the door I forced my way in, got the best of him and put the cuffs on him. After applying a little pressure he told me he was there when Smith and McDuffty killed Laslow and Rueben. He also admitted other information concerning the Rainer Investment Company and the Port of Tacoma. He complained about the cuffs being too tight so I took them off, he bolted and ran into the bedroom and locked the door. I forced the door open, he fired two shots and missed, I fired twice and didn't."

Phil sat for a few seconds contemplating what Reggie has just said then said, "And you did this all by yourself? I see you don't appear to be wounded so whose blood was on the floor?"

Reggie was caught! He didn't want to lie to Phil any more and wanted him to hear the tape he had recorded on that evening, so he was forced to tell him about Joe.

Reggie looked at Phil and smiled, then said, "No I wasn't alone. I'm sure you remember Joe Morrison, the policeman who was forced to retire a few years ago; he has been working for me for the past several months. He was there with me and it's his blood you found on the bedroom rug. I have a tape of the whole encounter and I think it will be enough to clear both of us, at least of murder. Phil, I'm asking you as a friend, to forget what I said about the killing of Hatcher. I promise you that when this is over I'll turn myself in and take any punishment the law says I deserve."

Without answering Reggie's question Phil said, "Yes, I know Joe, a good man, how bad was he hit?"

"Just a flesh wound in the upper arm, now let me play the other tape for you."

Reggie inserted the tape in the recorder. The tape ran for about ten minutes; as it played Phil sat silently, carefully listening to the recording.

When it was finished, Phil looked intently at Reggie then said, "I don't really understand everything you have told me or what I just heard, it will take a while for me to process all this information. At the present time I'm inclined to trust you and out of respect for your father and mother stay out of your investigation. I'm going to make several demands on you; first I want your assurance if anything else comes up during your investigation which involves Las Vegas you inform me immediately; secondly, if you are in any way implicated in Hatcher's murder by the Henderson Police, you will turn yourself in immediately to face charges."

Reggie breathed a sigh of relief, then responded to Phil's demands, "I agree, Phil, I will go one step further and let you know where I am as I have to go to Seattle to do some further investigating with my partner, Toby. I'm sincerely sorry I didn't include you from the start but I made the decision and had to live by it."

"I want you to know Reggie, if I didn't know and trust you I would turn you over to the Henderson Police right now. I owe your father a debt I could never repay, maybe this is one way I can try and repay him for all he did for me."

"Phil, now I owe you a debt of gratitude and I promise I'll not let you down." Reggie said, getting up from the chair, preparing to leave his office.

"Hold it a minute, Reggie," said Phil, as he walked over to Reggie, "I have a couple of other things to say, this is coming from Phil your friend and not the cop Phil. Be careful and if you need anything let me know. Last but not least, put those bastards where they belong!"

The two men shook hands and a very relieved Reggie walked out of the Las Vegas Police station.

They say confession is good for the soul and after confessing to Phil; Reggie felt like a large weight had been removed from his shoulders. He slowly drove back to his office contemplating his next move. Back at the office he informed Hilda he would only be in for a short time in order to clear up some paperwork from one of his other cases and then he was going home.

He sat at his desk for an hour trying to concentrate on the work without success and had just decided to leave when he heard the phone ring, and then Hilda, over the intercom informed him it was Toby.

Toby explained what he had been up to lately. He had visited the lost hunter's grandmother. He was the guy Lebowitz and Abbott had been hired to find.

"Keep on it, partner," said Reggie. "I've just finished up things here and will be in Bremerton shortly. I have a lot to tell you. I have a computer file I want you to see and some cassette tapes for you to hear. Also, I finally confessed to Phil what was going on, and for now he has given his blessing on our continuing the investigation."

"That's good," Toby responded.

"Oh, by the way," Reggie said, "We are getting their attention in a big way. I just received a call from Mr. Big himself; at least I think it was him. He threatened both of us and told me he was bringing in the first team."

"With what has been happening around here I'm sure we're getting their attention and I'm real flattered we have caught the attention of the big man." Toby responded.

After the call had ended Reggie called his travel agent to get tickets for him and Brandy to fly to Seattle in the morning. After confirming the tickets and getting the schedule he called Toby and gave him the flight information. His final call, before leaving the office was to Brandy to tell her the flight time.

The next morning a thoroughly rested Reggie picked up Brandy in a limousine he had rented for the purpose of transporting them to the airport. Depositing their luggage with the valet, they proceeded directly to their departure gate and fifteen minutes later boarded the flight to Seattle.

CHAPTER TWENTY-THREE

A surprise at the Port

HUDDLED IN THE corner of the tiny room the still figure gave all appearances of being dead. He had not moved for over an hour and had it been possible to see his face the haggard expression altering the once handsome features would have given credence to the supposition. A new day was dawning, but for Thomas Lincoln Graden, the third, each day was the same. A tiny beam of light made its way through one of the many cracks in the wall to the flimsy structure he called a bed. Nothing more than a few wooden slats lying over a crudely constructed frame; it had no mattress and was covered by two threadbare blankets incapable of supplying much heat. The solitary figure always welcomed the ray of sunshine, as it brought the only heat allowed in the room. It was like a friend to the emaciated, skeleton of a man. This room had been his dungeon for an indeterminable length of time, and the ray of sunshine his only companion, as he saw his captors only during meal times, with any talk kept to a minimum. He had discovered long ago his questions wouldn't be answered, as silence seemed to be the rule that was adhered to. The indistinguishable sound of voices yelling in the distance provided proof there was life outside his tiny quarters. As for food, the scarce fare was barely enough to subsist on, consisting of watered down gruel and dry bread. On occasion raw vegetables were served, but never meat or fish. Despite his growing physical weakness he kept his spirits strong with the knowledge his grandmother would never give up the search for him. *'You would be proud of me granny. This spoiled rich kid has proved his meddle.'* He slowly and painfully moved over to the ray of light, seeking the minuscule warmth it offered and dozed off wondering how much longer before they either killed him or he died of malnutrition.

Toby was jarred from his thoughts by the announcement of the arrival of Reggie's flight and looking around he saw Renie and Ruth engaged in idle chatter. They seemed to have formed a bond and had practically been inseparable since the shooting. Once again Toby became lost in his thoughts but this time he was brought to the present by Reggie's voice, "Hey, Preston, grab this bag, will you? These things are heavy."

As Toby reached over for Brandy's carry-on bag, Reggie continued, "No, not her bag, mine! Brandy can carry her own."

"Always the gentleman, my Reggie is," Brandy said, taking away the sting of his words by the affectionate hug she gave her traveling companion. "Where are these two women of yours I've been hearing so much about? You fellows wrestle the bags while we get to know each other."

Ruth and Renie had been standing apart watching the exchange between the friends and now walked up. Toby made the introductions between the women, commenting, "Ruth, you already know this big ape, so I'll ignore him. Renie, this is Reggie, the one you choose to refer as 'Uncle'."

The young girl glanced at her 'Uncle' Reggie and coyly asked, "Did you bring me a present?"

Not in the least offended or disturbed by either of the Preston clan's remarks, Reggie, simply stated, "I brought me, didn't I?" Reaching over he grabbed both women in a bear-like hug, planting a resounding kiss on their lips. "Say, you look pretty good for a lady who was in a hospital bed the last time I saw you," he said to Ruth. "And you young lady," he added to Renie, "Look just like you sounded on the phone."

"Maybe not as good as new," Ruth managed to say, recovering from the near bone-shattering embrace, "As I will have a minor limp for the rest of my life."

Toby chimed in, "We had better move if we are going to catch the Airporter. I've made reservations for the five of us, but when it's time to go they don't look around for you and we still have to get your luggage."

Toby and Reggie led the way through the terminal while the three females hung back, chatting as if they were long lost friends and had ages of gossip to catch up on. One would never know from the way they conversed that this was their first meeting. The two men talked also, but their tone was much more serious.

"From what you told me, Toby, and from what I myself have experienced since we last met, they're stepping things up a bit. The attempts on our lives would indicate we're in the middle of something pretty big. It makes me glad we are back together; there's security in numbers, even if it's only two. I never thought when my family was murdered that it would wind up being something this big. And we're still not even sure what *THIS* is yet."

Glancing back at the women, Toby, answered, "We now have extra people to be concerned about, but I have arranged for Chief Fisher to take Renie to Disney World along with his family; they leave tomorrow. The two women have already proved they know how to take care of themselves, but when we investigate the Port of Tacoma we need to leave them home."

"I agree," answered Reggie.

At this point the small entourage had arrived at the baggage carousel and their conversation turned to a lighter vein, with Reggie saying, "Do you folks in Washington believe in eating? My stomach thinks my throat has been cut."

Renie quickly reacted to this comment, "Uncle Reggie, that isn't original. I first heard that said in a movie, 'Quigley Down Under'." Turning to her father she asked, "Dad, what about Whiskey Creek? If Uncle Reggie is hungry he will love their steaks or salmon." Turning back to the older women she explained, "It's a small place out in the sticks, but they serve the best food in the county. When daddy feels like a steak that's where we go. We can celebrate your coming and my leaving; my father thinks I don't know it, but he's sending me away so I'll be safe."

The adults turned their gaze to the twelve-year-old girl, marveling at her maturity. All except Toby who raised his gaze toward heaven and said, "See what you left me with, Esther?"

When they arrived at the Preston's house they dropped their luggage off in their rooms and then climbed into Toby's Buick Roadmaster heading out in search of food.

The Sunday traffic was light; giving Toby the rising hope there wouldn't be too long of a wait at the popular eating-place. He had a hungry crowd with him and didn't want to hear any of their bellyaching Pulling into the parking lot of the restaurant he was thankful to find it practically empty and after entering the restaurant they were immediately seated. The meal proved to be everything the Preston duo had predicted. The steaks ordered by Toby and Reggie were tender enough to cut with a fork and the salmon chosen by the women was fresh and succulent. All passed on dessert and Reggie could be heard to groan as they collapsed in the car, "I'm stuffed. I couldn't possibly have eaten dessert, though that Peanut Butter Pie sure sounded scrumptious."

"Of course, you are stuffed, my sweet," declared Brandy. "After all you did finish my salmon and would have eaten Renie's if Toby didn't beat you to it."

"See what I have to put up with, Toby? Marriage to this one is going to be void of respect for my consummate skill as a member of the clean plate club."

The sound of laughter filled the car, causing Reggie to look askance at his companions. "See what I mean? I get no respect."

The short drive home was full of chatter, mostly at Reggie's expense and as Toby steered the car on its homeward path he felt he was blessed to be surrounded by friends and family, who in such a short time had become closely knit. His desire to protect them from the evil of the world filled him with such an intense feeling he found himself gripping the steering wheel tightly. He knew he was capable of anger and he also knew he would gladly kill to keep his daughter and friends from harm. This thought sobered him as he pondered what lay ahead.

Arriving home the two women fussed over Renie, preparing her for tomorrow and bed, while Toby and Reggie sat at the kitchen table drinking coffee and discussing the plans for tomorrow night's visit to the Port of Tacoma. A plan of attack was agreed upon, one that would afford an element of surprise with the least amount of physical confrontation. Neither of the men expected violence, as the people on the receiving end of the shipments were just drones necessary to see the cargo was routed to wherever it was DONE was preparing to mount their push.

Talk ceased as Ruth and Brandy entered the kitchen.

"And what kind of conspiracy are you two planning in here?" Brandy asked. "Probably how to shake us girls, so you can go off and play, I imagine."

"Actually," Reggie responded, "We were planning tomorrow's activities, which unfortunately don't include you. However, Toby has something for you to do, if you don't mind, which will keep you busy in our absence."

"It will even involve shopping, which most women thrive on," interjected Toby. "The events of the past days have impressed on me how important it is to move my end of our detective agency out of the house. I have an office space in mind downtown and need furniture and office equipment. I would probably pick everything wrong, so your good taste and judgment is being solicited. You will even get to meet a new friend—the lady, who I hope to have run the office."

"I believe we are up to the task; don't you, Ruth?' The excitement in Brandy's voice was evident as she pulled her new friend aside, already scheming over the color and décor of the yet unseen office.

"Which reminds me, I haven't called Joan yet," exclaimed Toby. "I'd better call her right away. Hopefully she doesn't go to bed too early. I have to go to my office to get her number."

As Toby walked into his office in search of Joan's phone number he could hear Reggie's voice badgering the women for not allowing him to have dessert after dinner. From the sound of the commotion they were both pummeling the hapless Reggie. Grinning with pleasure at the sound of the merriment he picked up the phone and punched in the number he had for Joan Naismith.

The phone was answered on the first ring, with Joan speaking in a terse voice. "This is Joan Naismith and no I will not work overtime tomorrow."

"Joan, this is Toby Preston, hope I didn't waken you, and I might ask you to work overtime on occasion, but not until you say yes."

"Toby, hi, I am just laying here in bed catching up on my reading, sorry about the way I answered the phone, but the only people who call me at this time of the night want me to either come to work and fix a problem or put in overtime to eliminate a problem arising. What do you mean, until I say yes?"

"I mean if you are ready to retire I have a position for you. I primarily need an assistant to run my detective agency office, but will mainly rely on your computer skills and contacts. I can put you to work yesterday, but will take you when you tell your current masters you are retiring."

The joy was evident in her voice and he could envision the almost sixty—year old woman jumping on her bed in joy as she said, "I've had my papers filled out and ready to turn in since the day you offered me a job. I can go on terminal leave tomorrow and can start work while my papers are being processed. You've just made my day. Uh, I mean night."

"I've already leased office space in the old Peoples bank building and have two eager young ladies who'll work with you in setting it up. We'll go over office procedures and salary in the next day or so. Let me put one of the ladies on the phone. Her name is Brandy Thomas. The two of you can set up a meeting place and time and begin with all the arrangements. Thanks Joan and welcome aboard."

"I can't believe I'll be starting a new career at my age, "the exuberant Joan exclaimed. "I feel like a kid again? Go ahead and put her on. Good night, boss."

Things appeared to have quieted down in the kitchen as he walked down the hall and handed the portable handset to Brandy, saying, "This is my friend Joan Naismith, who will be taking over the running of the office. Would you please talk to her and set up a meeting place and time for tomorrow?"

"Well folks, it is going to be a full day tomorrow and I'm going to turn in," Toby stated. "The Chief Fisher is coming by for Renie at eight and I need to see she is ready to go. Maria, our housekeeper will be in at seven to make breakfast for all. See you all in the morning."

"Goodnight, pal," Reggie said rising from the table. "I'm starting to drag a little myself and bed sounds good right now. How about you ladies, are you calling it a night?"

Ruth spoke up answering for both, "Not just now, when Brandy's finished talking with Joan we want to girl talk for a while."

The smell of bacon and the tantalizing aroma of brewing coffee brought the house to life the next morning. Renie had already joined Maria in preparing the morning meal and Reggie, drawn by the scent of coffee, was next to come into the kitchen. An acquaintance had once said, as long as there was coffee in the world, Reggie would be around. Nodding a good morning to the housekeeper and planting a perfunctory kiss on Renie's cheek he poured a steaming cup of java, and grabbed the morning newspaper Maria had brought in, snared a piece of bacon just out of reach of Maria and plopped down at the kitchen table.

By the time the rest of the group showed their faces Reggie was working on his second cup of coffee and Maria was starting the extra coffee maker, figuring this man was going to drink a pot by himself.

"Good morning sleepyheads," he greeted them, rising to plant a tender kiss on the lips of Brandy. "You had better watch out, Toby, I just might steal Maria away from you. She makes the best cup of coffee I have ever tasted. Little stingy with the bacon, though."

Maria waved her spatula at the effusive Reggie as she said; "This one would eat all the bacon if I let him. He is one mucho hungry hombre."

The ringing of the buzzer at the gate interrupted their morning conversations. On the close circuit monitor, Toby saw it was the Chief Fisher and pressed the button releasing the gate and then closed it after he drove through. He had changed the code but was still mindful of the fact the two DONE agents who had followed him around the previous day were still on the loose.

After brief introductions were made, followed by Renie's tearful good-byes, the chief and his family, with Renie, were on their way. For a few minutes silence prevailed, then Maria said, "Come eat, the food is getting cold. Already the little one has left without eating. Orange juice and toast, ha; what breakfast is that for a growing child."

Reggie and Toby had planned on being on the road by noon, but the conversation following the breakfast lasted much longer than either had planned on as both women were aware of the danger their men would be facing and were concerned for their welfare. No matter how much the two men tried to reassure them they refused to believe the possibility of danger wasn't ever prevalent. Finally at noon they headed out leaving behind two very worried women.

"They're right, you know," Toby commented as he headed the car down the highway toward Tacoma, a distant twenty-six miles away. "We can never be sure of what we'll be up against. I can't help but think about your near brush with death or the experience Ruth and Renie went through."

Reggie reached up and touched the side of his head where the bullet had delivered its glancing blow. "I suppose you're right, but there's more at stake than our lives. Besides I plan on living for a long time yet."

Toby offered no comment, as he knew Reggie was right. He had no desire to die, but he didn't fear the prospect. He carried the same fears as Reggie knowing that there were far more lives in jeopardy because of DONE's irresponsible actions, than just their own. If they knew a little more about them they might be able to discern motives and formulate a plan to combat them.

"Hey, Tob," Reggie asked, interrupting his thoughts, "How long has the green Expedition been following us?"

"I first picked him up at the head of the bay," Toby answered, "but I'll bet a nickel to a donut he's been with us since we left the house. It may be the same two guys only in a different vehicle who have been camped outside my house for a while. Be prepared for some heads up driving; as it looks they are aiming to ram us. They're picking up speed with no intentions of passing."

The big green SUV was accelerating at a speed well above the 60-mile per hour speed limit, Toby had been maintaining and would soon be on them unless he took evasive action.

"These guys are getting bolder, Reggie. Guess that means the word is out to quit playing games and eliminate us. I'm waiting until they are almost on us then I'm going to move into the passing lane and brake. We need to be sure they aren't just a couple of guys out on a road rage bender."

Traffic on the normally busy arterial was sparse, which allowed for some maneuverability, in fact there were no cars within Toby's limit of vision giving him the freedom to use his evasive skills. "I have never had the opportunity to check the ABS brake system. Sure hope Buick lives up to its reputation," Toby said.

The car following had reached to within twenty feet when Toby swerved into the adjacent lane and immediately applied the brakes. The Roadmaster fishtailed slightly, but Toby's firm grip kept it in check. The bigger vehicle's driver was caught unaware and shot by, but not so fast for Reggie, who saw a large automatic pistol gripped in the hand of the vehicle's passenger.

"These guys are for real, pal," Reggie yelled. "One of them has a gun in his hand." Reacting in a way that proved his reflexes were still functioning, Reggie took his own weapon from its position under his shirt and without a second thought emptied his magazine into the big car's rear end from the open passenger's side window. His accuracy was uncanny as all nine shots hit their mark; his first two blew out the back window, two more hit the approximate area of the fuel tank and the remaining five disintegrated the rear tires.

Out of control the big vehicle spun and rolled over three times before coming to rest in the median. It immediately caught fire, exploding with a tremendous sound.

"Keep driving, Toby," Reggie exclaimed, "those guys are done for and we can't afford to be questioned. My guess is it will be investigated as a rollover due to tire failure. When and if guns are discovered the State Patrol may wonder and even put the accident under investigation, but these DONE people cover their tracks pretty well and any investigation will most likely hit a dead end."

Not being callous at the extinguishing of two lives, Reggie sank back in his seat and heaved a big sigh, saying in a remorseful voice, "I never like this part, people dying, but it looked like it was them or us."

Toby, also shaken by the encounter, continued down the highway and after his breathing returned to normal looked over at his friend and said to break the tension; "At least we didn't get any scratches on my car."

They had only traveled a short distance from the rollover when they observed two State Patrol cruisers coming from the opposite direction with sirens blaring and lights flashing, apparently in response to the accident. As far as they could tell there had been no witnesses to their part in the vehicular mayhem, so they continued on, wanting to put some distance between themselves and the scene of the accident as quickly as possible.

Keeping an eye on the rearview mirror Toby proceeded up the highway toward the city of Fife and the Port of Tacoma careful to maintain the posted speed limit.

The two men had agreed it was important they arrive during daylight in order to make a reconnaissance of the port, as neither man was familiar with the area. They weren't sure what they were looking for, but from the information Reggie had forced from Peter Hatcher, the Office of Transportation and Movement would be a good place to start.

Arriving at the port area, Toby drove slowly along the thoroughfare looking for some sign of the building or yard housing the office in question. Reggie spotted it, exclaiming, "There it is, Toby, just ahead on the left."

Toby nosed the big car through the opening in the fence, noting the acres of imported cars waiting to be moved to their destinations and the long lines of boxcars sat on the railroad tracks while a dozen or more car-haulers lined the side of the road waiting to be filled with the new cars. Most of the drivers were in their cabs relaxing, with a few standing around talking. In an adjoining large yard were several other containers awaiting removal to their destinations, it was these containers, which interested Reggie and Toby the most.

Reggie remarked, "From what we learned in our discussions with Joel, it's in containers such as these that we're going to find the contraband DONE is sneaking into the country. I'm not sure how they're shipping the recruits, but what better way than disguised as deck hands. They've been doing this for a long time and there's no telling how big this army is, which means that we're going to need a lot of help."

"But for now it's up to us," Toby said. "We have no authority here and need to quietly nose around for a while. I can't understand the lack of security though; you would think with millions of dollars worth of cars sitting out here we would have seen some kind of security."

"You're right, Toby. It's almost as if everyone is on a coffee break," Reggie affirmed, also puzzled by the lack of security.

Toby had turned his gaze in the direction of a pile of gravel that had been dumped near the north side of the fence. It had been there long enough for grass to begin growing out of it. "I think I have our place to hide away until dark, Reg. Our only problem will be hiding the Buick and getting back here unobserved."

"Without knowing where everyone is we're going to have a devil of time knowing what to do. Surely they lock this gate at night and use a roving patrol car, or dogs to maintain security. If the note you found meant 10:30 pm we have time enough to plan our reentry. Sure hope there isn't any dogs, I really hate dogs not all kinds of dogs just guard dogs with big teeth."

"Why don't we drive the car down the road and leave it in the parking lot of the Emerald Queen Casino. There's traffic in and out of there until 6 am and no one will notice one more car in the lot. It's only about a mile away and the walk back will give us a chance to plan."

The plan was agreed upon and with one final look around, Toby turned the car and drove to the casino parking lot. The crowds had already begun arriving; making it slow going in finding a parking spot, but Toby finally spotted one and pulled into it.

Before climbing out of the vehicle both men crawled into black coveralls and black leather tennis shoes, as there was the possibility they would be scaling fences and running. Toby then pulled a dark tarpaulin out of the trunk, which they would use to lie on as they waited.

The sun was just disappearing over the Olympic Mountain range when Reggie and Toby approached the yard for the Office of Transportation and Movement. The gate hadn't yet been locked and the two friends were able to enter undetected. Mercury lights mounted on poles ringed the outer fence, dimly lighting the yard and a single light shone in the office of the yard manager. A vehicle with government plates was parked up against the building. Peering through the window they could make out the figure of a man sitting hunched over a desk.

In a hushed voice, Reggie commented, "This is the first activity of any type we've seen since our arrival. From what I know of the government they don't work overtime very often, so this dude may be the one DONE owns. As long as he's in there I doubt if there will be any kind of security around, so let's get into position and bed down for a couple of hours."

Both men settled down behind the pile of gravel creating as comfortable a niche in the loose material as was possible. Expecting to be there for at least three hours the two allowed themselves to doze fitfully, knowing their well-trained internal clocks wouldn't let them fall into a deep sleep.

They were instantaneously roused by the sound of tires spinning on gravel. Peering from their hiding place they observed two black vans roar through the still open gate. Armed men dressed in vests and carrying large intimidating weapons poured out of the back of the vans. Acting without voice commands some of them took up positions along the fence, while others surrounded the building. Two of the armed men kicked the door down pointing their weapons at the interior to the building. Two men dressed in conservative attire, void of any protective vests, stepped down from the front seat of one of the vans and entered the office through the splintered doorframe. From their hiding place Toby and Reggie could hear the voices of the men in the office.

Toby whispered to Reggie, "That's Samuelson and Jones, the FBI agents, what in the world are they doing here?"

The words had scarcely left his mouth when Jones stepped out onto the porch of the building and signaled the team surrounding the building to advance in the direction of the containers in the corner of the yard. From Toby's viewpoint there seemed to be fewer of the large steel containers than there had been earlier in the afternoon. Two of the men previously stationed along the fence took positions outside the building eliminating any chance of the two partners getting closer to hear the conversation taking place inside.

From the direction of the containers could be heard the sharp sound of metal snapping as bolt cutters were used to cut the locks securing the doors. Several minutes passed before the team returned to the building and the waiting vans. One of the black-garbed figures entered the building apparently relaying the findings of the search. The immediate raising of voices in the building gave indication the results weren't satisfactory as the barrage of words being shot at the official ended abruptly and the men doing the questioning, walked out of the building, climbed into the two vans and left.

The two partners remained where they were for a few minutes, to make sure the invaders had no intention of returning and then they rose from their place of concealment, advanced toward the office building, pausing under the window for a short period and then entered the building through the damaged doorway, startling the room's occupant. He started to rise from his chair, but was roughly pushed back down by Toby.

"Did you think we would leave believing your cock and bull story?" Toby belligerently asked. Dressed in their black clothing they gave the impression of being members of the assault team. "We know you were tipped off and that the goods have already left. We intend finding out what was in the shipment and how many men went with it. We aren't going to be nice guys like the others; my partner here has been trained in every type of torture known to man, so if you want to go home to the wife and kids you will cooperate."

Reggie looked askance at Toby as if to say, "Why do I have to be the bad guy?" But being up to the task and following Toby's lead, he roughly grasped the still bewildered Customs official pushing him deeper into his chair and started tying him up using nylon rope he had pulled from his coverall pocket.

He knelt in front of the bound man and removed his shoes and socks. Going around to the front of the desk, Reggie looked at the nameplate sitting there. "Timothy Heath, well, Mr. Heath when is the last time you had a pedicure? The way I do it you end up never needing another one for I remove the nails and sometimes I get a little carried away and one or two toes end up coming off also, but have no fear I'm improving. My last patient only lost two, whereas the one before that lost four."

As it turned out Reggie wouldn't have to live up to his threat for Mr. Timothy Heath truly believed every word Reggie had uttered and was eager to reveal his part in the night's deception. He wasn't a brave man and had only agreed to work with DONE for the promise of money. The words spilled out of his mouth so fast Reggie, at times, would have to slow him down in order to keep up with the information he was hearing. Toby furiously scribbled on a note pad hoping to keep a record of what was spilling out of the thoroughly frightened Heath's mouth.

After about thirty minutes Heath stopped and his head drooped to his chest. His breathing was irregular, so Reggie checked his pulse and said, "A little fast, but he'll be okay."

"Do you think we have it all?" Toby queried. "Not once did he mention names. And the only place mentioned is some compound located north of Glasgow, Montana."

"I'm reasonably sure he told us all he knows," Reggie answered. "I'm sure you caught the part about being tipped off about the raid? Which makes me wonder how the raid came about in the first place? Outside of DONE, we are the only ones who knew to expect activity here tonight."

"No, not the only ones," Toby replied, "there are two others, remember Jones told me he suspects his partner, Samuelson is a DONE operative and then how about our friend in Israel?"

"It could be the FBI guy and not Joel as he gave me his word he wouldn't have the plug pulled," Reggie protested.

"Why don't we set our friend here loose and talk about it on the way home," Toby insisted.

Reggie nodded and carefully loosened the man's bonds. Heath slumped forward almost tumbling to the floor, but an alert Reggie easily caught him, positioning him more securely in the chair. Reggie once again checked the pulse of the still figure satisfied it was okay he joined Toby outside for the walk back to the casino and the car.

Retrieving the car they headed for home. Reggie sat morosely in his seat; irritated to think his friend Joel could have gone against his word and instigated the raid. Toby sensing his friend's mood kept silent, knowing when Reggie was ready he would speak his mind. Finally when

Toby moved over to the right to exit at the 38th Street off ramp, Reggie broke his silence. "I wonder if Joel is still playing a game. First he lies to us; admittedly he ended up telling the truth, but was it the whole truth. Then he sends Ruth to spy on you. Now we're thinking he broke our trust and instigates this raid. He couldn't act on U.S. soil, so it had to have been him who alerted the Feds. No one else, except him and Samuelson could have known about a shipment coming in here."

"We have to go to the source to resolve this," Toby replied. "As soon as we get home we need to phone Joel and confront him. He has to realize the precarious position he may have put us in, should he be the one who provided the information to the Feds. Betrayal for any reason isn't acceptable."

They entered Bremerton and came to Toby's house and as he was making the turn into his driveway he noticed a strange car parked across the street. "Looks like we still have some snoops across the street," he commented to Reggie. "I saw a couple of guys inside. Maybe we could arrange a little surprise for them. I'll pull the car into the garage then we can go out the back door and scale the fence near the oak tree. We'll hit them before they know what happened."

"Lead on, buddy, I'm right behind you."

After parking the car both men then raced across the grass of Toby's back yard making good use of the concealment offered by the trees and shrubs scattered there. Scaling the fence they advanced on the two men in the car. Fortunately for Reggie and Toby the occupants of the car had attempted to place themselves as much out of the lights glow as possible and the two partners were able to come up behind the car without being observed.

Removing their weapons from hiding places under their shirts and with them in hand they simultaneously yanked open the doors of the car nearly spilling its unsuspecting occupants on the pavement.

"Don't reach for anything but the sky, dirt-bags," Reggie cried.

The startled men didn't hesitate to obey as their hands shot into the air. "We aren't armed, Nutsbagh!" exclaimed the man who had been behind the steering wheel.

"How do you know my name?" Reggie asked as he reached inside the car to turn on the dome light.

With the induction of light into the car Reggie caught a glimpse of the man who was behind the wheel, so Reggie sarcastically said, "Well what do you know, the elusive Lebowitz and Abbott, I presume. Thought you two had left the country the way you skipped out on me in Vegas."

"Take your guns out of our faces so we can talk," mumbled Abbott. He was finding it hard to talk with Toby's gun forced into this mouth. Toby, who had never met the two ex-cops, finally relented after receiving a signal from Reggie.

"I won't apologize for the rough treatment, gentlemen," Toby tersely said. "We have had a pretty rough few days and usually a strange car is the bearer of more bad tidings. You're lucky we didn't come with our guns smoking."

Lebowitz took a big gulp of air and began by saying, "We apologize for running out on you in Las Vegas, Nutsbagh, but we ran for our lives."

"Yeah," Abbott interrupted, "We must have seen something in Montana that made us targets. They shooed us out of there and followed us to Vegas expecting to eliminate us, only Sam recognized one of the goons who warned us off talking to the desk clerk in our hotel. We've been hiding out ever since."

"We're only back in the game," Lebowitz added. "Because we called Mrs. Graden and she told us you were on the job."

"I won't say your help isn't welcome, but we need someone who will stick and not run every time a gun goes off," Reggie's words were harsh and brought a quick retort from Abbott.

"Get off it, Nutsbagh, we were cops for over thirty years and have faced every kind of situation imaginable. But when we faced our enemies; we knew who they were. These guys we're up against are like ghosts. They could be anywhere. I will face anyone, even you, but I want to see my opponent."

"This has been a long night," Toby said, "Give us a phone number where we can contact you and we will get back to you one way or another."

With this said, and after receiving a contact number, the two men were dismissed and Reggie and Toby watched as the taillights of the car disappeared into the night. They turned toward the house reentering the yard in a more conventional manner.

It had been a little over twelve hours since they had said good-bye to the two women, but from the way Brandy threw herself into Reggie's arms one would think it had been twelve months. Toby stood aside and was noting the affectionate display and Reggie's red face when he too, was ambushed by the lithesome Ruth who nearly bowled him over.

"Wow!" Reggie managed to gasp out. "Imagine what kind of reception we are going to get when we are gone for more than a few hours."

"Not sure if I can stand up under it," responded Toby.

"Get use to it, guys," Brandy said. "We are here for the duration."

"For which we are thankful," Toby gratefully sighed. "Who could complain when beautiful women throw themselves into your arms?" Toby's voice then went hard as he continued, "The only thing you have to fear is what I'll do when I get my hands on your brother if he has betrayed us."

Ruth had last heard that tone when he had lit into her upon finding out that she was a Mossad agent and had been spying on him. Her face turned ashen; as she feared having to defend her brother to the man she loved.

Sensing more than seeing the conflict within her Toby gently touched her face. He wasn't able to completely regain control of his emotions, but his touch reassured her that his anger wasn't directed at her.

"We have reason to believe, my love," he finally said in as gentle a voice as he could muster, "that Joel ruined our chance to stop a shipment of men and supplies tonight. I want to call him and confront him with it, so I'm going to ask Reggie to fill you and Brandy in on what happened tonight. Be patient with me, I'm extremely upset over this setback, but there's no way I can kill your beloved brother over the phone."

Bending down he planted a soft kiss on her tender lips, taking time to wipe a tear from the corner of her eye. Giving her arm a squeeze he turned and walked into his office.

"Ruth, I'm sure Toby will do the right thing," Brandy said, trying to console Ruth.

"It's okay Ruth, I'll make sure Toby doesn't do anything rash," Reggie added.

Brandy's words seemed less than prophetic as at that very moment Toby was angrily shouting his first words to the Hebrew, Joel Garza. "What do you mean by blowing our chance to stop some of the movement of men and supplies?"

Without giving the man on the other end a chance to respond, Toby went on, "We had these guys and you—it had to be you that tipped them off."

At the other end a bewildered Joel finally managed to get a word in, "Are you high, Preston? What in Hades are you talking about?"

Toby had put the conversation on the speakerphone and Reggie, who had just walked in wanting to keep his promise to Ruth, responded, "Don't give us the innocent routine, Joel, only you could have told the Feds about the shipment coming into Tacoma."

Before Joel had time to respond, Toby once again chimed in, his voice still full of anger; "We had your word that you would wait until we had made some headway on our end, so much for being a man of your word."

There might have been several thousand miles separating the conversation, but the explosion from Joel's end could be heard as if the Mossad agent had been in the same room. "Do you think I run this country? I held my superiors off as long as I could. I almost got the axe covering your butts and all I get is this garbage."

"So you couldn't call and let us know?" Toby yelled back. "That would have been the right thing to do. At least we could have been more prepared."

"Why do you think I am at home at two in the afternoon?" Joel thundered back. "I have been confined to my quarters until news of the raid gets back here. And that was at the request of your FBI."

"Our FBI?" a subdued Toby asked.

"Yes, the agent in charge, Seth Samuelson, submitted a request to my superiors that I be kept under house arrest and all my calls out be intercepted. My own men are forced to keep their captain captive."

An enlightened Toby glanced at Reggie before responding to Joel's last declaration. "Joel, we both owe you a huge apology, I now see that the problem is on our end. Please forgive us for jumping without asking questions."

Somewhat mollified by the apology, Joel replied, "It is okay, my American friends, only your anger could have made me angry enough to reveal what I did, but maybe it is all for the best. I think I am ready to quit this business. It has made me use my sister in a shameful way. I have not only lost her respect but the respect of the man she loves for wanting to serve my country."

"If anything you have risen in my esteem," Toby came back. "If I respect and honor anything it is loyalty. Difficult decisions come with your job and you did what you had to do. Most of the damage to your reputation will be repaired soon, for we have a double-dealer in our midst. When his part is revealed your government and mine will owe you big-time."

At this point Reggie interrupted, saying, "Hey, big fellow, there's a little lady here who wants to talk to you."

Taking the phone off speaker, Toby handed the receiver to Ruth, who had entered the room at the sound of the raised voices, giving her a hug in the exchange. "Shalom," Ruth shyly said. Speaking only in Hebrew the brother and sister spoke for some time. Toby was unable to understand a single word, but from the expression on Ruth's face and her constant side-glances in his direction he had cause to believe he was a topic of their conversation. Feeling self-conscious he left his office walking back to the den to join Brandy and Reggie who had left immediately after Ruth came in.

"Well, Toby," Reggie commented, "Looks like we have some work to do. This FBI agent Samuelson needs to be dealt with. Just how do we propose doing that?"

"Jones!" Toby stated. "He suspected Samuelson long ago, but could never get hard evidence other than the tattoo on his arm. Today's revelation may not be irrefutable evidence of his complicity, but it lays the groundwork for an investigation and Jones would just love to hang him."

All talk of business ceased as a jubilant Ruth rushed into the room and flung herself on Toby's lap, excitedly saying, "Joel gave his blessing! We can get married! I was so afraid he would not allow it after you were so angry, but he loves you even more because you stood up against him."

By the time the laughter had ended the four friends realized how exhausted they were and slowly toddled off to their respective rooms and bed. Life continued to present its complications, but weathering each obstacle as it presented itself brought the friends into a closer bond.

CHAPTER TWENTY-FOUR

The Partners continue to apply pressure

REGGIE WOKE WITH a start, once again his night had been filled with dreams of demons chasing he and Brandy through an endless maze. *'What's it going to take to get a decent night's sleep?'* Climbing out of bed, he walked to the window of his bedroom and looked outside at the lush green foliage surrounding Toby's house. It had rained overnight and when he opened the window the cool fresh morning breeze brought the delightful smell of the rich fir and pine trees into his room. Finally looking at the clock, he knew he should hurry with his morning preparations, as he was sure Toby would already be up and about.

Toby was indeed awake for some time, and was sitting in his office contemplating their next move, while the disturbing conversation with Joel, the previous evening, weighed heavily on his mind. Sitting there a sudden inspiration came to him and he walked over to the file cabinet in the corner of the room, he moved it aside revealing the safe hidden underneath. Opening the safe he began going through the compartments within the safe; finally finding what he sought a sly smile came over his face, *'This should at least get us in the front door of RIC.'* He then removed a card from the stack of stock certificates then closed, locked the safe and moved the filing cabinet back to its original position.

Leaving his study Toby looked down the hallway and saw Reggie coming out of his room, "Good morning pal, I trust you slept well?"

"I slept okay," was Reggie's reply. "I would like to see more sunshine around here, but one thing I can say about your Pacific Northwest, it sure does smell nice in the morning. I haven't smelled anything this fresh since I was a kid and cut grass to earn money."

Arriving in the kitchen both men greeted Maria, who acknowledged their greetings by pouring them a cup of coffee.

Sipping his coffee Reggie asked, "Well what's on tap for this morning? Are we going to try and shake things up at RIC and watch them squirm? I'm primed and ready to go and really think it's about time we start pushing them for a change."

At Reggie's comment the sly smile returned to Toby's face as he responded, "I agree and also think it's time we go on the offensive. I have found a wedge which will allow us to at least get our feet in the front door of RIC, and then we'll have to wing it from there. It just dawned on me this morning that Esther, God Bless her, had bought a large block of stock in RIC when they first went public, I had completely forgotten about it until now. Checking my safe I found the stock certificates and a business card from the agent handling the stock. We're going to pay him a visit this morning and once we get in the door to RIC we can get lost and maybe wander into the wrong office and ask the right questions."

Ruth and Brandy, along with Joan had laid out plans among themselves for the day and were impatient to get started decorating Toby's new office. So as soon as breakfast was completed they shooed the men out of the house so they could get started.

On their way to Seattle, Toby chuckled out loud, "Can you believe that, seems like they couldn't wait for us to leave so they could go out and spend money. I don't care what country a woman is from or what nationality she is, they all have one thing in common, they all like to go shopping and spend money. And it's even better when it's not their money they're spending."

For their trip to Seattle Toby decided to use the ferry, wanting to show Reggie a different view of the area he called home. When Toby drove the jeep onto the ferry Reggie commented, "I sure hope the guy driving this thing knows what he's doing; I can swim but would sure hate to try in these cold choppy waters."

Toby assured him it was completely safe and that there hadn't been an accident with the Bremerton to Seattle ferry run that he could remember.

Driving off the ferry in Seattle they found the traffic slow and congested as usual, but Toby, despite his dislike of Seattle, managed to maneuver his way through the maze, and soon pulled in front of the Rainer Investment Company building.

"We don't have an appointment," said Toby, "but as an investor I should be able to bully my way in on some pretext. Not even sure what we expect to find in here."

The interior of the investment firm's lobby was impressive with many pictures and murals of Mt. Rainer done by local artists. Even the shiny granite floor was inlaid in different colors showing a to-scale picture of the mountain's craggy peaks. A large male receptionist was standing at a counter in the middle of the lobby talking to two middle-aged men. Their briefcases were open in front of them while the man behind the desk searched their contents. His position blocked access to a bank of elevators leading to the various floors of the building. A bulge under his arm was evidence he carried a large pistol.

"This doesn't look to be a very friendly place," commented Reggie quietly. "Maybe they're doing so well they don't welcome new investors."

Refraining from immediately responding to Reggie's sarcastic comment, Toby fingered the business card he had stuck in his shirt pocket earlier that morning. "Here, I hope is our ticket to the elevators," holding up the business card with the big letters RIC emblazoned on it. "This has my account number and agent on it and should get us past this hairy gorilla."

"What do you two want?" The receptionist demanded, his tone of voice and attitude raising Reggie's hackles.

"To start with a little improvement in your attitude," Reggie answered. And then without warning he grabbed the guard posing as a receptionist by the shirtfront and with a mighty heave, yanked him over the counter. With his free hand he removed the weapon from under his arm and ejected the clip. "Now my friend here just happens to be a client and we will be going up the elevator to see his agent." Scooping up the clip and pocketing it along with the weapon, he threw the guard back across the counter, where he crumpled to the floor. "If you're a nice boy and say please I may give your toy back to you when we come back down."

Turning his back Reggie walked over to the bank of elevators where Toby was waiting. "You really need to learn how to control that temper, Reggie," Toby quipped. "According to the directory, my agent is on the 16th floor and there are no listings above the 19th. However, before coming in I counted 20, so the people we are looking for must be on the 20th. What do you say we pay them a visit?"

Stepping back to the counter Reggie reached underneath and after a few seconds of studying the panel hidden there he pushed a button, which opened the doors of the one elevator that had been cordoned off. "This is the express to the top floor. We can expect a hostile reception when we arrive."

"Catch the doors before they close," Reggie said to his ever-amazed friend. "Maybe I can eliminate some of the hostility." Walking over to the guard, who was still groggy from the first encounter, he grabbed him by the collar, yanked him to his feet and pulled him into the waiting elevator.

"Gaining access shouldn't be a problem, you have an account and an agent and I have this idiot to vouch for me," Reggie said.

The elevator slowly rose to the top floor and stopped and when the door opened two more of the 'hairy gorillas' were positioned on either side of the open door of the elevator. Seeing them, Reggie, holding the other guard in front of him, walked out of the elevator, looked around and smiled, asking, "Is this the house-wares department?"

"I guess not," Toby spoke up, moving from behind Reggie, "You guys don't look like any store clerks I've seen lately. Take it easy, be good and nothing will happen. The first thing I want you to do is to remove the hardware from under your coats, slowly, or my partner will see to it that the first wrong move you make will be your last. We're here on business and your partner here seemed to take exception to the fact we weren't dressed for the occasion."

Seeing by the look in Toby's eyes he meant business, both men slowly reached under their coats and removed their handguns then bending over placed them on the floor in front of them.

"Now kick them in my direction," Reggie added.

Once that had been done the taller of the two men, spoke up, "What's this all about and who in the hell do you think you are?"

"I'm nothing more than an investor," was Toby's answer, "in fact a heavy investor, in this company, who was denied access to his agent by this idiot, who my partner disarmed and is now holding securely. I came here on business and was treated rather shabbily by this bumbling idiot and decided to plead my case with the man upstairs, so here I am, upstairs."

Spying a door down the hallway imprinted with the title 'Chief Executive Officer', Toby continued, "I see where I want to go, so if you two will just step into the elevator along with your friend here, we will be about our business."

Looking hard at Toby, with a look that said more than any words could, the two men moved into the elevator. Reggie shoved the other man in and still covering them, reached in through the open door and punched the button labeled G, for ground floor. The elevator door closed and started its journey to the ground floor.

Reggie took one of the guns from Toby and lodged it behind the elevator door insuring when the three returned to the top floor they would have a hard time getting the door open.

Both men then walked down the hall and without knocking, entered the door marked CEO. The first thing they saw was a pretty woman sitting behind a large desk working on a computer. As they walked through the door she looked up with a startled expression on her face and managed to stammer out, "What are you doing here, I wasn't told by security that they had authorized anyone to come to this floor."

Toby looked at the receptionist with a grin on his face and replied, "Well they really didn't have a choice in the matter and to answer your other question, no, I don't have an appointment. But I'm going in to see, what did you say his name was?"

"I didn't say and as you don't have an appointment I can't let you go into his office." The woman had overcome her initial shock and was attempting to gain control of the situation.

Toby stepped up in front of the desk and spoke in a very soft, yet firm voice, "Young lady, I happen to be the proud owner of a whole lot of stock in this company. The man listed as my agent, at the time, might have been promoted and could be sitting behind a very large desk in a wonderfully decorated office behind that door. I fully intend on going into that office and have a heart to heart discussion with him. Now you can admit us nicely or we'll be obligated to force our way in. One way or another we are going into that office."

The receptionist looked up with a very confused expression on her face and said, "But, Sir, Mr. Davenport is extremely busy at the present time and told me to see he wasn't disturbed for the next hour or until he called me. Do you want me to get fired?"

"No Ma'am, I don't want to see you get fired, but it's urgent I see him. I don't care how busy he is and what he's doing, he's going to see me."

Saying this Toby started for the door leading into the inner office. As he moved towards the door the receptionist flipped the switch on the intercom and hurriedly spoke into it, "Mr. Davenport there are two men out here that insist on seeing—"

Before she could finish her warning, Reggie reached across the desk and pulled the cord out of the back of the intercom box, as he did Toby opened the door to the CEO's office and stepped inside.

When Toby pushed the door open he heard the sound of a door being closed and the click of a lock being pushed into place.

Entering they were faced by a large man sitting behind a massive oaken desk. Two partially filled glasses of amber liquid sat on the edge of the desk. The nameplate on the desk proclaimed him to be, Hamilton Davenport, CEO, Rainer Investment Company.

The man they assumed was Davenport shoved his chair back from the desk and with anger evident in his voice said, "What in the hell is the meaning of this? How dare you force your way past my security guards and secretary then enter my office. You have five seconds to convince me why I shouldn't call the police and have you forcibly removed from my office and this building."

Glancing around the room, Toby saw a beautifully decorated office that included a large library of books and what appeared to be a well stocked bar in the corner of the office.

On one of the walls hung a large painting depicting the Olympic Mountains while on the other wall hung a large decorative mirror. If Toby could have seen through this mirror he would have observed the figure standing behind it.

The figure peering out through the two-way mirror had recognized Toby and Reggie as they entered. He barely managed to get into the hidden room before they barged in. As he watched he smiled wryly and said to himself, *"Well, well we finally meet. I must admit you are persistent, but you both have become a thorn in my side and it is time to extract the thorn."*

Hamilton broke into Toby's examination of the office, saying, "If you didn't hear me your time is almost up."

No sooner was this out of Hamilton's mouth, than Reggie broke into the conversation and said, in a voice filled with anger and disdain, "No, it's not our time that's almost up, it's yours and DONE's time, which is almost up!"

At this comment the figure standing behind the mirror quietly laughed to himself, *"Mister Nutsbagh, you have no idea what DONE is and what it can do. If you did you wouldn't be standing there saying things you can't possibly back up."*

"You two must be out of your minds coming in here accusing me of being part of some terrorist organization," was Hamilton's response.

At this point Toby entered the conversation, "In the first place who said DONE was a terrorist organization and who inferred you were part of this mysterious organization."

"Then, I have absolutely no idea what you are talking about and your five seconds are up, so why don't both of you get the hell out of my office, right now!"

Reggie gazed long and hard at the man who claimed to have no knowledge of DONE and its activities, his eyes narrowed, got hard and his voice was filled with hatred as he spoke in cold, calculating tones, "I'm sure you are up to your corporate neck in DONE and its many and diverse activities, so let me tell you a few things. My partner and I will stop you and will make you pay for what you have done to our families and are doing in this country. We will not stop until you and all of your friends are either dead or behind bars where you belong."

Pulling on his partner's arm, Toby was forced to physically restrain Reggie, saying, "Slow down, Reg, our turn will come and then we'll both grab them and turn them every which way but loose."

Reggie slowly gained control of his emotions and stepped back from Hamilton's desk saying with all the contempt he could muster, "Hamilton, both you and I are lucky Toby is here. You, because he stopped me from killing you right where you sit and me that he is such a good friend he couldn't allow me to commit cold-blooded murder, no matter how evil you are."

Toby placed his hand on Reggie's shoulder saying, "Well, I think we've found out all we need to know. The only thing I have left to do is divest myself of all the stock I own in this ill-begotten company and buy something which stands for America. Don't bother to get up, Hamilton we'll show ourselves out. And should we meet again you had better have more and better security around you than those idiots you have out in the hallway and that dummy on the ground floor."

The laughing figure behind the mirror was highly amused watching Hamilton squirm under the verbal assault of the two partners. He had known for a long time Hamilton didn't have the stomach for such a venture and sooner or later would outlive his usefulness and when that time came he would meet the same fate as Harold Johnson. *'These two, Preston and Nutsbagh, are good, but they have yet to meet the first team, but they will real soon!'*

The two partners stomped their way out of Hamilton's office not breaking stride as they walked past the secretary standing in the middle of her office with her mouth wide open. They retraced their steps down the hallway to the elevator and went back to the ground floor.

Upon reaching the ground floor they saw the same individual back at the reception desk and as they exited the elevator and walked towards the front door the man didn't say anything to them, in fact he averted his eyes and pretended to be occupied with some papers on his desk.

As the two partners left the building and headed for their vehicle, a limousine turned the corner coming out of the alley that ran along side of the RIC building. Toby and Reggie stopped and watched with curiosity as the limo came towards them. When the vehicle came abreast of their position the front passenger side window opened and the man sitting in the passenger seat put his hand out the window as if holding a pistol and his mouth formed the words, 'Bang you're dead'. It was one of the men, who Reggie and Toby had bested on the 20th floor of the RIC building.

Meanwhile, in the back of the limo the passenger was using his car phone. After the third ring the phone was answered, "Hello."

"Put Number One on."

After a brief pause, a voice came on, "Number One, Sir."

"Number One, I want you to have six good men ready for combat sitting in the safe house in Seattle the day after tomorrow."

After the limo passed the two partners, Toby turned to Reggie and said, "I sure would like to know who was sitting in the back seat of that limo. After our conversation with Hamilton I don't think he's smart enough or tough enough to run an organization as diverse as DONE. I suspect we were close enough to Mr. Big to spit on him."

A little over an hour later they pulled into the parking lot of the old Peoples Bank building in Bremerton, where Toby's new office was located. Entering the office Toby was amazed at the transformation it had under gone in just the few short hours he and Reggie had been in Seattle.

All three of the ladies were present attempting to rearrange the furniture and were pleasantly surprised to see the two men walk in the front door. Toby seeing Joan walked over to her and introduced her to Reggie as the one who would be running the office.

After Reggie and Joan acknowledged the introductions and greeted each other, Toby continued, "One of the first things we need to do is to give her your office phone numbers and have her touch base with Hilda, so they can at least recognize each other's voice. Then give her the rest of your phone numbers, cell phone, apartment and house." Glancing at Brandy to insure she was listening, Toby continued, "Although, I understand you will not be using the apartment much longer."

Reggie looked at Toby, grinned, then replied, "Not use my apartment, do you know something I don't?"

"See, Toby it's exactly like I told you he's a hard man to tie down," interjected Brandy with a smile on her face.

"I can see both of our guys are cut from the same cloth, I can not get Toby to set a date either." Ruth yelled from across the room.

Toby, looking at this watch, said, "Hey ladies, I hate to break this up, but I refuse to start Joan's first day off with overtime. So why don't we lock up and get out of here. Tomorrow is another day. By the way, Joan we are going to Tony Romas later for dinner, how about joining us?"

"I would love to, boss, what time are you going?"

"I'll pick you up around 7:30 pm, if that's alright."

Later that evening after all the others had said their 'goodnights' Toby sat in his study completing some last minute details concerning the leasing of the office space when his phone rang. He picked up the phone and said, "Preston."

"I see you are still playing around with the second team, huh Preston." The gravelly voice began the conversation without preamble. *"Hamilton was a pussy cat compared to what's in store for you and Nutsbagh later, both of you need to crawl back into your holes or you will be put in holes, permanently."* With a sadistic laugh the connection was broke

CHAPTER TWENTY-FIVE

A Strike in the Park

T HE LARGE GABLED house with its beautiful view of the
Puget Sound and majestic Olympic Mountain range sat serenely
nestled amidst the tall evergreen trees. A locked ornate gate and a 10-foot
high cyclone fence discouraged any who might be curious as to what went
on within the confines of the fenced area. Except for a caretaker who
maintained the yard there had been little activity at the house until today
when an airport limousine service arrived and delivered six passengers.
Once inside the men never left the house or showed their faces outside
or in one of the many windows. They had only been there a short time
when the phone rang, after ringing only twice it went silent, none of the
six men, sitting around the dining room table, moved or showed any
sign of having heard the shrill sound. Exactly thirty seconds later the
phone rang again but this time the receiver was picked up immediately
by the sallow-faced man sitting at the head of the table. He listened
intently, never interrupting, answering only in short syllables, as the
gravelly sounding voice at the other end spoke. The conversation lasted
only twenty seconds.

Hanging up, the evident leader looked at the five other men, and said,
"We have our mission. Two men across the water in Bremerton, names
of Nutsbagh and Preston, have been making a nuisance of themselves
and are to be eliminated. Get some sleep we leave at 0300."

No words were exchanged between the team of carefully selected
men; the only sounds heard were those of breeches being opened and
rammed shut as the team of assassins checked the tools of their trade.
Each of the assembled team members had killed before. Some of them
had killed in the service of their country, now it was for the thrill and

the money. They had no political affiliation or motivations in the name of loyalty, Nutsbagh and Preston were nothing more than a couple of names. It was just a job.

Toby awoke suddenly out of a deep sleep, he was attuned to every noise in his house, and an unfamiliar sound had reached his subconscious mind. He was used to the clocks chiming and the occasional hum of the refrigerator, all the normal sounds of the house, but what had roused him was none of those. Reaching under his pillow for the gun, which had just recently become part of his bedding, he silently slipped out of bed and edged toward the bedroom door. He very slowly turned the knob and inched the door open. There were no lights showing under the doors of the other rooms, so he assumed he was the only occupant of the house moving around. He held his gun in the ready position as he moved stealthily in the direction of the kitchen, advancing with extreme caution.

A single light over the kitchen sink dimly lit the room. Sweeping the kitchen with his eyes, always keeping the pistol pointing in the direction his eyes were moving, he detected nothing out of the ordinary and was moving toward the laundry room when he heard a voice behind him ask, "Do you always walk around the house wearing nothing but shorts and a pistol?"

Lowering his weapon at the sound of Reggie's voice, he turned around, staring at his friend in the dimly lit room and replied, "Only when I'm looking for vermin. What are you doing up?"

"Couldn't sleep," Reggie answered. "You must have pretty big rats to go hunting them with a .38."

"There seems to be rats lurking everywhere lately. I was sleeping soundly when a noise woke me. With all that has been going on I didn't want to leave it to chance. Now since we are both awake how about going down to Lion's Field and taking an early morning jog? I've been eating so much this last couple of days that I'm beginning to feel like a slug."

"Sounds good to me," Reggie returned.

After both men had dressed in jogging suits, Toby walked back into his office and removed a box from his floor safe. Tucking the box under his arm he hesitated long enough to leave a note for Ruth telling her where they had gone and approximately when they expected to return, and then headed for the garage.

Before backing his '57 Chevrolet out of the garage Toby reached into the box he had brought along removing two 32-caliber pistols both in ankle holsters. Handing one of them to Reggie, he commented, "It may not be a cannon, but it gives me a comfortable feeling knowing I have it."

With the exception of an ambulance entering the highway from the direction of Preble Street and two vehicles entering the Navy Shipyard, the traffic was minimal. A taxi joined them for a few blocks, leaving them when they turned onto Warren Avenue. The ambulance followed them over the Warren Avenue Bridge and down to Lebo Boulevard, and then turned right toward the hospital, while Toby turned left in the direction of the field.

"I don't envy those guys," commented Reggie, who had been watching the vehicle in the rearview mirror, "Especially when they have to give mouth-to-mouth. Remember riding with a couple of young EMT's once, they were responding to a call of a man in distress on the Strip."

When Toby turned the car into Lion's Field, the ambulance made a U-turn, following them with its lights off. The emergency vehicle stopped at the entrance to the playing field and six black-clad figures silently slipped out. All the interior lights had been turned off and the doors of the vehicle were left slightly ajar as the team of assassins took every precaution in their attempt at surprise. The move across the street was accomplished with military precision as each man zigzagged singly, using the parked cars and available shrubs in the yards of the bordering houses to conceal their actions. Their timing and movement had been so precisely carried out that Reggie and Toby had just emerged from the car when the first bullet struck Toby in the chest knocking him back against the car where he collapsed limply to the pavement.

Reacting on instinct Reggie hit the pavement and rolled under the car, yanking his downed partner under the car and out of the hail of bullets that followed. Not taking time to examine his fallen friend's wound he slid out from under the car on the opposite side of the attack and made for the utility shed just yards away darting to the left and then the right in an attempt to avoid the missiles of death aimed at him.

A bullet struck him in the leg causing him to stumble, regaining his balance he managed to limp to the shed where he immediately pulled the small caliber pistol from its hiding place.

'*The only way this peashooter is going to do any good is at close range,*' he mumbled. '*With the firepower they are throwing at me that's unlikely to happen.*'

Knowing that staying in one place would seal his fate he looked around for another place to move to when another hail of bullets nearly disintegrated the wooden shed. Keeping as low to the ground as possible he charged the twenty yards to the rocky shoreline receiving a glancing blow to his shoulder just as he dove for what cover the jutting boulders afforded.

From the direction of the demolished shed he had just left he heard a voice bellow, "Move in on him and finish him off and hurry it, we'll be having company soon."

So far Reggie had returned no fire, making his assailants wrongly assume he was unarmed. The morning sun was just beginning to show its head over the distant mountain range, but it was still dark enough for Reggie to raise his head over the boulder he was crouched behind and catch a glimpse of five figures advancing in his direction.

The sixth man had stayed behind to finish off the wounded or dead Toby, who was still lying under the car. Over confident, the black-garbed man lay on his stomach with his weapon on the pavement beside him and using both hands yanked the inert form toward him. It was to be the last mistake he would ever make, for Toby, using the .32, which he had managed to free from its ankle holster, put a bullet into his heart. The clothing the assailant wore and the fact that the pistol had been pressed forcefully into his chest muffled the sound of the shot.

From the intense pain in his chest Toby was sure he had at least some broken ribs. Feeling under his sweatshirt he ran his fingers over the indentation in the Kevlar vest, which he wore underneath. '*I sure am thankful Reggie insisted on our wearing our vests this morning.*' he thought.

Grabbing the dead man's weapon, he checked its load and then hastily searched the body, removing a large knife and two magazines for the Uzzi machine pistol. Taking dead aim at the nearest figure, he fired off half of the gun's magazine, striking his target and sending the others scurrying. One of the four remaining attackers made the mistake of diving for cover behind a boulder near Reggie and was met by the deadly shooting of Reggie and his little 'peashooter'.

Crawling to the fallen man, Reggie confiscated the weapon and unleashed a deadly fire of his own, catching one of the opposing forces in the chest as he rose from behind a shrub. The remaining two members of the team of assassins had seen their odds dwindle to two against two, not liking the even odds they retreated in the direction of the ambulance. Toby, though in pain from his chest wound, raced after them. Willing himself to go on despite the excruciating pain in his chest he caught the slower of the two and brought him down with a tackle.

As Toby wrestled with the man, Reggie, despite his wounds, took up pursuit of the other man as the sound of sirens could be heard approaching. It had taken long enough, but finally a concerned citizen had contacted the authorities. Wounded as he was Reggie managed to catch the man he was chasing just as he opened the door of the ambulance.

The sallow-faced man raised the .45 caliber pistol, which was tightly gripped in his fist and pointed it at Reggie, only to be met with a stream of bullets from the Uzzi machine gun Reggie had confiscated earlier. Turning, he ran back across the street to where he had left Toby grappling with the remaining assailant. As he neared he saw two figures lying still on the ground; the black-clad man lay across Toby's chest. Concerned about his friend, Reggie reached down and pulled the man aside; the knife, which Toby had confiscated earlier, was buried to the hilt in the man's chest.

"Thanks Pal," a winded Toby offered. "I didn't have the strength to push him off. I think I may have some busted ribs, but I would have been a goner if you hadn't advised wearing the Kevlar."

Four cars rolled up at that instant with the officers jumping out and surrounding the two friends. Both men were ordered to raise their hands and were in the process of being handcuffed when one of the arriving officers, Cpl. Terry Sloan, recognized his former lieutenant, and ordered them released.

"What went down here, lieutenant?" Cpl Sloan asked.

Old habits are hard to break and the respect Toby had earned during his time on the Force kept most of his former police officer subordinates using the title they had known him by.

"Right now I wish I knew, Terry," Toby answered, not wanting to mention or implicate DONE. "I, and my friend and partner here, Reggie

Nutsbagh, came down for an early morning jog and these six ambushed us. You can see what they were packing while all we had were a couple of .32's."

By then an emergency vehicle had arrived and both men's wounds were being tended. Even though Reggie had suffered some loss of blood his wounds were not serious enough to require hospitalization. One of the technicians tightly bound Toby's ribcage and he advised Toby to go in for x-rays later in the day. Two of the police officers lent Reggie and Toby their jackets upon request, ostensibly to ward off the possibility of shock.

Along with the police, Julie Stern, one of the local reporters, had also arrived on the scene. Recognizing Toby, she walked over to where he and Reggie were standing, "What brings you out this time of the morning, Preston? I understood you were no longer on the force, so why are you wearing a Police jacket?"

Rather than lie to the Press, Toby chose to be evasive and responded by saying, "I was getting a little chilly and the men in blue offered their jackets. As for what my friend Reggie and I are doing out this time of the morning we were out jogging and happened to get in the middle of a fracas. Since I'm no longer an officer I can't really tell you much more."

"You must have been in here before things happened to have your car shot up like that."

Turning away from the reporter, Toby looked at his automobile for the first time and spoke in a matter of fact voice, "Looks as if it's back to work for me, going to take a little more than paint to fix it up."

Perturbed at not having received any reportable facts from the former lieutenant, she folded her arms across her chest and addressed Reggie, "And what do you think, Mr.—"

"Just call me Reggie," he replied, "All this mister stuff is too formal. I agree with Toby, it's going to take more than a little paint this time, Ms Stern."

Completely exasperated, the pert reporter tried a new tactic. Batting her eyelashes she tried some of her feminine wiles, appearing to be the helpless female, "Come on you guys, I'm just trying to do a job here. I can't go back to the desk without a story."

Acting the part of a truly caring person, Toby took her by the elbow and guided her toward where the other reporters were gathered. As he directed her he said in a conspiratorial tone, "We are here making a movie and this is no real crime scene."

Knowing Toby was being flippant with her she jerked her elbow free of his grasp and made a beeline to where Terry Sloan had now gathered the reporters to give the standard police response to their many questions.

"Corporal Sloan, how do former lieutenant Preston and his friend fit into this? Were they involved in the shooting? Or are they just innocent bystanders?"

Caught in mid-sentence the Bremerton police officer continued on and then addressed the persistent questioner, "Ms Stern, apparently you were not here when I started this interview, so I will repeat what I have already said for your benefit. This entire incident where six men were slain is still under investigation. Involvement of any other individuals has not been established as yet. Thus far there has been no motive determined. No evidence of drugs was found on the scene therefore we have concluded it wasn't a drug deal gone sour. A full report will be released to the media once the investigation has advanced far enough to satisfy the Department. Thank you, ladies and gentlemen, this interview is over."

Having finished, the police officer strode over to where Toby and Reggie stood and asked, "What did you guys say to get Stern so riled up?"

"I think it's what we didn't say, Terry," Toby answered. "Thanks for loaning us the jackets, she noticed them right off the bat and would have been all over us if she had seen the blood. Is there any reason why we need to hang around here any longer?"

"No, just don't leave town without letting us know. And get those wounds tended to."

"Terry, about this going out of town, can't you forgo that order?" asked Toby. "We have a trip out of state planned for tomorrow and can't possibly delay it."

Looking at the two with a thoughtful expression, Cpl Sloan said, "I can't really make that decision, but since we have your statements and it seems clear you were the victims I'm sure the Captain will let you leave on your own cognizance. Check with me before you leave, okay?"

Agreeing to do as asked the two friends headed for the bullet-riddled convertible and the ride home, where it was certain two women anxiously waited.

"With all these bandages we're sporting, there'll be no way we can play this down," commented Reggie.

"Yeah," Toby said, "they may even begin to have second thoughts about marrying a couple guys who are always getting shot up. We certainly give them cause to worry."

"There must be an easier way for us to prove our manliness," stressed Reggie.

"A less painful way, at least," moaned Toby.

When they drove up to the house, Ruth and Brandy came out to meet them and after entering the house the men recounted the events of the morning, downplaying their own heroics. The women had chosen these men and voiced no regrets as they listened to their most recent brush with death, thankful, that even though wounded, they were home.

Still discussing the events of the morning they walked into the kitchen where Maria was preparing breakfast. Even though she seemed oblivious to everything, she was, however, sending prayers of her own to 'Dios' above for the safety of her benefactor and employer.

Breakfast was eaten in near silence as the four dealt with the morning activities in their own way and when the meal was finished Toby headed to his bed for some much-needed rest. Brandy and Ruth left to meet with Joan in the hopes of getting the office finished and Reggie went into Toby's office. Maria moved about the kitchen humming loudly as she began her other household duties.

The sound of the phone ringing interrupted the music of her humming. Answering it she said, "This is the Preston residence, how can I help you?"

"This is Agent Terry Jones of the FBI; may I speak to Mr. Preston, please?"

Speaking without thinking, Maria answered, "Mr. Toby has been shot and is in bed resting. Can you call back some more time?"

The alarmed FBI agent excitedly asked, "Shot? How? Where? When?"

"Excuse me Senor; I can not answer all these questions. I will get Senor Reggie. You will speak to him. Momento, please."

Setting the phone down she hurried to Toby's office catching Reggie just as he was about to call Joe.

"Senor Reggie, a man from the FBI wants to talk to Senor Toby; can you talk to him so the Senor can sleep?"

Putting down his cell phone, Reggie spoke to the concerned woman, "Yes, Maria, I will talk to him in here. Hang up the kitchen phone, please."

Picking up the phone sitting on Toby's desk, he began, "This is Reggie Nutsbagh, can I help you?"

"Mr. Nutsbagh, my name is Terry Jones; I'm an agent with the local office of the FBI. The Mexican housemaid told me Toby had been shot. What's the story?"

Reggie's response was to ask a question of his own. "Are you in your office now, Agent Jones?"

"Yes I am," Jones answered, "Why".

"Why don't you come here; I will meet you at the gate and let you in. By then Toby will have rested a little and the three of us will sit down and talk."

Agreeing to come right away, Jones hung up.

Reggie walked out of the house and had just reached the gate when a black Crown Victoria with government plates rounded the corner and started up the drive. The car stopped and the man behind the wheel stepped out. Reggie detected a shoulder holster under the conservative jacket of the agent.

"Put your weapon in the car and lock it," he ordered. "You can leave the car here and we can walk up to the house."

Not used to such brusque treatment, but recalling his previous reception at Toby's hands, he decided against protesting. After doing as he was instructed he entered the gate and walked with Reggie to the house.

No conversation passed between the two during the brisk walk. Reggie opened the door and directed Jones to Toby's office, stopping just long enough to tap lightly on Toby's bedroom door.

As soon as Toby's head hit the pillow he had immediately fallen into a deep sleep, yet the light tapping brought him out of his sleep just as quickly as he had fallen into it. Grasping the gun, which was nestled under his pillow, he asked, "Yes?"

"Sorry to wake you, pal, but you have a guest."

Gingerly sliding over the edge of the bed Toby arose and slipped into a pair of leisure pants. Not sure who the guest was he donned a robe, slid the pistol into one of the pockets and headed for his office.

Seeing the FBI man seated in one of the chairs in his office, he queried, "What brings you here, Agent Jones?"

Noting the heavily wrapped chest of Toby, he responded, "Actually your friend here did, but it was curiosity more than anything. Your maid mentioned you had been shot and Reggie wouldn't talk over the phone."

Receiving a nod of assent from Reggie, Toby briefly gave an account of the morning's activities, which led to Reggie and he being wounded. The account retelling left him a little dizzy and he glanced at Reggie signaling him to continue.

"So, Agent Jones, you called here not knowing what had gone down this morning, which means you had something on your mind. How about telling us what prompted your call."

From the pallor of Toby's face Terry Jones knew he would be dealing mostly with Reggie, so turning in his chair he looked at Reggie and answered his question.

"I had explained to Preston earlier that I have been suspicious of my station head, Seth Samuelson, for some time now. Well, a couple of days ago we had an operation at the Port of Tacoma, which should have yielded valuable information along with arms and supplies we believed were headed for DONE. We had confirmation from an impeccable source, yet when we arrived there was nothing, not even dust from recently departed vehicles. Our source, Samuelson and I, were the only ones who knew we would be conducting a raid that night. I was so livid I almost confronted him with my suspicions."

"I know," Reggie, responded, "we were there. In fact we used the memory of your visit to squeeze the truth out of Heath about what happened at the port prior to your raid. We know who your source is and deplore the way the FBI treated him."

Jones sat open-mouthed, stunned that the debacle, which had started out as a well-planned operation, had been witnessed by a couple of private investigators whose presence had gone undetected. He wasn't sure what upset him more; the revelation his humiliation had been witnessed or the knowledge two supposed amateurs had escaped detection by his men.

Finally finding the words to speak, he asked, "How did you find out about the shipment and how did you manage to slip by the team we had posted at the gate?"

"The how's and why's are not relevant, "Reggie shot back. "What we're concerned with here is the leaking of information from your office. I refuse to believe the FBI with all its tradition is rotten, but your man Samuelson is. He has caused a lot of damage and is being allowed to run around unchecked."

An angry Jones retorted, "And what do you expect me to do; just blow him away? The man is my boss and I can't even blow the whistle on him without feeling repercussions from the top down. The Bureau doesn't take lightly accusations of top-level agents; especially field chiefs with distinguished records."

Toby spoke for the first time, "It looks as if we are going to have to take things in our own hands then. We can't have someone with access to vital information blocking us at every turn. Where is he right now?"

Jumping in before the agent could answer, Reggie declared, "I know what you have in mind Toby, and in your condition I strongly advise against it."

It was as if the FBI agent didn't exist as the two friends faced each other. The one's face reflecting concerns for a wounded comrade while the other showed determination.

"Don't you see, Reggie, the only way we are going to be able to beat this guy is take him out ourselves. I don't mean kill him, for he is an official of the U.S. Government, but we have to get him out of the picture."

"And how do you intend doing that?" Reggie questioned.

"By using him," he said, pointing at Agent Jones. "He can set up a meeting for us with Samuelson. All he needs to say is that we have information about DONE, which we wish to share with the FBI. Once we have our audience with him we give him the full story on today's attack and let it slip, that in the search of one of the men we found information leading us back to Israel. Hopefully it will put them off guard while we make our plans for a look at Montana."

At the mention of Montana, Reggie gave his friend a look as if to remind him that their upcoming trip there wasn't for broadcasting. It had always been understood that they wouldn't divulge information to just anybody and Reggie wasn't yet ready to trust Jones.

Acknowledging his friend's look with a, 'please hear me out' smile, he continued on, "We want to force him into a mistake. This is where we will really need you, Terry. While we have Samuelson occupied with telling our story you need to electronically bug his phones both at home and in the office. Also we will need you to plant a tracking device on his car. It would be too much to hope for, but if you could disable any cellular phone he has it would make any surveillance we place on him easier."

With a heavy note of sarcasm, Jones responded with, "Yes, Master. And when am I expected to put my own gun to my head?"

Reggie had stood by silently long enough and with that comment he jumped to his feet exploding in anger, "Do you think we are in this for fun? We're putting our lives and the lives of loved ones and friends on the line doing a job the Fed's won't even touch and you sit there whining. Come hell or high water we intend to stop this bunch of murderers, with or without your help."

Few people could withstand a full blast of Reggie's anger and Jones was no exception. Trying to maintain his composure he responded, saying, "Alright, cool down, I have to get back to the office and pick up the necessary equipment from the supply room. Give me about an hour before contacting Samuelson. If you guys whet his appetite he more than likely will not want me around, so I should be free to do what you want. Once you begin your spiel I will need at least a couple of hours to do my bit."

Rising from his chair, he looked at the two men who were now standing side by side and commented, "Bandaged and bruised, but I would still rather be aligned with you two than anyone I know."

Later, using the phone number Agent Jones had given him before departing, Toby dialed Samuelson's personal number. An irritated sounding voice came on the line, "I'm in the middle of lunch, Jones. This had better be important."

"My name isn't Jones, but it's important. My name is Toby Preston and I got your number from Chief Fisher. He said I was to contact you if I had any information regarding DONE."

Toby's attempt at placating the FBI Station Chief with the mention of DONE had its desired effect, for Seth Samuelson responded so eagerly and loudly Toby had to move the earpiece away from his ear.

"What do you have, Preston?"

"I think we should agree to meet somewhere. What I have to tell you shouldn't be discussed over an open line. How about the Bremerton Boardwalk in twenty minutes? I'll have a friend with me." Hoping Jones had assessed his superior's reaction correctly, he added, "You can bring Jones if you need to."

"No, no," Samuelson quickly answered. "He is on surveillance in East Bremerton and isn't available right now," he lied.

"Fine with me," Toby replied. "See you in twenty minutes."

After hanging up Toby looked at Reggie who sat lolling in a chair, with one of his legs dangling over its arm. "I should have had that conversation on a speaker phone for you to listen to," he said. "He was a bit transparent. It's not going to be difficult to yank his chain."

When Reggie went to the closet in the foyer to get his jacket, Toby made a quick call to the police station hoping to catch Sergeant Vince. Fortunately Vince was in; Toby spoke a few words to him then hung up.

They decided to drive the Jeep, with Reggie driving, as it was the best vehicle for tailing their subject. It wasn't long before they reached their destination and Reggie parked the Jeep on Pacific Avenue. They then walked to the Boardwalk where they spotted a black Crown Victoria with government plates pull into a handicap spot near the ferry terminal.

As they drew close, Reggie looked at his friend and said, "This guy has got to be the world's biggest jerk. It's going to be fun watching his world crumble."

At the sound of approaching footsteps, Samuelson turned from his position at the handrail, which encompassed the Boardwalk. He looked in disdain at the two men approaching him.

"From the sound of your voice on the phone I expected you to be here waiting on me," Samuelson complained. "I don't care to be kept waiting. My time is extremely valuable."

Reggie took the measure of the tall, slightly overweight man, dressed in what appeared to be the standard wear for FBI personnel. He then replied in a caustic voice, "We would have been here sooner, but some jerk nearly caused an accident up on Washington Street and we were a little delayed."

"Whatever," the impatient agent muttered. "Let's hear what you have to say. From what I hear you two are preoccupied with this DONE group, which frankly I'm hard-pressed to believe even exists. I thought you PI's kept yourselves busy with snooping on errant husbands."

Toby replied, "You may find it hard to believe that DONE exists, but we know they exist. We have been in their den at Rainer Investment and this morning we were attacked by six of their group in East Bremerton."

With the many years Samuelson had spent in the Bureau he had no doubt learned how to hide his emotions, but no amount of training could hide the shocked look on his face when Toby made his declaration. Evidently he wasn't high enough up in the DONE hierarchy to know everything that transpired and Toby's revelation came as a total surprise.

Toby went on, "The Bremerton police probably didn't tell you about the attack because it's still being investigated. Before they carted off the bodies, I took a piece of paper out of a pocket of the man we believe was the leader and the information written on the paper is of such importance we feel we need to go back to Israel."

Still recovering from the shock of what he had first heard, the agent asked Toby, "Do you have that piece of paper with you?"

"No," Toby answered. "I burned it as soon as I read it. It only made reference to a shipment from Israel coming into the Port of Tacoma. Except for the weapons which the police confiscated we found nothing on the others."

"I should have you two jailed for obstruction," the agent spoke in a blustery manner. "I suppose you're going to Israel to confer with your Mossad buddy?"

Tired of listening to the pompous traitor, Toby gritted his teeth knowing they had to keep Samuelson a little longer in order to give Terry Jones more time to perform his deeds.

Reggie, who hadn't uttered a word during the exchange, looked at the over-bearing government agent and stated quietly, "We don't really want to take this trip to Israel, but we have to find out what they're up to. Between Toby's discovering the cache of weapons here and what was uncovered down my way we believe we are dealing with an organization, which is planning something big. You guys blew 9-11 and we can't let something like that happen again."

Reggie's reference to the terrorist attack on American soil on September 11th and the FBI's failure to prevent it caused Samuelson to bridle. "Go on get out of here! Go to Israel. Let's see how much difference you can make."

The two friends had heard enough of the agent's hypocrisy and decided to terminate the meeting before they lost control of their tempers.

Walking away rapidly Toby and Reggie put distance between themselves and Samuelson.

Reaching the ferry terminal they darted inside and removed their loud yellow jackets, reversing them to now reveal a black outside. Keeping back from the glass doors they observed the agent climb into his car and reach under his seat.

He fumbled around for a minute or two, then cursing he opened the car door, threw his gloves on the pavement and knelt on them to protect his suit pants from being soiled while he continued to search under the seat with an almost feverish pitch, still coming up empty handed.

"Looks like Jones succeeded in snatching Samuelson's cell phone," Reggie commented. "Now we have to get our transportation before we lose him."

"No need to worry about that," Toby replied. "Just before we left home I put in a call to a police friend who has no love for Samuelson and he let the air out of one of his tires. We should have plenty of time to get to the jeep."

The words had no sooner left Toby's mouth, when the government official, who had started his engine and had begun to move away from the curb, jerked to a stop as the car pulled to the right due to a flat right front tire. Hitting the steering wheel in frustration with the heel of his hand he caused the horn to sound, startling an elderly couple walking by. He cast them a dirty look and with total disregard for other traffic he left the official government vehicle half way into the street and while he strode into the ferry terminal in search of a phone.

The two amused friends quickly stepped behind a rack of brochures and as the agent headed for a phone booth they slipped out of the terminal and headed for the jeep.

Reggie moved the jeep to a spot where they could see the agent's vehicle. They watched as the irate and impatient Samuelson came out of the terminal and paced back and forth beside his car oblivious of the inconvenience he was causing other motorists.

"Besides betraying every oath he ever gave allegiance to this guy thumbs his nose at laws and common decency," Toby angrily declared.

"Maybe it's part of the criteria for admittance into DONE," an equally disturbed Reggie replied. "So far this character has flaunted his arrogance as if it was a badge of honor. How could someone like this have gotten in the position he's in without having been exposed long ago?"

Finally a Ford van with government markings pulled up alongside the disabled car. Two men in mechanics overalls got out; one opened the back door of the van and began removing tools while the other walked up to the car and its anxiously pacing driver. Toby and Reggie couldn't hear the conversation, but from the animation of his hands it was easy to guess the agitated Samuelson was taking his anger out on the hapless mechanic, who took the arrival of his co-worker and the accompanying tools as an excuse to turn away from Samuelson.

In minutes the two had the flat tire off and the spare put on. Then Samuelson, without a word of appreciation or even a glance in their direction, climbed into the car, started the engine and paying no heed to pedestrians pulled on to Washington Avenue, and headed north.

"Doesn't look like he's going to the office," Toby remarked. "Terry gave his address as 1040 Shore Drive, and I suspect he's going there to make his call."

As if on cue the black Crown Victoria turned right and crossed the Manette Bridge and from two cars back Toby saw the car turn right at the end of the bridge and on to Shore Drive.

"This is a narrow road traveled mostly by residents, so we need to give him a lot of distance," cautioned Toby. "There's a small park just ahead on the right where we can leave the Jeep while we proceed on foot. We'll walk along the shoreline to avoid curious neighbors."

After parking and locking the Jeep the two walked down toward the beach, their jackets tightly zipped against the brisk breeze that was whipping along the water's edge.

Shivering, Reggie turned to Toby saying, "Don't see how you can enjoy living in a climate like this. It has rained three out of the five days I've been here; if it isn't raining, it's freezing. You should pack up and move to Vegas where you're almost guaranteed sun 350 days out of the year."

The native Washingtonian looked at his friend but withheld his remarks about missing the blue skies and green fields of his beloved Pacific Northwest.

They arrived at their destination, recognizing the familiar black Crown Victoria parked in the carport and checked the house. Seeing the drapes on the window facing the shoreline were closed they quickly moved under the patio deck and up the concrete steps to the house.

They had spent too much time getting to the house and could hear Samuelson's voice from inside talking to someone. They moved to a window as near to the speaker as possible in an effort to hear what was being said. The one-sided conversation led them to believe he was talking on the telephone rather than to someone with him in the house.

Toby whispered to Reggie that he was going to try to get into the house to confront Samuelson. Moving off Toby entered the house through an unlocked kitchen door and soon found himself in what seemed to be the den. Toby could hear the voice of the agent coming from an adjoining room. Staying as close to the wall as he could to lessen the chance of the floor squeaking, he advanced in the direction of the voice.

For Reggie, on the outside of the house, time stood still. He had no way of knowing how far Toby had advanced into the house and the lack of movement was causing the cold to settle into his bones.

In the house, Toby had moved close enough to see Samuelson as he nervously paced in front of the closed drapes of the living room windows with a portable phone glued to his ear. Some inner feeling must have alerted him to a presence in the room and he turned to see the intruder in his house. Shocked by the invasion, he reacted too slowly in reaching for the pistol, which rested under his armpit, allowing Toby to leap across the room and snatch the weapon from him. Using it as a club he struck the senior FBI agent and he and the phone fell to the carpeted floor with a soft thud.

Toby quickly retrieved the phone and spoke in the mouthpiece, "Hello. Who is this?"

The gravelly voice at the other end responded in an authoritative manner, *"Who is this? Where is Samuelson?"*

"You needn't concern yourself with your little puppet Samuelson," answered Toby, "He's resting comfortably on the carpet."

"Ah, Preston is that you? You and your friend Nutsbagh have come to be more of a nuisance than I envisioned. At first you were no more than a couple pesky gnats who should have been swatted away, but now you have become more like two angry wasps. What shall I do with you two?"

"I wouldn't worry about what you are going to do with us I would start concerning myself with what we'll do with you when we catch up to you. And we will."

A raspy laugh was heard and the voice continued. *"Do you think you can frighten me with your petty threats? You should be glad that you don't know whom you are dealing with. The six men I sent after you today and the ones you managed to dispatch previously are nothing compared to what I can unleash. Consider yourselves fortunate that I have bigger fish to catch. Go to Israel; go to Tibet, for all I care!"*

With extreme effort Toby fought to gain control of his anger and fearing he would lose any advantage they might have by blowing up at their nameless adversary he handed the phone to Reggie, who had entered the house. When Reggie took the phone he turned back to Samuelson and using items he found around the room tied him up.

"In spite of all you have been able to throw at us it seems you are not invincible," Reggie began. "Tell us where you are and we'll send a dog-catcher over to put you out of your misery."

"Well, well, the indefatigable Reggie Nutsbagh; or should I say the other half of Abbott and Costello? But then you are not old enough to remember that comedy act, are you? That is all you two are, an outdated comedy act."

Reggie struggling to hold his anger in check responded to the attack with biting words of his own," This outdated pair, as you call us, will be around long enough to give you your final round of applause."

For the first time there was a note of anger in the voice of the man, *"Every dog has his day, young Nutsbagh, and you have pissed on your last fire hydrant. You are no better than your father was. You can't come up against me and expect to win. This conversation is over. Do me a favor and put a gun to Samuelson's head he is of no further use to me."*

The line then went dead. Slamming the phone down on its cradle he looked at Toby and said through clenched teeth, "If it's the last thing I do, this jerk is going down."

Toby nodded in agreement.

By this time the trussed up Samuelson was coming around demanding to be turned loose. "How dare you come into my home and treat me like this. Untie me this instant."

"Oh we'll turn you loose, alright," Toby answered, "just as soon as we turn over the taped conversation between you and your raspy-voiced conspirator to your fellow FBI agents."

"What do you mean taped?" The agent spluttered. Attempting to appear indignant he continued, "Wiretapping is illegal and not admissible as evidence."

"Oh, I don't think your fellow agents will be concerned about something as trivial as that," countered Reggie. "To think one of their own would go to such lengths to betray their beliefs, they might just assassinate you without the benefit of a trial."

"Besides," Toby interjected, "we don't think you're going to lodge a complaint. Your best bet is to clean out your bank account and head for the hills, get while the getting is good."

Removing the bullets from his gun, Toby threw the weapon on the sofa next to him while Reggie loosened his bonds.

With Samuelson looking on Toby calmly removed the bugging device from the telephone, sticking it in his pocket. Without a backward glance the two friends walked out the door not bothering to close it behind them.

"This has been some day," Reggie quipped, as they briskly walked back to the Jeep. "Remind me to decline the next time you suggest we go jogging."

"Yeah," the bone weary Toby replied. "And we never did get to jog."

As the two headed back to the house, Toby put in a call to Terry Jones. Expecting their call Jones answered on the first ring. Not waiting to introduce himself, he excitedly began, "I got it all. I wasn't able to trace the call, but every word they uttered is recorded. We have him by the short hairs."

"Good work, Terry. We put the fear into him and I believe you have seen the last of him. Wouldn't hurt to check on him, but I figure he is heading underground, probably to wherever the headquarters of DONE is. Thanks for the help."

"Wait,' Jones requested. "What do you suggest I do with what I have on Samuelson?"

"I suggest you duplicate it, putting one copy in a safe deposit box and send the other to your superiors. Be sure to cover all your bases for this mysterious guy who, I assume is the boss, professes to wield a big stick. None of us can say who else is in his employment?"

After he ended the call he turned to Reggie, "If Mr. Big (the name by which they had chosen to identify the anonymous man) took our bait he believes we are going back to Israel, now is the time to gather our forces."

"I agree," responded Reggie, "as soon as we get back to the house I'll call Joe; he's a good man to have in a fight. I'm sure he will jump at the chance to come up and lend a hand. We also have Lebowitz and Abbott, for what they are worth."

Toby pondered his friend's remarks about the two retired police officers before answering. "Admittedly they turned tail when things got hot, but we'll have to overlook that, I'm afraid. We'll need their knowledge of the area and most assuredly their guns. We aren't blessed with a lot of support as it is."

Entering the security gate Reggie drove up to the house where Toby noticed a car sitting in the circular driveway. "Looks like Joan brought the girls home," he commented. "That's her Toyota. I guess that means I'll get chewed out royally for not staying home in bed."

Brandy was the first one to notice the arrival of the two. Getting up from the table she greeted Reggie with a kiss, exclaiming, "Joan is teaching us a game called Progressive Rummy. It can be played with two players, but is more fun with three or more. Do you guys want to play?"

Walking around to where Ruth was seated; Toby knelt beside her chair and gave her a warm kiss; he then burrowed his head into her shoulder, letting out a big sigh.

"Now what was the sigh all about?" she asked.

Keeping his head nestled comfortably against her shoulder, he replied, "I'm going to miss the feel and smell of you while Reggie and I are in Montana."

Joan had been watching the coziness of her new boss and his lady and couldn't miss the look, which came over Ruth's face. Glancing at Brandy, she saw the same expression on her face. Rising from the table she excused herself, saying, "I think I had better scoot. There are some things I need to take care of while it's still daylight. Call me tomorrow, Toby."

Toby, who had felt Ruth stiffen at his announcement, rose from his position and acknowledged his assistant's request with a wave of his hand.

Ruth spoke up for the first time, directing her tirade at Toby, "And you, Toby Preston, should be ashamed of yourself. You came so close to death today that I felt I could have been a widow without having been married. I will not stand around waiting to hear of your death."

Ruth had barely finished when Brandy also lit into both men echoing Ruth's comments. The two partners were too flabbergasted to respond. Seeing the fire in the eyes of the women made them back off temporarily.

The four had been so caught up in the heated words they failed to notice Maria had come into the room. Looking at the people she had grown to love as her family she offered a temporary solution. "Why don't you peoples not yell and talk more tomorrow when you sleep on it?"

Without acquiescing to the opposite faction the four combatants yielded to the wisdom of the older woman and refrained from discussing the matter further.

As Toby walked toward the kitchen he could hear Reggie in the den talking to his friend Joe in Las Vegas. "Okay, Joe, I can count on your being there when we arrive. Right, the Quality Inn; bring a little extra hardware with you, too. We have some, but will need some heavy artillery and plenty of extra ammo. Do you think you can round up some tear gas canisters without raising an alarm? Thanks pal, same to you. See you soon."

Brandy sat at the kitchen table with her head in her hands looking dejected. Going over to her Toby touched her lightly on the shoulder saying, "He's off the phone now. Go on in and just love on him. You don't have to concede."

Immediately perking up she gave Toby a quick peck on the cheek and practically skipped into the den from where Toby heard a squeal of delight.

Taking a business card from his wallet he called the number written on the back. After the third ring the phone was answered by a gruff voice, "This had better not be one of them solicitors. I have two of everything I need."

"Is that you, Lebowitz?" replied Toby, leaning back in his chair with a smile on his face.

"Yeah, this is Sam Lebowitz. Who's asking?"

A little irritated with Lebowitz's phone manners, Toby responded in a brusque tone, "This is Toby Preston, Lebowitz. Quit acting like you are still a cop."

"Sorry, Preston," the retired policeman apologized. "We get so many calls from people trying to sell stuff that I try to put them on the defensive. To what do I owe the honor of this call?"

"If you and Abbott were sincere about wanting to help we could sure use you. We are going in tomorrow."

Toby wasn't entirely sure what kind of reaction his request would receive and was pleased to hear Abbott, who had picked up an extension bellow, "Count us in, Toby. How do you want to work this?"

"Glad you're both together," the encouraged Toby replied. "Copy these driving instructions I'm going to give you and we will go over it when we get together."

"Let me grab a pen and pencil," Lebowitz requested. After a short interval he said, "Okay, I got it. Go ahead."

"Real simple," Toby said as he gave the driving instruction, "take Interstate 90 into Billings, Montana, get off at Exit 446, and go to the Quality Inn at Homestead Park. Reggie and I will meet you there in two days. Bring as much heat as you can gather. God speed."

CHAPTER TWENTY-SIX

The Team is Assembled

IT WAS A morning typical of a lot of mornings in the Pacific Northwest, it had rained hard overnight and now the rain had settled into a slow drizzle creating an overcast and dreary sky. '*What an ugly way to start the day,*' Reggie thought, as he carried the last of his clothing and personal things out to the RV, parked in the garage.

Toby had finished loading his things and was sitting at the kitchen table when Brandy and Ruth entered; he stood up to greet them but was rebuffed in both attempts. It didn't take much of a detective to see the women were ready to wage a battle.

Before Toby could say anything about their actions, Brandy said, "Toby, Ruth and I have been talking and have decided, regardless of what we agreed to last night we'll not stay home while you and Reggie are out putting yourselves in danger. Both of us have proven we can handle ourselves in times of trouble and we believe we can be a valuable asset to you guys during your investigation in Montana."

"Brandy, I thought we had been over all of these things last night and it was settled." Before Toby could continue, Ruth broke in, "My dear Toby, I know we are soon to be wed and Jewish traditions allow the man is the boss of the family. However, right now there is one small problem, we are not yet married, and I will not be told what to do and where to go when the man I love is putting himself in danger!"

"And, I, "interjected Brandy, "Feel exactly the same way, where Reggie is concerned."

At this point Reggie walked into the kitchen from the garage and not having heard the comments made by either party had no idea what he had stepped into and was totally unprepared for the verbal onslaught, which hit him. Seeing Brandy, he walked over to her and attempted to kiss her good morning, but was rebuffed as she angrily turned her face away. Reggie looked at her saying, "Now what's this all about?"

Without preamble Brandy launched into her tirade, "Ruth and I have decided that we're going with you, no matter what you say. As we have already told Toby, we have proven we can be helpful and we want to be with our men. It would only drive us crazy to sit here while you two are out facing danger. Especially since we've witnessed how ruthless DONE's operatives are. What are we supposed to do? Sit around with our knitting needles and gossip? I don't think so!"

Reggie looked helplessly at Toby, but found no help there.

Silence prevailed until, with an audible sigh, Toby said, "You are certainly the most hardheaded women I've ever had the pleasure of knowing and I'm sure neither Reggie nor I knew what we were getting into when we decided to ask you to marry us. But the deed is done and I for one am glad I asked Ruth to marry me and will live with my decision. I'm not speaking for Reggie, he is his own man, but I will allow Ruth to come with us, but with conditions. First—If I even feel you are in danger I will send you away immediately and you will go with no argument. Secondly—you will this time, and most likely the only time, have to do as I tell you, without question. You must agree to these conditions before you can come along."

"I agree and it will only take me five minutes to put my bags into the RV, as they are already packed," said Ruth, as she walked over to Toby, kissed him on the mouth and hurried out of the kitchen.

A frustrated Brandy intoned, following Ruth's departure "Well, Reggie my love, what do you have to say?"

"I don't like the idea of putting you in danger either, but I can see there are some benefits of traveling with women; with you and Ruth along, we will look more like vacationers. However, I want to reiterate the conditions Toby laid down. You have to agree to them; I love you too much to put you in danger."

Brandy smiled and walked over to Reggie, kissed him, saying, "Good morning, my love, have some coffee. I'm going to my room and get my bags, which by the way, are also already packed."

The two men could only stand looking at each other in amazement as Brandy followed Ruth out of the kitchen.

An hour later the RV pulled out with four people aboard and towing Toby's Jeep, with Toby driving and Reggie sitting in the passenger's seat. Ruth and Brandy were in the rear completing the stowing of the last items brought on board, which included a large basket of food Maria had prepared for them last evening, evidently she knew who would win the battle.

Having previously planned their route it was just a matter of making the right turns and getting on the proper highway. Their planning included their route to Billings, Montana and the Quality Inn there, where they would meet the rest of the team in two days.

After the battle with the women had been lost and their travel plans adjusted to include them, neither one of the men would openly admit it, but having them along would be a big help for many different reasons. Brandy, a registered nurse, could provide them with the treatment of their wounds they had already received (hopefully there would be no further use for services of that nature) and Ruth could, because of her previous experience with the Mossad, help them in some of the planning.

Several hours later Toby pulled off the road at the summit of Snoqualmie Pass and shut down the engine of the RV, saying, "I think it's time we take a break and see what tasty treats Maria prepared for us."

They spent an hour eating fried chicken and tortillas, ending with strawberry turnovers and were finishing their meal with coffee, when Toby glancing at his watch said, "We should be getting a move on it." Reggie rose from the table, saying, "Pal, why don't you give it a break and let me drive for awhile?"

"That's a good idea; it will give me a little more time to work out a few details about our plan of attack."

The sun was just beginning to drop down behind the distant mountains, when Reggie pulled the large RV into the parking lot of a Holiday Inn, on the outskirts of Missoula, Montana. Shutting the engine down he said, "I think it would be nice to get out of this rolling bread box and sleep in a comfortable bed while we can and maybe enjoy a good meal."

After checking in and taking personal items to their rooms they met in the restaurant for dinner. After dinner Toby and Reggie said good night to the ladies, who went to their rooms, as Reggie and Toby went to Toby's room to further their discussion about their upcoming foray in Montana.

As soon as they were in the room and seated, Reggie said, "All during the drive down here, I was continually checking to see if we had a tail. Even though I haven't noticed anyone, I'm concerned we're being followed. We surely don't need DONE to be alerted to the fact we're going on the offensive. They will find out soon enough, but right now, especially since we're going to have a larger team, I think we need to rid ourselves of anyone who might be following."

"You're right, Reg, I've also been thinking about that and I might have a solution to resolve that problem. Joe has a cell phone and you have the number, don't you?"

"Sure do and I told him I would contact him when we got in range. What did you have in mind?"

"Tomorrow when we get close to Billings, call Joe and have him drive west on Highway 90 back towards Bozeman. He needs to find the last rest stop before Billings on the east side; once he gets to the rest stop have him park close to the entrance. We'll pull into the same rest stop, timing our arrival for after dark. Once in the rest stop we'll pull into a slot designated for RV's and if someone is following us Joe will be able to tell and alert us."

"Sounds like a good idea. If there is someone following us, what are we going to do?"

"Well, as we can't have them following us to our final destination, maybe it's time to take the gloves off and deal with them the same way they've been dealing with us."

Reggie looked at Toby when he made this last comment and noted the hard set to his eyes and jaw and realized his partner had his game face on and it was time to get down to business. "You're right partner it's definitely time to get down to business!"

The next morning, after breakfast, the four friends departed the motel with Reggie driving. Several hours later Toby took over the driving and Reggie called Joe. After several rings with no answer Reggie was about to hang up when he heard Joe, "Hello, this is Joe."

"Your voice is a welcome sound, Joe. I take it you are in Billings at the rendezvous point?"

"Sure am, boss, where are you guys?"

"We're about 180 miles out on I-90. The meeting place in Billings remains the same, but there is something we need you to do. We think we might be pulling a tail along with us from Bremerton. I'll put Toby on the line he'll explain what's going on and what we need for you to do. Are you packing?"

"Absolutely," Joe replied. "Packing heavy and traveling light, not knowing what I was getting into."

"Joe, let me tell you I feel a whole lot better having you with us on this, thanks."

Toby took the phone from Reggie and after exchanging pleasantries explained to Joe the situation and what he wanted him to do at the rest stop. He completed the conversation and after getting a description of Joe's vehicle, broke the connection laughing as he handed the phone to Reggie.

With a quizzical expression on his face Reggie, asked, "What's so funny?"

"When I asked Joe for a description of his vehicle he reminded me to tell you about getting him a new truck. He didn't tell me why but said you knew. Why do you owe Joe a new truck?"

"He must be driving his old truck. Remember I told you about Johnson, the partner to Goins, who was following me around Las Vegas. There came a time when I wanted to get Johnson off my tail so I could move about Las Vegas freely, so to do that we staged an accident with Joe's truck. Johnson followed me into a parking lot and Joe ran into him with his truck and of course the police just happened to be there with one of them being my friend, Phil. When the police confronted Johnson they found a gun on him and he was arrested, so Joe has been telling me since it was my idea he run into Johnson denting his truck, he says I owe him a truck."

Chuckling at the story, Toby asked, "I assume that means you'll be able to recognize Joe's vehicle when we pull into the rest stop?"

"I sure will, and now I really need to get him a new truck, for helping us out."

As the sun slowly dropped its rosy head over the distant mountains and dusk gave way to dark Toby spotted a highway sign showing the rest stop they were looking for was five miles ahead. Reaching over he lightly touched Reggie on the shoulder; who came awake instantly asking, "What's up, Toby?"

"We're about five miles from the rest stop so we need to get prepared," Toby said, as he reached into the center console to get his pistol. He checked to insure it was loaded and then placed it in his shoulder holster, he then removing a second pistol handing it to Reggie.

"I take it these rigs are going to be the designated wear from this day forward," Reggie said, as he stowed the pistol in his shoulder holster.

Reggie, then turned to the two women resting in the rear of the RV, "Ladies, we're going to stop in a minute, you need you to stay in back out of sight and don't show yourselves in any of the windows." Reggie had finished his instructions to the women as Toby swung the RV onto the off ramp leading into the rest stop.

Entering the parking area reserved for RV's and trucks; Reggie spotted Joe's truck sitting in the first parking place for smaller vehicles, but couldn't see anyone sitting in the truck. Toby pulled forward into a parking place as close as he could to the parked truck as Reggie punched in Joe's cell phone number, saying as soon as it was answered, "We're in. Did you pick us up?"

"Gotcha, boss, we'll get back to you as soon as we find out if there's someone following you, hang loose." Saying this Joe terminated the phone call.

'We'll get back to you? What does that mean? The way Joe talked there's another person with him. What's going on?' Reggie muttered under his breath.

Toby attempting to put the puzzle together from what he had heard Reggie mumble under his breath, asked, "Reg, what are you muttering about?"

"When Joe answered he told me he had picked us up coming into the rest stop, but then he said, 'we'll get back to you as soon as we find out if someone is following you', as if there was someone with him in the truck. Oh, well, right now there is nothing we can do about it, other than just sit here and wait until he contacts us."

In Joe's truck, Reggie's friend, Phil Warren, senior detective, Las Vegas Police Department, sat with Joe watching intently as a big Lincoln Continental pulled into a parking place about 75 feet from the RV.

"Well, Phil, looks like Reggie was right, they are being followed, at least it looks that way; or maybe those guys in the Lincoln just want to park close to an RV."

"Got'em," said Phil. "Now we wait and see what they're up to; let them make the first move and then we'll decide what we need to do to counter their opening move."

"Sounds like a plan."

Ten minutes later the two men got out of the parked Lincoln and slowly approached the RV with guns drawn. Not sure of the two men's intentions, Joe and Phil quietly got out of the truck with their guns also drawn and advanced toward the men. Getting within fifteen feet of the Lincoln they hid behind a bush watching as the two men walked to the rear of the RV and shone a small flashlight on the rear of the RV, evidently checking the license plate number.

Apparently satisfied it was the RV they had been following they returned to their vehicle, one man got into the car while the other walked over to a soda machine, purchased two sodas and then returned to the car.

Joe and Phil remained hidden behind the bush for another few minutes observing and giving the men in the car a chance to settle in and get comfortable. On signal, Joe began to move slowly around to the driver's side of the vehicle as Phil crept along the bush to a position alongside the passenger.

Simultaneously they opened both doors of the car reaching in and jerked the men out of the car onto the ground, warning them in muted voices not to move as they showed them their silenced pistols. On the driver's side of the car, Joe and his hostage were plainly visible to several cars and trucks parked at the rest stop, so he grabbed his man by the collar of his coat and pulled him across the pavement to the other side of the car depositing him next to his partner who Phil was covering.

Because of the element of surprise Joe and Phil had no problems getting the two men out of the car and onto the ground. However, as the surprise wore off the situation could get harder to control.

Wanting to maintain a degree of control and before either one of the men could say anything, Joe grabbed the man nearest to him pulling him up into a sitting position he began sifting through his pockets, with his pistol pointed at the man's head. He pulled a gun out of the man's waistband and then rummaging through his pockets, he found only the normal items. He put the man's wallet in his coat pocket to look at later.

"What in the hell are you doing with the artillery, going duck hunting? And why are you following our friends in the RV over there? Don't try and deny it we saw you walk over to the RV and read the plate number," Joe asked, in a muted voice.

"It's none of your business what we're doing. The question is what in the hell are you doing? Give me my things back and go about your business and we'll forget that you stuck your nose into something that has nothing to do with you," said the man Joe was holding hostage.

The other man being held by Phil spoke for the first time, "Why are you hassling us? We only pulled in here for a rest."

Phil, wanting to maintain the image portrayed by Joe, reached over and slapped the man alongside the head, telling him to shut up and speak only when spoken to.

Joe continued with his questioning, "Now why don't you be a good little boy and take off your jacket and roll up the sleeves of your shirt."

"Go to hell," was the reply.

Joe reached up and viciously slapped the man across the face saying, "I guess we'll have to do this the hard way, which is I shoot you, take your coat off and roll the sleeves up myself. You continue messing with me and you will be the one going to hell. You have no idea who you are dealing with, not only am I half crazy, but I'm a half crazy black man with a gun. Now do as you were told before I get real angry."

Feeling the first surge of fear the man slowly removed his jacket and rolled up his shirtsleeves revealing a large tattoo on his forearm reading DONE with a dagger through the word DONE.

"Now tell me why you were following our friends and who you are working for?" Joe asked.

"I told you before it's none of your business and if you think I'm going to tell you anything more you're in for a big surprise."

With a snarl, Joe grabbed the man and forced his mouth open; shoving the silenced end of the 38 half way down the man's throat. "Now you'll shut up. If we don't get some answers to our questions you'll be dead and have a good excuse for not answering."

Taking his cue from Joe, Phil grabbed his man and pulled him up into a sitting position, saying, "You see your partner sitting there sucking on a gun barrel; if you don't want to see how far the back of his head will fly with one bullet then you'll answer the questions." Phil stared intently at the man, as he continued, "I'm only going to ask one time and if I don't get a good answer, you'll have to find a new partner. Why were you following our friends in the RV?"

The man glanced at his partner and shrugged his shoulders as if to signify that their position was hopeless, and said, "We were spending the night at a Holiday Inn in Missoula and recognized Nutsbagh and Preston and decided to follow them."

Phil continued, "How did you recognize them?"

"About a week ago we were handed flyers with their names and pictures on it, stating there's a fifty thousand dollar bounty on each of their heads. So we thought we could follow them and collect the bounty."

"Who else knows about them being in Montana?" asked Joe, interrupting Phil's questioning.

"No one; we were going to do this ourselves, why would we want to share the bounty with anyone?"

Joe shoved the gun further down the throat of the man's partner, drawing blood, which began to flow freely out of the corners of his mouth. "I really don't believe you didn't tell anyone."

Shivering in fear as he watched the blood flow down his partner's face the man stammered, "I'm telling you the truth, I have no reason to lie. Neither of us wants to die."

"Joe, why don't you guard our two friends here and I'll go search their car and see if I can find anything interesting."

Phil walked over to the car, popped the trunk but found it empty; he then started to search the interior of the car finding only a gun and a folded piece of paper under the edge of the front seat. "Nothing in here except another one of those cannons some people call guns. Unfolding the paper he continued, "Maybe our friends are telling the truth. Here's the flyer they were talking about, the one with Reggie's picture and the picture of another guy who must be Toby."

Joe was momentarily distracted by Phil's comments and at the two men lying on the ground seized the opportunity to jump up in an attempt to overpower Joe. One man got his hands on Joe's weapon and attempted to turn the gun around and use it on Joe. He was able to wrestle the gun away from Joe and fired three shots, two of them striking Joe. Before he could do further damage Phil ran up to the man and swung his pistol and hit the man along side the head, rendering him unconscious.

The other man had joined the fight and Joe was still struggling with him but was losing the battle because of his wounds. Phil, in an attempt to assist Joe, reached over and jerked the man loose from Joe's grasp, as he came loose he came up with one of the pistols which had been on the ground and was bringing it around to take a shot at Phil. With no hesitation Phil brought his gun up and fired two shots directly into the man's head, killing him instantly.

Phil's first concern was for Joe; he rushed over but saw Joe was getting to his feet even though parts of his clothing were blood soaked. He then bent over the man he had hit over the head, feeling for a pulse, finding none, he said, "Must have hit him a little too hard."

"Joe, can you make it? We have to get to the truck, you're bleeding like a stuck hog and it won't be long before this place will be swarming with cops."

Phil had no sooner spoken than the door of the RV swung open revealing Reggie framed in the doorway holding his gun.

Phil and Joe recognized Reggie and heaved a sigh of relief and then saw Toby coming out of the RV on the other side they decided they had better just stay still waiting for their approach. They certainly didn't want to be mistaken for the enemy.

A short time later Phil and Joe heard a voice behind them saying, "Whoever you are just stand there quietly and place both of your hands on top of your heads, making sure your hands are empty; my partner has you both covered and will not hesitate to shoot, should you make a wrong move."

Recognizing the voice as that of his friend Reggie, Joe said, through clenched teeth, against the pain of his wounds, "Reggie would you stop playing games and get over here before this black man bleeds red blood all over this green grass, killing it. There has to be some kind of a law prohibiting that."

Reggie recognized Joe's voice and his sense of humor closed the distance in seconds, saying just loud enough for Toby to hear, "Come on in Toby, its Joe and Phil." Then looked directly at Phil, and asked, "What are you doing here?"

Reggie's question went unanswered as Toby hurriedly walked into the group saying, "No time for that right now, we need to get things moving. Joe, where are the keys to your truck?"

Joe reached his free hand into his pocket and gave the keys to Toby, who immediately turned to Phil, saying, "How do you do Phil, I'm Reggie's partner, Toby. I've heard a lot about you from Reggie. Take these keys then get the truck and yourself out of here fast. I assume you know where the meeting place is? We'll see you there."

Phil nodded at the instructions from Toby, took the keys and sprinted away into the darkness.

Snapping out of his bewilderment over seeing Phil at the rest stop and realizing the need for action, Reggie walked over to Joe and assisted him to the RV.

Before joining Reggie, Toby stooped down checking the pulses of each man, verifying they were dead. He then began a systematic search of the dead men's pockets removing anything he could find and placing it in the pocket of his jacket. He was completing the search of the bodies when he heard the engine of Joe's truck roar to life as Phil started the engine and drove out of the rest stop. He picked up the guns lying on the ground and ran back to the RV.

Arriving at the RV he jumped in, closed the door then nodded to Reggie who started the engine and pulled the RV out of the rest stop. As they began rolling down the freeway Toby walked over to where Joe sat with his shirt off while Brandy administered to his wounds. Squeezing Joe on the shoulder, he asked, "How are you doing, Joe?"

Before Joe could respond, Brandy said, "He has two flesh wounds, one in the side and another on the upper left arm. I'll clean both of them and then close them, other than loss of blood he'll recover. This is one tough man."

Joe said, "Oh by the way, Toby, there's one significant thing that came up during our encounter, you and Reggie are famous, just like the outlaws of the old west there is a wanted poster out on the two of you with a fifty thousand dollar bounty for your dead bodies."

"You're kidding me?" Toby questioned.

"No sir, I'm not and as soon as we meet Phil again he'll show you. He took the flyer out of the thug's car."

"I guess we've been causing someone enough problems that they want us out of the way."

"Sounds that way," Joe answered, then continued, "and you can tell Mr. Hard Head up front, Phil is on vacation and decided to come and visit an old friend, that's why he's here. He just came along for the ride and I for one sure am glad he did, he saved my bacon back there."

Toby smiled at this last comment, reached over to Joe and grabbed his good hand, saying, "Thanks Joe, with such good friends along we can't possibly go wrong."

Making his way to the front of the RV Toby felt it picking up speed as Reggie accelerated trying to put more distance between themselves and the rest stop.

Sitting down in the passenger's seat he briefed Reggie on what had transpired at the rest stop, Joe's condition and why Phil was with Joe. At the mention of Phil, he saw Reggie's eyes cloud up for a brief second. He reached over and squeezed Reggie's arm. "These are some good friends you have, I sure am glad they're on our side."

"I'm glad both of them are here, but I'm worried about Phil putting his career on the line to get into something like this. I sure wouldn't want to be responsible for him losing his job just because he feels he has an obligation to me."

Toby paused for a second, choosing his words very carefully," Reggie, I understand your concern, but, in my book that's what friendship is all about. Even though we have only been friends for a short time, think about what you would do for me should I be under duress. Oh, by the way, before I forget the most important part of the little drama, which played itself out at the rest stop, we are becoming famous in the DONE circles. We have reached the big time, there's a circular out with our pictures on it offering a fifty-thousand dollar reward to anyone who takes us out, that's fifty thousand apiece."

Reggie glancing at Toby, replied, "You're kidding me?"

"No, I'm not and we'll see the proof when we see Phil at the hotel, he has the flyer."

An hour later the RV slowed and exited the Freeway at Billings, Montana then pulled into the parking lot of the Qualify Inn, Homestead Park, where the team was going to assemble before moving into what they felt was DONE territory. Pulling into the parking lot, Reggie saw Joe's truck parked in the corner of the lot, signifying that Phil had also arrived at the Inn. Reservations had been made previously over the Internet, so it was just a matter of signing in and getting their room keys.

After parking the RV Reggie walked to the back and gave Joe a big hug, being careful to steer away from the bandages he proudly displayed.

"How is it that every time you and I get together, I have to get shot?" was Joe's comment after the show of affection by Reggie.

"Well, I guess growing up you didn't learn how to duck," was Reggie's response. "How are you, Joe?"

Before Joe could answer Brandy joined in, "As his nurse, I recommend a strong drink and some sleep. I would even suggest, if possible, several days rest would be in order, for all of you. Joe is not the only one trying to recover from being wounded."

"Reggie wounded! Boss, don't talk to me about ducking. Looks like you didn't learn that art either," said Joe, laughing.

"I agree as I feel the need for some rest. We want to be at peak efficiency when we face DONE," was Toby's response.

With this settled they grabbed what personal items they needed, exited the RV and walked into the Inn and checked in. Before going to their individual rooms they decided to meet in about fifteen minutes in the restaurant for a bite to eat.

Fifteen minutes later Reggie walked into the restaurant to find the others, with the exception of Phil already seated drinking coffee. Approaching the table, Reggie saw Lebowitz and Abbott sitting at a corner table watching him. He acknowledged their presence and waved them over to join the others. Ten minutes later Phil walked in.

When he entered the room Reggie got to his feet and walked over to his friend, looking him in the eye, he shook his hand and said one word, "Thanks."

Smiling Phil took out a folded piece of paper from his pocket and handed it to him without saying a word.

Reggie unfolded the piece of paper and saw a likeness of he and Toby printed on a wanted poster right out of the old west. It offered a fifty thousand-dollar reward, the price for their deaths.

After making the introductions, Reggie took control of the gathering. Starting he told them a planning session would be held in the morning after breakfast. He cautioned everyone that the bad guys were on the loose and to be very careful. He then told Sam and Jerod what had transpired at the rest stop just a few hours earlier.

Thirty minutes later the group headed for their rooms, with Joe accompanying Reggie and Brandy to her room to get his dressings changed prior to calling it a night.

Once in the room Reggie briefed Joe on all that had transpired after he left Las Vegas and told him about the big shoot out he and Toby had in the park in Bremerton and about RIC and Mr. Big. "We are certainly going to have to be careful these guys mean business and will not hesitate to kill. Firepower and manpower are on their side, so we will have to use stealth and cunning."

Early the next morning the members of the team gathered for breakfast and twenty minutes after breakfast was completed the women left with a shopping list provided by Toby and the six men assembled in Reggie's room. When they were seated, Toby began, "At one time or another we have all either been or are cops, so you all can understand the need for caution and the need to be aware of what's going on around you at all times. We also need to be sure we watch out for each other. As demonstrated last night at the rest stop, these people are extremely dangerous and don't mind taking a life. Most of you don't know the whole story about what's happening you just have bits and pieces of it. Hopefully over the next several minutes Reggie can fill in the pieces of the puzzle so you'll all understand what's going on and what we are up against. Needless to say these people are trying to disrupt the American way of life. We know it and are trying to stop them; they know we know and are trying to stop us, any way they can."

Reggie stood up looking at the assembled group, "This started for me when I wanted to find out why my parents were killed and what type of people would put a bomb in their airplane. Well, I found out what type of people they are and I will go to any extreme to stop whatever it is that they're attempting to do." Then Reggie went on, with input from Toby, to outline all that had happened to date.

After finishing he handed each man a map and then continued, "The first thing we have to do is set up a base of operations and try to establish some working teams. On your maps you will see Toby and I have decided to establish a base camp not too far from where we suspect DONE is operating. We chose the Fort Peck Recreation Area, outside Fort Peck, Montana. In order to get there without being too conspicuous we will use three different routes and as you are each familiar with your own partners you will travel together, for now. Sam, you and Jerod take Route #1 as marked on the map; Joe and Phil, you will use Route #2; Toby, the women and I will take Route #3."

Reggie took a deep breath then continued, "We will all meet in the campgrounds in three days. The women are bringing back the things you will need in order to set up your camp, including short-range radios. The base station will be located in the RV. Sam, Jerod, any questions about your route?"

"No, I think we can handle it," Sam replied.

Reggie cast a glance at Joe and Phil, "How about you two?"

Injecting a little humor into the meeting, Joe spoke, "I guess Phil will have to teach me about the great outdoors, I'm a city boy. Does Montana have snakes?"

Reggie laughed saying, "Joe, if there are snakes around they would take one look at you and run for their lives."

Toby stood up and asked, "Does anyone need any more artillery? We have some large caliber guns we took from the two agents at the rest stop, which will be kept in the RV. We are going to have to be extremely careful not to bring any undue attention on ourselves; we are tourist and nothing more. Another thing, we always need to keep the fact in the back of our minds, outside of this group trust no one and always be suspicious of everyone. One more thing, this group is into bomb making, make sure you check your vehicle every time you get into it. Once we break up here, we'll go and wander around a bit observing the people in the area and then eventually meet back in the RV parked in the rear."

The initial meeting broke up and everyone left Reggie's room only to reassemble fifteen minutes later in the RV.

Seeing that everyone had coffee, Toby resumed the meeting, "Reggie and I thought you needed to know some of the things which have been going on with DONE, how ruthless they are and how they are ready to kill for their cause, whatever it may be. We have had a lot of indicators, which point to DONE being here in force and planning something having to do with our country and our way of life. They need to be stopped, and right or wrong we are going to do something about it. You may ask why we don't turn this thing over to the federal government, that's been tried and Reggie's parents paid for it with their lives. You see, we know for a fact there are people in our government, foreign governments and people who work for federal law enforcement agencies who are involved. Reggie, do you want to add anything?"

There was a brief silence, and then before Reggie could speak, Phil spoke up, "Reggie, if you are looking for some way to convince us we have to do something, don't bother, I for one am totally convinced, or I wouldn't be here now. Not only am I your friend, but I too like living in this country and, even though this country has some faults, it isn't something, which can't be overcome. I'm with you to the end."

After that, one by one the assembled men spoke up with their pledges of support, vowing they were in the fight to the end.

Reggie stood and slowly looked around the crowded RV and words failed him as he saw in their faces the confirmation he sought. He cleared his throat several times in an effort to gain control of his emotions then said, "Your show of support has overwhelmed me, thanks."

Toby added his sincere appreciation; "I can only add my thanks to that of my partner. Once the women get back with the equipment you can move to the next location, whenever you feel like it. God bless each of you."

Two hours later Sam and Jerod dropped by Reggie's room and informed him they were leaving and would make a slow leisurely trip to the rendezvous point and set up camp.

Joe and Phil decided to wait until morning so Joe could give Brandy another chance to change his bandages and Joe to get one more day of rest to recover from his loss of blood.

The six friends ate dinner together later that night. The conversation was kept on a light note, with no discussion of the up-coming events. Joe briefed Reggie on some of his pending cases in Las Vegas, "Hey boss, I like this arrangement we have, with me working out of your office. If Toby doesn't mind why don't we make it a permanent thing?"

"Joe, I would like nothing better than for you to share my office, but remember the top billing is mine," said Reggie, laughing at his own joke.

Before Joe could answer, Toby piped up, "I agree, as Reggie's partner and a person who shares top billing it would be great to incorporate your skills into the firm."

Ten minutes later Phil and Joe left to retire for the night, with the rest of them following a few minutes later, their minds full of thoughts of the days to come.

The next morning the four met in the Inn restaurant for breakfast, as Joe and Phil had already departed, two hours later the RV towing the Jeep left the parking lot headed east, following the route outlined on the map.

Approximately ten hours later the RV pulled into the Fort Peck Recreation area, where they registered and were assigned a parking place pre-selected for its isolation. After setting up camp Toby turned on the base station radio and attempted to contact each team using the pre-arranged call names. After several attempts, Joe and Phil returned his call telling him they were in the area and setting up camp.

Toby couldn't contact the team of Sam and Jerod, so they asked Joe to take a spin around the encampment in an attempt to locate them. An hour later the base station radio crackled to life and much to Toby and Reggie's relief it was Sam and Jerod. They had problems inserting the battery in the radio but were on station and relaxing in their camp.

After realizing all the pieces were in place Toby looked at Reggie and said, "Well it looks like the game is on and there's no turning back now, time to get to work."

"I, for one, am glad," responded Reggie. "I'm a little apprehensive about what we're up against, so little against so much. We can only hope that the old saying is true, 'Good triumphs over Evil', because we are going to need all the help we can get."

CHAPTER TWENTY-SEVEN

Rescued

THE EYES OF the emaciated figure lying on the rickety bed snapped open with a start. Feebly lifting his head he slowly looked around the dim room. The door hadn't opened to admit one of his captors yet he felt a presence in the room. Unable to hold his head up any longer he let it fall back onto the soiled pillow. In barely audible words he called out, "Granny, is that you?" His eyes slowly closed and with a smile on his lips he fell into a dreamless sleep.

The feel of snow was in the air as Reggie stepped from the Winnebago to the ground. Wrapping his arms around himself in an effort to create warmth he slowly circled the vehicle, looking for nothing in particular, but ever mindful the enemy could be anywhere. It was unlikely that DONE was aware of their presence yet, but as easily as it had been for the two bounty hunters to chance upon them, there was a possibility they could have been spotted by others. Satisfied all was well he let himself back into the RV.

Inside the rest of the group had started stirring, so he set about making coffee. The walk in the brisk morning air made the coffee all the more inviting. As he was pouring water into the coffee maker he felt Brandy come up behind him and slip her arms around his waist.

"I love to see a man who knows his way around a kitchen," she mumbled against his broad back. "I guess I'm going to have to keep you."

"You'd better reserve any comment until you've tasted it," Reggie answered as he turned to face the tousle-haired beauty. "I'm using the same brand of coffee, but a Maria I'm not."

"Don't apologize, Reggie," Ruth said, covering her mouth to stifle a yawn. "In this marvelous fresh air everything has a way of taking on a new taste. I remember when I was a child during safer times we would often go up into the mountains and camp out. I cannot recall food ever tasting so good. Maybe we need to cook outside here."

"What a wonderful idea," Brandy echoed. "Maybe we can go out to town later and buy some steaks and have a barbecue."

It was nearing nine o'clock before everyone got up and decided to have a leisurely breakfast of coffee and toasted bagels. Conversation was kept to subjects that had no bearing on their reasons for being here, though each one in their minds was preparing for upcoming events.

When breakfast ended and Toby was collecting the dishes, there was a pounding on the door, followed by the voice of Phil; "This is the police open the door or we'll fill you full of icicles."

With plates and cups balanced in one hand Toby opened the door admitting Phil and Joe followed closely by Sam and Jerod. All were shivering from the cold morning air and Joe showed by the blanched look on his face, he was far from being recovered. He had insisted on sleeping in the tent, which Phil had erected for them, in spite of the objection of the others.

Brandy rushed over to Joe and led him to a soft armchair in the corner of the, now cramped room. Placing the palm of her hand on his forehead, she remarked, "You may look like death warmed over, but your temperature has gone down." Casting a poisonous glance at the other three men in the room, she stated emphatically, "He's too weak to go traipsing off with the rest of you."

Reggie made arrangements to meet Sam and Jerod at a restaurant in Glasgow, and decided to, on Brandy's recommendation, to leave a mournful Joe in her capable hands while the rest headed for town. "Did you ever see such a look of woe?" asked Reggie, describing the look on Joe's face. "However, we're going to be the woeful ones if she can't nurse the big guy back to health by the time any action begins."

They had no way of knowing what lay ahead for them, but it was readily accepted without argument, that Joe was a formidable member of the team and his presence would be sorely missed in any skirmish. He was inches taller and pounds heavier than any of them, but it wasn't his size, which made him a force to be reckoned with, it was his sure marksmanship and ability to react quickly under fire, which made him an invaluable member of this hastily assembled team. Their manpower situation wasn't impressive as it was and to be without someone of Joe's caliber would greatly hamper their efforts.

Toby himself wasn't fully mended. The X-rays his doctor had ordered before their departure showed no broken ribs but several were severely bruised and kept tightly bound and Brandy checked them daily.

Small flakes of snow were falling as Reggie maneuvered the Jeep through the campground. He waved to an elderly couple whose acquaintance he had made on the previous day. They were natives of Montana and were spending the weekend in the camping area while they fished the nearby lakes. Stopping beside them he opened his door and poked his head outside asking, "Hey, Jim, is this stuff going to stick?"

The man, replied, "It's not supposed to, that is, if you can believe the TV weather people, they say there will only be occasional flurries down here where we are, but the higher elevations can expect a heavier snow fall. It better hold off because I have my eye on a big trout down by the old snag. If I hook him be glad to share my catch with you."

"Thanks for the offer, but we have too many mouths to feed. If your trout is that big, you should have him mounted. Certainly hope you're right about the snow, this stuff is nice to look at, but only from a distance as far as I'm concerned. Good luck on your fishing."

Hastily closing the door, Reggie cranked up the heater to its maximum and slowly moved the Jeep out of the campground and onto the two-lane road leading to Glasgow. Jim's comments regarding the snow turned out to be prophetic as the snow dissipated and the clouds, which had been present, disappeared revealing a blue sky.

The twenty plus miles to Glasgow passed quickly and soon Reggie was pulling the Jeep into the parking lot of the local restaurant where they were to meet Lebowitz and Abbott. Recognizing Lebowitz's late model Land Rover Reggie parked next to it and the three climbed out of the Jeep hurrying into the inviting warmth of the restaurant.

The sound of country and western music blared from a jukebox in the corner of the room, looking around they spied their comrades sitting at a corner table and walked back to join them. They signaled a passing waitress to bring coffee for three and a menu for Phil, who hadn't yet eaten.

"This seems to be a popular eating place," Toby remarked, looking around at the crowded restaurant.

"This was the first place we found," spoke up Abbott through a mouthful of food. "Of the few eating places in town this is far and away the best. Music is a little loud, but the service is great and the food is even better. They have a chicken-fried steak topped with the best country gravy I've ever tasted."

The waitress arrived bearing three cups of steaming coffee and a menu tucked under her arm. She set the coffee down in front of the men and with a weary smile offered the menu to Phil, who rejected it, saying, "You know, I think I will try your chicken-fried steak, eggs over easy with wheat toast. Have your cook make those hash browns crisp, please."

A Seattle Times newspaper lay folded on the bench beside Lebowitz, and Toby, hungry for home news picked it up. As he did so the bold headlines caught his eye;

Rainier CEO Falls 20 Stories to His Death. Rainier Investment Company's Chief Executive Officer, Hamilton Davenport plummeted from his penthouse on the twentieth floor of the Rainier Building sometime during the early morning hours. A newspaper driver for the Times discovered his body at 3 PM. His personal secretary, Donnie Little, informed investigating officers Davenport ritually spent long hours in the garden area of the penthouse and police believe he was watering plants on the edge of the wall and lost his footing in water that had spilled onto the inlaid brick floor. Interviews taken from close friends gave no indication of despondency. His housekeeper, Teresa Lester, stated he had been in a good mood when she left for the day at 6 PM. The company was doing so well in the financial world that it had been rumored they were planning on linking up with WorldCompt.

Showing the article to Reggie, Toby uttered a single word, "Fell?"

After reading the article, Reggie commented in a like manner, "Pushed."

Without further comment Reggie cast the paper aside. Now wasn't a good time to go into Rainier Investment's involvement with DONE, but the mention of WorldCompt gave him cause to puzzle, that company's name had come up in his father's papers.

His thoughts were interrupted by the arrival of the waitress who sat a large platter heaped with food in front of a wide-eyed Phil.

Phil, despite his complaint of the size of the portion served, was placing the last morsel of food into his mouth when Lebowitz spoke up, "Don't make it too obvious, but when you can, turn around and look at the two guys who just sat down at the end of the counter. They're the same two who ordered us out of town and then followed us to Las Vegas."

Toby, from his seat against the wall, had a clear view of the doorway and had observed the two when they first came in. Both men were wearing camouflage trousers and Eddie Bauer woolen shirts worn under bulky, black coats. They must have been regulars for the waitress serving the counter knew not to offer them menus. She merely poured coffee into a couple of cups and moved off.

Rising from the table, Reggie suggested he and Toby make themselves scarce for a while in case the two were to recognize them and spread the alarm. Phil remained where he was sitting not wanting to create a mass exodus, which was certain to draw attention.

Oblivious to the two men walking behind him, the man at the end of the counter looked up from his coffee and casually glanced around the room. Spying Lebowitz and Abbott sitting in the back booth, he nudged the man beside him whispering something to him. Both of the suspected DONE agents stared at the men who had managed to elude them in Las Vegas. Leaving money on the counter in payment for their unfinished coffee they hurried out of the door.

Toby and Reggie, who were standing by the restroom door, saw them leave, and walked over to a window overlooking the parking lot and observed them getting into a mud-caked, Ford Broncho. The driver must have started the engine, as evidenced by the steam from the exhaust, but he made no effort to leave.

Walking back to the table, Toby picked up the checks, stating he would pay them, and then said, "Sam, we'll follow you in the Jeep to St. Marie. We'll meet there and go over what we want to accomplish today. Make sure your two-way is on. Phil, how about you walking out behind them but go the opposite direction they do, keeping your eyes on the two guys in the dirty 4X4 parked next to the phone booth."

Toby and Reggie remained inside until it was certain there would be no confrontation outside the café. After watching Sam pull out closely followed by the Broncho, they hastily left the concealment of the café's alcove and piled into the Jeep and not wanting to give themselves away to the men in the vehicle ahead, Reggie held back allowing a vehicle behind him to go around.

Reaching under his seat Toby took out the two-way radio he had put there earlier. Turning it on, he said, "Hope Sam or Jerod remembered to turn theirs on."

Bringing the small handset to his mouth he spoke into it, "Jerod, can you hear me?"

A short crackle was heard and the voice of Jerod came loudly through, "Gotcha loud and clear, how about me?"

"You're a little too loud. Turn the volume down a bit."

Seconds later the voice of Jerod came back, "How about now?"

"Perfect," Toby answered. "As you are aware, your former acquaintances are right behind you. Have Sam find a wide spot on the shoulder and pull off. Both of you get out, go to the front of the car and raise the hood as if you are having engine trouble. We have dropped far enough back that your tail shouldn't suspect they are being tailed. They are sure to stop also, don't attempt to take them alone."

"You're the boss. Sam says he sees a spot just ahead and will be pulling over. Let me sign off so I can get out with him."

"Slow down a bit, Reggie," Toby cautioned. "They should be just around the bend. We don't want them to see us, but we also don't want them to make a move on Sam and Jerod without us being in range to cover them."

Reggie slowly edged forward until they could see the Ford, as well as the Land Rover with its raised hood.

From the back seat Phil spoke up, "Let me out. I'll go across the road and use the ditch line to get as close as I can. I'll try to get abreast of the goons' car, so I can keep our guys out of the line of fire. When I'm in place how about you pulling right up behind them?"

Nodding in agreement Toby watched as Phil climbed out of the back, checked the load of his weapon and raced across the road to the ditch. Reggie was more concerned with the two men now stepping out of the dirty 4X4 but no weapons were visible, yet. As soon as Phil was in position he drove the Jeep back onto the roadway and slowly came to a stop behind the Ford.

The noise of the approaching vehicle didn't go unnoticed and both men turned around and observed the two men dismounting from the black Jeep.

One of the men yelled to the two men as they came near, "It's okay, fellas. Our friends are having some engine trouble, but we have it under control."

As Toby and Reggie drew nearer one of the men screamed to his partner, "Watch out its Nutsbagh and Preston!"

When they fumbled beneath their bulky coats, Phil stood up from his position across the street and ordered in a loud voice, "I wouldn't if I were you."

Neither man heeded the warning; coming up with what appeared, from a distance, to be .357 Magnums, they took aim at the man across the street, which was their first and last mistake. Phil had already cocked his weapon and fired five rapid shots at the over confident combatants; none of the shots went astray as the life of the nearest man was instantly snuffed out. As he fell, he bumped his companion causing Phil's shots to go off target, but they didn't miss altogether, as the second gunman fell to the ground with wounds to his thigh and stomach.

The whole episode had happened so fast neither Reggie nor Toby had been able to get off a shot. Sam and Jerod were just coming around the front of the car with their weapons in hand as the wounded man slipped to the ground. The occupants of a passing southbound car paid little heed, seeing only some cars parked on the shoulder, one with its hood up and men standing around. With the many splinter groups of militia in Montana most natives feared getting involved.

"We need to get these guys off the road before one of the passersby turns out to be a State trooper or a Sheriff's deputy," offered Reggie. "Let's load them in their own vehicle. Use gloves so we don't leave any finger prints."

Working together they lifted the dead man into the rear of the Broncho and the wounded man they laid on the back seat, covering him with a blanket found on the floor. This was a meaningless touch of kindness as the stomach wound was severe enough to eventually prove fatal.

While Toby was wadding clothing into the wound in an attempt to stem the flow of blood, he asked the man a question. "Where is your camp located?"

Weak, but defiant the dying man answered, "Go to hell, Preston. I'm not telling you anything. You're dead meat." Coughing violently he shuddered, jerked spasmodically and died.

As he spoke Toby was undertaking the unpleasant task of searching his clothing for any useable information. The wallet contained a driver's license made out to Trent Lofthus with an address in Helena, Montana, a couple of pictures of Trent with an attractive middle-aged woman (probably his mother) and a tattered, often folded copy of a dishonorable discharge from the Marine Corps.

The search of the other man revealed an ID card that identified him as Joel Richards, also from Helena. Other than the ID card his wallet contained only a metal Swastika wrapped in what appeared to be a piece of a U.S. flag.

"None of the DONE agents we've come up against has yielded a lot of useful information," Reggie noted. "They sure are a secretive organization; and this kid, only nineteen and dying, yet he refused to reveal anything. How do you get this kind of loyalty out of dirt bags? Is it fear, or money, or both?"

"I don't know," broke in Phil, "but we better get these cars off the road before a State Trooper happens by and we end up under the jail."

"Right," Toby agreed. "I'll drive the Broncho. We need to dispose of it where it will be found right away, but where we can do it without being seen. Reggie, how about you leading us and try to find a place for us to pull off, when you do I'll drop the vehicle off and walk up the road to meet you."

With Reggie in the lead the three vehicles headed up the road. They had driven about a mile when Reggie stuck his hand out the window and waved it high in the air. The single building on the lot was decaying, but there was evidence vehicles regularly used the grounds as a turn-around. Checking both ways for traffic, Toby drove the Broncho onto the lot and emerged locking the doors behind him.

The other vehicles in the convoy had stopped several hundred yards up the road, so Toby jogged up and joined them. Hurriedly climbing into the Jeep he encouraged Reggie to move quickly and put some distance between them and the vehicle they had just left behind.

Both cars, with Reggie still in the lead continued up the road maintaining the posted speed, until they arrived at the Fort Peck campgrounds. Pulling into a parking spot near the picnic area the five headed for a distant table.

Once they were seated, Toby addressed the group, "From what Sam and Jerod have related of their confrontation in this general area and with the presence of the two Phil disposed of this morning we have to believe that we are not far from DONE's base of operations."

Looking at Sam and Jerod, he continued, "I would like you guys to take us to the spot where you were confronted and sent packing. We need to have a starting point and I believe that would be our best bet."

"Sure, Toby," answered Jerod. "It's only about a half hour away. There's an old military installation there. The military left long ago and turned the base over to the State. Most of the base is grown over with brush and trees. The eastern boundary is where the missing hunter was last seen and where we saw the guys who told us to beat it."

"Phil, I would like to leave you here for this one," suggested Toby. "Reggie and I will go with Sam and Jerod for a short reconnaissance of the area. If all goes well we'll meet you back at the RV in about four hours. Fill Joe in on what transpired this morning, but when you do make sure the girls can't hear you; we don't need to alarm them more than necessary."

Unable to hide his disappointment, Phil pounded his fist on the table and angrily proclaimed, "I didn't come along to sit around."

Attempting to mollify his long-time friend, Reggie reached over and laid his hand on Phil's arm. "Nobody is asking you to sit around, Phil. We aren't expecting any trouble, but if we run into any and don't make it back we will need you here to direct operations."

"Sorry, fellas," Phil said apologetically. "Things have been happening so fast, it's hard to take the inaction. I've been around long enough to know somebody has to sit on the sidelines, now and then."

"Understood," responded Toby. "If things go as planned we should be back within four hours, but give us five hours before you start looking for us."

Agreeing, Phil took the keys for the Jeep from Reggie and departed, dejected, but determined to accept his part without further complaint.

Looking at the back of the retreating Las Vegas police officer, Sam commented, "I was a cop for over thirty years, but I never ran across a guy like Phil. Watching him in action this morning was something to behold. Never hesitated, just acted automatically. We all better be glad he's on our side."

The drive to the former Air Force base was made without incident, though the road was alive with law enforcement vehicles. Sam, keeping the car at the posted speed limit, arrived at the front of the base in less than thirty minutes.

Turning in to the base through an open gate Reggie looked at the now unused guard house and recalled with nostalgia the years of going on and off military bases with his father. His father always received a crisp salute from the Air Police and Reggie would salute back as if it were he receiving the rendering of respect. *'An unlikely place for a terrorist camp,'* he thought, *'but maybe the least suspected.'*

Driving around the inside of the fence on a badly deteriorated road, Sam commented, "Just beyond the end of the runway there are signs posted prohibiting entry into the woods beyond. If there's a camp back there we never found any sign of traffic going in." Stopping the car, he further commented, "We'd better walk in from here."

"Okay," Toby answered, "we'll make a short excursion into the trees on foot and determine if we can bring the car in."

In its active days the base was used for large transports and its runways stretched several thousand yards into the distance. Brush now pushed up through the tarmac that once welcomed the wheels of thunderous C130's headed for the battlefields of Vietnam. After walking for approximately five hundred yards, Jerod held up his hand, pointing outside the fence to where landing lights, now overgrown with brush and weeds were, he said, "It was right about here where we cut off into the woods. I remember looking through the fence and seeing those lights."

Looking toward the tree line, Reggie noticed what appeared to be an old path leading into the woods. "I'm not practiced at reading sign," he jokingly commented, "but it looks as if someone uses this path on a regular basis. What do you say we follow and see where it leads?"

With Toby leading the way the four moved out in single file. They had moved about a hundred yards when Toby motioned everyone down signaling for silence.

From his prone position he crept back to where Reggie lay and whispered, "I've spotted some movement ahead. Could be nothing more than an animal, but we need to check it out."

Motioning Sam and Jerod to stay put, Toby, with Reggie close behind, crawled forward to the spot from where Toby had first noticed the movement. From concealment behind a huckleberry bush the two looked down into a slight depression in the terrain. Nestled in the trees was a small shed, they continued to scan the area when they spotted a solitary figure, carrying a rifle, walk away from the building in an easterly direction.

They waited a few minutes and then slowly moved down the slight grade toward the ramshackle building. Without need for words they went around the building in opposite directions, weapons in hand. Sam and Jerod, who had moved forward to the spot vacated by their friends, took their weapons out and watched as Toby and Reggie circled the building. Soon they were both behind the building and hidden from view, causing Sam and Jerod to focus their attention on the bordering woods, acting as lookouts.

Down below Toby and Reggie met at a padlocked door, the only opening in the windowless shack. Curious as to why a small, dilapidated building had such a strong lock, they applied their combined strength and managed to pull the jamb from the weakened doorframe. The door opened inward from its own weight revealing a room with only a rickety wooden frame of some kind in the corner. A pile of rags lay heaped on the frame and what appeared to be a plastic plate with some type of mush in it sat on the dirt floor.

An unaccountably eerie feeling came over Toby. Slowly, almost reverently he shuffled toward the rickety frame knowing, even dreading what he would discover beneath the heap of rags. Carefully pulling back the thin, tattered blankets he was horrified by what was revealed. Even in the dimness of the room he was able to make out the figure of what once must have been a vibrant human being. The grossly emaciated figure lying there bore no resemblance to the person in the photo Lucille Graden had given him, but Toby unerringly knew this was Thomas Lincoln Graden, the Third. If there had been any doubt it would have been swept away by the weak voice, which greeted him, "Granny sent you, didn't she? I knew you would come."

Fighting back the tears welling in his eyes, Toby gingerly slipped his arms under the frail body and drew him tenderly to his chest; angrily kicking the plate lying on the floor and sending it and its contents splattering against the wall muttering, "These guys are worse than animals."

With Reggie leading the way and Toby gently carrying his precious burden they walked away from the shack, which had imprisoned Thomas, anger in their heart and vengeance on their mind.

His arms aching with weariness, but unwilling to relinquish Graden, Toby made the long haul back to the car without faltering. Reggie watched as his friend, near total exhaustion from his effort, slid into the back seat of the Land Rover still cradling the frail body, and thought, *'If I were you DONE, I would be worried.'*

Toby spoke for the first time since his display of anger in the tiny cabin, "I can't in my wildest dreams envision any one treating another human being in this fashion. With winter coming on he surely would have died of exposure. Why were they keeping him alive at all?"

"If you can call that living," retorted Reggie.

Heading back to the recreation area, none of the four had been paying attention to the time, but they knew it was well after five PM, when a black Jeep came tearing out of the entrance, nearly tipping as it rounded the corner.

"What did I tell you about the guy?" Reggie asked. "He's probably ticked off we're here and headed back."

Phil recognized Sam's car and made a U-turn on the highway and was pulling alongside the Land Rover before its doors were opened. A gasp of shock rose from his throat upon seeing what was on Toby's lap. "Who do you have there?"

As Jerod opened the door for Toby, Reggie explained to Phil who the person was and how he came to be here. Phil watched slack-jawed as Toby swiveled his legs around bringing himself erect and then carefully stood. Sam had already gone to the door of the RV and was about to open it when the door was flung open; the towering figure of Joe stood in the doorway looking down at the group below.

"Heard the sound of vehicles outside and thought I better check," Joe said a pistol visible in a hand, "Just wanted to make sure they were friendly vehicles."

Seeing the pathetic figure Toby was holding he stepped aside to make way. Reggie placed his hand on his friend's back to steady him as he climbed the two steps into the RV.

Both women moved efficiently about making room in the motor home's primary bedroom for Toby's burden. Once Toby had discharged his ward to the women's care he walked out of the RV stepping into the cool evening air. Reggie waved the others off and silently followed him, knowing he wanted solitude for the moment, but would eventually need to talk.

Finally Toby breaking the silence spoke, "During the entire time I held that young man in my arms I wasn't thinking of him. I was seething inside at the thought of anyone treating Renie that way and what I would do if I got my hands on them. What turns people into such animals, Reg?" Reggie had no response.

Arriving back at the RV they found the men gathered around the barbecue pit roasting hot dogs.

"The women threw us out while they bathed and dressed the young man," commented Joe, "so I figured we could feed the body a bit. Do you want me to put a couple on for you guys?"

"Thanks, Joe," replied Toby. "Come to think of it we haven't eaten since early this morning and then only a bagel."

Toby was stuffing the last morsel of food in his mouth when the door of the RV opened and Ruth beckoned him to come inside. Wiping his mouth on a paper towel he bounded up the steps.

It was Brandy who spoke when he came in. "I spoon fed him a little chicken broth and gave him a few bites of Jell-O. So far he has kept it down. He is awful weak, but he insists on talking to his grandmother. I tried to tell him he needed to conserve his strength, but he's adamant."

Walking over to the coffee table in the middle of the room Toby picked up the small cellular phone sitting there. "You are a marvelous nurse, Brandy, and are absolutely right, but with all he has been through I believe we need to indulge him on this."

From his wallet he took a slip of paper with a phone number written on it and dialed the number, the phone was answered on the first ring, "Hello."

"Mrs. Graden, this is Toby Preston, could you hold for just a minute? I have someone who wishes to speak to you."

Walking to Thomas's bedside he held the phone to his mouth. In a weak but joyous voice, the boy whispered, "Granny this is Thomas."

There must have been complete silence at the other end, for Thomas lay silently with a look of disappointment on his face. Putting the phone back to his mouth Toby asked, "Mrs. Graden, Lucille are you there?"

"Oh yes, Mr. Preston, I'm here. I was so shocked at being called Granny I dropped the phone. Was that really my Thomas? He sounds so different."

"That was Thomas, ma'am. He has gone through a lot and is very weak. Say a few words to him and then I'll come back on and tell you how to get here."

None of the three gathered in the room could hear what Thomas was hearing, but from the look on his face he was more than happy. Thomas repeated the same line over and over, "I knew you would find me. I never gave up hope."

Brandy tapped Toby on his back and softly whispered, "He needs to rest now. He has talked enough." Removing the phone from Thomas, Toby caught Lucille Graden in mid-sentence, "—come to take you home, son."

"Mrs. Graden, this is Toby Preston again. Thomas' nurse feels he needs to rest some more. Let's talk about your coming to take him home. He is too weak to travel unassisted, so I suggest you bring an able-bodied nurse and a wheel chair to the place I will give you directions to. I don't advise you to drive as it is too far; book a flight to Billings, Montana and from there charter a plane to Glasgow, Montana. If you use a travel agent they can make all the arrangements for you. In Glasgow hire a taxi to bring you to the Fort Peck Recreation area. We are at Site # 112."

"How can I ever thank you, Mr. Preston?"

"Its Toby, ma'am and the look on your face when you two are reunited will be payment enough. You should get started making your arrangements. See you soon."

"Good-bye and God bless you, Toby."

CHAPTER TWENTY-EIGHT

The Scales of Justice Begin to Tip

INSIDE THE DIMLY lit Sheriff's office the lone deputy on duty sat scratching his head as he tried to complete the crossword puzzle in the local newspaper. The telephone rang and after the fifth ring, the annoyed deputy picked up the instrument and spoke into the receiver. "Yellowstone County Sheriff's Office, Deputy Albers, can I help you?"

A harsh raspy voice came from the other end. *"Good evening deputy, can you give me any information concerning the two men who were killed at the rest stop outside of Billings yesterday evening?"*

"No sir, any information concerning those two murders, would have to come from the Federal Bureau of Investigation as they took over the case immediately after being notified."

The connection was broken without further conversation.

Thomas Lincoln Graden was safe and securely tucked away in the rear bedroom of the RV. His condition was stable but he was still very weak and emaciated and had to be hand fed every two or three hours until he regained his strength. Brandy had assumed the duties of helping nurture the young man. At first he resisted being cleaned and fed by a woman, but in his weakened condition he stood no chance against the strong will of Brandy, who as a nurse had handled many strong willed men.

Meanwhile in the living quarters of the RV undercurrents of exuberance flowed through the individuals gathered there. They had outsmarted his captors and successfully freed Thomas from the grasp of his jailers without firing a shot.

Toby and Reggie both sat on the fringes of the celebration knowing full well their work was hardly started and there really wasn't any reason to celebrate, but they didn't want to dampen the spirits of the assembled group. Finally Toby cleared his throat in an attempt to gain everyone's attention, "Gentlemen, I hate to put a damper on your celebration but we have some planning to do for tomorrow."

The group slowly quieted down and turned their attention to Toby and Reggie. "Reggie is going to outline what we hope to accomplish tomorrow. All of us will be involved with the exception of Joe, who will stay and provide security for the girls while he's on the mend from his wounds."

Joe bristled at Toby's remarks and growled, "No sir, I didn't come all this way to help and then be left out of the happenings just because I happened to have been nicked by a bullet or two. I think I should be the judge of my condition; if I don't think I can carry my weight, I'll be the first to say so."

Reggie turned to Brandy, "Brandy, you're the one who has been taking care of Joe; what do you have to say about his condition?"

"Joe shouldn't engage in any physical activity until he gets more time to mend. The key word being shouldn't. Joe is right about one thing, he's the only one who can judge if he feels strong enough to cope with the elements and the physical activity," Brandy answered, attempting to be diplomatic and appease everyone.

"I didn't come up here to be left behind, I'm going," declared Joe.

"Well, I guess it's settled; now here's what we are going to do in the morning. Sam and Jerod have been in this area before and will take us to the area where they met with the armed resistance on the south side of the base. We'll go as a group, dressed for warmth and action. We have no idea what we're going to run into, so we have to be prepared for anything. Bring what weapons you feel comfortable with and meet here at O-Six-Hundred. We'll use Sam's Rover and Toby's Wrangler as our method of transportation."

At this point Reggie looked at Toby, saying, "Toby do you have anything to add?"

Toby looked at the group, "As we have all been around law enforcement at one time or another and have seen the evil men do, I want to caution you not to get too carried away with the fact that rescuing Thomas was so easily accomplished. Evidently they weren't expecting anything to happen, so he wasn't guarded or watched. But believe me when I tell you that most of the men we'll encounter in the next several days are men who have no compunction when it comes to taking a life. Most of them have no love of country nor love for anything else but the almighty dollar." He paused for several seconds, and then said, "Reggie?"

"Toby and I have faced several of Mr. Big's hired killers on different occasions. They are ruthless and most of them owe loyalty only to the person that pays them the most money. We're going to be out-gunned and out-manned, but we have one thing in our favor, we are going to out-smart them. Joe, I would like you to bring the gas grenades and wire cutters, they might come in handy. Do any of you have any questions?"

"Reggie you might want to mention the types of weapons they will be using against us, that is if the weapons cache found in Las Vegas is a clue to what they'll be carrying," Phil said.

"Good idea, Phil. Using the arms cache taken out of Las Vegas, as a guide there should be a variety of weapons. The inventory list included machine guns, rocket launchers, and all types of explosives and small arms, with ample ammunition for them all. One of our initial goals has to be to try and locate their weapons; ammunition and explosive storage areas and try to take them out or at least render them useless. We also might try and liberate some of their weapons for our own use."

"Do we try and take some of them alive?" Sam questioned.

"I really don't think that will be possible, but if we can we will," commented Reggie. "We need to locate their headquarters or the place where their field commander is located and try and identify him. I tend to believe that Big doesn't personally run the entire show but passes his orders down. We need to find the guy running the show around here."

"I guess that's it," Toby said, "I think we should call it a day and get some rest; we're going to need it."

An hour later, after they had eaten every scrap of food the ladies had prepared; Sam and Jerod left followed shortly by Joe and Phil. After the RV had been straightened and all of the lunch dishes cleaned up and put away, Toby, Reggie and the women sat at the table drinking coffee and discussing the day's activities.

Toby looked at Ruth and Brandy sitting at the corner of the table engaged in conversation, interrupting them, he asked, "Would you ladies feel more comfortable if we left one of the guys here with you tomorrow?"

Brandy smiled at Toby and responded," I really don't think that would be necessary, for two reasons. Ruth and I can handle ourselves and should the need arise we can use the weapons stored around the RV. Secondly, I wouldn't want to be the one telling one of them they had to stay behind to look after us. Look what happened when you told Joe he was going to stay behind, and he was wounded."

Reggie laughed at her remarks, "Hey Toby your ribs are still on the mend, why don't you stay back and let me run the recon tomorrow?"

Toby bristled at Reggie's suggestion, then seeing the smile on his face, realized Reggie was pulling his leg, so he replied in kind, "My ribs are mending nicely, thanks to the great nursing I'm getting. But I saw from our recent venture your wounds must be slowing you down, you didn't seemed to be moving as fast as usual."

"Touché," Reggie said, laughing, "now that we have decided that neither one of us will be staying back, is there anything else for tomorrow?"

"No," Toby responded, "just what we went over with the guys; when we get to the area where Sam and Jerod were rousted the second time; we'll hide the vehicles as much as possible and travel by foot. The going will be slow because we have no idea where to find the men we're looking for; but from what Sam and Jerod are saying we shouldn't run into anything until we either get close to the fence or inside the fence."

Deciding there was nothing else to be gained by rehashing plans, the men got their weapons and began cleaning them, insuring they were all in good working order. A short time later the lights in the RV were extinguished as the last member of the foursome turned out the light and went to sleep for the night.

As the lights went out in the RV located at the Fort Peck Recreation Area they still shone brightly in the library of a large mansion located in the Rocky Mountains of Colorado. A middle-aged man, tall and slender with a build that made him appear much younger, sat at a large oak desk deep in thought. *'I wonder if my two friends, Nutsbagh and Preston had anything to do with the killings in Billings, Montana. Were those two killed trying to free lance and collect the reward that I offered? Offering it might have been a mistake. I was informed Nutsbagh and Preston were going back to Israel, but that might have been a ruse. I need to make a call to Israel; I should still have a contact there after the recent raids. I might even have to make a trip to my place in Montana.'*

Dawn was beginning to break in the east, barely creating an opening in the fog. A cool mist hung in the air providing for limited visibility. This was what greeted Toby as he stepped out of the RV the next morning. Smiling, he said to no one in particular, "this is just our type of morning. I sure hope this fog remains, especially in the area where we're going."

Engrossed in watching the fog banks roll off the lake he was joined by Reggie, who had walked up unnoticed behind him, "Good morning, pal; wonderful morning for a little walk in the woods."

"Sure is; I hope this fog is as thick there as it is here. It would make our jobs a lot easier."

The voice of Joe came quietly through the thick fog, "Is Brandy up yet? "She wants to change my bandages, so I came a little early. Phil is out at the truck bringing the rest of our gear around."

"Boy, this fog can be heaven sent," said Phil, walking out of the fog. "Sure hope it stays around for awhile. Hard to drive in but real nice when you're out looking for bad guys."

"Why don't both of you go into the RV, there's fresh coffee brewing, Reggie and I will be in shortly," Toby said, as he walked towards the Jeep parked at the rear of the RV.

As Joe and Phil entered the RV, Reggie and Toby began stowing their personal gear in the Jeep. When they finished, Sam and Jerod arrived in their vehicle and parked next to them. After exchanging greetings Toby told the two there was hot coffee waiting for them in the RV.

Sam and Jerod entered the RV and Toby climbed into the Jeep motioning Reggie to join him. "Reg, how do we want to handle things this morning?"

"I assume Phil and Joe would be more comfortable riding with Sam in the Land Rover. We'll let them lead the way until we get into the area, from there I would like to take the lead. Once we get there it's going to be a matter of following our nose and hope we stumble onto something. Probably the best thing for us to do would be to set up some type of search grid using a compass so we don't walk around in circles, especially if this fog stays around."

"Yeah, this fog is going to be helpful in one way and a hindrance in another," Toby responded, "we could walk right into the middle of something and never know it. We're going to have to stay alert."

"Why don't we join the rest of them in the RV, get another cup of coffee and lay out the ground work," said Reggie, "and then get on the move. We have about a thirty minute drive to the area."

Thirty minutes later breakfast was completed and plans finalized and the men loaded into the vehicles and headed out through the thickening fog. Negotiating through the fog was difficult, but forty-five minutes later the lead vehicle, with the Jeep following close behind, turned off the main road, and with headlights off, moved slowly down a narrow dirt road leading deeper into the woods.

After fifteen minutes of slowly navigating through the fog the Land Rover stopped and the engine was turned off; Toby in the Jeep behind them followed suit. Emerging from the vehicles the men huddled, and Sam said in a muted voice, "Can't say for sure if this is the exact spot because of the fog, but its close enough. After being warned off at the northern boundary we drove down this road then walked in for about twenty minutes before we met a group of armed men who weren't very diplomatic in asking us to leave. We insisted we were nothing more just naturalists looking at the wild life, but they had the guns and they persuaded us to leave."

"Okay," said Reggie, "Here's what we're going to do. I'll lead out with Joe bringing up the rear. Let's stay in single file and keep the noise down to a minimum. It looks like the fog is starting to lift, so we are going to have to be careful. If anything happens and we get separated, try and make it back to this spot. We have to assume that anyone we meet from now on is hostile, so take all precautions. Does everyone have their radio?" The men nodded, indicating they had their radios. "Good, make sure you turn off the squelch, we want to keep the noise level down."

The radios were checked then Reggie led out along the overgrown dirt road leading them deeper into the dense woods. As they began their march through the woods the fog began to dissipate with a few patches of bright sunlight shinning through the trees. Reggie, using his compass, attempted to keep their course basically northeast; which was the direction Sam had indicated earlier as the direction they had headed when they met the armed men.

Maneuvering down the overgrown trail was a tiring job and it wasn't long before Reggie decided it was time for a short break. The men waited while Toby tried to determine their exact location on the topographical map he had brought along, and Joe scouted around the immediate area.

328   Ronald Beach and Lee Pitts

He returned shortly and walked over to Reggie and Toby, saying quietly, "I was snooping around about a hundred yards from here and I heard someone talking in the distance. I didn't try and get any closer as I had no idea what was out there and I thought it would be smarter to come back here and alert you."

Reggie nodded, "Toby, why don't you move the men into the trees in front of us, out of sight, while Joe and I scout around and see what's out there."

Nodding, Toby motioned the other men to follow him as he walked into a dense grove of trees, while Joe and Reggie silently moved out with Joe in the lead.

Using the dense brush and trees for cover, Joe and Reggie slowly advanced to the spot where Joe had heard voices. Using his binoculars Reggie searched, what they now knew was a fence line and was about to tell Joe he couldn't see anything when he saw two men carrying what looked like AK-47's step out from behind a bush a few feet inside the six-foot high chain link fence. They appeared to be shooting the breeze as they walked along the fence parallel to Joe and Reggie; they then turned due north and disappeared into the trees.

"Joe, we're going to have to move closer to try and get a look into the woods where they disappeared. But first, why don't you go back and bring the rest of the guys up to this location; I'll stay and keep watch."

Joe nodded and headed back to where Toby and the rest of the men were waiting. When they joined Reggie they hunkered down around him, speaking in hushed tones, pointing to a distant point he briefed them on the situation. "There's a six-foot chain link fence about twenty-five feet in front of us, we saw two men carrying semi-automatic rifles come out from behind a bush. They walked along the fence line to a spot about two-hundred yards down and then turned north, disappearing into that grove of trees."

"What's the plan, Reggie?" asked Toby.

"You guys stay here, while Joe and I try to get closer to find out what we're up against. We're going to cut a hole in the fence just big enough to go through; hopefully we can do it without being spotted. If we are spotted I'm sure you'll know what to do."

"Is there anything you need?" asked Toby.

"Yeah," responded Reggie. "Phil, you have a silenced .38 like Joe's, I'd like to trade you. It would be better, should we run into trouble and have to take one of these guys out."

After Reggie and Phil exchanged guns, Joe and he moved up to the fence. Using wire cutters Joe cut a hole large enough to accommodate his large frame, then once through the fence, they covered the hole with brush and slowly moved toward the grove of trees where the men had disappeared.

Crawling a short distance into the trees they came to a large clearing. Lying down behind a large clump of bushes Reggie peered through the bush and could make out two men standing in front of what appeared to be a large bunker. Both of them were armed with semi-automatic rifles slung over their shoulders and .45 caliber pistols strapped to their waists.

Backing off Reggie motioned to Joe to come closer, "Joe, do you see those guys standing around? They appear to be guarding a bunker."

Joe acknowledged Reggie's comment with a nod.

Reggie continued, "We need to circle around and see if there are more guys and see if we can figure out what it is they find so precious it needs to be guarded."

"What about Toby and the rest?" Joe asked. "Wouldn't it be better if we brought them up to this location so they could provide support if needed?"

"You're right," Reggie acknowledged. "Why don't you go back and get them while I keep watch. Tell them to be extremely careful and not make any noise. Be sure to pile the brush back up against the fence after you come through."

Joe nodded and quietly went back the way they had come.

Reggie moved back to his original position behind the large bush. During the next few minutes, while he waited, he counted at least five men coming and going. There was no pattern to their movement so he had no idea what they were doing, except guarding the bunker.

Hearing a slight noise behind him, he hunkered further down in the dense undergrowth and stilled his breathing. Several seconds later another man armed with a sub-machine gun, walked within twenty-five feet of his location and joined the men on guard.

He breathed a sigh of relief as he watched the new arrival walk up to the two men, asking in a voice loud enough for Reggie to hear, "What's for breakfast this morning?"

One of the men replied, "Same old stuff, it all comes out of a can. I sure will be glad when we can get back to the main camp and have some decent food. I'm tired of eating out of a can. Hell, the Army didn't want those C-Rations any more, but here we are eating them."

"Where are the rest of the guys?"

"Back at camp I suppose. Bill and George just came back from scouting around, so they're probably out back having breakfast."

The other man of the duo spoke up for the first time, "One thing in our favor, at least we don't have to go through the training sessions with Haikim for the next several days. So what brings you out here this morning?"

"Word's been passed out from above that we need to use extreme caution. Two of the men who were supposed to be coming back to camp this morning didn't show up; someone sent them to their maker outside of Billings. The boss thinks someone is headed our direction to play some games with us. Speaking of bosses, rumor has it the big boss is coming here in the next day or two to see how everything is going."

"Well, I guess that means we have to be on our best behavior, whatever that is," replied the guard. Then patting his semi-automatic rifle, he said, "And as for anyone coming snooping around, I think I'll know how to deal with them. I have enough weapons and ammunition within my reach to start World War Three. By the way, who were the two guys that got killed up at Billings?"

"I don't know, I never heard of them. From what I hear through the rumor mill, someone out there is taking offense to what we're doing and have taken out a few of our guys. Do you remember the inseparable duo of Smith and McDuffy? They trained with us for about two weeks before they volunteered for an outside job?"

"Sure, they were some real bad guys, everyone walked around them on tip toes and we were all glad when they left camp."

"Well, they are no longer with us. Someone killed them, so I guess whoever is taking opposition to our little group is a force to be reckoned with."

"Does anyone know who took them out?"

"Yeah," replied the first man, taking a flyer out of his pocket, "It was probably one of these guys."

"Nutsbagh and Preston, I sure would like to meet up with them, that's good money for killing them."

"That's not all; I'm sure you remember Trent and Joe, two guys who have been in camp for about a month. They signed out the other day for a short trip into town and never came back." Then looking at his watch the messenger said, "I had better get on with my job and talk to the other guys and then get back to camp, don't want Number One on my back. You guys stay sharp."

Reggie remained where he was as he heard another slight noise coming from the direction Joe had taken. A few seconds later Joe sided up to him, crawling on his stomach. He moved in close enough to whisper in Reggie's ear, "That was close, some guy, coming this way, must have stepped on a dead branch laying on the ground, it warned us and we all ducked for cover just in time. Toby and the rest of the guys are about fifteen yards to the rear of us."

"Let's go back, we need to talk," was Reggie's muted reply.

Reversing his direction Joe slowly crawled back the way he had come with Reggie following. In just a few minutes he and Reggie crawled up next to Toby who was lying under cover in some dense underbrush with the rest of the team.

Reggie signaled the entire team to close in on him and then he briefed them on what he had seen and heard. At the mention of the part of the conversation involving Smith and McDuffy, Toby commented, "Well, it looks like we are in the right place. What's the plan?"

"This is probably a good place for the team to remain undercover, for now. You'll have to be real careful because the messenger who just arrived should be going back the same way he came, in just a few minutes. Once he has cleared, Joe and I are going to circle around and try to locate the camp the messenger was talking about. Once we do we'll come back and devise a plan. Toby, it might be wise, once the guy clears and heads back the way he came, to send someone up just a little closer to keep a watch on those two guards."

Just then Reggie heard someone cough in the distance. Looking through the brush he saw the messenger making his way past their location, evidently heading back to the 'main camp'.

"Good, he's out of the way," Reggie, whispered. Then he as Joe started moving out, Reggie held up his hand stopping Joe's movement, "Hold it a minute," he whispered, "Toby, I think it would be better to have those two guys standing guard out of the picture, then Joe and I won't have to worry about our backs. What do you think, can it be done?"

"Consider it done," was Toby's reply. "You and Joe go ahead and do what you have to do; we'll take care of those two jokers."

"Okay, Joe, let's go. On second thought we had better stay together. We'll move off to the left side of the bunker through those thick trees and see what we can find."

Reggie and Joe then moved silently around the far side of the bunker. As they left Toby said quietly, "Okay, guys, we have to take out those two guards."

Before he could continue Phil interjected, "Reggie gave me back my silenced pistol; I can move up and take them out, real quick."

"That's a good idea. We'll use that as a backup, but I'd like to try and take at least one of them alive if possible. Here's what we're going to do. Sam, Jerod, and I are going to move to a location just east of them, you get as close as you can without being detected and keep them covered at all times, in case my plan doesn't work. Once Sam and Jerod get into position, I'll move another twenty-five yards down from them and stand up; hopefully when they see me they will come over and Sam and Jerod can jump them. Okay?"

The three men nodded and then moved to their designated positions. Phil found a very comfortable spot under a large bush about thirty-five feet away from where the two men sat smoking and talking. When he saw the others move into position he rechecked the load in his gun and then got into a good firing position.

Seeing everyone was in position, Toby stood up and began a slow walk towards the two men, who were sitting on a bench. At first they didn't see him, so he yelled, "Hey guys, maybe you can help me?"

This brought a startled reaction from the two men, who jumped to their feet and swung their semi-automatic rifles into firing position covering the strangers. They started moving slowly toward him, casting furtive glances around to insure he was alone. One of the men asked, "Who the hell are you and what are you doing out here?"

"Well," Toby replied, "I'm new to the organization and was sent to deliver a message to someone named Bob, but got lost and ended up here and I don't know where I'm at. Can you help me?"

They weren't totally convinced as they continued to move slowly forward, keeping an eye on him while scanning the immediate vicinity. When they got within ten feet of him they stopped, "What did you say your name was, what is your designation, and what unit are you in?"

Toby replied, "I just came to camp yesterday and have no idea what you're talking about and I'm beginning to think I was sent out here on a lark; someone was trying to have fun with me. Now I'm lost and have no idea where I'm at."

Moving closer one of the guards looked real hard at Toby and Toby saw a flash of recognition come across his face. The guard yelled as he started to bring his weapon up into a firing position, "Hey, that's Preston we just saw his picture on that poster."

Hearing the man call Toby by name, Sam and Jerod burst from their positions and dove at both men. Jerod's dive was on target and he hit the man waist high driving him to the ground, a short uppercut knocked the man out. Sam wasn't as lucky for as he dove the man took a small step to the side causing Sam to miss full contact with his target. The rifle he was carrying fell to the ground, but spinning around he was able to get his .45 caliber pistol from his holster and get off two shots, both of them striking Sam. When the man turned to bring his gun up to bear on Toby, Phil put a bullet in his forehead and he fell to the ground.

As soon as Sam and Jerod had made their moves to tackle the two men, Phil had moved from his position. He was too late to keep Sam from being shot, but he didn't hesitate in firing and with deadly accuracy, killed the second man instantly.

Phil joined them and Toby rushed over to Sam to check his wounds. Sam had taken one bullet to the right shoulder and the other one creased his side. Neither wounds were life threatening but were bleeding profusely.

"Jerod, remove the sling from one of the weapons and tie up the wounded guy, then search him and remove everything from his pockets," Toby directed, as he tended to Sam's wound. "Phil, get into the bunker, see if there are any weapons or anything else we can use, then find some explosives and set the place to blow. We have to move quickly."

Meanwhile on the other side of the bunker, Reggie and Joe had just located a small encampment and were trying to devise a plan of attack when the sound of gunfire alerted the camp. Three men burst from the tent erected in the clearing. All three were in various states of undress, but carried semi-automatic rifles. Reggie and Joe stood up together ordering them to drop their weapons and stand still.

There was a split second of indecision and then all of them, as if on command, brought their weapons up to fire on the two strangers standing in front of them. Simultaneously Reggie and Joe opened fire, two of the three men were killed instantly, but the third man got off a burst of several rounds, which fanned the air just above Joe's head. Quickly Reggie fired a shot, which hit the man in the heart, killing him instantly.

Knowing they didn't have much time and wanting to see what was happening on the other side of the bunker, Reggie said, "Joe, it's obvious these three were the only ones here. You go into the tent and see if you can find anything important while I search the bodies."

Quickly finishing their searches they quickly ran back towards where they had left the rest of the team, hoping the gunfire they had heard did not bode ill for the rest of their team.

Back at the bunker, Phil had entered and stood looking inside the dimly lit bunker in amazement. He couldn't believe the vast array of weapons and ammunition he saw, '*Wow,*' he thought, '*I can't believe they were able to smuggle so much stuff into this area without someone getting wise to what they were doing.*'

Shaking his head he set aside several Uzzi's and plenty of ammunition along with two-dozen hand grenades. He then searched the bunker and found several boxes of C-4 explosives, blasting caps, wiring and a plunger. Arranging the boxes of C-4 around the interior, he broke open the boxes, inserted a blasting cap in one of the quarter pound blocks of C-4 in each box then ran the wire from the blasting caps back out the entrance of the bunker, connecting each wire to the plunger.

After putting the finishing touches to the explosives, he moved machine guns, ammunition and grenades to a safe location. While making his last trip with an arm full of ammunition he heard movement in the brush advancing towards him. He stopped, grabbed a magazine and loaded one of the Uzzi's and brought it up into a firing position prepared to take anyone out that showed his face. His finger was on the trigger as two men burst from cover. An instant before his finger caressed the trigger he recognized Reggie and Joe.

"Phil is everyone alright?" was Reggie's anxious question. "We heard gunfire and had to kill the three men in the camp."

"Sam took a couple of slugs, but is still alive. Toby is tending to him now. We're going to have to get out of here before all hell breaks loose and we're up to our rear end in more bad guys. Tell Toby, when you go over there, I'm ready to blow this thing. Joe, why don't you stick around to help me lug these weapons and ammunition?"

Reggie anxiously ran over to where Toby was tending to Sam. Toby looked up and saw the concern on his friend's face and said, "He took a couple of slugs, none of them in vital spots. It looks bad and he lost a lot of blood, but I've stopped the bleeding for now. What's your status?"

"When the firing started on this side, Joe and I had just moved into position when men there came out of a tent loaded for bear and wouldn't drop their weapons, so Joe and I dropped them."

"Good, we had better get a move on it; I know the noise of the firing is bound to bring more people this way. Jerod will need a hand, he has one of the men who were guarding the bunker tied up; I thought we would take him with us and see if we can get anything out of him. Did you stop and talk with Phil?"

"Yes, he told me to tell you he was ready with the explosives. Joe stayed with him to help carry some weapons and ammunition. If you think Jerod can handle the captive by himself for a bit I'll go over and tell Phil to give us about five minutes and then blow the bunker."

"We'll manage, but we have to move now. I think I hear some vehicles coming," said Toby, urgency in his voice.

Toby, Sam, Jerod and the captive began retracing their steps back to the hole in the fence while Reggie ran back to Phil with the information. He then turned and ran to catch up to Toby and his group.

Suddenly he heard a yell followed by several shot; he quickened his pace fearing the worst, when he cleared the dense underbrush he saw Jerod next to the fence bending over the body of a man. Not seeing Toby or Sam, Reggie's heartbeat went into overdrive as he raced toward Jerod, arriving he looked down and saw the face of the captive. Relief washed over him and he asked Jerod," Where are Toby and Sam? What happened here?"

Jerod looked up at Reggie with a grim look on his face," When our prisoner saw we were going through the fence he tried to get away. I yelled at him to stop but he wouldn't stop, so I fired one in the air and he still wouldn't stop, so I shot him."

Just then there was a tremendous explosion, the ground shook and a large fireball rose into the air. As soon as the sound of the explosion died down Phil and Joe came crashing through the underbrush, causing a startled Reggie to reach for his pistol. Recognizing the two men, he put it away and turned back to the fence.

336

Jerod, Phil, Joe and then Reggie crawled through the hole. When Reggie was about half way through there was another series of loud explosions and again the ground shook. In the distance they could hear men yelling in what sounded like total confusion. Running as fast as they could with the weapons and ammunition they had taken from the bunker, the four men made a beeline for their vehicles.

Thirty minutes later they arrived at the location of the vehicles to find Toby sitting in the Land Rover with Sam lying in the back seat. Toby breathed a sigh of relief as he saw the other men, turning to Sam he said, "The rest of the guys are here and it looks like they are all in one piece."

The four, out of breath, ran up to the vehicles, and Joe, always the joker, said, "I haven't had so much fun since the 4th of July. Man, Phil that was some fireworks display you touched off. I wonder if those secondary explosions got any of the bad guys."

"It would be nice to know," Reggie said, "but right now we should get loaded and get out of here. Sam is going to be okay, but he does need some medical attention for his wounds."

Reggie noticed Toby was looking at the map in his hand, deep in thought, and asked, "What's up, pal? Don't you think we should get on our horses and get out of here?"

"Sorry Reggie, I was thinking about what Joe said. We really have no idea how many men we're up against and I'm sure the sound of the gunfire and explosions brought a lot of those men to the bunker area. This would be a good chance to get a closer look at the opposition. I've been studying the map I brought and just east of here there's a rise in elevation and if my calculations are correct, from there we should be able to see the area where the bunker was and maybe we can get an idea of how many men they have."

"Sounds good, Toby; why don't you take Sam and Jerod back to camp in the RV and the rest of us will take a look and join you later at camp."

"No offense," Toby replied, "but I was talking about me going to take a look. So far you have done all the dirty work it's about time I earn my keep."

Reggie looked at his partner, before saying, "I was just thinking about your ribs, do you think—"

"Reggie, I appreciate your concern about my well being, but I can handle a short trek into the woods," said Toby, interrupting Reggie's comment.

Reggie smiled at Toby, "Never thought for a minute you weren't holding up your end. I stand corrected; I'll take Sam and Jerod back to camp, while you, Phil and Joe go on the scouting trip."

Looking at Phil and Joe, Reggie continued, "Take three of those Uzzi's and some ammunition out for you guys put the rest in the Land Rover and we'll be on our way."

When Reggie drove off the three men started walking toward the east with Toby in the lead. Each man, besides his own personal weapons, was now armed with an Uzzi machine gun, thanks to DONE. Twenty-five minutes later they reached the small knoll Toby had seen on the map. Looking to the north they could see a heavy pillar of smoke. Climbing the knoll proved to be difficult due to the heavy underbrush and it took almost an hour for them to reach the crest and find a spot from which they could view the area of the bunker.

Meanwhile, Reggie along Jerod and the wounded Sam arrived back at the RV. One look at Sam sent Brandy into action and she had the men place him on the other bed in the second bedroom while getting Ruth busy with hot water and bandages.

As Brandy worked on Sam, Ruth looked outside the RV and not seeing Toby asked Reggie, "Where is Toby?"

"He had to look at something and took Phil and Joe; they should be here in a little while. Don't worry, Sam is the only one wounded, Toby is okay."

"Thanks Reggie," Ruth said, heaving a sigh of relief.

"How's Thomas doing?"

"Gaining more strength every hour; we have been feeding him about every two hours and his color is returning and he's now able to eat by himself," Ruth replied.

"That's great."

Brandy looked up from administering to Sam and said to Reggie, "A hospital would be the best place for him, but the wounds don't look serious; he's weak from loss of blood, but his pulse is strong. I've cleaned, disinfected and bandaged his wounds, so right now he needs rest and plenty of it."

Back on the hillside, Toby, Phil and Joe lay concealed in the brush while Toby surveyed the scene around the bunker with binoculars. He counted fifteen men heavily armed men digging through the rubble of what was once the ammunition bunker. He swept the binoculars around and located one man who seemed to be directing the search. Handing the binoculars to Phil, he said, "You sure did a good job setting those explosives, there isn't enough left down there to put in a small trash can."

Phil acknowledged Toby's accolade then responded, "Did you see anything interesting down there?"

"Not really, although I saw one man who seems to be providing leadership to the group. I guess he's the one in charge and is the guy we need to talk to."

Phil took a quick look and then passed the binoculars to Joe. He started to scan the area and then excitedly broke into their conversation, "Toby, you need to see this. It looks like Phil blew up more than the weapons and ammunition." Joe quickly handed the binoculars back to Toby and directed him to look at the far eastern edge of the clearing next to a large truck.

Toby took the binoculars and looked in the direction Joe had indicated. At first he couldn't make out what it was he was seeing, but as he continued to look he saw two men walk up to a stack of what looked to be logs, and threw a—body on top of the stack. Toby strained to get a clearer picture of what he was looking at, and then he was hit with the sickening realization that what he was seeing were dead bodies being stacked like cordwood.

"There must be fourteen or fifteen bodies stacked up next to that truck," Toby exclaimed. "They must have gotten too close to the bunker when the secondary explosion went off. I don't like what those men are doing and don't like who they are working for, but that's no way to die, especially in this country."

Handing the binoculars to Phil, Toby closed his eyes momentarily, his lips moving in silent prayer. Phil took the binoculars and slowly panned the scene of devastation below. He had known when he set the charges it was going to be a big explosion, but he had no way of knowing other men would come and get caught up in secondary explosions. The look of so much death in one place took the hardened policeman's breath away. He muttered to no one in particular, '*live by the sword, and die by the sword.*'

After a few minutes of silence, Toby said, "Let's all take one last look at the man in charge down there and try to commit his face to memory, so if we ever see him again we'll be able to recognize him. Then let's get out of here."

After Joe and Phil took a long look, they departed, moving down the slope the same way they came up.

An hour and a half later they neared the Jeep, but drew up short as they saw a young man and woman standing beside it talking. Parked a few feet away was a motorcycle which was evidently their mode of transportation. Toby handing his weapons to Joe walked out of the brush, yelling, "Hey, what are you two doing around my jeep?"

The startled pair jerked around and saw Toby advancing on them. The man managed to stutter out, "Nothing, we meant no harm. We were out riding and just happened upon the Jeep. We haven't touched anything, we were just curious."

"No problem," said Toby. "I just drove off the main road and down here. It's such a beautiful morning I thought I would take a walk in the woods. Do you live near here?"

"No, my girlfriend and I, were out riding and heard a loud explosion and drove in here to see if we could find out what happened."

"Probably just some loggers blowing up some stumps," Toby replied.

"Well, we'll be going, you have a nice day," the young man said.

"You too and be careful," was Toby's response.

The two got on the motorcycle, started the engine and roared off down the dirt road in a cloud of dust.

After they left Toby signaled Phil and Joe and when they arrived at the Jeep they all climbed in and followed the motorcycle down the dirt road, breathing a sigh of relief to be out of the woods and back on the road again.

An hour later they were back at the RV. They briefed Reggie and Jerod on what had taken place after they left and then they went over the day's events. Although there was a feeling of sadness about the deaths of so many men, they all knew in their hearts they had done what needed to be done. Tomorrow was another day; a day of reckoning and the odds were becoming a little better as the Scales of Justice were slowly righting themselves in favor of the team. They had almost lost one good man today for their effort, but they had taken out many of the opposition.

Toby had one more thing to do before he would be able to relax. He picked up his cell phone and walked outside, motioning Reggie to join him. He dialed the number Agent Jones had given him and immediately the phone was answered, "Jones."

Toby briefly explained to Jones the day's activities. He then recommended to Jones he bring his task force in a little closer to the action, suggesting they come into the Glasgow airport, which would put them within striking distance. He also made sure that Jones would not come in until either Toby or Reggie requested he do so.

CHAPTER TWENTY-NINE

Taking the Battle to DONE

THE SMALL CELLULAR phone sitting on the counter reverberated, startling Brandy, who was in the middle of preparing breakfast for Sam and Thomas. Picking up the phone she answered, "Hello?"

A raspy voice came on the line: *"So which little sparrow is this? The pretty nurse or the little Hebrew girl?"* Answering his own question the gravelly voiced man laughingly continued, *"No accent, therefore it must be the nurse. Where is your beau Mr. Nutsbagh, or Mr. Preston, the two flies in my ointment?"*

So overcome by the tenor of the voice on the phone she beckoned for Ruth to follow and raced outside to where the men had gathered to plan for the next strike at DONE. Handing the phone to Reggie, she said in a tremulous voice, "It's him."

Taking the phone from Brandy's trembling hand, Reggie asked, "Are you calling to give up?"

Laughter could be heard over the phone as the gravelly voiced man replied, *"Well, well, aren't we the devious ones? It isn't often that I'm fooled. You had me believing you were headed back to Israel. You two are proving to be worthy adversaries. Give up, never! Thus far you have parried my every move, but you can't begin to know whom you are up against. I always come out on top."*

"We're dealing with deranged people, that much we know," Reggie shot back. "To us you are at the bottom of the heap. Anyone who would take a man hostage and then almost starve him to death is mentally unbalanced."

"What are you blithering about?" the voice demanded.

"I'm talking about how your bunch of sadists fools treated Thomas Graden, you jackass."

The line went silent for a long interval, during which time Toby took the phone from Reggie's hand, and yelled into the mouthpiece, "A nineteen-year old kid with his whole life still ahead of him and your apes turned him into a bag of skin and bones."

"Believe me that was not my wish, I truly regret that it happened and you may be assured heads will roll because of it. But just as the perpetrators of such a deed will not go unpunished you must know that your days are also numbered, my friend."

With that statement the connection was broken. Toby looked down at the instrument in his hand then raised his eyes to the men around him. "We have just been threatened. He never even gave us an option to back off."

"As if we would," Jerod vehemently declared.

"If our problems were only that simple," Phil commented. "We had the advantage of surprise initially, now they know what we're capable of and we can expect to meet stiffer opposition the next time."

"Which means," Toby added, "we can't afford to split ourselves this time; we must stick together. Unless one of you has a better idea I think we should drive around to the west side and come through the fence there."

"Are you suggesting we drive through the woods as far as we can and then hike into the area where we suspect they are located?" asked Joe.

"Exactly," confirmed Toby. "By now they have found the hole in the fence and have it covered. They may even have the west side of the fence patrolled, but they will be spreading themselves thin in order to cover all the directions from which we could attack. With the four-wheel drive vehicles we don't need roads. Once we are close enough we hike in as a unit and make our strike."

"Phil and Joe this is where your silenced weapons will come in," offered Reggie. "I don't need to tell you that surprise will be the key to our success."

"We have no idea what the size of the force is we're up against," interjected Toby, "but we know they have more guys than us."

"What about your friend from the FBI?" asked Jerod. "Can't the Feds come in on this?"

"I called Agent Jones last night and told him what had happened so far. Right now we are here without authority and on private property. The Bureau suffered a lot of setbacks as a result of the incidents in Waco and Northern Idaho and he's a little gun-shy, but has agreed to bring in a tactical force to assist. Our problem is he doesn't expect to get here before late afternoon and won't come in to assist us until we call. We can't afford to wait; we have to move now."

"Okay," Joe, said, "It's time for action. Let's get this show on the road."

"All right men," said Reggie, "Toby and I will take the lead. We'll go around the base on the main road until we find a likely place to go into the brush; stay close behind and keep your weapons ready."

After an hour on the main road and another thirty minutes on a dirt road they finally reached a place where they could angle through the woods toward the western boundary of what was once Billy Mitchell Air Force Base. Using his compass Toby directed Reggie off onto a barely detectable set of tracks leading in the direction he wanted to go. Several hundred yards ahead the tree line was visible. This would offer some protection, but could also be expected to slow down the advance. They had only penetrated two hundred yards into the dense forest when it was evident they could no longer use the motorized transport and would be forced to proceed on foot.

"By my calculations we are still about half a mile from the fence line," Toby pointed out. "Let's spread out to about five yards apart and move forward until one of us sights the fence or any enemy force. We aren't out to take prisoners, but we don't want to stoop to their level either. Use your own judgment when facing one of them. We should stay close together to watch each other's backs, but we all know there'll be no time for questions. We'll have to make snap decisions."

They had moved deeper into the woods when Joe suddenly stopped; raising his arm he motioned the others to get down. He remained standing; touching his fingers to his nose he indicated he had caught the smell of something and then bringing his fingers to his mouth parodying a smoker. Dropping to one knee and using a nearby bush for concealment he scanned the area, unable to find any telltale movement or distinctive shape, which would betray the location of the smoker.

One by one the others had risen to crouching positions and as Toby did so, he gestured toward a large pine tree ten yards distant, from behind which a thin vapor of smoke could be seen curling into the air.

Motioning the others to follow, he began a slow low-crawl toward where the smoke had been detected; noise would travel far in the thick forest with its bed of brush and twigs, so the advancement was a slow tedious process. Toby reached a position only ten feet away when a man garbed in camouflage fatigues arose from behind the tree extinguishing a cigarette in the earth. Toby, fearing he had made some noise to alert the guard held his breath, remaining deathly still.

Their movements were severely restricted as the guard, with a machine gun cradled in his arms, circled the tree apparently stretching his legs. No amount of training can totally conquer boredom and from the way he lazily looked around at his surroundings it was evident he was seeing nothing but forest. This proved to be his undoing, for as he turned back to the tree, the big arm of Joe encircled his neck shutting off his air supply. His weapon fell harmlessly to the earth and was quickly picked up by Toby.

"We have to assume he's not out here alone," Reggie noted. Turning to Joe he said, "Gag him and bind him to the tree. Phil, you and Jerod make a check off to the left and see if we have another outpost nearby."

While Joe was trussing their captive, Toby reached into his backpack and extracted one of the hand grenades that had been confiscated from DONE's ammo bunker. Holding it in front of the prisoner's face he pulled the pin. Still holding the spoon tightly he said to the wide-eyed prisoner, "Just to ensure you don't try to escape I'm going to place this between you and the tree. I suggest you remain very still, for tomorrow will never come if you jar this loose."

The man was in such an abject state of terror that he never saw the exchange of a green pinecone from the hand of Reggie for the grenade. As Toby slid the pinecone between the man and the tree, Reggie carefully replaced the pin in the grenade. Joe took one more wrap around the tree and the man's midriff to prevent an accidental drop of the cone, thus revealing the ruse.

A loud rustling in the brush caused the three men to dive to the ground their weapons out in front of them in a defensive pose. Looking in the direction from which the noise came they were relieved to see Phil tromping through the brush dragging a body with Jerod close behind carrying an array of weapons.

"Was forced to leave one of them behind," Phil commented. "We found two of them passing around a bottle of Johnny Walker. When I advised them to drop the bottle and their weapons one of them felt brave and raised his weapon. He's the one we left behind."

"Lash him on the opposite side of the tree from his compatriot," Reggie directed. "As big as this tree is we're going to have to waste another grenade. Toss me one will you, Toby?" Once again the subterfuge was reenacted for the benefit of the new captive.

Warily they resumed their advance to the battle they knew lay ahead. With three of the enemy down and an unknown number still ahead they eagerly yet apprehensively moved out. To stay as mobile as possible some of the heavier weapons they had began with were left behind, hastily camouflaged to avoid detection. Regretting the necessity of parting with some of their firepower they still realized the disadvantage of being slowed by the weightier weapons. Handguns and the lighter Uzzis made up the bulk of their arsenal. The backpacks were kept, but lightened for expediency's sake.

Beams of sunlight could be seen through the dense woods and it was one of these beams, which saved the team from almost certain death. As cautious as they had been during the advance they would have stumbled onto the three men burrowed beneath a large bush, had it not been for the sunbeam reflecting off something metallic.

The time for stealth and silence was past. The fence could be seen only yards away. A series of bursts from the weapons they held in their hands might eliminate the nest of suspected terrorist, but would consume too much valuable time in the process and give other members of the opposing force time to assemble. Simultaneously Phil and Toby removed hand grenades from their backpacks and in unison removed the safety pins. Releasing the spoon they cocked their arms back and on a silent count of three both men lobbed the deadly missiles at the spot where the metallic reflection had been spotted.

The accuracy of their throws and the explosive charges served their purpose well as three forms leaped from their hiding place just as the grenades exploded. Rushing forward the members of the team stopped just long enough to examine the mangled bodies for signs of life and finding none they ran toward the fence. A gate was discovered just to the left of where the DONE men had been laying in wait. Phil quickly checked the gate for possible booby traps, finding nothing they entered the gate.

Glancing around Toby stated the obvious, "Our element of surprise is gone, but we still have to proceed with caution. It looks like there are two paths through the brush going in different directions, Phil, you take Joe and Jerod and go to the left, Reggie and I will go to the right. We have to be extremely careful we don't get caught in our own crossfire."

Shortly after they parted gunfire sounded from the direction taken by Phil and his team, but Toby and Reggie proceeded knowing there was nothing they could do to help. Splitting up had been the best thing to do at this point and they had to continue and hope for the best. They soon realized the confrontation between Phil's team and the terrorists was to their advantage. A few yards ahead of them a group of three men hastily arose from their hiding places in an apparent attempt to join in the fray. Without hesitation Toby and Reggie used the Uzzi's they were holding.

Moving forward with caution they checked for signs of life, finding none. Noting the facial features and attire of one of the bodies, Reggie remarked, "Looks as if DONE is making use of Middle Eastern terrorist cells to make up some of their fighting force."

Using evasive tactics to avoid detection, they once more advanced in the direction of a large clearing. On the outskirts of the field they lay in a prone position, scanning what appeared to be a training site; skeleton's of cars and burnt out false building fronts lent truth to the fact.

There was nothing stirring, but both men were aware that death could be waiting for them so they maintained caution. Removing binoculars from his backpack, Reggie slowly scanned the woods on the opposite side of the field. About to lower them he halted and whispered to Toby, "Just to the right of the burnt out Cadillac, about five yards into the woods, I can't tell how many men are there, but I see at least two."

Using no more motion than necessary, Toby pulled his binoculars from the side pocket of his coat and was focusing the lens when he detected movement to the left of the spot where Reggie had directed him.

It was Phil. Was he aware of the men lying in wait? Turning to Reggie he said, "Phil and his team are moving in on the left. They may not know about those men hiding in the grass, is your throwing arm accurate enough to throw a grenade right to that spot?"

"Would like to have a couple of practice tosses," he replied, "but guess I don't have time for that, huh?"

Handing Reggie a grenade from his backpack, Toby stated, "This is my last one, make it good."

Reggie was starting to rise to his feet to gain the leverage needed to throw the projectile when Toby restrained him, exclaiming, "Phil has seen us, hold the grenade."

Relieved, Reggie resumed his prone position, as Toby made use of sign language to indicate to Phil the presence of the person or persons lurking just beyond.

An interminable amount of time passed as Reggie and Toby waited for the conflict to take place between the two forces. They couldn't see their friends, but movement could be seen in the brush as one or more of the team slowly advanced. Patience is a learned trait and the two friends practiced that trait with clenched teeth as they waited for the outcome. A long burst of fire came from the vicinity they had last spotted movement, followed by a short burst from the opposition's position, then silence.

Through their binoculars, Reggie and Toby watched the tall figure of Joe run toward the area they had just fired upon. A shot rang out and Joe was jolted back slightly only to recover and send a quick burst from his Uzzi into the area where the shot had come from. Phil and Jerod had only been steps behind the big man and were seen tending Joe's wound. Sure it was safe Reggie and Toby raced across the field at top speed to join their friends and check on Joe's condition. All were relieved to discover that the Kevlar vest Joe wore had deflected the round, knocking him off balance but not drawing blood.

After insuring Joe was okay, Phil briefed Toby and Reggie on what his team had encountered to this point, "We met two pockets of resistance when we first started out. This twosome makes three and each group had at least one person of Middle Eastern descent. What do you make of that?"

"We ran across one also," Reggie answered. "We think DONE has been importing these guys on container ships under the guise of being crew members. They come into Tacoma and a Customs agent, who is obviously on their payroll, closes his eyes to allow them off the ship. Most of the stuff we blew up yesterday came through the same channels."

"What can you do when people in your own government entrusted with responsible positions help a scumbag organization like this," Jerod asked.

"They do it for the green stuff, man," responded Joe. "Most of them don't look at the long range damage of their actions, their greed runs too deep. I don't think any of the traitors realize what they're doing."

After regrouping and on the move once again they had only advanced about 100 meters when they spotted several buildings in the distance. The buildings gave the impression of having been hastily erected, barely more than lean-to's. However well trained the group of terrorists may be in the cowardly acts attributed to them, they weren't trained as carpenters.

"I just caught some movement under the near building," Phil said quietly.

"We still have several grenades, let's use them to our advantage," Joe suggested.

"Okay," Toby said in agreement. "Reggie, you have the better arm, you take the building farthest back to the left. Joe and I will take the middle one and Phil and Jerod get the nearest one."

Wanting to make sure all the grenades were launched at the same time Toby counted down and then with deadly accuracy the five grenades hit their intended targets achieving the desired effect of partially destroying the buildings.

After the dust settled the group slowly advanced, weapons at the ready position and began a thorough search of the demolished structures uncovering fifteen bodies. A moan was heard coming from beneath a pile of rubble. Removing the debris they discovered a young man with a large piece of timber protruding from his chest. Unable to stem the flow of blood from the wound, Toby took his poncho from his backpack and tucked it in and around the chest wound as best he could and then leaned and down spoke to him, "We're sorry it has to end this way, but we intend putting an end to this now. Where is your leader and how many more of you are there?"

Whether it was Toby's act of kindness or the knowledge he was dying and the need to make amends, the young man answered in a weak voice. "Number One has four men with him at the headquarters building. Someone from the FBI is there too." Flecks of blood spewed from his mouth as he continued, "And the guards are dug in behind a stump just in front of the door." The last words were barely audible, accompanied by convulsions as he went into the throes of death.

In a luxurious cabin some miles distant a wiry muscular man of middle age sat in a position of silent repose behind an oak desk. An array of telephones took up one corner of the desk. As if on cue the red one rang. Picking up the receiver, he spoke into it in his raspy voice, *"I expect this to be news of the demise of Nutsbagh and Preston, Number One."* After a brief hesitation the voice on the other end of the line detailed the events of the morning. In an unusual display of temper the man behind the desk angrily swiped at a stack of papers sitting on the desk, sending them flying across the room. Screaming into the phone he berated the caller, *"With all the firepower and personnel I have provided you with you are telling me you are defeated? Destroy all evidence and meet me at the rendezvous point in one hour. Bring that worthless Samuelson with you."*

Slamming the receiver onto its cradle he stared blankly out the window for a few moments, then spoke into the nearby intercom, *"George, warm up the chopper, I'll be down in five minutes. Get Bob on the phone and tell him to have the jet warmed up."*

The others had gathered around as Toby was bent over the dying man, Joe looked down and commented, "In a different setting the guy could have been a hero. Too bad his loyalties were misplaced."

Standing in the middle of the ruin, Reggie looked around and remarked, "As I look around I see a lot of carnage, but with all the waste of human lives I thankfully reflect on the one life we saved; Thomas Graden. I would love to be there for the reunion with his grandmother."

An elderly woman stepped down from the six-seat Cessna plane. The energy she exhibited belied her eighty plus years. She had reason to rejoice as she was going to see her Thomas. A burly young man climbed out behind her. Daniel, the male nurse she had hired, didn't look quite as enthusiastic. The rough ride in the small aircraft had caused him to regret accepting this assignment no matter how lucrative the offer. Behind him two men dressed in business suits disembarked. The two had been at the counter of the small independent airline when Lucille Graden and the medical aide she brought along arrived. They had been on the same flight from Seattle, but had gone unnoticed by the excited woman and her companion. Claiming to have urgent business in Glasgow they offered to pay well to share the chartered aircraft. Feeling extremely generous in light of receiving her grandson back she assented refusing any offer of money.

A battered Dodge Caravan awaited them at the building, which served as a terminal for the Glasgow Airport. The driver, a grizzled veteran who owned and operated the single taxi business, greeted them with a toothless smile, "Howdy, folks. I'm Alex Grant, welcome to the thriving city of Glasgow. Let's get your stuff loaded and then we can head for the campgrounds. What brings you up our way? Fishing is good, but you don't have any gear, so you must be just visiting. Who's the wheelchair for?" The loquacious old-timer was wearing on the young nurse, but Lucille Graden was in such a state of euphoria that she was oblivious to the chatter.

Back at the camp, Brandy was sitting at the picnic table adjoining the big RV when the van pulled up. The vehicle hadn't quite come to a full stop when the back door opened and Lucille bounded out. Without the benefit of introductions, she excitedly questioned, "Where is he?" The actions of the joyous grandmother seemed to be the only force that could end the continuous talk of Grant, for he stared slack-jawed as his gray haired passenger jumped from the moving vehicle. Daniel sat stunned with incredulity as he beheld the vivacity of his employer. If she wasn't more careful he feared he would have two patients to tend to.

As Lucille was being escorted into the motor home, the two men who had traveled with them, had parked their car some distance away and were now wending their way through the camp areas of the other campers as unobtrusively as possible. Grant had stayed with his vehicle while Daniel accompanied the elder Graden inside, the sounds of a joyful reunion distracted him and he didn't know there was a presence behind him until something hard slammed into the side of his head rendering him unconscious. Quickly trussing him with tape found in the weathered vehicle, the assailants threw his bound body into the back of the vehicle on top of the wheelchair.

Scanning the area to be certain their activities hadn't been witnessed they walked up to the large camper and knocked on its door. The lead man asked Ruth, who had responded to the knock, "May we speak to Mr. Nutsbagh or Mr. Preston? We're with the FBI."

Not willing to trust anyone, she stepped down to the ground and asked for identification. As the man who spoke was reaching for his wallet the second man overpowered her, clamping his hand over her mouth. Speaking in a muted voice, he said, "Now if you are a good girl I won't hurt you. The three of us are going inside where we'll wait for your friends, who evidently aren't here."

Keeping her in a tight grip he beckoned his friend to open the door. Pushing Ruth up the steps in front of him he hurled her to the floor. As he brandished his weapon at the RV's occupants, he ordered, "I want to see everyone's hands; even yours, old lady. If there's someone in the back room they had better come out with their hands high or we'll to kill all of you."

With fire in her eyes and anger in her voice, Brandy answered the gunman. "There's a very sick man in there. He can't get up to come in, but I'll open the door for you."

Blocking the way, Brandy said in a loud voice, "He's very sick, he can't harm you. Leave him alone."

Gentlemanly behavior wasn't one of the better sides of the two so the man forcefully pushed Brandy to one side and barged into the bedroom where Sam was lying peacefully with his eyes closed. "The guy looks dead," he yelled back to the other man.

"Well make sure he is dead," the obvious leader of the duo, commanded. "Shoot him!"

Standing in the doorway to the bedroom he obscured the ringleader's view of Sam and as he turned back to Sam he found himself staring into the barrel of a Police .38. Without warning the recumbent ex-police officer sent four evenly spaced bullets into the man's chest. Seeing his companion fall the other intruder emptied his weapon at the body on the bed. Supposing the other occupants of the motor home would be cowed at his presence he began to reload his empty gun with bullets he removed from his jacket pocket. While he confidently was in the process Ruth came up behind him kicking him hard in the groin, as he was falling Thomas pulled a snub-nosed .32 caliber pistol from under his blankets and fired pointblank into his face. No one could have been more shocked at Thomas's actions than his grandmother, but had she experienced the long weeks of isolation he had undergone she would have applauded him.

The first shots fired must have alerted neighbors for the sound of sirens approaching could be heard. Brandy retreated quickly to the bedroom to check on Sam and finding him dead she yanked the torn bloody covers off him, replacing them with clean ones. She then smoothed his features giving him the appearance of one in deep sleep.

Leaving the room she left the door halfway open knowing investigating officers would want to see the room's contents. Just as she finished there was a loud pounding at the door, Daniel, still reeling from the shock of the events, was the closest to the door and opened it admitting two law officers. "We are responding to your neighbor's report of gunshots," an officer wearing sergeant chevrons stated. "Is there a problem here?"

Moving around the speechless medical aide, Ruth explained to the sheriff's deputy what had transpired, leaving out only the shooting of Sam. Brandy had taken the weapon Sam had used and was prepared to claim credit for the shooting of the first intruder. Another deputy had discovered the trussed up Grant and was getting his story as curious campers gathered around.

Lucille explained the presence of the two men on her chartered plane commenting she knew no reason why they had followed her. The officers spent an hour questioning the vehicle's occupants, only once glancing in at Sam. A hearse arrived from the coroner's office and carted away the bodies, leaving Brandy and Ruth to restore a semblance of order to the RV.

Granny looked at her Thomas with adoration and newfound respect. He would always be her baby, but he, in his weakened condition had shown he possessed the strength of his departed father and grandfather.

Ruth and Brandy sat on the couch, looking at each other as the adrenaline drained out of them, Brandy released a big sigh and spoke with anguish in her voice, "Will this madness never end? Now we sit and wait when our men are still out there battling these maniacs."

As the small band sifted through the debris in search for weapons and ammunition, Jerod looked up then glancing over at Reggie made the observation, "Would have been nice for Sam to have been in on this. He took it real hard when we let these guys chase us off. He really wanted to be here when we squashed these guys."

"Yeah, I suppose I would feel bad too, but knowing he's back there with the ladies and Thomas makes me feel good," Reggie replied. "I'll feel better when we are out of here."

"One more small pocket of resistance and we should be there," remarked Phil, as he stuffed his pockets with loose shells. "We have been fortunate thus far, but the leader of this pack has probably fortified himself real well. It will take more than a couple of grenades to dislodge him."

"Maybe not," offered Joe. "The kid told us four men were dug in behind a stump; which limits their mobility. Why don't we spread out and surround their location. Phil and Reggie are the only ones of us least hampered by wounds or age, so if they were to skinny up a couple of trees and act as snipers and spotters we could do the rest from the ground. The two men in the building will either give up or run for it once their protectors are eliminated."

They all agreed there was no other feasible plan short of using armored tanks, which were in short supply at the moment. Toby took out his cell phone and made the call to Agent Jones, alerting him to come in and mop up and then the plan was put in motion. They spread out as they moved toward the location of their last point of resistance.

There was no pre-arranged signal to start firing, but each member of the ground crew was ready when Reggie and Phil began the assault from their positions high in the trees. The men hiding behind the stump weren't prepared for being shot at from above and after the first shots they returned fire and then attempted to gain entrance into the building only to be cut down by the ground unit.

One of the enemy shots clipped a branch near Reggie causing him to lose his balance, nearly sending him tumbling to the ground. It was his quick reaction and disregard for his weapon that allowed him to catch himself on a branch below.

The situation suddenly turned serious again when Jerod shouted, "Over there, coming out of a hole in the ground—two men! One of them is dressed in a suit, must be Samuelson."

"They are too far for our weapons to reach them," Reggie said. "Toby, how about you and I give chase on foot?" Turning to Phil, he continued, saying, "Take Joe and Jerod and scour the building. Confiscate papers and anything else of importance. Be careful of booby-traps. Meet us at the south fence as soon as you're finished."

The fleeing duo had a large head start on Reggie and Toby, but the two friends possessed greater speed and physical endurance, so were able to slowly gain ground. The man in the lead was dressed in the same camouflage uniform of the men they had encountered previously and was carrying a large valise, which he set down as he stopped and turned to face his pursuers. Pulling a large pistol from the holster on his hip he took aim at the charging pair, but before he squeezed off his first round the air around him was full of flying lead as Toby and Reggie cut loose. Samuelson had abandoned the man, who Toby recognized as the man called Number One, from the cleanup effort at the blown up bunker and continued to run in the direction they had been headed. The bullets from Reggie and Toby's guns forced the man to be driven away from the bag he had set down and he decided running was better than death. After firing until his weapon was empty he ran after Samuelson.

Arriving at the discarded bag, Toby stooped down to examine its contents. On top he found a sheath of papers, some maps of locations throughout the United States and what appeared to be applications forms. Looking further he discovered numerous bundles of crisp U.S. currency. Glancing up at Reggie, he commented, "Looks like we have found a way to cut our losses and help finance the fight against terrorism."

It would be an understatement to say Reggie wasn't interested, but he was dismayed, for the stop to check the valise had given Samuelson and Number One the opportunity to disappear from sight. Dejected, despair in his heart, Reggie stared intently at the spot where they had been seen last, he vowed in silence, '*I will not let you get away from me. Mom, dad, I swear you will rest in peace soon. This isn't over!*' Hearing the sound of a helicopter approaching from the west, Reggie beckoned Toby to follow. '*Samuelson, you are mine.*'

CHAPTER THIRTY

The Chase is on

TOBY AND REGGIE ran towards the spot where the two men had disappeared but were stopped by a shout from behind them. Suspecting the worst and as if by some unseen signal Reggie broke to his left diving down behind a small tree and Toby broke to the right also finding cover behind another tree. Peering from their covered positions they saw the rest of the team coming toward them at a fast clip. Arriving at Toby and Reggie's positions, the men stopped to catch their breath. Phil used the time to relate what had happened when they searched the building.

"We checked the building; all we found were some papers and maps. As we started to gather them up we heard gunfire. We checked and saw the FBI starting to move in. Not wanting to get caught up in their business we beat a hasty retreat."

"Good thinking, Phil," Reggie replied. "Joe, do you still have the wire cutters?"

"Sure do," Joe replied.

"Good. Go over to the fence and cut a hole in it so we can get out of here."

A few minutes later Joe had the hole cut and they were on the other side of the fence. Once they were through Toby handed the bag containing the papers, maps and money to Phil saying, "You guys get to the vehicles and get out of here as fast as possible. Reggie and I have one more thing we need to do. Take both vehicles, we'll find our own way back when the time comes."

Joe looked up as Toby spoke and said, "We aren't going to leave you two here facing trouble alone."

"Joe, we appreciate your concern, but this is something Reggie and I have to do; no arguments, just get on your way, we'll see you back at the camp in a little bit."

The appearance of Agent Jones and his FBI force on the scene indicated they all should be leaving, but Toby and Reggie had to find out where Samuelson and the infamous Number One went when they disappeared.

After the rest of the men departed Reggie and Toby turned to resume the chase, when Toby said, the strain of the past few hours evident in his voice, "Things look like there're going to get tight."

Reggie's body sagged out of weariness, his mud caked face revealing the disgust that the job was coming to an end and he was no closer to finding out who ordered his parents killed than when this escapade started months before in a coffee shop in Las Vegas.

He sighed, not out of the weariness his body felt, but that he had failed to mete out the final justice to Samuelson. Now he was gone, as was the other man they desperately wanted to take alive—Number One.

Suddenly he caught a glimpse of two people running down the inside of the fence. "I wonder who that could be?" he questioned.

Toby quickly turned to look but saw nothing. "What did you see, Reggie?"

"Out of the corner of my eyes I picked up two men running along the inside of the fence, moving east. I couldn't make out any features but one of the men was in a suit which fits Samuelson's description."

"Okay, let's go."

Toby and Reggie started at a fast lope along the outside of the fence moving in the same direction as the two men. Close to the fence there wasn't a lot of brush, because of the outer boundary road, so they were able to maintain a very fast pace and within a matter of minutes, they saw the two men on the inside of the fence. The run must have been too much for them, because they had slowed down and were taking deep gulps of air.

Advancing to within fifty feet of the two Reggie yelled, "Stop right where you are!"

Both men jerked around in complete surprise, not believing they were still being pursued. When they turned, Reggie and Toby recognized

Samuelson. Toby, taking a second look at the other man realized he was looking at Number One.

Within seconds both Samuelson and Number One brought their weapons up and began firing at Reggie and Toby but in their haste all of their shots were high and wide. Reggie took deliberate aim and pulled the trigger of the .357 Magnum he was carrying. Samuelson fell to the ground as the bullet from Reggie's gun struck him in the leg tearing away a large chunk of his left kneecap. Number One dropped his weapon and moved into the trees dragging Samuelson behind him.

"We have to get on the other side of the fence, if we hope to get them," Reggie said.

"Give me your jacket. We'll use it to cover the barbed wire so we can crawl over."

By the time Reggie got his jacket off Toby was already halfway up the fence; catching the thrown jacket he threw it across the barbed wire and crawled over jumping to the ground on the other side. Reggie threw the weapons to Toby and started climbing the fence. Halfway up he hesitated, watching a low flying helicopter pass directly over their heads, after it passed Reggie completed his climb and jumped to the other side. When they picked their weapons up and begin moving once again they saw the helicopter descending about two hundred yards in front of them behind a grove of trees.

Looking at the helicopter as it descended, Reggie commented, "That doesn't have the markings of a FBI helicopter. I wonder? Damn, it must be coming in to pick up our two friends. We better get a move on, if we want to finish what we started."

Within seconds the partners were at full speed, dodging trees and clumps of under brush.

In a few minutes they broke into the clear to see the helicopter, its rotors still turning sitting on the side of a long unused runway. Also sitting on runway was a sleek Gulf Stream jet, its engines running apparently waiting for the helicopter's passengers.

They stopped and watched as one man walked from the helicopter and up the steps of the jet. The two men they had been chasing, Samuelson and Number One were making their way across the tarmac heading towards the jet. Samuelson was limping badly and couldn't keep up with Number One, who was no longer helping him. Number One bounded up the steps of the Jet and disappeared inside.

358 RONALD BEACH AND LEE PITTS
Its mission completed the helicopter lifted off, creating a terrible down wash, which momentarily blinded Reggie and Toby with the blowing dust and debris. When the air cleared they saw Samuelson almost to the bottom step of the jet. Suddenly a lone figure, carrying a semi-automatic rifle appeared in the doorway of the jet; it wasn't Number One, but rather a slender middle-aged man, with a full head of white hair.

As he appeared Toby shouted a warning and both he and Reggie hit the ground seeking what cover they could find. Looking up they saw the man deliberately point the rifle at them, then slowly swung the muzzle back to a startled Samuelson, who attempted to reverse his course, but was hampered by his bad leg. The man pulled the trigger and Samuelson was dead before he hit the ground.

Even from where Toby and Reggie lay on the ground they could see the sadistic grin on the man's face. He then waved his free hand at them as the door was pulled closed and the jet started to move down the runway.

The two partners lay motionless transfixed by the drama which had played out before their eyes. They didn't move as the jet lifted off the runway and disappeared into the clouds.

Moving over to Reggie, Toby, his eyes showing anger, said, "I think we just saw Mr. Big!"

With a sigh and a shake of his head, Reggie replied, "Winners but losers; we fought a good fight and won a battle today but lost the war. I have an eerie feeling we haven't heard the last from those two."

We'd better get going; it's going to be a long walk back to the RV," Toby said. "Before we start I want to give Jones a quick call and tell him about his ex-side kick, I'm sure he would like to bring his body back."

"While you're making the call I'll check down by those old buildings at the far end of the runway to see if there's a faster way out of here."

As Reggie jogged off in the direction of the distant buildings, Toby placed his call. On the third ring it was answered, "Jones."

"Terry, Toby here, did you see a small jet take off just a few minutes ago?"

"Sure did. Was that something included in this business we're in the middle of right now?" questioned Terry Jones.

"Yes, in fact it left here carrying the Big Man and his number one."

"Damn, I should have called it in and tried to get an intercept on them, but I was rather busy at the time, someone was trying to separate my head with a semi-automatic rifle."

"Okay, I just wanted to tell you your ex-friend Samuelson, is lying over here where the plane took off from. Evidently he outlived his usefulness or didn't remember to buy a ticket because the Mr. Big took him out with a semi-automatic rifle before the plane lifted off."

"I was wondering what happened to him. After all that's happened I can only say, it couldn't have happened to a nicer guy," was Jones reply. "By the way, before I forget, we found some papers indicating there were other cells of these people practically from coast to coast. When we finally get this mess cleaned up I'll have more of an opportunity to read and digest the material and let you know exactly what we found."

"We're out of here but we also have some papers you need to see, give me a call later this evening and we'll make arrangements to get them to you. We're going back to camp and then heading back home. Thanks, Terry for all your help. Come see us when you get a chance, and keep your head down."

Toby signed off and started at a trot toward the old buildings where Reggie had headed. He was about halfway down the runway when he heard an engine roar to life and saw an old military Jeep come around the corner of one of the buildings.

Driven by instinct he dove into a nearby drainage ditch seeking cover. Kneeling in the icy water he watched shivering as the Jeep came roaring down the runway at full speed. Not wanting to be seen by the occupant of the speeding Jeep, Toby flattened further down into the ditch until his body was covered with water and only his head showed above the water line. There he remained until the Jeep roared past his location.

Toby was just about to crawl out of the cold, muddy water when the Jeep's brakes squealed and the vehicle came to a sudden halt fifty yards from where he lay shivering in the ice-cold water.

Several seconds later when he heard Reggie's voice yelling his name he realized it was Reggie driving the Jeep. Shivering and dripping with muddy water he got up from the icy waters and crawled up the side of the steep drainage ditch and through chattering teeth he managed to squeak out, "Over here, Reggie."

Approaching the Jeep he looked at his partner, saying, "Well, I needed a bath anyway." He then sat down in the seat of the Jeep and said, "Let's go home, I forgot the towels."

Reggie looked at his partner, who was still dripping water from head to foot saying, "Don't tell me I have to take that kind of a bath before we get home."

Driving over the overgrown dirt road along the fence line they came to a small, unused vehicular gate that stood wide open. Driving through, Reggie made his way back to the main road and pointed the Jeep towards the camp grounds.

An hour later Reggie pulled the Jeep into the Fort Peck Recreation area, making his way to where the RV was parked. Nearing the RV they were overcome with anxiety when they saw a crowd of people milling around their campsite engaged in animated conversations, accompanied by finger pointing and hand waving.

Reggie quickly parked the Jeep then Toby and he hurried toward the RV. They were closing in on the RV when Ruth came bounding out of the door straight into Toby's arms, followed by an equally excited Brandy, who jumped at Reggie almost causing him to fall to the ground.

Both women began talking at once, trying to relay what had happened at the RV several hours earlier. Fifteen minutes later a very subdued group made their way into the RV; with the death of Sam turning the joyous reunion into a more somber one. When final preparations had been made Jerod pulled out of the recreation area driving Sam's Land Rover, with the body of his friend wrapped in a blanket laying in the rear of the vehicle. He carried with him Agent Jones's private cell phone number should he encounter any problems during the long trip back to Seattle.

Daniel, the male nurse who had accompanied Lucille Graden to take care of Thomas, was dismissed and sent back to Seattle with a large bonus for his involvement. Grant, the loquacious guide was handsomely rewarded for his bump on the head.

Two hours later the RV pulled out of the campgrounds with the women in the rear of the RV along with Thomas. Toby was driving with Reggie riding quietly in the passenger seat. Phil and Joe followed in Joe's battered pickup. They drove to Billings and pulled into a Holiday Inn where they secured rooms for the night.

After dinner and by mutual agreement they all retired to their rooms for hot showers and a long restful night hopefully with no interruptions.

Late the next morning everyone met in the Motel restaurant for breakfast. Nothing was mentioned of the incidents leading up to now, the conversation revolved around their trip back and how soon they would all be getting together again. The plan was when they came to the Interstate 15 cutoff, Brandy and Reggie would take Toby's Jeep Wrangler and head for Las Vegas with Joe and Phil following. Toby and the rest of the party would continue on to Seattle and then Bremerton in the RV.

Suddenly Reggie spoke up, "Hey Joe, let's you, me and Toby take a little trip. We can leave Phil here to entertain the ladies for awhile."

A puzzled Joe looked up from his coffee and replied, "Why, what's up, Reg?"

An equally puzzled Toby got up from the table and accompanied Reggie and Joe out of the restaurant into the Motel parking lot. Toby started to walk to the RV, but was halted by Reggie's next comment.

"Joe, let's take your truck it's too much trouble to unhook the Jeep."

Shaking their heads in puzzlement both Toby and Joe walked over to the truck, Joe sliding behind the wheel, Reggie sliding into the center of the seat with Toby squeezing into the seat beside Reggie.

"Where to, Reggie?" asked Joe, still confused.

"Go out to the street and take a right."

Three blocks later Reggie said to Joe, "Pull into the Dodge dealership on the right side."

Joe did as Reggie instructed, still not knowing what Reggie was up to.

"Okay, Joe, we are here to fulfill my bargain with you. With no questions asked, I want you to go find the truck that you want and when you do I'll buy it for you."

Joe looked at Reggie, saying, "But, but—."

"No buts about it Joe, you deserve that and more. What I truly owe you I can never repay, so this is in a very small way a 'Thank You' from Toby and myself."

The next morning the RV towing the Jeep Wrangler, followed by a beaming Joe Morrison, driving his brand new truck, headed west following the sun.

EPILOGUE

A S THE LARGE motor home moved west on Interstate 90 its six occupants rejoiced, thankful they had survived the events of the last few days. The elderly woman sitting on the couch tenderly clung to the frail body of her grandson humming as she rocked him much the way she had when she soothed his injuries as a small child. The olive-skinned Ruth sat next to Toby, possessively clinging to his free hand as he guided the RV toward home. Together they voiced thanks that the mission had met with such success, yet sorrowful that their friend Sam wasn't returning to his beloved Seattle alive. His sacrifice had ensured that others would live and he would always hold a place in their hearts. Reggie and Brandy were holding hands across the table speaking in low voices, with eyes only for each other. Suddenly the phone lying on the table rang. Freeing one of his hands from Brandy's grasp Reggie picked up the small cellular device, expecting to hear the voice of either Joe or Phil, instead a raspy voice spoke, *"I am not a forgiving person, nor do I forget a slight. You and your friends are to be congratulated on your success, but your meddling has done nothing more than deter me temporarily. You are formidable adversaries, but interfere again and I will squash you."* Reggie spoke no words, but the expression on his face revealed more than words. It wasn't over yet.

Edwards Brothers Malloy
Thorofare, NJ USA
February 17, 2015